Anthony Trollope

The Complete Short Stories

VOLUME IV

Courtship and Marriage

Edited, with introduction, by
Betty Jane Slemp Breyer

Texas Christian University Press
Fort Worth, Texas 76129

Published by Texas Christian University Press

Manufactured in the United States of America

Trollope, Anthony, 1815-1882.
   The complete short stories.

   Contents: v. 1. The Christmas stories—v. 2. Editors
and writers—[etc.]—v. 4. Courtship and marriage.
   I. Breyer, Betty Jane. II. Title.
PR5682.B73   823'.8   79-15519
ISBN 0-912646-56-X (v. 1)

Contents

Introduction

OF HIS COURTSHIP AND MARRIAGE, Trollope has left us but scant record. Though he was ever writing of courtship and marriage in his fiction, he practiced a careful reticence about his own. Those going to his autobiography for that personal and intimate glimpse so beloved of twentieth century readers come away disappointed. Of his literary life he was willing to tell much — indeed, some have thought too much. About his life as a civil servant he was not, perhaps, as reticent as he should have been; but about his personal life he not only refused to inform his readers, he made it quite clear that he thought it was none of their business: ". . . of what matter," he says in *An Autobiography*, "is that to any reader."

And on the rare occasions when he does write of his own courtship and marriage, he does so in pragmatic and practical terms:

> My marriage was like the marriage of other people, and of no special interest to anyone except my wife and me. It took place at Rotherham in Yorkshire, where her father was the manager of a bank. We were not very rich, having about £400 a year on which to live. Many people would say that we were two fools to encounter such poverty together. I can only reply that since that day I have never been without money in my pocket, and that I soon acquired the means of paying what I owed.

Underlying the objective pragmatism of this account is an unregenerate believer in the power of love and the beneficence of marriage. He was in this, as in so many things, the perfect Victorian, for no age believed more firmly in the fitness of the married state nor had a more ardent examplar than their Queen.

Despite the very little that he has told us about his married life, one thing seems certain. Whether among the villagers of Ireland, or the strawberries and asparagus of Waltham House, or the book-lined rooms of Harding Grange, Trollope seems to have led a life of domestic equanimity. Sometimes there are glimpses of his satisfaction in the married state. In a letter to George Lewes in 1861 he writes, perhaps forgetting for a moment Lewes's own difficulties: "As to myself personally, I have daily to wonder at the continual run of domestic and worldly happiness which has been granted me; — to wonder at it as well as to be thankful for it." Here is none of the shambling, red-faced, ursine Englishman seen by his contemporaries, but rather a man humble in the acknowledgement of his happy condition—the latter a much more accurate picture of the man than the former.

Whatever may have been the limits of his own domestic happiness and sorrow, and his own domestic virtues and vices, his readers are never in any doubt about the fact that Trollope approved of marriage. "A woman's life is not perfect or whole," he says in *Miss Mackenzie*, "till she has added herself to a husband. Nor is a man's life perfect or whole till he has added to himself a wife." R. C. Terry has commented that all Trollope's fiction "revolves on this axiom of Victorian felicity." But though Trollope was committed to the idea that it was man's duty as well as his destiny to marry, in love stories the focus is more often on his women than on his men. In one sense, the stakes are higher for women than for men. Women in love are about to be launched on their one important career — at least, according to Trollope's view their one important career — marriage, to which courtship is a risky and difficult apprenticeship.

Accordingly, he had little to say in favor of women's rights as a movement. He was not unsympathetic to the plight of women left without the means or education to support themselves. Indeed, "Journey to Panama" is a poignant study of such circumstances. (See Volume V.) He had contributed stories to the two albums published by Miss Emily Faithfull and the Victoria Press for the Employment of Women. On his visit to the States in 1861 he had even distributed Miss Faithfull's card to those interested in the English movement. Even so, Trollope seldom wrote about the "working girl."

The notable exceptions are found in his story "The Telegraph Girl." Even here he is true to his opinion that the best career for a woman is marriage. Nevertheless, he makes a good case for Lucy Graham as a working girl. She is industrious, honest, generous, determined, and sturdy and with a spirit willing to be independent:

> She was driven to consider what else she could do to earn her bread. She might become a nursemaid, or perhaps a nursery governess. . . . To be a servant was distasteful to her. . . . To work and work hard she was quite willing, so that there might be some hours of her life in which she might not be called upon to obey. . . . Why should she not be independent, and respectable and safe? . . . During a third of the day she was, as she proudly told herself, a servant of the Crown. During the other two-thirds she was lord, — or lady, — of herself.

There is a certain amount of proprietorial pride in Trollope's description of the girls in the Telegraph Office, part of the General Post Office. In an article on that service for *Good Words* he remarked that women there could "be employed with equal advantage to the employer and to themselves." While Trollope was certainly not for women's rights, he was not the hostile anti-feminist some have tried to make him.

Trollope's philosophy may have committed him to espouse the rightness of marriage, but his creative genius committed him to write about it with the same steady vision with which he wrote about life generally. He has filled his fiction with an amazing array of marriages. They run the gamut from the comic marriage of the Proudies of Barsetshire to the tragic, tortuous marriage of the Trevelyans in *He Knew He Was Right*. Trollope's particular talent was the ability to build from the bits and pieces of ordinary English life an accurate picture of that peculiar alchemy which transforms two people into a married couple. He was able to do so because he was never sentimental about hearth and home, nor was he sentimental about women and marriage. His women never obtain pedestals unless they themselves construct them. On the other hand, there is no sexual equality in the marriages he created. In theory, at least, it was the woman's job to be submissive to her husband. But Trollope was always shrewd enough to separate the theory of his philosophy from the reality of his fiction:

> The theory of man and wife — that special theory in accor-
> dance with which the wife is to bend herself in loving sub-
> mission before her husband — is very beautiful; and would
> be good altogether if it could only be arranged that the hus-
> band should be the stronger and the greater of the two. The
> theory is based upon that hypothesis; — and the hypothesis
> sometimes fails of confirmation. In ordinary marriages the
> vessel rights itself, and the stronger and the greater takes
> the lead, whether clothed in petticoats, or in coat, waist-
> coat, and trousers. . . . [The Belton Estate]

Not surprisingly, in many of the marriages Trollope wrote about, they in petticoats led. He delighted to create such women — sharp-witted, vigorous women who knew their own minds, or even better, those of their husbands. Perhaps he created only one Lady Glencora, but her sisters fill his pages. Critics have often commented on Trollope's English girls, praising them for their naturalness: they seldom lavish the same praise on his matrons. And yet, in each English maiden is a potential English matron than which there is no one more formidable in the full panoply of her rights. Whatever else Trollope had to say about marriage, he has stated in clear, bold terms his admiration for the English matron. On her shoulders rested the grave responsibilities of making the sun run its appointed course and the eggs appear on the table in due season. She was the arbiter of taste and the repository of the most sacred Victorian household god — Duty. The influence of this figure is so pervasive and her sway so mighty that many of Trollope's love stories must be played out in her absence.

Indeed, it is strange that no one has as yet commented on the fact that so many of Trollope's young girls manage their loves without the benefit of a mother or any other worthy matron to take a strong hand in their affairs. Eleanor Harding (The Warden), Mary Thorne (Doctor Thorne), Lucy Robarts (Framley Parsonage), Caroline Waddington (The Bertrams), Clara Amed-roz (The Belton Estate), Alice Vavasour (Can You Forgive Her?), Mary Lovelace (Is He Popenjoy?), Ayala and Lucy Domer (Ayala's Angel) — to name a few — manage to fall in love without the help of a feminine guide. In the short stories of this volume, half the young ladies in love have no mother to guide them. Moreover, when conflicts and difficulties do arise in love stories, they often come from the young men's mothers. Lucy Robarts must overcome the objections of Lady Lufton; Mary Thorne those of Lady Arabella Gresham; Bessy Pryor those of Mrs. Miles, and to some degree Alice Dugdale those of Mrs. Rossiter. When young ladies in love, about to be in love, or just looking for husbands appear accompanied by their mothers an interesting adjustment in the dynamics of characterization takes place. Either the young lady has a mother weak, widowed, ineffectual or once-removed from power by virtue of being a step-mother, or the mother assumes the dominant role and the young lady becomes colorlessly indifferent. Arabella Trefoil (*The American Senator*), Rachel Ray (*Rachel Ray*), Lily Dale (*The Small House at Allington*), Alice Dugdale, Susan Bell all appear with their mothers in their wakes. Of one such mother Trollope wrote: "Ophelia Gledd's mother was, for a living being, the nearest thing to a nonentity that I ever met." Young ladies with mothers who assume the dominant role in matchmaking either assume statuesque poses as does Georgiana Wanless (*Alice Dugdale*) or they become such a one as Griselda Grantley (*Framley Parsonage*) of whom her mother says: "I don't think she will ever allow herself to indulge in an unauthorized passion."

Trollope's fiction is too good to be reduced to formulae and categorical statements, and the thorough reader may quickly point to exceptions to the hypothesis that Trollope does not allow two strong female characters (the matron and the maiden) to act in concert. Mrs. O'Hara's actions culminate in the final tragedy of Kate O'Hara's story (*An Eye for an Eye*); Lady Anna is tormented by her mother throughout the novel (*Lady Anna*); and the strong, dark emotions of Lady Desmond make her daughter's story a curious tangle (*Castle Richmond*).

Still, Trollope seems only too willing to let his matron have full play for her power and do battle where she sees fit, even against an adversary of the opposite sex if he be worthy of her talents. Trollope seems equally willing to allow his young woman in love to stand on her own feet and be guided only by her virtues and the power of her love. When maid and matron do battle, for

Trollope the outcome is a foregone conclusion. No one, however great, can stand against his girl in love:

> "Must I go back to him, Lucy, and tell him that there is some other objection — something besides a stern old mother; some hindrance, perhaps, not so easily overcome?"
>
> "No," said Lucy, and it was all which at the moment she could say.
>
> "What shall I tell him then? Shall I say yes—simply yes?"
>
> "Simply yes," said Lucy.
>
> "And as to the stern old mother who thought her only son too precious to be parted with at the first word — is nothing to be said to her?"
>
> "Oh, Lady Lufton!"
>
> "No forgiveness to be spoken, no sign of affection to be given? Is she always to be regarded as stern and cross, vexatious and disagreeable. . . . Lucy, dearest Lucy, you must be very dear to me now." [Framley Parsonage]

Of all the hundreds of characters Trollope created the ones he liked best were those in love and of those in love undoubtedly his favorite was the English girl. Critics early in his career credited him with the power to portray the "feminine heart," but it was Henry James, reviewing Trollope's whole career in 1888, who wrote the most definitive description of his talent:

> . . . Trollope settled down steadily to the English girl; he took possession of her, and turned her inside out . . . he bestowed upon her the most patient, the most tender, the most copious consideration. He is always more or less in love with her, and it is a wonder how under these circumstances he should make her so objective, plant her so well on her feet. . . . She is always definite and natural. She plays her part most properly. She has always health in her cheek and gratitude in her eye. She has not a touch of the morbid, and is delightfully tender, modest and fresh.

James's assessment is an elegant tribute to Trollope's skill. Trollope has made his characters seem real — so real that Hugh Walpole called him the supreme English novelist of "average humanity." His girls are not "average humanity," but they seem to be — "the usual young lady of *Punch*" as one writer put it. To James's catalogue of virtues possessed by Trollope's girl in love must be added those of steadfastness (to the point of stubbornness at times), honesty and unquestioning faith in the rightness of love itself. Bessy Pryor of "The Lady of Launay" is one such girl. She is soft and pretty, but in no way above the ordinary in her softness and prettiness. She is devoted to her adopted mother, but has the temerity to fall in love with the son of the house who has been destined by his mother for greater things than the orphaned daughter of a poor friend. Now Bessy can show her mettle. She can display that love which Trollope said his heroines should have — "downright honest love in which there is no pretense on the part of the lady that she was too ethereal to be fond of a man. . . ." And so she does, despite opposition and exile:

> "I owe you everything." [Bessy says to her adopted mother.]
> "Then say that you will give him up."
> "I owe you everything, except this. I will not speak to him, I will not write to him, I will not even look at him, but I will not give him up. When one loves, one cannot give it up."

As though the exception proves the rule, Trollope has created one girl who, while she loves with a "downright honest love" does in the end give it up. Of the many girls in love that he created none other is tried in quite the same way as Patience Woolsworthy in "The Parson's Daughter of Oxney Colne." In a brief story he has drawn a character who meets all of James's criteria for a Trollopian heroine. Furthermore, she declares her love forthrightly:

> She stood opposite him for a moment, and then placing her two hands on his shoulders, she answered him "I do, I do, I do," she said, "with all my heart; with all my heart — with all my heart and strength."

She is not met with equal fervor by her young man and thereby hangs the tale.

Trollope's girl in love is unafraid to show her love when it is returned. She may be modest and meek before the prospect of some worthy suitor, but once the declaration has been made she assumes quite a different pose. She is bold in her love and exalted in her mood — "a triumphant conqueror." The gentle satire of this exaggeration from *Kept in the Dark* is a more accurate description than it was meant to be:

> The happiness of a girl in her lover is something wonderful to behold. He is surely the only man, and she the only woman born worthy of such a man. She is to be the depository of all his secrets, and the recipient of all his thoughts. That other young ladies should accept her with submission in this period of her ecstasy would be surprising were it not that she is so truly exalted by her condition as to make her for a short period an object to them of genuine worship.

It is hardly surprising to find that Trollope's young lady is happy at being in love. Trollope's delight in the English girl seems only to be exceeded by her delight in being in love. His heroine does not regret her state — even Lily Dale had her hour of happiness before she was deserted. If she is unhappy, she is so in the cause of love. If she is disappointed, the imperfection of her own heart is not the cause. Whatever may be the final judgment on the conduct of Patience Woolsworthy in "The Parson's Daughter," no one can deny the loving tribute Trollope, at the end of the story, pays to her and to all those like her who have been disappointed in their love:

> In her own eyes she is a confirmed old maid; and such is my opinion also. The romance of her life was played out in that summer. She never sits now lonely on the hill-side thinking how much she might do for one whom she really loved. But with a large heart she loves many, and with no romance, she works hard to lighten the burdens of those she loves.

Those who read Trollope to be entertained will not be disappointed in the young ladies found in these stories. They are a fair sampling of the kind. Even his transatlantic young ladies carry much the same qualities of character found in his English girls. That there are differences is part of their charm. Trollope never betrays his young women or invites his readers to laugh at their concerns. He has shown their weaknesses and strengths, their virtues and shortcomings, but he has made them honest about their love and honest about being in love. They never pretend that being in love is something too common or vulgar for them or that they are too spiritual for such things. He has created seemingly ordinary young ladies, but young ladies of such truth of

mind and soul that they stand as patterns of their kind. They have admirably fulfilled their creator's wishes when he said in *An Autobiography:* ". . . if I can make young men and women believe that truth in love will make them happy, then, if my writing be popular, I shall have a very large class of pupils." There are still among us many pupils to Mr. Trollope.

The O'Conors of Castle Conor, County Mayo

I SHALL NEVER FORGET MY FIRST INTRODUC-
TION to country life in Ireland, my first day's hunting there, or
the manner in which I passed the evening afterward. Nor shall
I ever cease to be grateful for the hospitality which I received
from the O'Conors of Castle Conor. My acquaintance with that
family was first made in the following manner. But before I begin
my story let me inform my reader that my name is Archibald
Green.

I had been for a fortnight in Dublin, and was about to proceed
into County Mayo on business which would occupy me there for
some weeks. My headquarters would, I found, be at the town of
Ballyglass; and I soon learned that Ballyglass was not a place in
which I should find hotel accommodation of a luxurious kind, or
much congenial society indigenous to the place itself.

"But you are a hunting man, you say," said old Sir P——
C——; "and in that case you will soon know Tom O'Conor. Tom
won't let you be dull. I'd write you a letter to Tom, only he'll certainly make you out without my taking the trouble."

I did think at the time that the old baronet might have written
the letter for me, as he had long been a friend of my father's in
former days; but he did not, and I started for Ballyglass with no
other introduction to anyone in the county than that contained

in Sir P——'s promise that I should soon know Mr. Thomas O'Conor.

I had already provided myself with a horse, groom, saddle, and bridle; and these I sent down, *en avant*, that the Ballyglassians might know that I was somebody. Perhaps before I arrived Tom O'Conor might learn that a hunting man was coming into the neighborhood, and I might find at the inn a polite note intimating that a bed was at my service at Castle Conor. I had heard so much of the free hospitality of the Irish gentry as to imagine that such a thing might be possible.

But I found nothing of the kind. Hunting gentlemen in those days were very common in County Mayo, and one horse was no great evidence of a man's standing in the world. Men there, as I learned afterward, are sought for themselves quite as much as they are elsewhere; and though my groom's top boots were neat, and my horse a very tidy animal, my entry into Ballyglass created no sensation whatever.

In about four days after my arrival, when I was already infinitely disgusted with the little pothouse in which I was forced to stay, and had made up my mind that the people of County Mayo were a churlish set, I sent my horse on to a meet of the foxhounds, and followed after, myself, on an open car.

No one but an erratic fox-hunter such as I am—a fox-hunter, I mean, whose lot it has been to wander about from one pack of foxhounds to another—can understand the melancholy feeling which a man has when he first intrudes himself, unknown by any one, among an entirely new set of sportsmen. When a stranger falls thus, as it were out of the moon, into a hunt, it is impossible that men should not stare at him and ask who he is—and it is disagreeable to be stared at, and to have such questions asked! This feeling does not come upon a man in Leicestershire or Gloucestershire, where the numbers are large, and a stranger or two will always be overlooked; but in small hunting fields it is so painful that a man has to pluck up much courage before he encounters it.

We met on the morning in question at Bingham's Grove. There were not above twelve or fifteen men out, all of whom, or nearly all, were cousins to each other. They seemed to be all Toms and Pats and Larrys and Micks. I was done up very know-

2

ingly in pink, and thought that I looked quite the thing, but for two or three hours nobody noticed me.

I had my eyes about me, however, and soon found out which of them was Tom O'Conor. He was a fine looking fellow, thin and tall, but not largely made, with a piercing gray eye and a beautiful voice for speaking to a hound. He had two sons there also — short, slight fellows, but exquisite horsemen. I already felt that I had a kind of acquaintance with the father, but I hardly knew on what ground to put in my claim.

We had no sport early in the morning. It was a cold, bleak February day, with occasional storms of sleet. We rode about from cover to cover, but all in vain.

"I am sorry, Sir, that we are to have such a bad day, as you are a stranger here," said one gentleman to me. This was Jack O'Conor, Tom's eldest son, my bosom friend for many a year after. Poor Jack! I fear that the Encumbered Estates Court sent him altogether adrift upon the world.

"We may still have a run from Poulnaroe, if the gentleman chooses to come on," said a voice coming up behind with a sharp trot. It was Tom O'Conor.

"Wherever the hounds go I'll follow," said I.

"Then come on to Poulnaroe," said Mr. O'Conor. I trotted on quickly by his side, and before we reached the cover had managed to slip in something about Sir P —— C ——.

"What the deuce!" said he — "What! a friend of Sir P ——'s? Why the deuce didn't you tell me so? What are you doing down here? Where are you staying?" etc., etc., etc.

At Poulnaroe we found a fox; but before we did so Mr. O'Conor had asked me over to Castle Conor; and this he did in such a way that there was no possibility of refusing him, or, I should rather say, of disobeying him. For his invitation came quite in the tone of a command.

"You'll come to us, of course, when the day is over; and — let me see — we're near Ballyglass now, but the inn will be right away in our direction. Just send word for them to send your things to Castle Conor."

"But they're all about and unpacked," said I.

"Never mind — write a note and say what you want now, and go and get the rest tomorrow yourself. Here's Patsey: Patsey, run into Ballyglass for this gentleman at once. Now don't be long, for the chances are we shall find here." And then, after giving some further hurried instructions, he left me to write a line in pencil to the innkeeper's wife on the bank of a ditch.

This I accordingly did: "Send my small portmanteau," I said, "and all my black dress clothes and shirts and socks and all that, and, above all, my dressing things which are on the little table, and the satin neck-handkerchief, and, whatever you do, mind you send my *pumps*;" and I underscored the latter word, for Jack O'Conor, when his father left me, went on pressing the invitation. "My sisters are going to get up a dance," said he, "and if you are fond of that kind of thing perhaps we can amuse you." Now in those days I was very fond of dancing—and very fond of young ladies too, and therefore glad enough to learn that Tom O'Conor had daughters as well as sons. On this account I was very particular in underscoring the word pumps.

"And hurry, you young devil!" Jack O'Conor said to Patsey.

"I have told him to take the portmanteau over in a car," said I.

"All right; then you'll find it there on our arrival."

We had an excellent run, in which I may make bold to say that I did not acquit myself badly. I stuck very close to the hounds, as did the whole O'Conor brood; and when the fellow contrived to earth himself, as he did, I received those compliments on my horse which is the nearest approach to praise which one fox-hunter ever gives to another.

"We'll buy that fellow of you before we let you go," said Peter, the younger son.

"I advise you to look sharp after your money if you sell him to my brother," said Jack.

And then we trotted slowly off to Castle Conor, which, however, was by no means near to us.

"We have ten miles to go — good Irish miles," said the father. "I don't know that I ever remember a fox from Poulnaroe taking that line before."

"He wasn't a Poulnaroe fox," said Peter.

"I don't know that," said Jack; and then they debated that question hotly.

Our horses were very tired, and it was late before we reached Mr. O'Conor's house. That getting home from hunting with a thoroughly wearied animal, who has no longer sympathy or example to carry him on, is very tedious work. In the present instance I had company with me; but when a man is alone — when his horse toes at every ten steps — when the night is dark and the rain pouring, and there are yet eight miles of road to be conquered — at such times a man is almost apt to swear that he will give up hunting.

At last we were in the Castle Conor stableyard, for we had approached the house by some back way; and as we entered by a door leading through a wilderness of back passages, Mr. O'Conor said out loud,

"Now, boys, remember I sit down to dinner in twenty minutes." And then, turning expressly to me, he laid his hand kindly upon my shoulder, and said, "I hope you will make yourself quite at home at Castle Conor; and whatever you do, don't keep us waiting for dinner. You can dress in twenty minutes, I suppose?"

"In ten," said I, glibly.

"That's well. Jack and Peter will show you your room." And so he turned away and left us.

My two young friends made their way into the front hall, and thence into the drawing room, and I followed them. We were all dressed in pink, and had waded deep through bog and mud. I did not exactly know whither I was being led in this guise, but I soon found myself in the presence of two young ladies and of a girl about thirteen years of age.

"My sisters," said Jack, introducing me very laconically. "Miss O'Conor, Miss Kate O'Conor, Miss Tizzy O'Conor."

"My name is not Tizzy," said the younger; "it's Eliza. How do you do, Sir? I hope you've had a fine hunt. Was papa well up, Jack?"

Jack did not condescend to answer this question, but asked one of the elder girls whether my things had come, and whether a room had been made ready for me.

"Oh yes," said Miss O'Conor, "they have come, I know, for I saw them brought into the house; and I hope Mr. Green will find everything comfortable."

5

As she said this I thought I saw a slight smile steal across her remarkably pretty mouth.

They were both exceedingly pretty girls. Fanny, the elder, wore long glossy curls — for I write, O reader, of bygone days, as long ago as that when young ladies wore curls if it pleased them so to do, and gentlemen danced in pumps, with black handkerchiefs round their necks — yes, long black, or nearly black, silken curls; and then she had such eyes! — I never knew whether they were most wicked or most bright; and her face was all dimples, and each dimple was laden with laughter and laden with love. Kate was probably the prettier girl of the two, but on the whole not so attractive. She was fairer than her sister, and wore her hair in braids, and was also somewhat more demure in her manner.

In spite of the special injunctions of Mr. O'Conor, Sen., it was impossible not to loiter for five minutes over the drawing room fire talking to these houris; more especially as I seemed to know them intimately by intuition *before* half the five minutes was over. They were so easy, so pretty, so graceful, so kind; they seemed to take it so much as a matter of course that I should stand there talking in my red coat and muddy boots.

"Well, do go and dress yourselves," at last said Fanny, pretending to speak to her brothers, but looking more especially at me. "You know how mad papa will be. And remember, Mr. Green, we expect great things from your dancing tonight. Your coming just at this time is such a godsend!"

And again that *soupçon* of a smile passed over her face.

I hurried up to my room, Peter and Jack coming with me to the door.

"Is everything right?" said Peter, looking among the towels and water-jugs.

"They've given you a decent fire, for a wonder," said Jack, stirring up the red-hot turf which blazed in the grate.

"All right as a trivet," said I.

"And look alive, like a good fellow," said Jack. We had scowled at each other in the morning, as very young men do when they are strangers, and now, after a few hours, we were intimate friends.

I immediately turned to my work, and was gratified to find that all my things were laid out ready for dressing. My portmanteau had, of course, come open, as my keys were in my pocket; and therefore some of the excellent servants of the house had been able to save me all the trouble of unpacking. There was my shirt hanging before the fire; my black clothes were spread upon the bed, my socks and collar and handkerchief beside them; my brushes were on the toilet-table, and every thing prepared exactly as though my own man had been there. How nice!

I immediately went to work at getting off my spurs and boots, and then proceeded to loosen the buttons at my knees. In doing this I sat down in the armchair, which had been drawn up for me opposite to the fire. But what was the object on which my eyes then fell? — the objects I should rather say.

Immediately in front of my chair was placed, just ready for my feet, an enormous pair of shooting boots — half boots, made to lace up round the ankles, with thick double-leather feet, and each bearing half a stone of iron in the shape of nails and heel-pieces. I had superintended the making of these shoes in Burlington Arcade with the greatest diligence. I was never a good shot, and, like some other sportsmen, intended to make up for my deficiency in performance by the excellence of my sporting apparel. "Those nails are not large enough," I had said; "not nearly large enough." But when the boots came home they struck even me as being too heavy, too metalsome. "He-he-he!" laughed the boot-boy, as he turned up the soles for me to look at. It may therefore be imagined of what nature were the articles which were thus set out for my evening's dancing.

And then the way in which they were placed! When I saw this, the conviction flew across my mind like a flash of lightning that the preparation had been made under other eyes than those of the servant. The great big boots were placed so prettily before the chair, and the strings of each were made to dangle down at the sides, as though just ready for tying. They seemed to say — the boots did — "Now, make haste; we at any rate are ready; you can not say that you were kept waiting for us." No mere servant's hand had ever enabled a pair of boots to laugh at one so completely.

But what was I to do? I rushed at the small portmanteau, thinking that my pumps also might be there. The woman surely could not have been such a fool as to send me those tons of iron for my evening wear! But alas! alas! no pumps were there. There was

7

nothing else in the way of covering for my feet; not even a pair of slippers.

And now what was I to do? The absolute magnitude of my misfortune only loomed upon me by degrees. The twenty minutes allowed by that stern old paterfamilias was already gone, and I had done nothing toward dressing. And indeed it was impossible that I should do any thing that would be of avail. I could not go down to dinner in my stocking feet, nor could I put on my black dress trowsers over a pair of mud-painted top boots. As for those iron-soled horrors — and then I gave one of them a kick with the side of my bare foot which sent it halfway under the bed.

But what was I to do? I began washing myself and brushing my hair with this horrid weight upon my mind. My first plan was to go to bed, and send down word that I had been taken suddenly ill in the stomach; then to rise early in the morning and get away unobserved. But by such a course of action I should lose all chance of any further acquaintance with those pretty girls. That they were already aware of the extent of my predicament, and were now enjoying it — of that I was quite sure.

What if I boldly put on the shooting boots, and clattered down to dinner in them? What if I took the bull by the horns, and made myself one in the joke? This might be very well for the dinner, but it would be but a bad joke for me when the hour for dancing came. And, alas! I felt that I lacked the courage. It is not every man that can walk down to dinner, in a strange house full of ladies, wearing such boots as those I have described.

Should I not attempt to borrow a pair? This, all the world will say, should have been my first idea. But I have not yet mentioned that I am myself a large-boned man, and that my feet are especially well developed. I had never for a moment entertained a hope that I should find any one in that house whose boot I could wear. But at last I rang the bell; I would send for Jack, and if every thing else failed, I would communicate my grief to him.

I had to ring twice before any body came. The servants, I well knew, were putting the dinner on the table. At last a man entered the room, dressed in rather shabby black, whom I afterward learned to be the butler.

"What is your name, my friend?" said I, determined to make an ally of the man.

"My name? why, Larry to be sure, yer honor. And the masther is out of his sinses in a hurry, becase yer honor don't come down."

"Is he though? Well, now, Larry, tell me this, which of all the gentlemen in the house has got the largest feet?"

"Is it the largest feet, yer honor?" said Larry, altogether surprised by my question.

"Yes; the largest feet." And then I proceeded to explain to him my misfortune. He took up, first my top boot, and then the shooting boot, in looking at which he gazed with wonder at the nails, and then he glanced at my feet, measuring them with his eye; and after this he pronounced his opinion.

"Yer honor couldn't wear a morsel of leather belonging to ere a one of 'em, young or ould. There niver was a foot like that yet among the O'Conors."

"But are there no strangers staying here?"

"There's three or four on 'em come in to dinner; but they'll be wanting their own boots, I'm thinking. And there's young Misther Dollor, he's come to stay. But Lord love you" — and he again looked at the enormous extent which lay between the heel and the toe of the shooting apparatus which he still held in his hand — "I niver see sich a foot as that in the whole barony," he said, "barring my own."

Now Larry was a large man, much larger altogether than myself; and as he said this I looked down involuntarily at his feet, or rather at his foot, for as he stood I could only see one. And then a sudden hope filled my heart. On that foot there glittered a shoe — not indeed such as were my own, which were now resting ingloriously at Ballyglass while they were so sorely needed at Castle Conor, but one which I could wear before ladies without shame, and in my present frame of mind with infinite contentment.

"Let me look at that one of your own," said I to the man, as though it were merely a subject for experimental inquiry. Larry, accustomed to obedience, took off the shoe and handed it to me. My own foot was immediately in it, and I found that it fitted me like a glove.

"And now the other," said I, not smiling, for a smile would have put him on his guard; but somewhat sternly, so that that habit of obedience should not desert him at this perilous moment. And then I stretched out my hand.

"But yer honor can't keep 'em, you know," said he. "I haven't the ghost of another shoe to my foot." But I only looked more sternly than before, and still held out my hand. Custom prevailed. Larry stooped down slowly, looking at me the while, and pulling off the other slipper handed it to me with much hesitation. Alas, as I put it to my foot I found that it was old, and worn, and irredeemably down at heel; that it was in fact no counterpart at all to that other one which was to do duty as its fellow. But nevertheless I put my foot into it, and felt that a descent to the drawing-room was now possible.

"But yer honor will give 'em back to a poor man?" said Larry, almost crying. "The masther's mad this minute becase the dinner's not up. And, glory be to God, only listhen to that!" and as he spoke a tremendous peal rang out from some bell down stairs that had evidently been shaken by an angry hand.

"Larry," said I — and I endeavored to assume a look of very grave importance as I spoke — "I look to you to assist me in this matter."

"Och, wirra sthrue thin, and will you let me go? Jist listhen to that!" and another peal rang out, loud and repeated.

"If you do as I ask you," I continued, "you shall be well rewarded. Look here! look at these boots," and I held up the shooting shoes, new from Burlington Arcade. "They cost thirty shillings — thirty shillings! and I will give them to you for the loan of this pair of slippers."

"They'd be no use at all to me, yer honor; not the laist use in life."

"You could do with them very well for to-night, and then you could sell them. And here are ten shillings besides;" and I held out half a sovereign, which the poor fellow took into his hand.

I waited no further parley, but immediately writhed out of the room. With one foot I was sufficiently pleased; as regarded that I felt that I had overcome my difficulty. But the other was not so satisfactory. Whenever I attempted to lift it from the ground the horrid slipper would fall off, or only just hang by the toe. As for dancing, that would be out of the question.

"Oh, murther, murther!" sang out Larry, as he heard me going down stairs; "what will I do at all? Tare and 'ounds! there — he's at it again as mad as blazes!" This last exclamation had reference to another peal, which was evidently the work of the master's hand.

I confess I was not quite comfortable as I walked down stairs. In the first place, I was nearly half an hour late, and I knew from the sign of the peals that had sounded that my slowness had already been made the subject of strong remarks. And then my left shoe went flop, flop on every alternate step of the stairs; by no exertion of my foot in the drawing up of my toe could I induce it to remain permanently fixed upon my foot. But over and above, and worse than all this, was the conviction, strong upon my mind, that I should become a subject of merriment to the girls as soon as I entered the room. They would understand the cause of my distress; and probably at this moment were expecting to hear me clatter through the stone hall with those odious metal boots.

However, I hurried down and entered the drawing-room, determined to keep my position near the door, so that I might have as little as possible to do on entering, and as little as possible in going out. But I had other difficulties in store for me. I had not as yet been introduced to Mrs. O'Conor, nor to Miss O'Conor, the squire's unmarried sister.

"Upon my word I thought you were never coming," said Mr. O'Conor, as soon as he saw me. "It is just one hour since we entered the house. Jack, I wish you would find out what has come to that fellow Larry!" and again he rang the bell. He was too angry, or it might be too impatient, to go through the ceremony of introducing me to any body.

I saw that the two girls looked at me very sharply; I stood, however, at the back of an arm-chair, so that no one could see my feet. But that little imp Tizzy walked round deliberately, looked at my heels, and then walked back again. It was clear that she was in the secret.

There were eight or ten people in the room, but I was too much fluttered to notice well who they were.

"Mamma," said Miss O'Conor the elder, "let me introduce Mr. Green to you."

11

It luckily happened that Mrs. O'Conor was on the same side of the fire as myself, and I was able to take the hand which she offered me without coming round into the middle of the circle. Mrs. O'Conor was a little woman, apparently not of much importance in the world; but, if one might judge from first appearances, very good-natured.

"And my aunt Die, Mr. Green," said Kate, pointing to a very straight-backed, grim-looking lady, who occupied a corner of a sofa on the opposite side of the hearth. I knew that politeness required that I should walk across the room and make acquaintance with her; but, under the existing circumstances, how was I to obey the dictates of politeness? I was determined, therefore, to stand my ground, and merely bowed from a respectful distance at Miss O'Conor. In so doing I made an enemy who never deserted me during the whole of my intercourse with the family. But for her, who knows who might have been sitting opposite to me as I now write?

"Upon my word, Mr. Green, the ladies will expect much from an Adonis who takes so long over his toilet!" said Tom O'Conor, in that cruel tone of banter which he so well knew how to use.

"You forget, father, that men in London can't jump in and out of their clothes as quick as we wild Irishmen!" said Jack.

"Mr. Green knows that we expect a great deal from him this evening. I hope you polk well, Mr. Green?" said Kate.

I muttered something about never dancing; but I knew that what I said was unaudible.

"I don't think Mr. Green will dance," said Tizzy; "at least, not much!" The impudence of that child was, I think, unparalleled by any that I have ever witnessed.

"But, in the name of all that's holy, why don't we have dinner?" And Mr. O'Conor thundered at the door. "Larry! Larry! Larry!" he screamed.

"Yes, yer honor; it'll be all right in two seconds!" answered Larry, from some bottomless abyss. "Tare an' ages! what'll I do at all?" I heard him continuing, as he made his way into the hall. Oh what a clatter he made upon the pavement, for it was all stone! And how the drops of perspiration stood upon my brow as I listened to him!

And then there was a pause, for the man had gone into the dining-room. I could see now that Mr. O'Conor was becoming very angry; and Jack, the eldest son — oh how often he and I have laughed over all this since! — left the drawing-room for the second time. Immediately afterward Larry's footsteps were again heard hurrying across the hall; and then there was a great slither, and an exclamation, and the noise of a fall! and I could plainly hear poor Larry's head strike against the stone floor.

"Ochone! ochone!" he cried at the top of his voice. "I'm murthered with'em now, and d—— 'em for boots! St. Peter be good to me!"

There was a general rush into the hall, and I was carried with the stream. The poor fellow who had broken his head would be sure to tell them how I had robbed him of his shoes. The coachman was already helping him up, and Peter good-naturedly lent a hand.

"What on earth is the matter?" said Mr. O'Conor.

"He must be tipsy," whispered Miss O'Conor, the maiden sister.

"I ain't tipsy at all, thin," said Larry, getting up, and rubbing the back of his head and sundry other parts of his body. "Tipsy, indeed!" And then added, when he was quite upright, "The dinner is sarved — at last."

And he bore it all without telling! "I'll give that fellow a guinea to-morrow morning," said I to myself, "if it's the last that I have in the world."

I shall never forget the countenances of the Misses O'Conor as Larry scrambled up, cursing the unfortunate boots. "What on earth has he got on?" said Mr. O'Conor. "Sorrow take 'em for shoes!" ejaculated Larry. But his spirit was good, and he said not a word to betray me.

We all then went in to dinner how we best could. It was useless for us to go back into the drawing-room that each might seek his own partner. Mr. O'Conor, "the masther," not caring much for the girls who were around him, and being already half-beside himself with the confusion and delay, led the way by himself. I, as a stranger, should have given my arm to Mrs. O'Conor; but as it was I took her eldest daughter instead, and contrived to shuffle along into the dining-room without exciting much attention;

and when there, I found myself happily placed between Kate and Fanny.

"I never knew any thing so awkward," said Fanny. "I declare I can't conceive what has come to our old servant Larry. He's generally the most precise person in the world, and now he is nearly an hour late—and then he tumbles down in the hall."

"I am afraid I am responsible for the delay," said I.

"But not for the tumble, I suppose," said Kate, from the other side. I felt that I blushed up to the eyes, but I did not dare to enter into an explanation.

"Tom," said Tizzy, addressing her father across the table, "I hope you had a good run to-day." It did seem odd to me that a young lady should call her father Tom, but such was the fact.

"Why, pretty well," said Mr. O'Conor.

"And I hope you were up with the hounds."

"You may ask Mr. Green that. He, at any rate, was with them, and therefore he can tell you."

"Oh, he wasn't before you, I know. No Englishman could get before you; I am quite sure of that."

"Don't you be impertinent, miss," said Kate. "You can easily see, Mr. Green, that papa spoils my sister Eliza."

"Do you hunt in top boots, Mr. Green?" said Tizzy.

To this I made no answer. She would have drawn me into a conversation about my feet in half a minute, and the slightest allusion to the subject threw me into a fit of perspiration.

"Are you fond of hunting, Miss O'Conor?" asked I, blindly hurrying into any other subject of conversation.

Miss O'Conor owned that she was fond of hunting—just a little—only papa would not allow it. When the hounds met anywhere within reach of Castle Conor she and Kate would ride out to look at them; and if papa was not there that day—an omission of rare occurrence—they would ride a few fields with the hounds.

"But he lets Tizzy keep with them the whole day," said she, whispering.

"And has Tizzy a pony of her own?"

"Oh yes, Tizzy has every thing. She's papa's pet, you know."

"And whose pet are you?" I asked.

14

"Oh, I am nobody's pet; unless sometimes Jack makes a pet of me, when he's in a good humor. Do you make pets of your sisters, Mr. Green?"

"I have none; but if I had, I should not make pets of them."

"Not of your own sisters?"

"No. As for myself, I'd sooner make a pet of my friend's sister — a great deal."

"How very unnatural!" said Miss O'Conor, with the prettiest look of surprise imaginable.

"Not at all unnatural, I think," said I, looking tenderly and lovingly into her face. Where does one find girls so pretty, so easy, so sweet, so talkative as the Irish girls? And then, with all their talking and all their ease, who ever hears of their misbehaving? They certainly love flirting as they also love dancing; but they flirt without mischief and without malice.

I had now quite forgotten my misfortune, and was beginning to think how well I should like to have Fanny O'Conor for my wife. In this frame of mind I was bending over toward her, as a servant took away a plate from the other side, when a sepulchral note sounded in my ear. It was like the *memento mori* of the old Roman — as though some one pointed, in the midst of my bliss, to the sword hanging over me by a thread. It was the voice of Larry whispering in his agony, just above my head.

"They's desthroying my poor feet intirely — intirely; so they is. I can't bear it much longer, yer honor."

I had committed murder, like Macbeth, and now my Banquo had come to disturb me at my feast, as another Banquo had once disturbed Macbeth.

"What is it he says to you?" asked Fanny.

"Oh, nothing," I answered, once more in my misery.

"There seems to be some point of confidence between you and our Larry," she remarked.

"Oh no," said I, quite confused. "Not at all."

"You need not be ashamed of it. Half the gentlemen in the county have their confidences with Larry, and some of the ladies too, I can tell you. He was born in this house, and never lived any where else; and I am sure he has a larger circle of acquaintance than any one else in it."

15

I could not recover my self-possession for the next ten minutes. Whenever Larry was on our side of the table I was afraid that he was coming to me with another agonized whisper. When he was opposite I could not but watch him as he hobbled in his misery. It was evident that the boots were too tight for him; and had they been made throughout of iron, they could not have been less capable of yielding to the feet. I pitied him from the bottom of my heart; and I pitied myself also, wishing that I was well in bed up stairs with some feigned malady, so that Larry might have had his own again.

And then for a moment I missed him from the room. He had doubtless gone to relieve his tortured feet in the servants' hall, and as he did so was cursing my cruelty. But what mattered it? Let him curse. If he would only stay away, and do that, I would appease his wrath, when we were alone together, with pecuniary satisfaction.

But there was no such rest in store for me.

"Larry! Larry!" shouted Mr. O'Conor. "Where on earth has the fellow gone to?" They were all cousins at the table except myself, and Mr. O'Conor was not therefore restrained by any feeling of ceremony. "There is something wrong with that fellow to-day. What is it, Jack?"

"Upon my word, Sir, I don't know," said Jack.

"I think he must be tipsy," whispered Miss O'Conor, the maiden sister, who always sat at her brother's left hand. But a whisper though it was, it was audible all down the table.

"No, ma'am; it ain't dhrink at all," said the coachman. "It's his feet as does it."

"His feet!" shouted Tom O'Conor.

"Yes, I know it's his feet," said that horrid Tizzy. "He's got on great thick, nailed boots. It was that that made him tumble down in the hall."

I glanced at each side of me, and could see that there was a certain consciousness expressed on the face of each of my two neighbors. On Kate's mouth there was decidedly a smile, or rather, perhaps, the slightest possible inclination that way; whereas, on Fanny's part, I thought I saw something like a rising sorrow at my distress. So, at least, I flattered myself.

16

"Send him back into the room immediately," said Tom, who looked at me as though he had some idea that I had introduced all this confusion into his household. What should I do? Would it not be best for me to make a clean breast of it before them all? But alas! I lacked the courage.

The coachman went out, and then we were left for five minutes without any servant, and Mr. O'Conor the while became more and more savage. I attempted to say a word to Fanny, but failed. *Vox faucibus haesit.*

"I don't think he has got any others," said Tizzy; "at least, none others left."

On the whole, I am glad that I did not marry into the family, as I could not have endured that girl to stay in my house as a sister-in-law.

"Where the d—— has that other fellow gone to?" said Tom. "Jack, do go out and see what is the matter. If any body is drunk, send for me."

"Oh, there's nobody drunk," said Tizzy.

Jack went out, and the coachman returned; but what was done and said I hardly remember. The whole room seemed to swim round and round; and as far as I can recollect, the company sat mute, neither eating nor drinking. Presently Jack returned.

"It's all right," said he.

I always liked Jack. At the present moment he just looked toward me and laughed slightly.

"All right?" said Tom. "But is the fellow coming?"

"We can do with Richard, I suppose?" said Jack.

"No, I can't do with Richard," said the father. "And I will know what it all means. Where is that fellow Larry?"

Larry had been standing just outside the door, and now he entered gently as a mouse. No sound came from his football, nor was there in his face that look of pain which it had worn for the last fifteen minutes. But he was not the less abashed, frightened, and unhappy.

"What is all this about, Larry?" said his master, turning to him. "I insist upon knowing."

"Och, thin, Mr. Green, yer honor, I wouldn't be afther telling agin yer honor; indeed I would not, thin, av the masther would only let me hould my tongue." And he looked across at me, deprecating my anger.

"Mr. Green!" said Mr. O'Conor.

"Yes, yer honor. It's all along of his honor's thick boots;" said Larry, stepping backward toward the door, lifted them up from some corner, and coming well forward, exposed them, with the soles uppermost, to the whole table.

"And that's not all, yer honor; but they've squoze the very toes of me into a jelly."

There was now a loud laugh, in which Jack, and Peter, and Fanny, and Kate, and Tizzy all joined, as, too, did Mr. O'Conor, and I also, myself, after a while.

"Whose boots are they?" demanded Miss O'Conor, Senior, with her severest tone and grimmest accent.

"Deed, thin, and the divil may have them for me," answered Larry. "They wor Mr. Green's, but the likes of him won't wear them ag'in afther the likes of me — barring he wanted them very particular," added he, remembering his own pumps.

I began muttering something, feeling that the time had come when I must tell the tale. But Jack, with great good-nature, took up the story and told it so well that I hardly suffered in the telling.

"And that's it!" said Tom O'Conor, laughing till I thought he would have fallen from his chair. "So you've got Larry's shoes on —"

"And very well he fills them," said Jack.

"And it's his honor that's welcome to 'em," said Larry, grinning from ear to ear now that he saw that the "masther" was once more in a good humor.

"I hope they'll be nice shoes for dancing," said Kate.

"Only there's one down at the heel, I know," said Tizzy.

"The servant's shoes!" this was an exclamation made by the maiden lady, and intended apparently only for her brother's ear. But it was clearly audible by all the party.

"Better that than to have no dinner," said Peter.

"But what are you to do about the dancing?" said Fanny, with an air of dismay in her face, which flattered me with an idea that she did care whether I danced or not.

18

In the mean time, Larry, now as happy as an emperor, was tripping round the room without any shoes to encumber him as he withdrew the plates from the table.

"And it's his honor that's welcome to 'em," said he again, as he pulled off the table-cloth with a flourish. "And why wouldn't he, and he able to folly the hounds betther un any Englishman that iver was in these parts before? — anyways, so Mick says."

Now Mick was the huntsman, and this little scrap of eulogy from Larry went far toward curing my grief. I had ridden well to the hounds that day, and I knew it.

There was nothing more said about the shoes, and I was soon again at my ease, although Miss O'Conor did say something about the impropriety of Larry walking about in his stocking-feet. The ladies, however, soon withdrew, to my sorrow, for I was getting on swimmingly with Fanny, and then we gentlemen gathered round the fire and filled our glasses.

In about ten minutes a very light tap was heard, the door was opened to the extent of three inches, and a female voice which I readily recognized called to Jack.

Jack went out, and in a second or two put his head back into the room and called to me: "Green," he said, "just step here a moment; there's a good fellow." I went out, and there I found Fanny standing with her brother.

"Here are the girls at their wit's ends," said he, "about your dancing. So Fanny has put a boy on one of the horses and proposes that you should send another line to Mrs. Mechan, at Ballyglass. It's only ten miles, and he'll be back in two hours."

I need hardly say that I acted in conformity with this advice. I went into Mr. O'Conor's back room with Jack and his sister, and there scribbled a note. It was delightful to feel how intimate I was with them, and how anxious they were to make me happy.

"And we won't begin till they come," said Fanny.

"Oh, Miss O'Conor, pray don't wait," said I.

"Oh, but we will," she answered. "You have your wine to drink, and then there's the tea; and then we will have a song or two. I'll spin it out, see if I don't!" And so we went to the front door, where the boy was already on his horse — her own nag, as I afterward found.

"And Patsey," said she, "ride for your life, now; and Patsey, whatever you do, don't come back without Mr. Green's pumps — his dancing shoes, you know."

And in about two hours the pumps did arrive, and I don't think that I ever spent a pleasanter evening or got more satisfaction out of a pair of shoes. They had not been two minutes on my feet before Larry was carrying a tray of negus across the room in those which I had worn at dinner.

"The Dillon girls are going to stay here," said Fanny, as I wished her good-night at two o'clock, "and we'll have dancing every evening as long as you remain."

"But I shall leave to-morrow," said I.

"Indeed you won't! Papa will take care of that."

And so he did. "You'd better go over to Ballyglass yourself to-morrow," said he, "and collect your own things; there's no knowing else what you may have to borrow from Larry."

I staid there three weeks, and in the middle of the third I thought that every thing would be arranged between me and Fanny. But the aunt interfered; and in about a twelvemonth after my adventures she consented to make a more fortunate man happy for his life.

"The O'Conors of Castle Conor, County Mayo" appeared first in the May issue of *Harper's New Monthly Magazine* for 1860.

The Parson's Daughter of Oxney Colne

T HE PRETTIEST SCENERY IN ALL ENGLAND
— and if I am contradicted in that assertion, I will say in all
Europe — is in Devonshire, on the southern and southeastern
skirts of Dartmoor, where the rivers Dart and Avon and Teign
form themselves, and where the broken moor is half cultivated,
and the wild-looking uplands fields are half moor. In making this
assertion I am often met with much doubt, but it is by persons
who do not really know the locality. Men and women talk to me
on the matter who have travelled down the line of railway from
Exeter to Plymouth, who have spent a fortnight at Torquay, and
perhaps made an excursion from Tavistock to the convict prison
on Dartmoor. But who knows the glories of Chagford? Who has
walked through the parish of Manaton? Who is conversant with
Lustleigh Cleeves and Withycombe in the moor? Who has
explored Holne Chase? Gentle reader, believe me that you will
be rash in contradicting me unless you have done these things.

There or therabouts — I will not say by the waters of which
little river it is washed — is the parish of Oxney Colne. And for
those who would wish to see all the beauties of this lovely country
a sojourn in Oxney Colne would be most desirable, seeing that
the sojourner would then be brought nearer to all that he would
delight to visit, than at any other spot in the country. But there
is an objection to any such arrangement. There are only two

decent houses in the whole parish, and these are — or were when I knew the locality — small and fully occupied by their possessors. The larger and better is the parsonage in which lived the parson and his daughter; and the smaller is the freehold residence of a certain Miss Le Smyrger, who owned a farm of a hundred acres which was rented by one Farmer Cloysey, and who also possessed some thirty acres round her own house which she managed herself, regarding herself to be quite as great in cream as Mr. Cloysey, and altogether superior to him in the article of cider. "But yeu has to pay no rent, Miss," Farmer Cloysey would say, when Miss Le Smyrger expressed this opinion of her art in a manner too defiant. "Yeu pays no rent, or yeu couldn't do it." Miss Le Smyrger was an old maid, with a pedigree and blood of her own, a hundred and thirty acres of fee-simple land on the borders of Dartmoor, fifty years of age, a constitution of iron, and an opinion of her own on every subject under the sun.

And now for the parson and his daughter. The parson's name was Woolsworthy — or Woolathy as it was pronounced by all those who lived around him — the Rev. Saul Woolsworthy; and his daughter was Patience Woolsworthy, or Miss Patty, as she was known to the Devonshire world of those parts. That name of Patience had not been well chosen for her for she was a hot-tempered damsel, warm in her convictions, and inclined to express them freely. She had but two closely intimate friends in the world, and by both of them this freedom of expression had been fully permitted to her since she was a child. Miss Le Smyrger and her father were well accustomed to her ways, and on the whole well satisfied with them. The former was equally free and equally warm-tempered as herself, and as Mr. Woolsworthy was allowed by his daughter to be quite paramount on his own subject — for he had a subject — he did not object to his daughter being paramount on all others. A pretty girl was Patience Woolsworthy at the time of which I am writing, and one who possessed much that was worthy of remark and admiration had she lived where beauty meets with admiration, or where force of character is remarked. But at Oxney Colne, on the borders of Dartmoor, there were few to appreciate her, and it seemed as though she herself had but little idea of carrying her talent further afield, so that it might not remain for ever wrapped in a blanket.

She was a pretty girl, tall and slender, with dark eyes and black hair. Her eyes were perhaps too round for regular beauty, and her hair was perhaps too crisp; her mouth was large and expressive; her nose was finely formed, though a critic in female form might have declared it to be somewhat broad. But her countenance altogether was very attractive — if only it might be seen without that resolution for dominion which occassionally marred it, though sometimes it even added to her attractions.

It must be confessed on behalf of Patience Woolsworthy that the circumstances of her life had peremptorily called upon her to exercise dominion. She had lost her mother when she was sixteen, and had had neither brother nor sister. She had no neighbours near her fit either from education or rank to interfere in the conduct of her life, excepting always Miss Le Smyrger. Miss Le Smyrger would have done anything for her, including the whole management of her morals and of the parsonage household, had Patience been content with such an arrangement. But much as Patience had ever loved Miss Le Smyrger, she was not content with this, and therefore she had been called on to put forth a strong hand of her own. She had put forth this strong hand early, and hence had come the character which I am attempting to describe. But I must say on behalf of this girl that it was not only over others that she thus exercised dominion. In acquiring that power she had also acquired the much greater power of exercising rule over herself.

But why should her father have been ignored in these family arrangements? Perhaps it may almost suffice to say, that of all living men her father was the man best conversant with the antiquities of the county in which he lived. He was the Jonathan Oldbuck of Devonshire, and especially of Dartmoor, — but without that decision of character which enabled Oldbuck to keep his womenkind in some kind of subjection, and probably enabled him also to see that his weekly bills did not pass their proper limits. Our Mr. Oldbuck, of Oxney Colne, was sadly deficient in these respects. As a parish pastor with but a small cure he did his duty with sufficient energy to keep him, at any rate, from reproach. He was kind and charitable to the poor, punctual in his services, forbearing with the farmers around him, mild with his brother clergymen, and indifferent to aught that bishop or arch-

deacon might think or say of him. I do not name this latter attrib-
ute as a virtue, but as a fact. But all these points were as nothing
in the known character of Mr. Woolsworthy, of Oxney Colne.
He was the antiquarian of Dartmoor. That was his line of life. It
was in that capacity that he was known to the Devonshire world;
it was as such that he journeyed about with his humble carpet-
bag, staying away from his parsonage a night or two at a time; it
was in that character that he received now and again stray visitors in the single spare bedroom — not friends asked to see him
and his girl because of their friendship — but men who knew
something as to this buried stone, or that old land-mark. In all
these things his daughter let him have his own way, assisting and
encouraging him. That was his line of life, and therefore she
respected it. But in all other matters she chose to be paramount
at the parsonage.

Mr. Woolsworthy was a little man, who always wore, except
on Sundays, grey clothes — clothes of so light a grey that they
would hardly have been regarded as clerical in a district less
remote. He had now reached a goodly age, being full seventy
years old; but still he was wiry and active, and shewed but few
symptoms of decay. His head was bald, and the few remaining
locks that surrounded it were nearly white. But there was a look
of energy about his mouth, and a humour in his light grey eye,
which forbade those who knew him to regard him altogether as
an old man. As it was, he could walk from Oxney Colne to Pries-
town, fifteen long Devonshire miles across the moor; and he who
could do that could hardly be regarded as too old for work.

But our present story will have more to do with his daughter
than with him. A pretty girl, I have said, was Patience
Woolsworthy; and one, too, in many ways remarkable. She had
taken her outlook into life, weighing the things which she had
and those which she had not, in a manner very unusual, and, as
a rule, not always desirable for a young lady. The things which
she had not were very many. She had not society; she had not a
fortune; she had not any assurance of future means of livelihood;
she had not high hope of procuring for herself a position in life
by marriage; she had not that excitement and pleasure in life
which she read of in such books as found their way down to
Oxney Colne Parsonage. It would be easy to add to the list of the

things which she had not; and this list against herself she made out with the utmost vigour. The things which she had, or those rather which she assured herself of having, were much more easily counted. She had the birth and education of a lady, the strength of a healthy woman, and a will of her own. Such was the list as she made it out for herself, and I protest that I assert no more than the truth in saying that she never added to it either beauty, wit, or talent.

I began these descriptions by saying that Oxney Colne would, of all places, be the best spot from which a tourist could visit those parts of Devonshire, but for the fact that he could obtain there none of the accommodation which tourists require. A brother antiquarian might, perhaps, in those days have done so, seeing that there was, as I have said, a spare bedroom at the parsonage. Any intimate friend of Miss Le Smyrger's might be as fortunate, for she was also so provided at Oxney Combe, by which name her house was known. But Miss Le Smyrger was not given to extensive hospitality, and it was only to those who were bound to her, either by ties of blood or of very old friendship, that she delighted to open her doors. As her old friends were very few in number, as those few lived at a distance, and as her nearest relations were higher in the world than she was, and were said by herself to look down upon her, the visits made to Oxney Combe were few and far between.

But now, at the period of which I am writing, such a visit was about to be made. Miss Le Smyrger had a younger sister who had inherited a property in the parish of Oxney Colne equal to that of the lady who lived there; but this younger sister had inherited beauty also, and she therefore, in early life, had found sundry lovers, one of whom became her husband. She had married a man even then well to do in the world, but now rich and almost mighty; a Member of Parliament, a Lord of this and that board, a man who had a house in Eaton-square, and a park in the north of England; and in this way her course of life had been very much divided from that of our Miss Le Smyrger. But the Lord of the Government board had been blessed with various children, and perhaps it was now thought expedient to look after Aunt Penelope's Devonshire acres. Aunt Penelope was empowered to leave them to whom she pleased; and though it was thought in Eaton-square that she must, as a matter of course, leave them to one of the family, nevertheless a little cousinly intercourse might make the thing more certain. I will not say that this was the sole cause for such a visit, but in these days a visit was to be made by Captain Broughton to his aunt. Now Captain John Broughton was the second son of Alfonso Broughton, of Clapham Park and Eaton-square, Member of Parliament, and Lord of the aforesaid Government Board.

And what do you mean to do with him? Patience Woolsworthy asked of Miss Le Smyrger when that lady walked over from the Combe to say that her nephew John was to arrive on the following morning.

"Do with him? Why, I shall bring him over here to talk to your father."

"He'll be too fashionable for that, and papa won't trouble his head about him if he finds that he doesn't care for Dartmoor."

"Then he may fall in love with you, my dear."

"Well, yes; there's that resource at any rate, and for your sake I dare say I should be more civil to him than papa. But he'll soon get tired of making love to me, and what you'll do then I cannot imagine."

That Miss Woolsworthy felt no interest in the coming of the Captian I will not pretend to say. The advent of any stranger with whom she would be called on to associate must be matter of interest to her in that secluded place; and she was not so absolutely unlike other young ladies that the arrival of an unmarried young man would be the same to her as the advent of some patriarchal pater-familias. In taking that outlook into life of which I have spoken she had never said to herself that she despised those things from which other girls received the excitement, the joys, and the disappointment of their lives. She had simply given herself to understand that very little of such things would come in her way, and that it behoved her to live — to live happily if such might be possible — without experiencing the need of them. She had heard, when there was no thought of any such visit to Oxney Colne, that John Broughton was a handsome clever man — one who thought much of himself and was thought much of by others — that there had been some talk of his marrying a great heiress, which marriage, however had not taken place through unwillingness on his part, and that he was on the whole a man of more mark in the world than the ordinary captains of ordinary regiments.

Captain Broughton came to Oxney Combe, stayed there a fortnight — the intended period for his projected visit having been fixed at three or four days — and then went his way. He went his way back to his London haunts, the time of the year then being the close of the Easter holy-days; but as he did so he told his aunt that he should assuredly return to her in the autumn.

"And assuredly I shall be happy to see you, John — if you come with a certain purpose. If you have no such purpose, you had better remain away."

"I shall assuredly come," the Captain had replied, and then he had gone on his journey.

The summer passed rapidly by, and very little was said between Miss Le Smyrger and Miss Woolsworthy about Captain Broughton. In many respects — nay, I may say, as to all ordinary matters, — no two women could well be more intimate with each other than they were; and more than that, they had the courage each to talk to the other with absolute truth as to things concerning themselves — a courage in which dear friends often fail. But, nevertheless, very little was said between them about Captain John Broughton. All that was said may be here repeated.

"John says that he shall return here in August," Miss Le Smyrger said as Patience was sitting with her in the parlour at Oxney Combe, on the morning after that gentleman's departure.

"He told me so himself," said Patience; and as she spoke her round dark eyes assumed a look of more than ordinary self-will. If Miss Le Smyrger had intended to carry the conversation any further she changed her mind as she looked at her companion. Then, as I said, the summer ran by, and towards the close of the warm days of July, Miss Le Smyrger, sitting in the same chair in the same room, again took up the conversation.

"I got a letter from John this morning. He says that he shall be here on the third."

"Does he?"

"He is very punctual to the time he named."

"Yes; I fancy that he is a punctual man," said Patience.

27

"I hope that you will be glad to see him," said Miss Le Smyrger.

"Very glad to see him," said Patience, with a bold clear voice; and then the conversation was again dropped, and nothing further was said till after Captain Broughton's second arrival in the parish.

Four months had then passed since his departure, and during that time Miss Woolsworthy had performed all her usual daily duties in their accustomed course. No one could discover that she had been less careful in her household matters than had been her wont, less willing to go among her poor neighbours, or less assiduous in her attentions to her father. But not the less was there a feeling in the minds of those around her that some great change had come upon her. She would sit during the long summer evenings on a certain spot outside the parsonage orchard, at the top of a small sloping field in which their solitary cow was always pastured, with a book on her knees before her, but rarely reading. There she would sit, with the beautiful view down to the winding river below her, watching the setting sun, and thinking, thinking, thinking — thinking of something of which she had never spoken. Often would Miss Le Smyrger come upon her there, and sometimes would pass her even without a word; but never — never once did she dare to ask her of the matter of her thoughts. But she knew the matter well enough. No confession was necessary to inform her that Patience Woolsworthy was in love with John Broughton — ay, in love, to the full and entire loss of her whole heart.

On one evening she was so sitting till the July sun had fallen and hidden himself for the night, when her father came upon her as he returned from one of his rambles on the moor. "Patty," he said, "you are always sitting there now. Is it not late? Will you not be cold?"

"No papa," she said, "I shall not be cold."

"But won't you come to the house? I miss you when you come in so late that there's no time to say a word before we go to bed."

She got up and followed him into the parsonage, and when they were in the sitting-room together, and the door was closed, she came up to him and kissed him. "Papa," she said, "would it make you very unhappy if I were to leave you?"

"Leave me!" he said, startled by the serious and almost solemn tone of her voice. "Do you mean for always?"

"If I were to marry, papa?"

"Oh, marry! No; that would not make me unhappy. It would make me very happy, Patty, to see you married to a man you would love; — very, very happy; though my days would be desolate without you."

"That is it, papa. What would you do if I went from you?"

"What would it matter, Patty? I should be free, at any rate, from a load which often presses heavy on me now. What will you do when I shall leave you? A few more years and all will be over with me. But who is it, love? Has anybody said anything to you?"

"It was only an idea, papa. I don't often think of such a thing; but I did think of it then." And so the subject was allowed to pass by. This had happened before the day of the second arrival had been absolutely fixed and made known to Miss Woolsworthy.

And then that second arrival took place. The reader may have understood from the words with which Miss Le Smyrger authorised her nephew to make his second visit to Oxney Combe that Miss Woolsworthy's passion was not altogether unauthorised. Captain Broughton had been told that he was not to come unless he came with a certain purpose; and having been so told, he still persisted in coming. There can be no doubt but that he well understood the purport to which his aunt alluded. "I shall assuredly come," he had said. And true to his word, he was now there.

Patience knew exactly the hour at which he must arrive at the station at Newton Abbot, and the time also which it would take to travel over those twelve up-hill miles from the station to Oxney. It need hardly be said that she paid no visit to Miss Le Smyrger's house on that afternoon; but she might have known something of Captain Broughton's approach without going thither. His road to the Combe passed by the parsonage-gate, and had Patience sat even at her bedroom window she must have seen him. But on such an evening she would not sit at her bedroom window; — she would do nothing which would force her to accuse herself of a restless longing for her lover's coming. It was for him to seek her. If he chose to do so, he knew the way to the parsonage.

Miss Le Smyrger — good, dear, honest, hearty Miss Le Smyrger, was in a fever of anxiety on behalf of her friend. It was not
that she wished her nephew to marry Patience, — or rather that
she had entertained any such wish when he first came among
them. She was not given to match-making, and moreover
thought, or had thought within herself, that they of Oxney
Colne could do very well without any admixture from Eaton-
square. Her plan of life had been that when old Mr. Woolsworthy
was taken away from Dartmoor, Patience should live with her,
and that when she also shuffled off her coil, the Patience
Woolsworthy should be the maiden-mistress of Oxney Combe
— of Oxney Combe and of Mr. Cloysey's farm — to the utter detriment of all the Broughtons. Such had been her plan before
nephew John had come among them — a plan not to be spoken
of till the coming of that dark day which should make Patience
an orphan. But now her nephew had been there, and all was to
be altered. Miss Le Smyrger's plan would have provided a companion for her old age; but that had not been her chief object.
She had thought more of Patience than of herself, and now it
seemed that a prospect of a higher happiness was opening for her
friend.

"John," she said, as soon as the first greetings were over, "do
you remember the last words that I said to you before you went
away?" Now, for myself, I much admire Miss Le Smyrger's harti-
ness, but I do not think much of her discretion. It would have
been better, perhaps, had she allowed things to take their course.

"I can't say that I do," said the Captain. At the same time the
Captain did remember very well what those last words had been.

"I am so glad to see you, so delighted to see you, if — if — if
—," and then she paused, for with all her courage she hardly
dared to ask her nephew whether he had come there with the
express purport of asking Miss Woolsworthy to marry him.

To tell the truth — for there is no room for mystery within the
limits of this short story, — to tell, I say, at a word the plain and
simple truth, Captain Broughton had already asked that question. On the day before he left Oxney Colne he had in set terms
proposed to the parson's daughter, and indeed the words, the hot
and frequent words, which previously to that had fallen like
sweetest honey into the ears of Patience Woolsworthy, had made

it imperative on him to do so. When a man in such a place as that has talked to a girl of love day after day, must not he talk of it to some definite purpose on the day on which he leaves her? Or if he do not, must he not submit to be regarded as false, self-fish, and almost fraudulent? Captain Broughton, however, had asked the question honestly and truly. He had done so honestly and truly, but in words, or, perhaps, simply with a tone, that had hardly sufficed to satisfy the proud spirit of the girl he loved. She by that time had confessed to herself that she loved him with all her heart; but she had made no such confession to him. To him she had spoken no word, granted no favour, that any lover might rightfully regard as a token of love returned. She had listened to him as he spoke, and bade him keep such sayings for the drawing-rooms of his fashionable friends. Then he had spoken out and had asked for that hand, — not, perhaps, as a suitor tremulous with hope, — but as a rich man who knows that he can command that which he desires to purchase.

"You should think more of this," she had said to him at last. "If you would really have me for your wife, it will not be much to you to return here again when time for thinking of it shall have passed by." With these words she had dismissed him, and now he had again come back to Oxney Colne. But still she would not place herself at the window to look for him, nor dress herself in other than her simple morning country dress, nor omit one item of her daily work. If he wished to take her at all, he should wish to take her as she really was, in her plain country life, but he should take her also with full observance of all those privileges which maidens are allowed to claim from their lovers. He should curtail no ceremonious observance because she was the daughter of a poor country parson who would come to him without a shill-ing, whereas he stood high in the world's books. He had asked her to give him all that she had, and that all she was ready to give, without stint. But the gift must be valued before it could be given or received. He also was to give her as much, and she would accept it as being beyond all price. But she would not allow that that which was offered to her was in any degree the more precious because of his outward worldly standing.

She would not pretend to herself that she thought he would come to her that afternoon, and therefore she busied herself in the kitchen and about the house, giving directions to her two maids as though the day would pass as all other days did pass in that household. They usually dined at four, and she rarely, in these summer months, went far from the house before that hour. At four precisely she sat down with her father, and then said that she was going up as far as Helpholme after dinner. Helpholme was a solitary farmhouse in another parish, on the border of the moor, and Mr. Woolsworthy asked her whether he should accompany her.

"Do, papa," she said, "if you are not too tired." And yet she had thought how probable it might be that she should meet John Broughton on her walk. And so it was arranged; but, just as dinner was over, Mr. Woolsworthy remembered himself.

"Gracious me," he said, "how my memory is going! Gribbles, from Ivybridge, and old John Poulter, from Bovey, are coming to meet here by appointment. You can't put Helpholme off till to-morrow?"

Patience, however, never put off anything, and therefore at six o'clock, when her father had finished his slender modicum of toddy, she tied on her hat and went on her walk. She started forth with a quick step, and left no word to say by which route she would go. As she passed up along the little lane which led towards Oxney Combe she would not even look to see if he was coming towards her; and when she left the road, passing over a stone stile into a little path which ran first through the upland fields, and then across the moor ground towards Helpholme, she did not look back once, or listen for his coming step.

She paid her visit, remaining upwards of an hour with the old bedridden mother of the farmer of Helpholme. "God bless you, my darling!" said the old lady as she left her; "and send you some one to make your own path bright and happy through the world." These words were still ringing in her ears with all their significance as she saw John Broughton waiting for her at the first stile which she had to pass after leaving the farmer's haggard.

"Patty," he said, as he took her hand, and held it close within both his own, "what a chase I have had after you!"

"And who asked you, Captain Broughton?" she answered, smiling. "If the journey was too much for your poor London strength, could you not have waited till to-morrow morning, when you would have found me at the parsonage?" But she did not draw her hand away from him, or in any way pretend that he had not a right to accost her as a lover.

"No, I could not wait. I am more eager to see those I love than you seem to be."

"How do you know whom I love, or how eager I might be to see them? There is an old woman there whom I love, and I have thought nothing of this walk with the object of seeing her." And now, slowly drawing her hand away from him, she pointed to the farmhouse which she had left.

"Patty," he said, after a minute's pause, during which she had looked full into his face with all the force of her bright eyes; "I have come from London to-day, straight down here to Oxney, and from my aunt's house close upon your footsteps after you to ask you that one question. Do you love me?"

"What a Hercules!" she said, again laughing. "Do you really mean that you left London only this morning? Why, you must have been five hours in a railway carriage and two in a postchaise, not to talk of the walk afterwards. You ought to take more care of yourself, Captain Broughton!"

He would have been angry with her, — for he did not like to be quizzed, — had she not put her hand on his arm as she spoke, and the softness of her touch had redeemed the offence of her words.

"All that have I done," said he, "that I may hear one word from you."

"That any word of mine should have such potency! But, let us walk on, or my father will take us for some of the standing stones of the moor. How have you found your aunt? If you only knew the cares that have sat on her dear shoulders for the last week past, in order that your high mightyness might have a sufficiency to eat and drink in these desolate half-starved regions."

"She might have saved herself such anxiety. No one can care less for such things than I do."

"And yet I think I have heard you boast of the cook of your club." And then again there was silence for a minute or two.

"Patty," said he, stopping again in the path; "answer my question. I have a right to demand an answer. Do you love me?"

33

"And what if I do? What if I have been so silly as to allow your perfections to be too many for my weak heart? What then, Captain Broughton?"

"It cannot be that you love me, or you would not joke now."

"Perhaps not, indeed," she said. It seemed as though she were resolved not to yield an inch in her own humour. And then again they walked on.

"Patty," he said once more, "I shall get an answer from you to-night, — this evening; now, during this walk, or I shall return to-morrow, and never revisit this spot again."

"Oh, Captain Broughton, how should we ever manage to live without you?"

"Very well," he said; "up to the end of this walk I can bear it all; — and one word spoken then will mend it all."

During the whole of this time she felt that she was ill-using him. She knew that she loved him with all her heart; that it would nearly kill her to part with him; that she had heard his renewed offer with an ecstacy of joy. She acknowledged to herself that he was giving proof of his devotion as strong as any which a girl could receive from her lover. And yet she could hardly bring herself to say the word he longed to hear. That word once said, and then she knew that she must succumb to her love for ever! That word once said, and there would be nothing for her but to spoil him with her idolatry! That word once said, and she must continue to repeat it into his ears, till perhaps he might be tired of hearing it! And now he had threatened her, and how could she speak it after that? She certainly would not speak it unless he asked her again without such threat. And so they walked on again in silence.

"Patty," he said at last. "By the heavens above us you shall answer me. Do you love me?"

She now stood still, and almost trembled as she looked up into his face. She stood opposite to him for a moment, and then placing her two hands on his shoulders, she answered him. "I do, I do, I do," she said, "with all my heart; with all my heart — with all my heart and strength." And then her head fell upon his breast.

Captain Broughton was almost as much surprised as delighted by the warmth of the acknowledgement made by the eager-hearted passionate girl whom he now held within his arms. She had said it now; the words had been spoken; and there was nothing for her but to swear to him over and over again with her sweetest oaths, that those words were true — true as her soul. And very sweet was the walk down from thence to the parsonage gate. He spoke no more of the distance of the ground, or the length of his day's journey. But he stopped her at every turn that he might press her arm the closer to his own, that he might look into the brightness of her eyes, and prolong his hour of delight. There were no more gibes now on her tongue, no raillery at his London finery, no laughing comments on his coming and going. With downright honesty she told him everything: how she had loved him before her heart was warranted in such a passion; how, with much thinking, she had resolved that it would be unwise to take him at his first word, and had thought it better that he should return to London, and then think over it; how she had almost repented of her courage when she had feared, during those long summer days, that he would forget her; and how her heart had leapt for joy when her old friend had told her that he was coming.

"And yet," said he, "you were not glad to see me!"

"Oh, was I not glad? You cannot understand the feelings of a girl who has lived secluded as I have done. Glad is no word for the joy I felt. But it was not seeing you that I cared for so much. It was the knowledge that you were near me once again. I almost wish now that I had not seen you till to-morrow." But as she spoke she pressed his arm, and this caress gave the lie to her last words.

"No, do not come in to-night," she said, when she reached the little wicket that led up the parsonage. "Indeed you shall not. I could not behave myself properly if you did."

"But I don't want you to behave properly."

"Oh! I am to keep that for London, am I? But, nevertheless, Captain Broughton, I will not invite you either to tea or to supper to-night."

"Surely I may shake hands with your father."

"Not to-night — not till —. John, I may tell him, may I not? I must tell him at once."

"Certainly," said he.

"And then you shall see him to-morrow. Let me see—at what hour shall I bid you come?"

"To breakfast."

"No, indeed. What on earth would your aunt do with her broiled turkey and the cold pie? I have got no cold pie for you."

"I hate cold pie."

"What a pity! But, John, I should be forced to leave you directly after breakfast. Come down — come down at two, or three; and then I will go back with you to Aunt Penelope. I must see her to-morrow." And so at last the matter was settled, and the happy Captain, as he left her, was hardly resisted in his attempt to press her lips to his own.

When she entered the parlour in which her father was sitting, there still were Gribbles and Poulter discussing some knotty point of Devon lore. So Patience took off her hat, and sat herself down, waiting till they should go. For full an hour she had to wait, and then Gribbles and Poulter did go. But it was not in such matters as this that Patience Woolsworthy was impatient. She could wait, and wait, and wait, curbing herself for weeks and months, while the thing waited for was in her eyes good; but she could not curb her hot thoughts or her hot words when things came to be discussed which she did not think to be good.

"Papa," she said, when Gribbles' long-drawn last word had been spoken at the door. "Do you remember how I asked you the other day what you would say if I were to leave you?"

"Yes, surely," he replied, looking up at her in astonishment.

"I am going to leave you now," she said. "Dear, dearest father, how am I to go from you?"

"Going to leave me," said he, thinking of her visit to Help-holme, and thinking of nothing else.

Now there had been a story about Helpholme. That bed-ridden old lady there had a stalwart son, who was now the owner of the Helpholme pastures. But though owner in fee of all those wild acres and of the cattle which they supported, he was not much above the farmers around him, either in manners or edu-cation. He had his merits, however; for he was honest, well to do in the world, and modest withal. How strong love had grown up, springing from neighbourly kindness, between our Patience and his mother, it needs not here to tell; but rising from it had come another love — or an ambition which might have grown to love. The young man, after much thought, had not dared to speak to Miss Woolsworthy, but he had sent a message by Miss Le Smyrger. If there could be any hope for him, he would present himself as a suitor — on trial. He did not owe a shilling in the world, and had money by him — saved. He wouldn't ask the parson for a shilling of fortune. Such had been the tenor of his message, and Miss Le Smyrger had delivered it faithfully. "He does not mean it," Patience had said with her stern voice. "Indeed he does, my dear. You may be sure he is in earnest," Miss Le Smyrger had replied; "and there is not an honester man in these parts."

"Tell him," said Patience, not attending to the latter portion of her friend's last speech, "that it cannot be, — make him understand, you know — and tell him also that the matter shall be thought of no more." The matter had, at any rate, been spoken of no more, but the young farmer still remained a bachelor, and Helpholme still wanted a mistress. But all this came back upon the parson's mind when his daughter told him that she was about to leave him.

"Yes, dearest," she said; and as she spoke, she now knelt at his knees. "I have been asked in marriage, and I have given myself away."

"Well, my love, if you will be happy —"

"I hope I shall; I think I shall. But you, papa?"

"You will not be far from us."

"Oh, yes; in London."

"In London?"

"Captain Broughton lives in London generally."

"And has Captain Broughton asked you to marry him?"

"Yes, papa — who else? Is he not good? Will you not love him? Oh, papa, do not say that I am wrong to love him?"

He never told her his mistake, or explained to her that he had not thought it possible that the high-placed son of the London great man shall have fallen in love with his undowered daughter; but he embraced her, and told her, with all his enthusiasm, that he rejoiced in her joy, and would be happy in her happiness. "My own Patty," he said, "I have ever known that you were too good for this life of ours here." And then the evening wore away into the night, with many tears but still with much happiness.

Captain Broughton, as he walked back to Oxney Combe, made up his mind that he would say nothing on the matter to his aunt till the next morning. He wanted to think over it all, and to think it over, if possible, by himself. He had taken a step in life, the most important that a man is ever called on to take, and he had to reflect whether or no he had taken it with wisdom.

"Have you seen her?" said Miss Le Smyrger, very anxiously, when he came into the drawing-room.

"Miss Woolsworthy you mean," said he. "Yes, I've seen her. As I found her out I took a long walk and happened to meet her. Do you know, aunt, I think I'll go to bed; I was up at five this morning, and have been on the move ever since."

Miss Le Smyrger perceived that she was to hear nothing that evening, so she handed him his candlestick and allowed him to go to his room.

But Captain Broughton did not immediately retire to bed, nor when he did so was he able to sleep at once. Had this step that he had taken been a wise one? He was not a man who, in worldly matters, had allowed things to arrange themselves for him, as is the case with so many men. He had formed views for himself, and had a theory of life. Money for money's sake he had declared to himself to be bad. Money, as a concomitant to things which were in themselves good, he had declared to himself to be good also. That concomitant in this affair of his marriage, he had now missed. Well; he had made up his mind to that, and would put up with the loss. He had means of living of his own, though means not so extensive as might have been desirable. That it would be well for him to become a married man, looking merely to that state of life as opposed to his present state, he had fully resolved. On that point, therefore, there was nothing to repent. That Patty Woolsworthy was good, affectionate, clever, and beautiful, he was sufficiently satisifed. It would be odd indeed if he were not so satisifed now, seeing that for the last four months he had declared to himself daily that she was so with many inward asseverations. And yet though he repeated now again that he was satisfied, I do not think that he was so fully satisifed of it as he had been throughout the whole of those four months. It is sad to say so, but I fear — I fear that such was the case. When you have your plaything how much of the anticipated pleasure vanishes, especially if it have been won easily!

He had told none of his family what were his intentions in this second visit to Devonshire, and now he had to bethink himself whether they would be satisifed. What would his sister say, she who had married the Honourable Augustus Gumbleton, gold-stick-in-waiting to Her Majesty's Privy Council? Would she receive Patience with open arms, and make much of her about London? And then how far would London suit Patience, or would Patience suit London? There would be much for him to do in teaching her, and it would be well for him to set about the lesson without loss of time. So far he got that night, but when the morning came he went a step further, and began mentally to criticise her manner to himself. It had been very sweet, that warm, that full, that ready declaration of love. Yes; it had been very sweet; but—but—; when, after her little jokes, she did confess her love, had she not been a little too free for feminine excellence? A man likes to be told that he is loved, but he hardly wishes that the girl he is to marry should fling herself at his head!

Ah me! yes; it was thus he argued to himself as on that morning he went through the arrangements of his toilet. "Then he was a brute," you say, my pretty reader. I have never said that he was not a brute. But this I remark, that many such brutes are to be met with in the beaten paths of the world's high highway. When Patience Woolsworthy had answered him coldly, bidding him go back to London and think over his love; while it seemed from her manner that at any rate as yet she did not care for him; while he was absent from her, and, therefore, longing for her, the possession of her charms, her talent, and bright honesty of purpose had seemed to him a thing most desirable. Now they were his own. They had, in fact, been his own from the first. The heart of this country-bred girl had fallen at the first word from his mouth. Had she not so confessed to him? She was very nice, — very nice indeed. He loved her dearly. But had he not sold himself too cheaply?

I by no means say that he was not a brute. But whether brute or no he was an honest man, and had no remotest dream, either then, on that morning, or during the following days on which such thoughts pressed more thickly on his mind — of breaking away from his pledged word. At breakfast on that morning he told all to Miss Le Smyrger, and that lady, with warm and gracious intentions, confided to him her purpose regarding her property. "I have always regarded Patience as my heir," she said, "and shall do so still."

"Oh, indeed," said Captain Broughton.

"But it is a great, great pleasure to me to think that she will give back the little property to my sister's child. You will have your mother's, and thus it will all come together again."

"Ah!" said Captain Broughton. He had his own ideas about property, and did not, even under existing circumstances, like to hear that his aunt considered herself at liberty to leave the acres away to one who was by blood quite a stranger to the family.

"Does Patience know of this?" he asked.

"Not a word," said Miss Le Smyrger. And then nothing more was said upon the subject.

On that afternoon he went down and received the parson's benediction and congratulations with a good grace. Patience said very little on the occasion, and indeed was absent during the greater part of the interview. The two lovers then walked up to Oxney Combe, and there were more benedictions and more congratulations. "All went merry as a marriage bell," at any rate as far as Patience was concerned. Not a word had yet fallen from that dear mouth, not a look had yet come over that handsome face, which tended in any way to mar her bliss. Her first day of acknowledged love was a day altogether happy, and when she prayed for him as she knelt beside her bed there was no feeling in her mind that any fear need disturb her joy.

I will pass over the next three or four days very quickly, merely saying that Patience did not find them so pleasant as that first day after her engagement. There was something in her lover's manner, — something which at first she could not define, — which by degrees seemed to grate against her feelings. He was sufficiently affectionate, that being a matter on which she did not require much demonstration; but joined to his affection there seemed to be —; she hardly liked to suggest to herself a harsh word, but could it be possible that he was beginning to think that she was not good enough for him? And then she asked herself the question — was she good enough for him? If there were doubt about that, the match should be broken off, though she tore her own heart out in the struggle. The truth, however, was this, — that he had begun that teaching which he had already found to be so necessary. Now, had any one essayed to teach Patience German or mathematics, with that young lady's free consent, I believe that she would have been found a meek scholar. But it was not probable that she would be meek when she found a self-appointed tutor teaching her manners and conduct without her consent.

So matters went on for four or five days, and on the evening of the fifth day, Captain Broughton and his aunt drank tea at the parsonage. Nothing very especial occurred; but as the parson and Miss Le Smyrger insisted on playing backgammon with devoted perseverance during the whole evening, Broughton had a good opportunity of saying a word or two about those changes in his lady-love which a life in London would require—and some word he said also—some single slight word, as to the higher station in life to which he would exalt his bride. Patience bore it—for her father and Miss Le Smyrger were in the room—she bore it well, speaking no syllable of anger, and enduring, for the moment, the implied scorn of the old parsonage. Then the evening broke up, and Captain Broughton walked back to Oxney Combe with his aunt. "Patty," her father said to her before they went to bed, "he seems to me to be a most excellent young man." "Dear papa," she answered, kissing him. "And terribly deep in love," said Mr. Woolsworthy. "Oh, I don't know about that," she answered, as she left him with her sweetest smile. But though she could thus smile at her father's joke, she had already made up her mind that there was still something to be learned as to her promised husband before she could place herself altogether in his hands. She would ask him whether he thought himself liable to injury from this proposed marriage; and though he should deny any such thought, she would know from the manner of his denial what his true feelings were.

And he, too, on that night, during his silent walk with Miss Le Smyrger, had entertained some similar thoughts. "I fear she is obstinate," he had said to himself, and then he had half accused her of being sullen also. "If that be her temper, what a life of misery I have before me!"

"Have you fixed a day yet?" his aunt asked him as they came near to her house.

"No, not yet: I don't know whether it will suit me to fix it before I leave."

"Why, it was but the other day you were in such a hurry."

"Ah — yes — I have thought more about it since then."

"I should have imagined that this would depend on what Patty thinks," said Miss Le Smyrger, standing up for the privileges of her sex. "It is presumed that the gentleman is always ready as soon as the lady will consent."

"Yes, in ordinary cases it is so; but when a girl is taken out of her own sphere —"

"Her own sphere! Let me caution you, Master John, not to talk to Patty about her own sphere."

"Aunt Penelope, as Patience is to be my wife and not yours, I must claim permission to speak to her on such subjects as may seem suitable to me." And then they parted — not in the best humour with each other.

On the following day Captain Broughton and Miss Woolsworthy did not meet till the evening. She had said, before those few ill-omened words had passed her lover's lips, that she would probably be at Miss Le Smyrger's house on the following morning. Those ill-omened words did pass her lover's lips, and then she remained at home. This did not come from sullenness, nor even from anger, but from a conviction that it would be well that she should think much before she met him again. Nor was he anxious to hurry a meeting. His thought — his base thought — was this; that she would be sure to come up to the Combe after him; but she did not come, and therefore in the evening he went down to her, and asked her to walk with him.

They went away by the path that led to Helpholme, and little was said between them till they had walked some mile together. Patience, as she went along the path, remembered almost to the letter the sweet words which had greeted her ears as she came down that way with him on the night of his arrival; but he remembered nothing of that sweetness then. Had he not made an ass of himself during these last six months? That was the thought which very much had possession of his mind.

"Patience," he said at last, having hitherto spoken only an indifferent word now and again since they had left the parsonage, "Patience, I hope you realize the importance of the step which you and I are about to take?"

"Of course I do," she answered: "what an odd question that is for you to ask!"

"Because," said he, "sometimes I almost doubt it. It seems to me as though you thought you could remove yourself from here to your new home with no more trouble than when you go from home up to the Combe."

"Is that meant for a reproach, John?"

"No, not for a reproach, but for advice. Certainly not for a reproach."

"I am glad of that."

"But I should wish to make you think how great is the leap in the world which you are about to take." Then again they walked on for many steps before she answered him.

"Tell me, then, John," she said, when she had sufficiently considered what words she would speak; — and as she spoke a dark bright colour suffused her face, and her eyes flashed almost with anger. "What leap do you mean? Do you mean a leap upwards?"

"Well, yes; I hope it will be so."

"In one sense, certainly, it would be a leap upwards. To be the wife of the man I loved; to have the privilege of holding his happiness in my hand; to know that I was his own — the companion whom he had chosen out of all the world — that would, indeed, be a leap upward; a leap almost to heaven, if all that were so. But if you mean upwards in any other sense —"

"I was thinking of the social scale."

"Then, Captain Broughton, your thoughts were doing me dishonour."

"Doing you dishonour!"

"Yes, doing me dishonour. That your father is, in the world's esteem, a greater man than mine is doubtless true enough. That you, as a man, are richer than I am as a woman is doubtless also true. But you dishonour me, and yourself also, if these things can weigh with you now."

"Patience, — I think you can hardly know what words you are saying to me."

"Pardon me, but I think I do. Nothing that you can give me — no gifts of that description — can weigh aught against that which I am giving you. If you had all the wealth and rank of the greatest lord in the land, it would count as nothing in such a scale. If — as I have not doubted — if in return for my heart you have given me yours, then — then — then, you have paid me fully. But when gifts such as those are going, nothing else can count even as a make-weight."

"I do not quite understand you," he answered, after a pause. "I fear you are a little high-flown." And then, while the evening was still early, they walked back to the parsonage almost without another word.

Captain Broughton at this time had only one more full day to remain at Oxney Combe. On the afternoon following that he was to go as far as Exeter, and thence return to London. Of course it was to be expected, that the wedding day would be fixed before he went, and much had been said about it during the first day or two of his engagement. Then he had pressed for an early time, and Patience, with a girl's usual diffidence, had asked for some little delay. But now nothing was said on the subject; and how was it probable that such a matter could be settled after such a conversation as that which I have related? That evening, Miss Le Smyrger asked whether the day had been fixed. "No," said Captain Broughton harshly; "nothing has been fixed." "But it will be arranged before you go." "Probably not," he said; and then the subject was dropped for the time.

"John," she said, just before she went to bed, "if there be anything wrong between you and Patience, I conjure you to tell me."

"You had better ask her," he replied. "I can tell you nothing."

On the following morning he was much surprised by seeing Patience on the gravel path before Miss Le Smyrger's gate immediately after breakfast. He went to the door to open it for her, and she, as she gave him her hand, told him that she came up to speak to him. There was no hesitation in her manner, nor any look of anger in her face. But there was in her gait and form, in her voice and countenance, a fixedness of purpose which he had never seen before, or at any rate had never acknowledged.

"Certainly," said he. "Shall I come out with you, or will you come up stairs?"

"We can sit down in the summer-house," she said; and thither they both went.

"Captain Broughton," she said — and she began her task the moment that they were both seated — "You and I have engaged ourselves as man and wife, but perhaps we have been over rash."

"How so?" said he.

"It may be — and indeed I will say more — it is the case that we have made this engagement without knowing enough of each other's character."

"I have not thought so."

"The time will perhaps come when you will so think, but for the sake of all that we most value, let it come before it is too late. What would be our fate — how terrible would be our misery, if such a thought should come to either of us after we have linked our lots together."

There was a solemnity about her as she thus spoke which almost repressed him, — which for a time did prevent him from taking that tone of authority which on such a subject he would choose to adopt. But he recovered himself. "I hardly think that this comes well from you," he said.

"From whom else should it come? Who else can fight my battle for me; and, John, who else can fight that same battle on your behalf? I tell you this, that with your mind standing towards me as it does stand at present you could not give me your hand at the altar with true words and a happy conscience. Is it not true? You have half repented of your bargain already. Is it not so?"

He did not answer her; but getting up from his seat walked to the front of the summer-house, and stood there with his back turned upon her. It was not that he meant to be ungracious, but in truth he did not know how to answer her. He had half repented of his bargain.

"John," she said, getting up and following him so that she could put her hand upon his arm, "I have been very angry with you."

"Angry with me!" he said, turning sharp upon her.

"Yes, angry with you. You would have treated me like a child. But that feeling has gone now. I am not angry now. There is my hand; — the hand of a friend. Let the words that have been spoken between us be as though they had not been spoken. Let us both be free."

"Do you mean it?" he asked.

"Certainly I mean it." As she spoke these words her eyes were filled with tears in spite of all the efforts she could make to restrain them; but he was not looking at her, and her efforts had sufficed to prevent any sob from being audible.

"With all my heart," he said; and it was manifest from his tone that he had no thought of her happiness as he spoke. It was true that she had been angry with him — angry, as she had herself declared; but nevertheless, in what she had said and what she had done, she had thought more of his happiness than of her own. Now she was angry once again.

"With all your heart, Captain Broughton! Well, so be it. If with all your heart, then is the necessity so much the greater. You go to-morrow. Shall we say farewell now?"

"Patience, I am not going to be lectured."

"Certainly not by me. Shall we say farewell now?"

"Yes, if you are determined."

"I am determined. Farewell, Captain Broughton. You have all my wishes for your happiness." And she held out her hand to him.

"Patience!" he said. And he looked at her with a dark frown, as though he would strive to frighten her into submission. If so, he might have saved himself any such attempt.

"Farewell, Captain Broughton. Give me your hand, for I cannot stay." He gave her his hand, hardly knowing why he did so. She lifted it to her lips and kissed it, and then, leaving him, passed from the summer-house down through the wicket-gate, and straight home to the parsonage.

During the whole of that day she said no word to anyone of what had occurred. When she was once more at home she went about her household affairs as she had done on that day of his arrival. When she sat down to dinner with her father he observed nothing to make him think that she was unhappy, nor during the evening was there any expression in her face, or any tone in her voice, which excited his attention. On the following morning Captain Broughton called at the parsonage, and the servant-girl brought word to her mistress that he was in the parlour. But she would not see him. "Laws, miss, you ain't a quarrelled with your beau?" the poor girl said. "No, not quarrelled," she said; "but give him that." It was a scrap of paper containing a word or two in pencil. "It is better that we should not meet again. God bless you." And from that day to this, now more than ten years, they never have met.

"Papa," she said to her father that afternoon, "dear papa, do not be angry with me. It is all over between me and John Broughton. Dearest, you and I will not be separated."

It would be useless here to tell how great was the old man's surprise and how true his sorrow. As the tale was told to him no cause was given for anger with anyone. Not a word was spoken against the suitor who had on that day returned to London with a full conviction that now at least he was relieved from his engagement. "Patty, my darling child," he said, "may God grant that it be for the best!"

"It is for the best," she answered stoutly. "For this place I am fit; and I much doubt whether I am fit for any other."

On that day she did not see Miss Le Smyrger, but on the following morning, knowing that Captain Broughton had gone off, — having heard the wheels of the carriage as they passed by the parsonage gate on his way to the station, — she walked up to the Combe.

"He has told you, I suppose?" said she.

"Yes," said Miss Le Smyrger. "And I will never see him again unless he asks your pardon on his knees. I have told him so. I would not even give him my hand as he went."

"But why so, thou kindest one? The fault was mine more than his."

"I understand. I have eyes in my head," said the old maid. "I have watched him for the last four or five days. If you could have kept the truth to yourself and bade him keep off from you, he would have been at your feet now, licking the dust from your shoes."

"But, dear friend, I do not want a man to lick dust from my shoes."

"Ah, you are a fool. You do not know the value of your own wealth."

"True; I have been a fool. I was a fool to think that one coming from such a life as he has led could be happy with such as I am. I know the truth now. I have bought the lesson dearly, — but perhaps not too dearly, seeing that it will never be forgotten."

There was but little more said about the matter between our three friends at Oxney Combe. What, indeed, could be said? Miss Le Smyrger for a year or two still expected that her nephew would return and claim his bride; but he has never done so, nor has there been any correspondence between them. Patience Woolsworthy had learned her lesson dearly. She had given her whole heart to the man; and, though she so bore herself that no one was aware of the violence of the struggle, nevertheless the struggle within her bosom was very violent. She never told herself that she had done wrong; she never regretted her loss; but yet — yet! — the loss was very hard to bear. He also had loved her, but he was not capable of a love which could much injure his daily peace. Her daily peace was gone for many a day to come.

Her father is still living; but there is a curate now in the parish. In conjunction with him and with Miss Le Smyrger she spends her time in the concerns of the parish. In her own eyes she is a confirmed old maid; and such is my opinion also. The romance of her life was played out in that summer. She never sits now lonely on the hill-side thinking how much she might do for one whom she really loved. But with a large heart she loves many, and, with no romance, she works hard to lighten the burdens of those she loves.

As for Captain Broughton, all the world knows that he did marry that great heiress with whom his name was once before connected, and that he is now a useful member of Parliament, working on committees three or four days a week with zeal that is indefatigable. Sometimes, not often, as he thinks of Patience Woolsworthy a smile comes across his face.

"The Parson's Daughter of Oxney Combe" appeared first in the March 2 issue of *The London Review* for 1861.

Malachi's Cove

O N THE NORTHERN COAST OF CORNWALL, between Tintagel and Bossiney, down on the very margin of the sea, there lived not long since an old man who got his living by saving sea-weed from the waves, and selling it for manure. The cliffs there are bold and fine, and the sea beats in upon them from the north with a grand violence. I doubt whether it be not the finest morsel of cliff scenery in England, though it is beaten by many portions of the west coast of Ireland, and perhaps also by spots in Wales and Scotland. Cliffs should be nearly precipitous, they should be broken in their outlines, and should barely admit here and there of an insecure passage from their summit to the sand at their feet. The sea should come, if not up to them, at least very near to them, and then, above all things, the water below should be blue, and not of that dead leaden colour which is so familiar to us in England. At Tintagel all these requisites are there, except that bright blue colour which is so lovely. But the cliffs themselves are bold and well broken, and the margin of sand at high water is very narrow, — so narrow that at spring tides there is barely a footing there.

But close upon this margin was the cottage or hovel of Malachi Trenglos, the old man of whom I have spoken. But Malachi, or old Glos as he was commonly called by the people around him, had not built his house absolutely upon the sand. There was a fissure in the rock so great that at the top it formed a narrow ravine, and so complete from the summit to the base that it afforded an opening for a steep and rugged track from the top of the rock to the bottom. This fissue was so wide at the bottom that it had afforded space for Trenglos to fix his habitation on a foundation of rock, and here he had lived for many years. It was told of him that in the early days of his trade he had always carried the weed in a basket on his back to the top, but latterly he had been possessed of a donkey which had been trained to go up and down the steep track with a single pannier over his loins, for the rocks would not admit of panniers hanging by his side; and for this assistant he had built a shed adjoining his own, and almost as large as that in which he himself resided.

But as years went on old Glos procured other assistance than that of the donkey, or, as I should rather say, Providence supplied him with other help; and, indeed, had it not been so, the old man must have given up his cabin and his independence and gone into the workhouse at Camelford. For rheumatism had afflicted him, old age had bowed him till he was nearly double, and by degrees he became unable to attend the donkey on its upward passage to the world above, or even to assist in rescuing the coveted weed from the waves. At the time to which our story refers Trenglos had not been up the cliff for twelve months, and for the last six months he had done nothing towards the furtherance of his trade, except to take the money and keep it, if any of it was kept, and occasionally to shake down a bundle of fodder for the donkey. The real work of the business was done altogether by Mahala Trenglos, his granddaughter. Mally Trenglos was known to all the farmers round the coast, and to all the small tradespeople in Camelford. She was a wild-looking, almost unearthly creature, with wild flowing, black, uncombed hair, small in stature, with small hands and bright black eyes; but people said that she was very strong, and the children around declared that she worked day and night and knew nothing of fatigue. As to her age there were many doubts. Some said she was ten, and others five and twenty, but the reader may be allowed to know that at this time she had in truth passed her twentieth birthday. The old people spoke well of Mally, because she was so good to her grandfather, and it was said of her that though she carried to him a little gin and tobacco almost daily, she bought nothing for herself; and as to the gin, no one who looked at her would accuse her of meddling with that. But she had no friends and but few acquaintances among people of her own age. They said that she was fierce and ill-natured, that she had not a good word for any one, and that she was, complete at all points, a thorough little vixen. The young men did not care for her, for, as regarded dress, all days were alike with her. She never made herself smart on Sundays. She was generally without stockings, and seemed to care not at all to exercise any of those feminine attractions which might have been hers had she studied to attain them. All days were the same to her in regard to dress, and, indeed, till lately, all days had I fear been the same to her in other respects. Old Malachi had never been seen inside a place of worship since he had taken to live under the cliff. But within the last two years Mally had submitted herself to the teaching of the clergyman at Tintagel, and had appeared at church on Sundays, if not absolutely with punctuality, at any rate so often that no one who knew the peculiarity of her residence was disposed to quarrel with her on that subject. But she made no difference in her dress on these occasions. She took her place on a low stone seat just inside the church door, clothed as usual in her thick red serge petticoat and loose brown serge jacket, such being the apparel which she had found to be best adapted for her hard and perilous work among the waters. She had pleaded to the clergyman when he attacked her on the subject of church attendance with vigour that she had got no church-going clothes. He had explained to her that she would be received there without distinction to her clothing. Mally had taken him at his word, and had gone, with a courage which certainly deserved admiration, though I doubt whether there was not mingled with it an obstinacy which was less admirable.

For people said that old Glos was rich, and that Mally might have proper clothes if she chose to buy them. Mr. Polwarth, the clergyman, who, as the old man could not come to him, went down the rocks to the old man, did make some hint on the matter, in Mally's absence. But old Glos, who had been patient with him on other matters, turned upon him so angrily when he made an allusion to money, that Mr. Polwarth found himself obliged to give that matter up, and Mally continued to sit upon the stone bench in her short serge petticoat, with her long hair streaming down her face. She did so far sacrifice to decency as on such occasions to tie up her back hair with an old shoestring. So tied it would remain through the Monday and Tuesday, but by Wednesday afternoon Mally's hair had generally managed to escape.

As to Mally's indefatigable industry there could be no manner of doubt, for the quantity of seaweed which she and the donkey amassed between them was very surprising. Old Glos, it was declared, had never collected half what Mally gathered together; but then the article was becoming cheaper, and it was necessary that the exertion should be greater. So Mally and the donkey toiled, and toiled, and the seaweed come up in heaps which surprised those who looked at her little hands and light form. Was there not some one who helped her at nights, some fairy, or demon, or the like? Mally was so snappish in her answers to people, that she had no right to be surprised if ill-natured things were said to her.

No one ever heard Mally Trenglos complain of her work, but about this time she was heard to make great and loud complaint of the treatment she received from some of her neighbours. It was known that she went with her plaints to Mr. Polwarth; and when he could not help her, or did not give her such instant help as she needed, she went — ah, so foolishly — to the office of a certain attorney at Camelford, who was not likely to prove himself a better friend than Mr. Polwarth.

Now the nature of her injury was as follows: — The place in which she collected her seaweed was a little cove; the people had come to call it Malachi's Cove from the name of the old man who lived there, which was so formed, that the margin of the sea therein could only be reached by the passage from the top down to Trenglos's hut. The breadth of the cove when the sea was out might perhaps be two hundred yards, and on each side the rocks ran out in such a way that, both from north and south, the domain of Trenglos was guarded from intruders. And this locality had been well chosen for its intended purpose. There was a rush of the sea into the cove which carried there large, drifting masses of seaweed, leaving them among the rocks when the tide was out. During the equinoctial winds of the spring and autumn the supply would never fail; and even when the sea was calm, the long, soft, salt-bedewed, trailing masses of the weed could be gathered there when they could not be found elsewhere for miles along the coast. The task of getting the weed from the breakers was often difficult and dangerous, — so difficult that much of it was left to be carried away by the next incoming tide. Mally doubtless did not gather half the crop that was there at her feet. What was taken by the returning waves she did not regret; but when interlopers came upon her cove, and gathered her wealth, — her grandfather's wealth, — beneath her eyes, then her heart was broken. It was this interloping, this intrusion, that drove poor Mally to the Camelford attorney. But, also, though the Camelford attorney took Mally's money, he could do nothing for her, and her heart was broken!

She had an idea, in which no doubt her grandfather shared, that the path to the cove was, at any rate, their property. When she was told that the cove, and sea running into the cove, were not the freeholds of her grandfather, she understood that the statement might be true. But what then as to the use of the path? Who had made the path what it was? Had she not painfully, wearily, with exceeding toil, carried up bits of rock with her own little hands, that her grandfather's donkey might have footing for his feet? Had she not scraped together crumbs of earth along the face of the cliff, that she might make easier to the animal the track of that rugged way? And now, when she saw big farmers' lads coming down with other donkeys, — and, indeed, there was one who came with a pony, — no boy, but a young man, old enough to know better than rob a poor old man and a young girl, — she reviled the whole human race, and swore that the Camelford attorney was a fool.

Any attempt to explain to her that there was still weed enough for her was worse than useless. Was it not all hers and his, or, at any rate, was not the sole way to it his and hers? And was not her trade stopped and impeded? Had she not been forced to back her laden donkey down, — twenty yards, she said, but it had, in truth, been five, — because Farmer Gunliffe's son had been in the way with this thieving pony? Farmer Gunliffe had wanted to buy her weed at his own price; and because she had refused, he had set on this thieving son to destroy her in this wicked way. "I'll hamstring the beast the next time as he's down here!" said Mally to old Glos, while the angry fire literally streamed from her eyes. Farmer Gunliffe's small homestead, — he held about fifty acres of land, — was close by the village of Tintagel, and not a mile from the cliff. The sea-wrack, as they call it, was pretty well the only manure within his reach, and no doubt he thought it hard that he should be kept from using it by Mally Tenglos and her obstinacy. "There's heaps of other coves, Barty," said Mally to Barty Gunliffe, the farmer's son. "But none so nigh, Mally, nor yet none that fills 'emselves as this place." Then he explained to her that he would not take the weed that came up close to hand. He was bigger than she was, and stronger, and would get it from the outer rocks, with which she never meddled. Then, with scorn in her eye, she swore that she could get it where he durst not venture, and repeated her threat of hamstringing the pony. Barty laughed at her wrath, jeered her because of her wild hair, and called her a mermaid. "I'll mermaid you!" she cried. "Mermaid, indeed! I wouldn't be a man to come and rob a poor girl and an old cripple. But you're no man, Barty Gunliffe! You're not half a man."

Nevertheless, Bartholomew Gunliffe was a very fine young fellow as far as the eye went. He was about five feet eight inches high, with strong arms and legs, with light curly brown hair and blue eyes. His father was but in a small way as a farmer, but, nevertheless, Barty Gunliffe was well thought of among the girls around. Everybody liked Barty, — excepting only Mally Trenglos, and she hated him like poison.

Barty, when he was asked why so good-natured a lad as he persecuted a poor girl and an old man, threw himself upon the justice of the thing. It wouldn't do at all, according to his view, that any single person should take upon himself to own that which God Almighty sent as the common property of all. He would do Mally no harm, and so he had told her. But Mally was a vixen, a wicked little vixen; and she must be taught to have a civil tongue in her head. When once Mally would speak him civil as he went for weed, he would get his father to pay the old man some sort of toll for the use of the path. "Speak him civil?" said Mally. "Never; not while I have a tongue in my mouth!" And I fear old Glos encouraged her rather than otherwise in her view of the matter.

But her grandfather did not encourage her to hamstring the pony. Hamstringing a pony would be a serious thing, and old Glos thought it might be very awkward for both of them if Mally were put into prison. He suggested, therefore, that all manner of impediments should be put in the way of the pony's feet, surmising that the well-trained donkey might be able to work in spite of them. And Barty Gunliffe, on his next descent, did find the passage very awkward when he came near to Malachi's hut, but he made his way down, and poor Mally saw the lumps of rock at which she had laboured so hard pushed on one side or rolled out of the way with a steady persistency of injury towards herself that almost drove her frantic.

"Well, Barty, you're a nice boy," said old Glos, sitting in the doorway of the hut, as he watched the intruder.

"I ain't a doing no harm to none as doesn't harm me," said Barty. "These a's free to all, Malachi."

"And the sky's free to all, but I mustn't get up on the top of your big barn to look at it," said Mally, who was standing among the rocks with a long hook in her hand. The long hook was the tool with which she worked in dragging the weed from the waves. "But you ain't got no justice, nor yet no sperrit, or you wouldn't come here to vex an old man like he."

"I didn't want to vex him, nor yet to vex you, Mally. You let me be for a while, and we'll be friends yet."

"Friends!" exclaimed Mally. "Who'd have the likes of you for a friend? What are you moving them stones for? Them stones belongs to grandfather." And in her wrath she made a movement as though she were going to fly at him.

"Let him be, Mally," said the old man; "let him be. He'll get his punishment. He'll come to be drownded some day if he comes down here when the wind is in shore."

"That he may be drownded then!" said Mally, in her anger. "If he was in the big hole there among the rocks, and the sea running in at half-tide, I wouldn't lift a hand to help him out."

"Yes, you would, Mally; you'd fish me up with your hook like a big stick of sea-weed."

She turned from him with scorn as he said this, and went into the hut. It was time for her to get ready for her work, and one of the great injuries done her lay in this, — that such a one as Barty

Gunliffe should come and look at her during her toil among the breakers.

It was an afternoon in April, and the hour was something after four o'clock. There had been a heavy wind from the north-west all the morning, with gusts of rain, and the sea-gulls had been in and out of the cove all the day, which was a sure sign to Mally that the incoming tide would cover the rocks with weed. The quick waves were now returning with wonderful celerity over the low reefs, and the time had come at which the treasure must be seized, if it was to be garnered on that day. By seven o'clock it would be growing dark, at nine it would be high water, and before daylight the crop would be carried out again if not collected. All this Mally understood very well, and some of this Barty was beginning to understand also. As Mally came down with her bare feet, bearing her long hook in her hand, she saw Barty's pony standing patiently on the sand, and in her heart she longed to attack the brute. Barty at this moment, with a common three-pronged fork in his hand, was standing down on a large rock, gazing forth towards the waters. He had declared that he would gather the weed only at places which were inaccessible to Mally, and he was looking out that he might settle where he would begin. "Let 'un be, let 'un be," shouted the old man to Mally, as he saw her take a step towards the beast, which she hated almost as much as she hated the man. Hearing her grandfather's voice through the wind, she desisted from her purpose, if any purpose she had had, and went forth to her work. As she passed down the cove, and went in among the rocks, she saw Barty still standing on his perch; out beyond, the white-curling waves were cresting and breaking themselves with violence, and the wind was howling among the caverns and abutments of the cliff. Every now and then there came a squall of rain, and though there was sufficient light, the heavens were black with clouds. A scene more beautiful might hardly be found by those who love the glories of the coast. The light for such objects was perfect. Nothing could exceed the grandeur of the colours, — the blue of the open sea, the white of the breaking waves, the yellow sands, or the streaks of red and brown which gave such richness to the cliff! But neither Mally or Barty were thinking of such things as these. Indeed, they were hardly thinking of their trade after its ordinary forms.

Barty was meditating how he might best accomplish his purpose of working beyond the reach of Mally's feminine powers, and Mally was resolving that wherever Barty went she would go further.

And, in many respects, Mally had the advantage. She knew every rock in the spot, and was sure of those which gave a good foothold, and sure also of those which did not. And then her activity had been made perfect by practice for the purpose to which it was to be devoted. Barty, no doubt, was stronger than she, and quite as active. But Barty could not jump among the waves from one stone to another as she could do, nor was he as yet able to get aid in his work from the very force of the water as she could get it. She had been hunting seaweed in that cove since she had been an urchin of six years old, and she knew every hole and corner and every spot of vantage. The waves were her friends, and she could use them. She could measure their strength, and knew when and where it would cease. Mally was great down in the salt pools of her own cove, — great, and very fearless. As she watched Barty make his way forward from rock to rock, she told herself, gleefully, that he was going astray. The curl of the wind as it blew into the cove would not carry the weed up to the northern buttresses of the cove; and then there was the great hole just there, — the great hole of which she had spoken when she wished him evil.

And now she went to work, hooking up the dishevelled hairs of the ocean, and landing many a cargo on the extreme margin of the sand, from whence she would be able in the evening to drag it back before the invading waters would return to reclaim the spoil. And on his side also Barty made his heap up against the northern buttresses of which I have spoken. Barty's heap became big and still bigger, so that he knew, let the pony work as he might, he could not take it all up that evening. But still it was not as large as Mally's heap. Mally's hook was better than his fork, and Mally's skill was better than his strength. And when he forked in some haul Mally would jeer him with a wild, weird laughter, and shriek to him through the wind that he was not half a man. At first he answered her with laughing words, but before long, as she boasted of her success and pointed to his failure, he became angry, and then he answered her no more. He became angry with himself, in that he missed so much of the plunder before him. The broken sea was full of the long straggling growth which the waves had torn up from the bottom of the ocean, but the masses were carried past him, away from him, — nay, once or twice over him; and then Mally's weird voice would sound in his ear jeering him. The gloom among the rocks was now becoming thicker and thicker, the tide was beating in with increased strength, and the gusts of wind came in with quicker and greater violence. But still he worked on. While Mally worked he would work, and he would work for some time after she was driven in. He would not be beaten by a girl.

The great hole was now full of water, but of water which seemed to be boiling as though in a pot. And the pot was full of floating masses, — large treasures of sea-weed which were thrown to and fro upon its surface, but lying there so thick that one would seem almost able to rest upon it without sinking. Mally knew well how useless it was to attempt to rescue aught from the fury of that boiling caldron. The hole went in under the rocks, and the side of it towards the shore lay high, slippery, and steep. The hole, even at low water, was never empty; and Mally believed that there was no bottom to it. Fish thrown in there could escape out to the ocean, miles away, — so Mally in her softer moods would tell the visitors to the cove. She knew the hole well. Poulnadioul she was accustomed to call it; which was supposed, when translated, to mean that this was the hole of the Evil One. Never did Mally attempt to make her own of weed which had found its way into that pot.

But Barty Gunliffe knew no better, and she watched him as he endeavoured to steady himself on the treacherously slippery edge of the pool. He fixed himself there and made a haul, with some small success. How he managed it she hardly knew, but she stood still for a while watching him anxiously, and then she saw him slip. He slipped, and recovered himself; — slipped again, and again recovered himself. "Barty, you fool," she screamed, "if you get yourself pitched in there, you'll never come out no more." Whether she simply wished to frighten him, or whether her heart relented and she had thought of his danger with dismay, who shall say? She could not have told herself. She hated him as much as ever, — but she could hardly have wished to see him drowned before her eyes. "You go on, and don't mind me," said he, speaking in a hoarse angry tone. "Mind you! — who minds you?" retorted the girl. And then she again prepared herself for her work.

But as she went down over the rocks with her long hook balanced in her hands, she suddenly heard a splash, and turning quickly round saw the body of her enemy tumbling amidst the eddying waves in the pool. The tide had now come up so far that every succeeding wave washed into it and over it from the side nearest to the sea, and then ran down again back from the rocks, as the rolling wave receded, with a noise like the fall of a cataract. And then, when the surplus water had retreated for a moment, the surface of the pool would be partly calm, though the fretting bubbles would still boil up and down, and there was ever a simmer on the surface, as though, in truth, the caldron were heated. But this time of comparative rest was but a moment, for the succeeding breaker would come up almost as soon as the foam of the preceding one had gone, and then again the waters would be dashed upon the rocks, and the sides would echo with the roar of the angry wave.

Instantly Mally hurried across to the edge of the pool, crouching down upon her hands and knees for security as she did so. As a wave receded, Barty's head and face was carried round near to her, and she could see that his forehead was covered with blood. Whether he were alive or dead she did not know. She had seen nothing but his blood, and the light coloured hair of his head lying amidst the foam. Then his body was drawn along by the suction of the retreating wave; but the mass of water that escaped was not on this occasion large enough to carry the man out with it. Instantly Mally was at work with her hook, and getting it fixed into his coat, dragged him towards the spot on which she was kneeling. During the half minute of repose she got him so close that she could touch his shoulder. Straining herself down, laying herself over the long bending handle of the hook, she strove to grasp him with her right hand. But she could not do it; — she could only touch him. Then came the next breaker, forcing itself on with a roar, looking to Mally as though it must certainly knock her from her resting-place, and destroy them both. But she had nothing for it but to kneel, and hold by her hook. What

59

prayer passed through her mind at that moment for herself or for him, or for that old man who was sitting unconsciously up at the cabin, who can say? The great wave came and rushed over her as she lay almost prostrate, and when the water was gone from her eyes, and the tumult of the foam, and the violence of the roaring breaker had passed by her, she found herself at her length upon the rock, while his body had been lifted up, free from her hook, and was lying upon the slippery ledge, half in the water, and half out of it. As she looked at him — in that instant, she could see that his eyes were open and that he was struggling with his hands. "Hold by the hook, Barty," she cried, pushing the stick of it before him, while she seized the collar of his coat in her hands. Had he been her brother, her lover, her father, she could not have clung to him with more of the energy of despair. He did contrive to hold by the stick which she had given him, and when the succeeding wave had passed by, he was still on the ledge. In the next moment she was seated a yard or two above the hole, in comparative safety, while Barty lay upon the rocks with his still bleeding head resting upon her lap.

What could she do now? She could not carry him; and in fifteen minutes the sea would be up where she was sitting. He was quite insensible, and very pale, — and the blood was coming slowly, very slowly, from the wound on his forehead. Ever so gently she put her hand upon his hair to move it back from his face; and then she bent over his mouth to see if he breathed, and as she looked at him she knew that he was beautiful. What would she not give that he might live? Nothing now was so precious to her as his life — as this life which she had so far rescued from the waters. But what could she do? Her grandfather could scarcely get himself down over the rocks, if indeed he could succeed in doing so much as that. Could she drag the wounded man backwards, if it were only a few feet, so that he might lie above the reach of the waves till further assistance could be procured? She set herself to work and she moved him, almost lifting him. As she did so she wondered at her own strength, but she was very strong at that moment. Slowly, tenderly, falling on the rocks herself so that he might fall on her, she got him back to the margin of the sand, to a spot which the waters would not reach for the next two hours!

Here her grandfather met them, having seen at last what had happened from the door. "Dada," she said, "he fell into the pool younder, and was battered against the rocks. See there at his forehead."

"Mally, I'm thinking that he's dead already," said old Glos, peering down over the body.

"No, dada; he is not dead; but mayhap he's dying. But I'll go at once up to the farm."

"Mally," said the old man, "look at his head. They'll say we murdered him."

"Who'll say so? Who'll lie like that? Didn't I pull him out of the hole?"

"What matters that? His father'll say we killed him."

It was manifest to Mally that whatever any one might say hereafter her present course was plain before her. She must run up the path to Gunliffe's farm and get necessary assistance. If the world were as bad as her grandfather said, it would be so bad that she would not care to live longer in it. But be that as it might, there was no doubt as to what she must do now. So away she went as fast as her naked feet could carry her up the cliff. When at the top she looked round to see if any person might be within ken, but she saw no one. So she ran with all her speed along the headland of the corn-field which led in the direction of old Gunliffe's house, and as she drew near the homestead she saw that Barty's mother was leaning on the gate. As she approached she attempted to call, but her breath failed her for any purpose of loud speech, so she ran on till she was able to grasp Mrs. Gunliffe by the arm. "Where's himself?" she said, holding her hand upon her beating heart that she might husband her breath.

"Who is it you mean?" said Mrs. Gunliffe, who participated in the family feud against Trenglos and his granddaughter. "What does the girl clutch me for in that way?"

"He's dying then, that's all."

"Who is dying? Is it old Malachi? If the old man's bad, we'll send some one down."

"It ain't dada, it's Barty; where's himself? where's the master?"

But by this time Mrs. Gunliffe was in an agony of despair, and was calling out for assistance lustily. Happily Gunliffe, the father, was at hand, and with him a man from the neighbouring village.

61

"Will you not send for the doctor?" said Mally. "Oh, man, you should send for the doctor!" Whether any orders were given for the doctor she did not know, but in a very few minutes she was hurrying across the field again towards the path to the cove, and Gunliffe with the other man and his wife were following her. As Mally went along she recovered her voice, for their step was not quick as hers, and that which to them was a hurried movement, allowed her to get her breath again. And as she went she tried to explain to the father what had happened, saying but little however of her own doings in the matter. The wife hung behind listening, exclaiming every now and again that her boy was killed, and then asking wild questions as to his being yet alive. The father, as he went, said little. He was known as a silent, sober man, well spoken of for diligence and general conduct, but supposed to be stern and very hard when angered. As they drew near to the top of the path the other man whispered something to him, and then turned round upon Mally and stopped her. "If he has come by his death between you, your blood shall be taken for his," said he. Then the wife shrieked out that her child had been murdered, and Mally looking round into the faces of the three saw that her grandfather's words had come true. They suspected her of having taken the life, in saving which she had nearly lost her own!

She looked round at them with awe in her face, and then, without saying a word, preceded them down the path. What had she to answer when such a charge as that was made against her? If they chose to say that she pushed him into the pool, and hit him with her hook as he lay amidst the waters, how could she show that it was not so? Poor Mally knew little of the law of evidence, and it seemed to her that she was in their hands. But as she went down the steep track with a hurried step, — a step so quick that they could not keep up with her, — her heart was very full, very full and very high. She had striven for the man's life as though he had been her brother. The blood was yet not dry on her own legs and arms, where she had torn them in his service. At one moment she had felt sure that she would die with him in that pool. And now they said that she had murdered him! It may be that he was not dead, and what would he say if ever he should speak again? Then she thought of that moment when his eyes had opened, and he had seemed to see her. She had no fear for herself, for her heart was very high. But it was full also, — full of scorn, disdain, and wrath. When she had reached the bottom, she stood close to the door of the hut waiting for them, so that they might precede her to the other group, which was there in front of them, at a little distance, on the sand. "He is there, and dada is with him. Go and look at him," said Mally. The father and mother ran on, stumbling over the stones, but Mally remained behind by the door of the hut.

Barty Gunliffe was lying on the sand where Mally had left him, and old Malachi Trenglos was standing over him, resting himself with difficulty upon a stick. "Not a move he's moved since she left him," said he; "not a move. I put his head on the old rug as you see, and I tried 'un with a drop of gin, but he wouldn't take it; — he wouldn't take it."

"Oh, my boy! — my boy!" said the mother, throwing herself beside her son upon the sand.

"Haud your tongue, woman," said the father, kneeling down slowly by the lad's head; "whimpering that way will do 'un no good." Then having gazed for a minute or two upon the pale face beneath him, he looked up sternly into that of Malachi Trenglos. The old man hardly knew how to bear this terrible inquisition. "He would come," said Malachi; "he brought it all upon hisself."

"Who was it struck him?" said the father.

"Sure he struck hisself, as he fell among the breakers."

"Liar!" said the father, looking up at the old man.

"They have murdered him! they have murdered him!" shrieked the mother.

"Haud your peace, woman!" said the husband again. "They shall give us blood for blood."

Mally, leaning against the corner of the hovel, heard it all, but did not stir. They might say what they liked. They might make it out to be murder. They might drag her and her grandfather to Camelford gaol, and then to Bodmin, and the gallows; but they could not take from her the conscious feeling that was her own. She had done her best to save him, — her very best. She remembered her threat to him before they had gone down on the rocks together, and her evil wish. Those words had been very wicked; but since that she had risked her life to save his. They might say what they pleased of her, and do what they pleased. She knew what she knew.

Then the father raised his son's head and shoulders in his arms, and called on the others to assist him in carrying Barty towards the path. They raised him between them carefully and tenderly, and lifted their burden on towards the spot at which Mally was standing. She never moved, but watched them at their work; and the old man followed them, hobbling after them with his crutch. When they had reached the end of the hut she looked upon Barty's face, and saw that it was very pale. There was no longer blood upon the forehead, but the great gash was to be seen there very plainly, with its jagged cut, and the skin livid and blue round the orifice. His light brown hair was hanging back, as she had made it to hang when she had gathered it with her hand after the big wave had passed over them. Ah, how beautiful he was in Mally's eyes with that pale face, and the sad scar upon his brow! She turned her face away, that they might not see her tears; but she did not move, nor did she speak.

But now, when they had passed the end of the hut, shuffling along with their burden, she heard a sound which stirred her. She roused herself quickly from her leaning posture, and stretched forth her head, as though to listen; then she moved to follow them. Yes, they had stopped at the bottom of the path, and had again laid the body on the rocks. She heard that sound again, as of a long, long sigh, and then, regardless of any of them, she ran to the wounded man's head. "He is not dead," she said. "There; —he is not dead."

As she spoke, Barty's eyes opened, and he looked about him. "Barty, my boy, speak to me," said the mother. Barty turned his face upon his mother, smiled, and then stared about him wildly.

"How is it with thee, lad?" said his father. Then Barty turned his face again to the latter voice, and as he did so his eyes fell upon Mally. "Mally!" he said, "Mally!" It could have wanted nothing further to any of those present to teach them that, according to Barty's own view of the case, Mally had not been his enemy; and, in truth, Mally herself wanted no further triumph. That word had vindicated her, and she withdrew back to the hut. "Dada," she said, "Barty is not dead, and I'm thinking they won't say anything more about our hurting him." Old Glos shook his head. He was glad the lad hadn't met his death there; he didn't want the young man's blood, but he knew what folk would say. The poorer he was the more sure the world would be to trample on him. Mally said what she could to comfort him, being full of comfort herself. She would have crept up to the farm if she dared, to ask how Barty was. But her courage failed her when she thought of that, so she went to work again, dragging back the weed she had saved to the spot at which, on the morrow, she would load the donkey. As she did this she saw Barty's pony still standing patiently under the rock, so she got a lock of fodder and threw it down before the beast.

It had become dark down in the cove, but she was still dragging back the sea-weed, when she saw the glimmer of a lantern coming down the pathway. It was a most unusual sight, for lanterns were not common down in Malachi's Cove. Down came the lantern rather slowly, — much more slowly than she was in the habit of descending, and then through the gloom she saw the figure of a man standing at the bottom of the path. She went up to him, and saw that it was Gunliffe, the father.

"Is that Mally?" said Gunliffe.

"Yes; it is Mally; and how is Barty, Mr. Gunliffe?"

"You must come to 'un yourself, — now at once," said the farmer. "He won't sleep a wink till he's seed you. You must not say but you'll come."

"Sure I'll come if I'm wanted," said Mally.

Gunliffe waited a moment, thinking that Mally might have to prepare herself, but Mally needed no preparation. She was dripping with salt water from the weed which she had been dragging, and her elfin locks were streaming wildly from her head; but, such as she was, she was ready. "Dada's in bed," she said, "and I can go now if you please." Then Gunliffe turned round and followed her up the path, wondering at the life which this girl led, so far away from all her sex. It was now dark night, and he had found her working at the very edge of the rolling waves, by herself, in the darkness, while the only human being who might seem to be her protector had already gone to his bed.

When they were at the top of the cliff Gunliffe took her by her hand, and led her along. She did not understand this, but she made no attempt to take her hand from his. Something he said about falling on the cliffs, but it was muttered so lowly that Mally hardly understood him. But in truth the man knew that she had saved his boy's life, and that he had injured her instead of thanking her. He was now taking her to his heart, and as words were wanting to him, he was showing his love after this silent fashion. He held her by the hand as though she were a child, and Mally tripped along at his side, asking him no questions.

When they were at the farm-yard gate he stopped there for a moment. "Mally, my girl," he said, "he'll not be content till he sees thee, but thou must not stay long wi' him, lass. Doctor says he's weak like, and wants sleep badly." Mally merely nodded her head, and then they entered the house. Mally had never been in it before, and looked about with wondering eyes at the furniture of the big kitchen. Did any idea of her future destiny flash upon her then, I wonder? But she did not pause here a moment, but was led up to the bedroom above stairs, where Barty was lying on his mother's bed. "Is it Mally herself?" said the voice of the weak youth. "It's Mally herself," said the mother, "so now you can say what you please."

"Mally," said he, "Mally, it's along you that I'm alive this moment."

"I'll not forget it on her," said the father, with his eyes turned away from her. "I'll never forget it on her."

"We hadn't a one but only him," said the mother, with her apron up to her face.

"Mally, you'll be friends with me now?" said Barty. To have been made lady of the manor of the cove for ever, Mally couldn't have spoken a word now. It was not only that the words and presence of the people there cowed her and made her speechless, but the big bed, and the looking glass, and the unheard-of wonders of the chamber, made her feel her own insignificance. But she crept up to Barty's side, and put her hand upon his.

"I'll come and get the weed, Mally; but it shall all be for you," said Barty.

"Indeed, you won't then, Barty dear," said the mother; "you'll never go near the awsome place again. What would we do if you were took from us?"

"He mustn't go near the hole if he does," said Mally, speaking at last in a solemn voice, and imparting the knowledge which she had kept to herself while Barty was her enemy; "'specially not if the wind's any way from the nor'rard."

"She'd better go down now," said the father.

Barty kissed the hand which he held, and Mally, looking at him as he did so, thought that he was like an angel.

"You'll come and see us to-morrow, Mally," said he.

To this she made no answer, but followed Mrs. Gunliffe out of the room. When they were down in the kitchen the mother had tea for her, and thick milk, and a hot cake, — all the delicacies which the farm could afford. I don't know that Mally cared much for the eating and drinking that night, but she began to think that the Gunliffes were good people, — very good people. It was better thus, at any rate, than being accused of murder, and carried off to Camelford prison.

"I'll never forget it on her — never," the father had said.

Those words stuck to her from that moment, and seemed to sound in her ears all the night. How glad she was that Barty had come down the cove; — oh yes, how glad! There was no question of his dying now, and as for the blow on his forehead, what harm was that to a lad like him? "But father shall go with you," said Mrs. Gunliffe, when Mally prepared to start for the cove by herself. Mally, however, would not hear of this. She could find her way to the cove whether it was light or dark. "Mally, thou art my child now, and I shall think of thee so," said the mother, as the girl went off by herself. Mally thought of this, too, as she walked home. How could she become Mrs. Gunliffe's child; — ah, how?

I need not, I think, tell the tale any further. That Mally did become Mrs. Gunliffe's child, and how she became so, the reader will understand; and in process of time the big kitchen and all the wonders of the farm-house were her own. The people said that Barty Gunliffe had married a mermaid out of the sea, but when it was said in Mally's hearing I doubt whether she liked it; and when Barty himself would call her a mermaid she would frown at him, and throw about her black hair, and pretend to cuff him with her little hand.

Old Glos was brought up to the top of the cliff, and lived his few remaining days under the roof of Mr. Gunliffe's house; and as for the cove, and the right of sea-weed, from that time forth all that has been supposed to attach itself to Gunliffe's farm, and I do not know that any of the neighbours are prepared to dispute the right.

"Malachi's Cove" appeared first in the December issue of *Good Words* for 1864.

The Telegraph Girl

T

Chapter I
Lucy Graham and Sophy Wilson

hree shillings a day to cover all expenses of life, food, raiment, shelter, a room in which to eat and sleep, and fire and light, — and recreation if recreation there might be, — is not much; but when Lucy Graham, the heroine of this tale, found herself alone in the world, she was glad to think that she was able to earn so much by her work, and that thus she possessed the means of independence if she chose to be independent. Her story up to the date with which we are dealing shall be very shortly told. She had lived for many years with a married brother, who was a bookseller in Holborn, — in a small way of business, and burdened with a large family, but still living in decent comfort. In order, however, that she might earn her own bread she had gone into the service of the Crown as a "Telegraph Girl" in the Telegraph Office.* And there she had remained till the present time, and there she was earning eighteen shillings a week by eight hours' continual work daily. Her life had been full of occupation, as in her spare hours she had been her brother's assistant in his shop, and had made herself familiar with the details of his trade. But the brother had suddenly died, and it had been quickly decided that the widow and the children should take themselves off to some provincial refuge.

*I presume my readers to be generally aware that the head-quarters of the National Telegraph Department are held at the top of one of the great buildings belonging to the General Post Office, in St. Martin's-le-Grand.

Then it was that Lucy Graham had to think of her independence and her eighteen shillings a week on the one side, and of her desolation and feminine necessities on the other. To run backwards and forwards from High Holborn to St. Martin's-le-Grand had been very well as long as she could comfort herself with the companionship of her sister-in-law and defend herself with her brother's arm; — but how would it be with her if she were called upon to live all alone in London? She was driven to consider what else she could do to earn her bread. She might become a nursemaid, or perhaps a nursery governess. Though she had been well and in some respects carefully educated, she knew that she could not soar above that. Of music she did not know a note. She could draw a little and understood enough French, — not to read it, but to teach herself to read it. With English literature she was better acquainted than is usual with young women of her age and class; and, as her only personal treasures, she had managed to save a few books which had become hers through her brother's kindness. To be a servant was distasteful to her, not through any idea that service was disreputable, but from a dislike to be subject at all hours to the will of others. To work and work hard she was quite willing, so that there might be some hours of her life in which she might not be called upon to obey.

When, therefore, it was suggested to her that she had better abandon the Telegraph Office and seek the security of some household, her spirit rebelled against the counsel. Why should she not be indpendent, and respectable, and safe? But then the solitude! Solitude would certainly be hard, but absolute solitude might not perhaps be necessary. She was fond too of the idea of being a Government servant, with a sure and fixed salary, — bound of course to her work at certain hours, but so bound only for certain hours. During a third of the day she was, as she proudly told herself, a servant of the Crown. During the other two-thirds she was lord, — or lady, — of herself.

But there was a quaintness, a mystery, even an awe, about her independence which almost terrified her. During her labours she had eight hundred female companions, all congregated together in one vast room, but as soon as she left the Post Office she was to be all alone! For a few months after her brother's death she continued to live with her sister-in-law, during which time this great question was being discussed. But then the sister-in-law and the children disappeared, and it was incumbent on Lucy to fix herself somewhere. She must begin life after what seemed to her to be a most unfeminine fashion, — "just as though she were a young man," — for it was thus that she described to herself her own position over and over again.

At this time Lucy Graham was twenty-six years old. She had hitherto regarded herself as being stronger and more steadfast than are women generally of that age. She had taught herself to despise feminine weaknesses, and had learned to be almost her brother's equal in managing the affairs of his shop in his absence. She had declared to herself, looking forward then to some future necessity which had become present to her with terrible quickness, that she would not be feckless, helpless, and insufficient for herself as are so many females. She had girded herself up for a work-a-day life, — looking forward to a time when she might leave the telegraphs and become a partner with her brother. A sudden disruption had broken up all that.

She was twenty-six, well made, cheery, healthy, and to some eyes singularly good-looking, though no one probably would have called her either pretty or handsome. In the first place her complexion was — brown. It was impossible to deny that her whole face was brown, as also was her hair, and generally her dress. There was a pervading brownness about her which left upon those who met her a lasting connection between Lucy Graham and that serviceable, long-enduring colour. But there was nobody so convinced that she was brown from head to foot as was she herself. A good lasting colour she would call it, — one that did not require to be washed every half-hour in order that it might be decent, but could bear real washing when it was wanted; for it was a point of her inner creed, of her very faith of faith, that she was not to depend upon feminine good looks, or any of the adventitious charms of dress for her advance in the world. "A good strong binding," she would say of certain dark-visaged books, "that will stand the gas, and not look disfigured even though a blot of ink should come in its way." And so it was that she regarded her own personal binding.

But for all that she was to some observers very attractive. There was not a mean feature in her face. Her forehead was spacious and broad. Her eyes, which were brown also, were very bright, and could sparkle with anger or solicitude, or perhaps with love. Her nose was well formed, and delicately shaped enough. Her mouth was large, but full of expression, and seemed to declare without speech that she could be eloquent. The form of her face was oval, and complete, not as though it had been moulded by an inartistic thumb, a bit added on here and a bit there. She was somewhat above the average height of women, and stood upon her legs, — or walked upon them, — as though she understood that they had been given to her for real use.

Two years before her brother's death there had been a suitor for her hand, — as to whose suit she had in truth doubted much. He also had been a bookseller, a man in a larger way of business than her brother, some fifteen years older than herself, — a widower, with a family. She knew him to be a good man, with a comfortable house, an adequate income, and a kind heart. Had she gone to him she would not have been required then to live among the bookshelves or the telegraphs. She had doubted much whether she would not go to him. She knew she could love the children. She thought that she could buckle herself to that new work with a will. But she feared, — she feared that she could not love him.

Perhaps there had come across her heart some idea of what might be the joy of real, downright, hearty love. If so, it was only an idea. No personage had come across her path thus to disturb her. But the idea, or the fear, had been so strong with her that she had never been able to induce herself to become the wife of this man; and when he had come to her after her brother's death, in her worse desolation, — when the prospect of service in some other nursery had been strongest before her eyes, — she had still refused him. Perhaps there had been a pride in this — a feeling that, as she had rejected him in her comparative prosperity, she should not take him now when the renewal of his offer might probably be the effect of generosity. But she did refuse him; and the widowed bookseller had to look elsewhere for a second mother for his children.

Then there arose the question, How and where she should live? When it came to the point of settling herself, that idea of starting in life like a young man became very awful indeed. How was she to do it? Would any respectable keeper of lodgings take her in upon that principle? And if so, in what way should she plan out her life? Sixteen hours a day were to be her own. What should she do with them? Was she or was she not to contemplate the enjoyment of any social pleasures? And if so, how were they to be found of such a nature as not to be discreditable? On rare occasions she had gone to the play with her brother, and had then enjoyed the treat thoroughly. Whether it had been *Hamlet* at the Lyceum or *Lord Dundreary* at the Haymarket she had found herself equally able to be happy. But there could not be for her now even such rare occasions as these. She thought that she knew that a young woman all alone could not go to the theatre with propriety, let her be ever so brave. And then those three shillings a day, though sufficient for life, would hardly be more than sufficient.

But how should she begin? At last chance assisted her. Another girl, also employed in the Telegraph Office, with whom there had been some family acquaintance over and beyond that formed in the office, happened at this time to be thrown upon the world in some such fashion as herself, and the two agreed to join their forces.

She was one Sophy Wilson by name, — and it was agreed between them that they should club their means together and hire a room for their joint use. Here would be a companionship, —and possibly after a while sweet friendship. Sophy was younger than herself, and might probably need, perhaps be willing to accept, assistance. To be able to do something that should be of use to somebody would, she felt, go far towards giving her life that interest which it would otherwise lack.

When Lucy examined her friend, thinking of the closeness of their future connection, she was startled by the girl's prettiness and youth and thorough unlikeness to herself. Sophy had long black glossy curls, large eyes, a pink complexion, and was very short. She seemed to have no inclination for that strong service-able brown binding which was so valuable in Lucy's eyes, but rather to be wedded to bright colours and soft materials. And it soon became evident to the elder young woman that the younger looked upon her employment simply as a stepping-stone to a husband. To get herself married as soon as possible was unblushingly declared by Sophy Wilson to be the one object of her ambition,

— and, as she supposed, that of every other girl in the telegraph department. But she seemed to be friendly and at first docile, to have been brought up with aptitudes for decent life, and to be imbued with the necessity of not spending more than her three shillings a day. And she was quick enough at her work in the office, — quicker even than Lucy herself, — which was taken by Lucy as evidence that her new friend was clever, and would therefore probably be an agreeable companion.

They took together a bedroom in a very quiet street in Clerkenwell, — a street which might be described as genteel because it contained no shops; and here they began to keep house, as they called it. Now the nature of their work was such that they were not called upon to be in their office till noon, but that then they were required to remain there till eight in the evening. At two a short space was allowed them for dinner, which was furnished to them at a cheap rate in a room adjacent to that in which they worked. Here for eightpence each they could get a good meal; or, if they preferred it, they could bring their food with them, and even have it cooked upon the premises. In the evening tea and bread and butter were provided for them by the officials; and then at eight or a few minutes after they left the building and walked home. The keeping of house was restricted in fact to providing tea and bread and butter for the morning meal, and perhaps when they could afford it for the repetition of such comfort later in the evening. There was the Sunday to be considered, — as to which day they made a contract with the keeper of the lodging-house to sit at her table and partake of her dishes. And so they were established.

From the first Lucy Graham made up her mind that it was her duty to be a very friend of friends to this new companion. It was as though she had consented to marry that widowered bookseller. She would then have considered herself bound to devote herself to his comfort and his welfare. It was not that she could as yet say that she loved Sophy Wilson. Love with her could not be so immediate as that. But the nature of the bond between them was such that each might possibly do so much either for the happiness or the unhappiness of the other! And then though Sophy was clever — for as to this Lucy did not doubt — still she was too evidently in many things inferior to herself, and much in want of such assistance as a stronger nature could give her. Lucy, in acknowledging this, put down her own greater strength to the score of her years and the nature of the life which she had been called upon to lead. She had early in her days been required to help herself, to hold her own, and to be as it were a woman of business. But the weakness of the other was very apparent to her. That doctrine as to the necessity of a husband, which had been very soon declared, had—well, almost disgusted Lucy. And then she found cause to lament the peculiar arrangement which the requirements of the office had made as to their hours. At first it had seemed to her to be very pleasant that they should have their morning hours for needle-work and perhaps for a little reading; but when she found that Sophy would lie in bed till ten because early rising was not obligatory, then she wished that they had been classed among those whose presence was demanded at eight.

After a while there was a little difference between them as to what might or what might not be done with propriety after their office hours were over. It must be explained that in that huge room in which eight hundred girls were at work together there was also a sprinkling of boys and young men. As no girls were employed there after eight there would always be on duty in the afternoon an increasing number of the other sex, some of whom remained there till late at night, — some indeed all the night. Now, whether by chance or, as Lucy feared, by management, Sophy Wilson had her usual seat next to a young lad with whom she soon contracted a certain amount of intimacy. And from this intimacy arose a proposition that they two should go with Mr. Murray—he was at first called Mister, but the formal appellation soon degenerated into a familiar Alec — to a music-hall. Lucy Graham at once set her face against the music-hall.

"But why?" asked the other girl. "You don't mean to say that decent people don't go to music-halls?"

"I don't mean to say anything of the kind, but then they go decently attended."

"How decently? We should be decent."

"With their brothers," said Lucy; — "or something of that kind."

"Brothers!" ejaculated the other girl with a tone of thorough contempt. A visit to a music-hall with her brother was not at all the sort of pleasure to which Sophy was looking forward. She did her best to get over objections which to her seemed to be fastidious and absurd, observing, "that if people were to feel like that there would be no coming together of people at all." But when she found that Lucy could not be instigated to go to the music-hall, and that the idea of Alec Murray and herself going to such a place unattended by others was regarded as a proposition too monstrous to be discussed, Sophy for a while gave way. But she returned again and again to the subject, thinking to prevail by asserting that Alec had a friend, a most excellent young man, who would go with them, — and bring his sister. Alec was almost sure that the sister would come. Lucy, however, would have nothing to do with it. Lucy thought that there should be very great intimacy indeed before anything of that kind should be permitted.

And so there was something of a quarrel. Sophy declared that such a life as theirs was too hard for her, and that some kind of amusement was necessary. Unless she were allowed some delight she must go mad, she must die, she must throw herself off Waterloo Bridge. Lucy, remembering her duty, remembering how imperative it was that she should endeavour to do good to the one human being with whom she was closely concerned, forgave her, and tried to comfort her; — forgave her even though at last she refused to be guided by her monitress. For Sophy did go to the music-hall with Alec Murray, — reporting, but reporting falsely that they were accompanied by the friend and the friend's sister. Lucy, poor Lucy, was constrained by certain circumstances to disbelieve this false assertion. She feared that Sophy had gone with Alec alone, — as was the fact. But yet she forgave her friend. How are we to live together at all if we can not forgive each other's offences?

Chapter II
Abraham Hall

As there was no immediate repetition of the offence the forgiveness soon became complete, and Lucy found the interest of her life in her endeavours to be good to this weak child whom chance had thrown in her way. For Sophy Wilson was but a weak child. She was full of Alec Murray for a while, and induced Lucy to make the young man's acquaintance. The lad was earning twenty shillings a week, and if these two poor young creatures chose to love each other and get themselves married, it would be respectable though it might be unfortunate. It would at any rate be the way of the world, and was a natural combination with which she would have no right to interfere. But she found that Alec was a mere boy, with no idea beyond the enjoyment of a bright scarf and a penny cigar, with a girl by his side at a music-hall. "I don't think it can be worth your while to go much out of your way for his sake," said Lucy.

"Who is going out of her way? Not I. He's as good as anybody else, I suppose. And one must have somebody to talk to some-times." These last words she uttered so plaintively, showing so plainly that she was unable to endure the simple unchanging dul-ness of a life of labour, that Lucy's heart was thoroughly softened towards her. She had the great gift of being not the less able to sympathize with the weakness of the weak because of her own abnormal strength. And so it came to pass that she worked for her friend, — stitching and mending when the girl ought to have stitched and mended for herself, — reading to her, even though but little of what was read might be understood, — yielding to her and assisting her in all things, till at last it came to pass that in truth she loved her. And such love and care were much wanted, for the elder girl soon found that the younger was weak in health as well as weak in spirit. There were days on which she could not, or at any rate did not, go to her office. When six months had passed by Lucy had not once been absent since she had begun her new life.

"Have you seen that man who has come to look at our house?" asked Sophy one day as they were walking down to the office. Lucy had seen a strange man, having met him on the stairs. "Isn't he a fine fellow?"

"For anything that I know. Let us hope that he is very fine," said Lucy, laughing.

"He's about as handsome a chap as I think I ever saw."

"As for being a chap the man I saw must be near forty."

"He is a little old I should say, but not near that. I don't think he can have a wife or he wouldn't come here. He's an engineer, and he has the care of a steam-engine in the City Road, — that great printing place. His name is Abraham Hall, and he's earning three or four pounds a week. A man like that ought to have a wife."

"How did you learn all about him?"

"It's all true. Sally heard it from Mrs. Green." Mrs. Green was the keeper of the lodging-house and Sally was the maid. "I couldn't help speaking to him yesterday because we were both at the door together. He talked just like a gentleman although he was all smutty and greasy."

"I am glad he talked like a gentleman."

"I told him we lodged here and that we were telegraph girls, and that we never got home till half-past eight. He would be just the beau for you because he is such a big steady-looking fellow."

"I don't want a beau," said Lucy angrily.

"Then I shall take him myself," said Sophy as she entered the office.

Soon after that it came to pass that there did arise a slight acquaintance between both the girls and Abraham Hall, partly from the fact of their near neighbourhood, partly perhaps from some little tricks on Sophy's part. But the man seemed to be so steady, so solid, so little given to lightnesses of flirtation or too dangerous delights, that Lucy was inclined to welcome the accident. When she saw him on a Sunday morning free from the soil of his work, she could perceive that he was still a young man, probably not much over thirty; — but there was a look about him as though he were well inured to the cares of the world, such as is often produced by the possession of a wife and family, — not a look of depression by any means, but seeming to betoken an appreciation of the seriousness of life. From all this Lucy unconsciously accepted an idea of security in the man, feeling that it might be pleasant to have some strong one near her, from whom in case of need assistance might be asked without fear. For this man was tall and broad and powerful, and seemed to Lucy's eyes to be a very pillar of strength when he would stand still for a moment to greet her in the streets.

But poor Sophy, who had so graciously offered the man to her friend at the beginning of their intercourse, seemed soon to change her mind and to desire his attention for herself. He was certainly much more worthy than Alec Murray. But to Lucy—to whom it was a rule of life, as strong as any in the commandments, that a girl should not throw herself at a man, but should be sought by him—it was a painful thing to see how many of poor Sophy's much-needed sixpences were now spent in little articles of finery by which it was hoped that Mr. Hall's eyes might be gratified, and how those glossy ringlets were brushed, and made to shine with pomatum, and how the little collars were washed and rewashed and starched and re-starched, in order that she might be smart for him. Lucy, who was always neat, endeavoured to become browner and browner. This she did by way of reproach and condemnation, not at all surmising that Mr. Hall might possibly prefer a good solid wearing colour to glittering blue and pink gewgaws.

At this time Sophy was always full of what Mr. Hall had last said to her; and after a while broached an idea that he was some gentleman in disguise. "Why in disguise? Why not a gentleman not in disguise?" asked Lucy, who had her own ideas, perhaps a little exaggerated, as to Nature's gentlemen. Then Sophy explained herself. A gentleman, a real gentleman, in disguise would be very interesting; — one who had quarrelled with his father, perhaps, because he would not endure paternal tyranny, and had then determined to earn his own bread till he might happily come into the family honours and property in a year or two. Perhaps, instead of being Abraham Hall, he was in reality the Right Honourable Russell Howard Cavendish; and if, during his temporary abeyance, he should prove his thorough emancipation from the thraldom of his aristocracy by falling in love with a telegraph girl, how fine it would be! When Lucy expressed an opinion that Mr. Hall might be a very fine fellow though he were fulfilling no more than the normal condition of his life at the present moment, Sophy would not be contented, declaring that her friend, with all her reading, knew nothing of poetry. In this way they talked very frequently about Abraham Hall, till Lucy would often feel that such talking was indecorous. Then she would be silent for a while herself, and rebuke the other girl for her constant mention of the man's name. Then again she would be brought back to the subject; — for in all the little intercourse which took place between them and the man, his conduct was so simple and yet so civil that she could not really feel him to be unworthy of a place in her thoughts. But Sophy soon declared frankly to her friend that she was absolutely in love with the man. "You wouldn't have him, you know," she said when Lucy scolded her for the avowal.

"Have him! How can you bring yourself to talk in such a way about a man? What does he want of either of us?"

"Men do marry you know, — sometimes," said Sophy; "and I don't know how a young man is to get a wife unless some girl will show that she is fond of him."

"He should show first that he is fond of her."

"That's all very well for talkee-talkee," said Sophy, "but it doesn't do for practice. Men are awfully shy. And then, though they do marry sometimes, they don't want to get married particularly, — not as we do. It comes like an accident. But how is a man to fall into a pit if there's no pit open?"

In answer to this Lucy used many arguments and much scolding. But to very little effect. That the other girl should have thought so much about it and be so ready with her arguments was horrid to her. "A pit open!" ejaculated Lucy; "I would rather never speak to a man again than regard myself in such a light." Sophy said that all that might be very well, but declared that it "would not wash."

The elder girl was so much shocked by all this that there came upon her gradually a feeling of doubt whether their joint life could be continued. Sophy declared her purpose openly of entrapping Abraham Hall into a marriage, and had absolutely induced him to take her to the theatre. He had asked Lucy to join them; but she had sternly refused, basing her refusal on her inability to bear the expense. When he offered to give her the treat, she told him with simple gravity that nothing would induce her to accept such a favour from any man who was not either a very old friend or a near relation. When she said this he so looked at her that she was sure that he approved of her resolve. He did not say a word to press her; — but he took Sophy Wilson, and, as Lucy knew, paid for Sophy's ticket.

All this displeased Lucy so much that she began to think whether there must not be a separation. She could not continue to live on terms of affectionate friendship with a girl whose conduct she so strongly disapproved. But then again, though she could not restrain the poor light thing altogether, she did restrain her in some degree. She was doing some good by her companionship. And then, if it really was in the man's mind to marry the girl, that certainly would be a good thing, — for the girl. With such a husband she would be steady enough. She was quite sure that the idea of preparing a pit for such a one as Abraham Hall must be absurd. But Sophy was pretty and clever, and if married would at any rate love her husband. Lucy thought that she had heard that steady, severe, thoughtful men were apt to attach themselves to women of the butterfly order. She did not like the way in which Sophy was doing this; but then who was she that she should be a judge? If Abraham Hall liked it, would not that be much more to the purpose? Therefore she resolved that there should be no separation at present, and, if possible, no quarrelling.

But soon it came to pass that there was another very solid reason against separation. Sophy, who was often unwell, and would sometimes stay away from the office for a day or two on the score of ill-health, though by doing so she lost one of her three shillings on each such day, gradually became worse. The superintendent at her department had declared that in case of further absence a medical certificate must be sent, and the doctor attached to the office had called upon her. He had looked grave, had declared that she wanted considerable care, had then gone so far as to recommend rest, — which meant absence from work, — for at least a fortnight, and had ordered her medicine. This of course meant the loss of a third of her wages. In such circumstances and at such a time it was not likely that Lucy should think of separation.

While Sophy was ill Abraham Hall often came to the door to inquire after her health; — so often that Lucy almost thought that her friend had succeeded. The man seemed to be sympathetic and anxious, and would hardly have inquired with so much solicitude had he not really been careful as to poor Sophy's health. Then, when Sophy was better, he would come in to see her, and the girl would deck herself out with some little ribbon and would

81

have her collar always starched and ironed, ready for his recep-
tion. It certainly did seem to Lucy that the man was becoming
fond of her foolish little friend.

During this period Lucy of course had to go to the office alone,
leaving Sophy to the care of the lodging-house keeper. And, in
her solitude, troubles were heavy on her. In the first place
Sophy's illness had created certain necessarily increased
expenses, and at the same time their joint incomes had been
diminished by one shilling a week out of six. Lucy was in general
matters allowed to be the dispenser of the money; but on occasions the other girl would assert her rights, — which always meant
her right to some indulgence out of their joint incomes which
would be an indulgence to her and her alone. Even those bright
ribbons could not be had for nothing. Lucy wanted no bright ribbons. When they were fairly prosperous she had not grudged
some little expenditure in this direction. She had told herself
that young girls like to be bright in the eyes of men, and that she
had no right even to endeavour to make her friend look at all
these things with her eyes. She even confessed to herself some
deficiency on her own part, some want of womanliness in that
she did not aspire to be attractive, — still owning to herself,
vehemently declaring to herself, that to be attractive in the eyes
of a man whom she could love would of all delights be the most
delightful. Thinking of all this she had endeavoured not to be
angry with poor Sophy; — but when she became pinched for shillings and sixpences and to feel doubtful whether at the end of
each fortnight there would be money to pay Mrs. Green for lodgings and coal, then her heart became sad within her, and she told
herself that Sophy, though she was ill, ought to be more careful.

And there was another trouble which for a while was very
grievous. Telegraphy is an art not yet perfected among us and is
still subject to many changes. Now it was the case at this time
that the pundits of the office were in favour of a system of com-
municating messages by ear instead of by eye. The little dots and
pricks, which even in Lucy's time had been changed more than
once, had quickly become familiar to her. No one could read and
use her telegraphic literature more rapidly or correctly than Lucy
Graham. But now that this system of little tinkling sounds was
coming up, — a system which seemed to be very pleasant to those

females who were gifted with musical aptitudes, — she found her-self to be less quick, less expert, less useful than her neighbours. This was very sad, for she had always been buoyed up by an unconscious conviction of her own superior intelligence. And then, though there had been neither promises or threats, she had become aware, — at any rate had thought that she was aware, — that those girls who could catch and use the tinkling sounds would rise more quickly to higher pay than the less gifted ones. She had struggled therefore to overcome the difficulty. She had endeavoured to force her ears to do that which her ears were not capable of accomplishing. She had failed, and to-day had owned to herself that she must fail. But Sophy had been one of the first to catch the tinkling sounds. Lucy came back to her room sad and down at heart and full of troubles. She had a long task of needle-work before her, which had been put by for a while through causes consequent on Sophy's illness. "Now she is better perhaps he will marry her and take her away, and I shall be alone again," she said to herself, as though declaring that such a state of things would be a relief to her, and almost a happiness.

"He has just been here," said Sophy to her as soon as she entered the room. Sophy was painfully, cruelly smart, clean and starched, and shining about her locks, — so prepared that, as Lucy thought, she must have evidently expected him.

"Well; — and what did he say?"

"He has not said much yet, but it was very good of him to come and see me, — and he was looking so handsome. He is going out somewhere this evening to some political meeting with two or three other men, and he was got up quite like a gentleman. I do like to see him look like that."

"I always think a working man looks best in his working clothes," said Lucy. "There's some truth about him then. When he gets into a black coat he is pretending to be something else, but everybody can see the difference."

There was a severity, almost a savageness, in this which sur-prised Sophy so much that at first she hardly knew how to answer it. "He is going to speak at the meeting," she said after a pause, "and of course he had to make himself tidy. He told me all that he is going to say. Should you not like to hear him speak?"

"No," said Lucy very sharply, setting to work instantly upon her labours, not giving herself a moment for preparation or a moment for rest. Why should she like to hear a man speak who could condescend to love so empty and so vain a thing as that? Then she became gradually ashamed of her own feelings. "Yes," she said; "I think I should like to hear him speak;—only if I were not quite so tired. Mr. Hall is a man of good sense and well educated and I think I should like to hear him speak."

"I should like to hear him say one thing I know," said Sophy. Then Lucy in her rage tore asunder some fragment of a garment on which she was working.

Chapter III
Sophy Wilson Goes to Hastings

Sophy went back to her work, and in a very few days was permanently moved from the seat which she had hitherto occupied next to Alec Murray and near to Lucy to a distant part of the chamber in which the tinkling instruments were used. And, as a part of the arrangement consequent on this, she was called on to attend from ten till six instead of from noon till eight; and her hour for dining was changed also. In this way a great separation between the girls was made, for neither could they walk to the office together, nor walk from it. To Lucy, though she was sometimes inclined to be angry with her friend, this was very painful. But Sophy triumphed in it greatly. "I think we are to have a step up to 21s. in the musical box," she said, laughing. For it was so that she called the part of the room in which the little bells were always ringing. "Won't it be nice to have 3s. 6d. instead of 3s.?" Lucy said solemnly that any increase of income was always nice, and that when such income was earned by superiority of acquirement it was a matter of just pride. This she enunciated with something of a dogmatic air; having schooled herself to give all due praise to Sophy although it had to be given at the expense of her own feelings. But when Sophy said in reply that that was just what she had been thinking herself, and that as she could do her work by ear she was of course worth more than those who could not, then the other could only with difficulty repress the soreness of her heart.

But to Sophy I think the new arrangements were most pleasant because it enabled her to reach the street in which she lived just when Abraham Hall was accustomed to return from his work. He would generally come home, — to clean himself as she called it, — and would then again go out for his employment or amusement for the evening; and now, by a proper system of lying in wait, by creeping slow or walking quick, and by watching well, she was generally able to have a word or two with him. But he was so very bashful! He would always call her Miss Wilson; and she of course was obliged to call him Mr. Hall. "How is Miss Graham?" he asked one evening.

"She is very well. I think Lucy is always well. I never knew anybody so strong as she is."

"It is a great blessing. And how are you yourself?"

"I do get so tired at that nasty office. Though of course I like what I am doing now better than the other. It was that rolling up the bands that used to kill me. But I don't think I shall ever really be strong till I get away from the telegraphs. I suppose you have no young ladies working where you are?"

"There are I believe a lot of them in the building, stitching bindings; but I never see them."

"I don't think you care much for young ladies, Mr. Hall."

"Not much — now."

"Why not now? What does that mean?"

"I dare say I never told you or Miss Graham before. But I had a wife of my own for a time."

"A wife! You!"

"Yes indeed. But she did not stay with me long. She left me before we had been a year married."

"Left you!"

"She died," he said, correcting very quickly the false impression which his words had been calculated to make.

"Dear me! Died before a year was out. How sad!"

"It was very sad."

'And you had no, — no, — no baby, Mr. Hall?"

"I wish she had had none, because then she would have been still living. Yes, I have a boy. Poor little mortal! It is two years old I think today."

"I should so like to see him. A little boy! Do bring him some day, Mr. Hall." Then the father explained that the child was in the country, down in Hertfordshire; but nevertheless he promised that he would some day bring him up to town and show him to his new friends.

Surely having once been married and having a child he must want another wife! And yet how little apt he was to say or do any of those things by saying and doing which men are supposed to express their desire in that direction! He was very slow at making love; — so slow that Sophy hardly found herself able to make use of her own little experiences with him. Alec Murray, who, how-ever, in the way of a husband was not worth thinking of, had a great deal more to say for himself. She could put on her ribbons for Mr. Hall, and wait for him in the street, and look up into his face, and call him Mr. Hall; — but she could not tell him how she would love that little boy and what an excellent mother she would be to him, unless he gave her some encouragement.

When Lucy heard that he had been a married man and that he had a child she was gratified though she knew not why. "Yes, I should like to see him of course," she said, speaking of the boy. "A child, if you have not the responsibility of taking care of it, is always nice."

"I should so like to take care of it."

"I should not like to ask him to bring the boy up out of the country." She paused a moment, and then added, "He is just the man whom I should have thought would have married, and just the man to be made very serious by the grief of such a loss. I am coming to think it does a person good to have to bear troubles."

"You would not say that if you always felt as sick as I do after your day's work."

About a week after that Sophy was so weak in the middle of the day that she was obliged to leave the office and go home. "I know it will kill me," she said that evening, "if I go on with it. The place is so stuffy and nasty, and then those terrible stairs. If I could get out of it and settle down, then I should be quite well. I am not made for that kind of work; — not like you are."

"I think I was made for it certainly."

"It is such a blessing to be strong," said poor Sophy.

"Yes; it is a blessing. And I do bless God that He has made me so. It is the one good thing that has been given to me, and it is better, I think, than all the others." As she said this she looked at Sophy and thought that she was very pretty; but she thought also that prettiness had its dangers and its temptations, and that good strong serviceable health might perhaps be better for one who had to earn her bread.

But through all these thoughts there was a great struggle going on within her. To be able to earn one's bread without personal suffering is very good. To be tempted by prettiness to ribbons, pomatum, and vanities which one cannot afford is very bad. To do as Sophy was doing in regard to this young man, setting her cap at him and resolving to make prey of him as a fowler does of a bird, was, to her way of thinking, most unseemly. But to be loved by such a man as Abraham Hall, to be chosen by him as his companion, to be removed from the hard, outside, unwomanly work of the world to do the indoor occupations which a husband would require from her — how much better a life according to her real tastes would that be than anything which she now saw before her! It was all very well to be brown and strong while the exigencies of her position were those which now surrounded her; but she could not keep herself from dreaming of something which would have been much better than that.

A month or two passed away during which the child had on one occasion been brought up to town on a Saturday evening, and had been petted and washed and fed and generally cared for by the two girls during the Sunday, — all which greatly increased their intimacy with the father. And now, as Lucy quickly observed, Abraham Hall called Sophy by her Christian name. When the word was first pronounced in Lucy's presence Sophy blushed and looked round at her friend. But she never said that the change had been made at her own request. "I do so hate to be called Miss Wilson," she had said. "It seems among friends as though I were a hundred years old." Then he had called her Sophy. But she did not dare — not as yet — to call him Abraham. All which the other girl watched very closely, saying nothing.

But during these two months Sophy had been away from her office more than half the time. Then the doctor said she had better leave town for a while. It was September, and it was desired that she should pass that month at Hastings. Now it should be explained that in such emergencies as this the department has provided a most kindly aid for young women. Some five or six at a time are sent out for a month to Hastings or to Brighton, and are employed in the telegraph offices in those towns. Their railway fares are paid for them, and a small extra allowance is made to them to enable them to live away from their homes. The privilege is too generally sought to be always at the command of her who wants it; nor is it accorded except on the doctor's certificate. But in the September Sophy Wilson was sent down to Hastings.

In spite, however, of the official benevolence which greatly lightened the special burden which illness must always bring on those who have to earn their bread, and which in Sophy Wilson's case had done so much for her, nevertheless the weight of the misfortune fell heavily on poor Lucy. Some little struggle had to be made as to clothes before the girl could be sent away from her home; and, though the sick one was enabled to support herself at Hastings, the cost of the London lodgings which should have been divided fell entirely upon Lucy. Then at the end of the month there came worse tidings. The doctor at Hastings declared that the girl was unfit to go back to her work, — was, indeed, altogether unfit for such effort as eight hours continued attendance required from her. She wanted at any rate some period of perfect rest, and therefore she remained down at the sea-side without the extra allowance which was so much needed for her maintenance.

Then the struggle became very severe with Lucy, — so severe that she began to doubt whether she could long endure it. Sophy had her two shillings a day, the two-thirds of her wages, but she could not subsist on that. Something had to be sent to her in addition, and this something could only come from Lucy's wages. So at least it was at first. In order to avoid debt she gave up her more comfortable room and went up-stairs into a little garret. And she denied herself her accustomed dinner at the office, contenting herself with bread and cheese, — or often simply with bread, — which she could take in her pocket. And she washed her own clothes and mended even her own boots, so that still she might send a part of her earnings to the sick one.

"Is she better?" Abraham asked her one day.

"It is so hard to know, Mr. Hall. She writes just as she feels at the moment. I am afraid she fears to return to the office."

"Perhaps it does not suit her."

"I suppose not. She thinks some other kind of life would be better for her. I dare say it would."

"Could I do anything?" asked the man very slowly.

Could he do anything? well; yes. Lucy at least thought that he could do a great deal. There was one thing which, if he would do it, would make Sophy at any rate believe herself to be well. And this sickness was not organic, — was not, as it appeared, due to any cause which could be specified. It had not as yet been called by any name, — such as consumption. General debility had been spoken of both by the office doctor and by him at Hastings. Now Lucy certainly thought that a few words from Mr. Hall would do more than all the doctors in the way of effecting a cure. Sophy hated the telegraph office and she lacked the strength of mind necessary for doing that which was distasteful to her. And that idea of a husband had taken such hold of her that nothing else seemed to her to give a prospect of contentment. "Why don't you go down and see her, Mr. Hall?" she said.

Then he was silent for a while before he answered, — silent and very thoughtful. And Lucy, as the sound of her own words rested on her ears, felt she had done wrong in asking such a question. Why should he go down, unless indeed he were in love with the girl and prepared to ask her to be his wife? If he were to go down expressly to visit her at Hastings unless he were so prepared, what false hopes he would raise; what damage he would do instead of good! How indeed could he possibly go down on such a mission without declaring to all the world that he intended to make the girl his wife? But it was necessary that the question should be answered. "I could do no good by that," he said.

"No; perhaps not. Only I thought—"

"What did you think?" Now he had asked a question and showed plainly by his manner that he expected an answer.

"I don't know," said Lucy, blushing. "I suppose I ought not to have thought anything. But you seemed fond of her."

"Fond of her! Well; one does get fond of kind neighbours. I suppose you would think me impertinent, Miss Lucy," — he had never made even this approach to familiarity before, — "if I were to say that I am fond of both of you."

"No indeed," she replied, thinking that as a fondness declared by a young man for two girls at one and the same moment could not be interesting, so neither could it be impertinent.

"I don't think I should do any good by going down. All that kind of thing costs so much money."

"Of course it does, and I was very wrong."

"But I should like to do something, Miss Lucy." And then he put his hands into his trowsers-pocket, and Lucy knew that he was going to bring forth money.

She was very poor; but the idea of taking money from him was shocking to her. According to her theory of life, even though Sophy had been engaged to the man as his promised wife, she should not consent to accept maintenance from him or pecuniary aid till she had been made, in very truth, flesh of his flesh and bone of his bone. Presents an engaged girl might take of course, but hardly even presents of simple utility. A shawl might be given, so that it was a pretty thing and not a shawl merely for warmth. An engaged girl should rather live on bread and water up to her marriage than take the means of living from the man she loved till she could take it by right of having become his wife. Such were her feelings, and now she knew that this man was about to offer her money. "We shall do very well," she said, "Sophy and I together."

"You are very hard pinched," he replied. "You have given up your room."

"Yes, I have done that. When I was alone I did not want so big a place."

"I suppose I understand all about it," he said somewhat roughly, or perhaps gruffly would be the better word. "I think there is one thing poor people ought never to do. They ought never to be ashamed of being poor among themselves."

Then she looked up into his face, and as she did so a tear formed itself in each of her eyes. "Am I ashamed of anything before you?" she asked.

"You are afraid of telling the truth lest I should offer to help you. I know you don't have your dinner regular as you used."

"Who has dared to tell you that, Mr. Hall? What is my dinner to anybody?"

"Well. It is something to me. If we are to be friends of course I don't like seeing you go without your meals. You'll be ill next yourself."

"I am very strong."

"It isn't the way to keep so, to work without the victuals you're used to." He was talking to her now in such a tone as to make her almost feel that he was scolding her. "No good can come of that. You are sending your money down to Hastings to her."

"Of course we share everything."

"You wouldn't take anything from me for yourself I dare say. Anybody can see how proud you are. But if I leave it for her I don't think you have a right to refuse it. Of course she wants it if you don't." With that he brought out a sovereign and put it down on the table.

"Indeed I couldn't, Mr. Hall," she said.

"I may give it to her if I please."

"You can send it to her yourself," said Lucy, not knowing how else to answer him.

"No, I couldn't. I don't know her address." Then without waiting for another word he walked out of the room leaving the sovereign on the table. This occurred in a small back parlour on the ground floor, which was in the occupation of the landlady, but was used sometimes by the lodgers for such occasional meetings.

What was she to do with the sovereign? She would be very angry if any man were to send her a sovereign; but it was not right that she should measure Sophy's feelings by her own. And then it might still be that the man was sending the present to the girl whom he intended to make his wife. But why—why—why, had he asked about her dinner? What were her affairs to him? Would she not have gone without her dinner for ever rather than have taken it at his hands? And yet, who was there in all the world of whom she thought so well as of him? And so she took the sovereign upstairs with her into her garret.

Chapter IV
Mr. Brown the Hairdresser

Lucy when she got up to her own little room with the sovereign sat for a while on the bed, crying. But she could not in the least explain to herself why it was that she was shedding tears at this moment. It was not because Sophy was ill, though that was cause to her of great grief; — nor because she herself was so hard put to it for money to meet her wants. It may be doubted whether grief or pain ever does of itself produce tears, which are rather the outcome of some emotional feeling. She was not thinking much of Sophy as she cried, nor certainly were her own wants present to her mind. The sovereign was between her fingers, but she did not at first even turn her mind to that, or consider what had best be done with it. But what right had he to make inquiry as to her poverty? It was that, she told herself, which now provoked her to anger so that she wept from sheer vexation. Why should he have searched into her wants and spoken to her of her need of victuals? What had there been between them to justify him in tearing away that veil of custom which is always supposed to hide our private necessities from our acquaintances till we ourselves feel called upon to declare them? He had talked to her about her meals. He ought to know that she would starve rather than accept one from him. Yes; — she was very angry with him, and would henceforth keep herself aloof from him.

But still, as she sat, there were present to her eyes and ears the form and words of an heroic man. He had seemed to scold her; but there are female hearts which can be better reached and more surely touched by the truth of anger than the patent falseness of flattery. Had he paid her compliments she would not now have been crying, nor would she have complained to herself of his usage; but she certainly would not have sat thinking of him, wondering what sort of woman had been that young wife to whom he had first given himself, wondering whether it was possible that Sophy should be good enough for him.

Then she got up, and looking down upon her own hand gazed at the sovereign till she had made up her mind what she would do with it. She at once sat down and wrote to Sophy. She had made up her mind. There should be no diminution in the contribution made from her own wages. In no way should any portion of that sovereign administer to her own comfort. Though she might want her accustomed victuals ever so badly, they should not come to her from his earnings. So she told Sophy in the letter that Mr. Hall had expressed great anxiety for her welfare, and had begged that she would accept a present from him. She was to get anything with the sovereign that might best tend to her happiness. But the shilling a day which Lucy contributed out of her own wages was sent with the sovereign.

For an entire month she did not see Abraham Hall again so as to do more than just speak to him on the stairs. She was almost inclined to think that he was cold and unkind in not seeking her; — and yet she wilfully kept out of his way. On each Sunday it would at any rate have been easy for her to meet him; but with a stubborn purpose which she did not herself understand she kept herself apart, and when she met him on the stairs, which she would do occasionally when she returned from her work, she would hardly stand till she had answered his inquiries after Sophy. But at the end of the month one evening he came up and knocked at her door. "I am sorry to intrude, Miss Lucy."

"It is no intrusion, Mr. Hall. I wish I had a place to ask you to sit down in."

"I have come to bring another trifle for Miss Sophy."

"Pray do not do it. I cannot send it her. She ought not to take it. I am sure you know that she ought not to take it."

"I know nothing of the kind. If I know anything, it is that the strong should help the weak, and the healthy the sick. Why should she not take it from me as well as from you?"

It was necessary that Lucy should think a little before she could answer this; — but, when she had thought, her answer was ready. "We are both girls."

"Is there anything which ought to confine kindness to this or the other sex? If you were knocked down in the street would you let no one but a woman pick you up?"

"It is not the same. I know you understand it, Mr. Hall. I am sure you do."

Then he also paused to think what he would say, for he was conscious that he did "understand it." For a young woman to accept money from a man seemed to imply that some return of favours would be due. But, — he said to himself, — that feeling came from what was dirty and not from what was noble in the world. "You ought to lift yourself above all that," he said at last.

93

"Yes; you ought. You are very good, but you would be better if you would do so. You say that I understand, and I think that you, too, understand." This again was said in that voice which seemed to scold, and again her eyes became full of tears. Then he was softer on a sudden. "Good night, Miss Lucy. You will shake hands with me; — will you not?" She put her hand in his, being per-fectly conscious at the moment that it was the first time that she had ever done so. What a mighty hand it seemed to be as it held hers for a moment! "I will put the sovereign on the table," he said, again leaving the room and giving her no option as to its acceptance.

But she made up her mind at once that she would not be the means of sending his money to Sophy Wilson. She was sure that she would take nothing from him for her own relief, and there-fore sure that neither ought Sophy to do so, — at any rate unless there had been more between them than either of them had told to her. But Sophy must judge for herself. She sent, therefore, the sovereign back to Hall with a little note as follows: —

Dear Mr. Hall, — Sophy's address is at

"Mrs. Pike's,

"19, Paradise Row,

"Fairlight, near Hastings.

"You can do as you like as to writing to her. I am obliged to send back the money which you have so *very generously* left for her, because I do not think she ought to accept it. If she were quite in want it might be different, but we have still five shillings a day between us. If a young woman were starving perhaps it ought to be the same as though she were being run over in the street, but it is not like that. In my next letter I shall tell Sophy all about it.

"Yours truly,

"Lucy Graham."

The following evening, when she came home, he was standing at the house door evidently waiting for her. She had never seen him loitering in that way before, and she was sure that he was there in order that he might speak to her.

"I thought I would let you know that I got the sovereign safely," he said. "I am so sorry that you should have returned it."

"I am sure that I was right, Mr. Hall."

"There are cases in which it is very hard to say what is right and what is wrong. Some things seem right because people have been wrong so long. To give and take among friends ought to be right."

"We can only do what we think right," she said as she passed in through the passage up-stairs.

She felt sure from what had passed that he had not sent the money to Sophy! But why not? Sophy had said that he was bashful. Was he so far bashful that he did not dare himself to send the money to the girl he loved, though he had no scruple as to giving it to her through another person? And, as for bashfulness, it seemed to her that the man spoke out his mind clearly enough. He could scold her, she thought, without any difficulty, for it still seemed that his voice and manner were rough to her. He was never rough to Sophy; but then she had heard so often that love will alter a man amazingly!

Then she wrote her letter to Sophy, and explained as well as she could the whole affair. She was quite sure that Sophy would regret the loss of the money. Sophy, she knew, would have accepted it without scruple. People, she said to herself, will be different. But she endeavoured to make her friend understand that she, with her feelings, could not be the medium of sending on presents of which she disapproved. "I have given him your address," she said, "and he can suit himself as to writing to you." In this letter she enclosed a money order for the contribution made to Sophy's comfort out of her own wages.

Sophy's answer, which came in a day or two, surprised her very much. "As to Mr. Hall's money," she began, "as things stand at present perhaps it is as well that you didn't take it." As Lucy had expected that grievous fault would be found with her, this was comfortable. But it was after that, that the real news came. Sophy was a great deal better; that was also good tidings; — but she did not want to leave Hastings just at present. Indeed, she thought that she did not want to leave it at all. A very gentle-manlike young man, who was just going to be taken into part-nership in a hair-dressing establishment, had proposed to her; — and she had accepted him. Then there were two wishes expressed; — the first was that Lucy would go on a little longer with her kind generosity, and the second, that Mr. Hall would not feel it very much.

As regarded the first wish, Lucy resolved that she would go on at least for the present. Sohpy was still on sick leave from the office, and, even though she might be engaged to a hair-dresser, was still to be regarded as an invalid. But as to Mr. Hall, she thought that she could do nothing. She could not even tell him, — at any rate till that marriage at Hastings was quite a settled thing. But she thought that Mr. Hall's future happiness would not be lessened by the event. Though she had taught herself to love Sophy, she had been unable not to think that her friend was not a fitting wife for such a man. But in telling herself that he would have an escape, she put it to herself as though the fault lay chiefly in him. "He is so stern and so hard that he would have crushed her, and she never would have understood his justness and honesty." In her letter of congratulation, which was very kind, she said not a word of Abraham Hall, but she promised to go on with her own contribution till things were a little more settled.

In the meantime she was very poor. Even brown dresses won't wear for ever, let them be ever so brown, and in the first flurry of sending Sophy off to Hastings, — with that decent apparel which had perhaps been the means of winning the hair-dresser's heart, — she had got somewhat into debt with her landlady. This she was gradually paying off, even on her reduced wages, but the effort pinched her closely. Day by day, in spite of all her effort with her needle, she became sensible of a deterioration in her outward appearance which was painful to her at the office, and which made her most careful to avoid any meeting with Abraham Hall. Her boots were very bad, and she had now for some time given up even the pretence of gloves as she went backwards and forwards to the office. But perhaps it was her hat that was most vexatious. The brown straw hat which had lasted her all the summer and autumn could hardly be induced to keep its shape now when November was come.

One day, about three o'clock in the afternoon, Abraham Hall went to the Post-office, and, having inquired among the messengers, made his way up to the telegraph department at the top of the building. There he asked for Miss Graham, and was told by the doorkeeper that the young ladies were not allowed to receive visitors during office hours. He persisted, however, explaining that he had no wish to go into the room, but that it was a matter of importance, and that he was very anxious that Miss Graham should be asked to come out to him. Now it is a rule that the staff of the department who are engaged in sending and receiving messages, the privacy of which may be of vital importance, should be kept during the hours of work as free as possible from communication with the public. It is not that either the girls or the young men would be prone to tell the words which they had been the means of passing on to their destination, but that it might be worth the while of some sinner to offer great temptation, and that the power of offering it should be lessened as much as possible. Therefore, when Abraham Hall pressed his request the doorkeeper told him that it was quite impossible.

"Do you mean to say that if it were an affair of life and death she could not be called out?" Abraham asked in that voice which had sometimes seemed to Lucy to be so impressive. "She is not a prisoner!"

"I don't know as to that," replied the man; "you would have to see the superintendent, I suppose."

"Then let me see the superintendent." And at last he did succeed in seeing some one whom he so convinced of the importance of his message as to bring Lucy to the door.

"Miss Graham," he said, when they were at the top of the stairs, and so far alone that no one else could hear him, "I want you to come out with me for half an hour."

"I don't think I can. They won't let me."

"Yes they will. I have to say something which I must say now."

"Will not the evening do, Mr. Hall?"

"No; I must go out of town by the mail train from Paddington, and it will be too late. Get your hat and come with me for half an hour."

Then she remembered her hat, and she snatched a glance at her poor stained dress, and she looked up at him. He was not dressed in his working clothes, and his face and hands were clean, and altogether there was a look about him of well-to-do manly tidiness which added to her feeling of shame.

"If you will go on to the house I will follow you," she said.

"Are you ashamed to walk with me?"

"I am, because —"

He had not understood her at first, but now he understood it all. "Get your hat," he said, "and come with a friend who is really a friend. You must come; you must, indeed." Then she felt herself compelled to obey, and went back and got her old hat and followed him down the stairs into the street. "And so Miss Wilson is going to be married," were the first words he said in the street.

"Has she written to you?"

"Yes; she has told me all about it. I am so glad that she should be settled to her liking, out of town. She says that she is nearly well now. I hope that Mr. Brown is a good sort of man, and that he will be kind to her."

It could hardly be possible, Lucy thought, that he should have taken her away from the office merely to talk to her of Sophy's prospects. It was evident that he was strong enough to conceal any chagrin which might have been caused by Sophy's apostasy. Could it, however, be the case that he was going to leave London because his feelings had been too much disturbed to allow of his remaining quiet? "And so you are going away? Is it for long?" "Well, yes; I suppose it is for always." Then there came upon her a sense of increased desolation. Was he not her only friend? And then, though she had refused all pecuniary assistance, there had been present to her a feeling that there was near to her a strong human being whom she could trust, and who in any last extremity would be kind to her.

"For always! And you go to-night!" Then she thought that he had been right to insist on seeing her. It would certainly have been a great blow to her if he had gone without a word of farewell.

"There is a man wanted immediately to look after the engines at a great establishment on the Wye, in the Forest of Dean. They have offered me four pounds a week."

"Four pounds a week!"

"But I must go at once. It has been talked about for some time, and now it has come all in a clap. I have to be off without a day's notice, almost before I know where I am. As for leaving London, it is just what I like. I love the country."

"Oh, yes," said Lucy, "that will be nice;—and about your little boy?" Could it be that she was to be asked to do something for the child?

They were now at the door of their house. "Here we are," he said, "and perhaps I can say better inside what I have got to say." Then she followed him into the back sitting-room on the ground floor.

Chapter V

"Yes;" he said; — "about my little boy. I could not say what I had to say in the street, though I had thought to do so." Then he paused, and she sat herself down, feeling, she did not know why, as though she would lack strength to hear him if she stood. It was then the case that some particular service was to be demanded from her, — something that would show his confidence in her. The very idea of this seemed at once to add a grace to her life. She would have the child to love. There would be something for her to do. And there must be letters between her and him. It would certainly add a grace to her life. But how odd that he should not take his child with him! He had paused a moment while she thought of all this, and she was aware that he was looking at her. But she did not dare to return his gaze, or even to glance up at his face. And then gradually she felt that she was shivering and trembling. What was it that ailed her, — just now when it would be so necessary that she should speak out with some strength? She had eaten nothing since her breakfast when he had come to her, and she was afraid that she would show herself to be weak. "Will you be his mother?" he said.

What did it mean? How was she to answer him? She knew that his eyes were on her, but hers were more than ever firmly fixed upon the floor. And she was aware that she ought briskly to have acceded to his request, — so as to have shown by her ready alacrity that she had attributed no other meaning to the words than they had been intended to convey, — that she had not for a moment been guilty of rash folly. But though it was so imperative upon her to say a word, yet she could not speak. Everything was swimming round her. She was not even sure that she could sit upon her chair. "Lucy," he said; — then she thought she would have fallen; — "Lucy, will you be my wife?"

There was no doubt about the word. Her sense of hearing was at any rate not deficient. And there came upon her at once a thorough conviction that all her troubles had been changed for ever and a day into joy and blessings. The word had been spoken from which he certainly would never go back, and which of course, — must be a commandment to her. But yet there was an unfitness about it which disturbed her, and she was still powerless to speak. The remembrance of the meanness of her clothes and poorness of her position came upon her, — so that it would be her duty to tell him that she was not fit for him; and yet she could not speak.

"If you will say that you want time to think about it, I shall be contented," he said. But she did not want a moment to think about it. She could not have confessed to herself that she had learned to love him, — oh, so much too dearly, — if it were not for this most unexpected, most unthought of, almost impossible revelation. But she did not want a moment to make herself sure that she did love him. Yet she could not speak. "Will you say that you will think of it for a month?"

Then there came upon her an idea that he was not asking this because he loved her, but in order that he might have a mother whom he could trust for his child. Even that would have been flattering, but that would not have sufficed. Then when she told herself what she was, or rather what she thought herself to be, she felt sure that he could not really love her. Why should such a man as he love such a woman? Then her mouth was opened. "You cannot want me for myself," she said.

"Not for yourself! Then why? I am not the man to seek any girl for her fortune, and you have none." Then again she was dumbfounded. She could not explain what she meant. She could not say, — because I am brown, and because I am plain, and because I have become thin and worn from want, and because my clothes are old and shabby. "I ask you," he said, "because with all my heart I love you."

It was as though the heavens had been opened to her. That he should speak a word that was not true was to her impossible. And as it was so she would not coy her love to him for a moment. If only she could have found words with which to speak to him! She could not even look up at him, but she put out her hand so as to touch him. "Lucy," he said, "stand up and come to me." Then she stood up and with one little step crept close to his side. "Lucy, can you love me?" And as he asked the question his arm was pressed round her waist, and as she put up her hand to welcome rather than to restrain his embrace, she again felt the strength, the support, and the warmth of his grasp. "Will you not say that you love me?"

"I am such a poor thing," she replied.

"A poor thing, you are? Well, yes; there are different ways of being poor. I have been poor enough in my time but I never thought myself a poor thing. And you must not say it ever of yourself again."

"No?"

"My girl must not think herself a poor thing. May I not say, my girl?" Then there was just a little murmur, a sound which would have been "yes" but for the inability of her lips to open themselves. "And if my girl, then my wife. And shall my wife be called a poor thing? No, Lucy. I have seen it all. I don't think I like poor things; — but I like you."

"Do you?"

"I do. And now I must go back to the City Road and give up charge and take my money. And I must leave this at seven — after a cup of tea. Shall I see you again?"

"See me again! Oh, to-day, you mean. Indeed you shall. Not see you off? My own, own, own man!"

"What will they say at the office?"

"I don't care what they say. Let them say what they like. I have never been absent a day yet without leave. What time shall I be here?" Then he named an hour. "Of course I will have your last words. Perhaps you will tell me something that I must do."

"I must leave some money with you."

"No; no; no; not yet. That shall come after." This she said smiling up at him, with a sparkle of a tear in each eye, but with such a smile! Then he caught her in his arms and kissed her. "That may come at present at any rate," he said. To this, though it was repeated once and again, there was no opposition. Then in his own masterful manner he put on his hat and stalked out of the room without any more words.

She must return to the office that afternoon of course, if only for the sake of explaining her wish to absent herself the rest of the day. But she could not go forth into the streets just yet. Though she had been able to smile at him and to return his caress and for a moment so to stand by him that he might have something of the delight of his love, still she was too much flurried, too weak from the excitement of the last half hour, to walk back to the Post-office without allowing herself some minutes to recruit her strength and collect her thoughts. She went at once up to her own room and cut for herself a bit of bread which she began to eat, — just as one would trim one's lamp carefully for some night work even though oppressed by heaviest sorrow, or put fuel on the fire that would be needed. Then having fed herself, she leaned back in her chair, throwing her handkerchief over her face, in order that she might think of it.

Oh, — how much there was to fill her mind with many thoughts! Looking back to what she had been even an hour ago, and then assuring herself with infinite delight of the certain happiness of her present position, she told herself that all the world had been altered to her within that short space. As for loving him; — there was no doubt about that! Now she could own to herself that she had long since loved him, even when she thought that he might probably take that other girl as his wife. That she should love him, — was it not a matter of course, he being what he was? But that he should love her, — that, that was the marvel! But he did. She need not doubt that. She could remember distinctly each word of assurance that he had spoken to her. "I ask you because with all my heart I love you." "May I not say my girl? — and, if my girl, then my wife?" "I do not think that I like poor things; but I like you." No. If she were regarded by him as good enough to be his wife then she would certainly never call herself a poor thing again.

In her troubles and her poverty, — especially in her solitude, she had often thought of that other older man, who had wanted to make her his wife, — sometimes almost with regret. There would have been duties for her and a home, and a mode of life more fitting to her feminine nature than this solitary, tedious existence. And there would have been something for her to love, some human being on whom to spend her human solicitude and sympathies. She had leagued herself with Sophy Wilson and she had been true to the bond; — but it had had in it but little satisfaction. The other life, she had sometimes thought, would have been better. But she had never loved the man, and, could not have loved him as a husband should, she thought, be loved by his wife. She had done what was right in refusing the good things which he had offered her, — and now she was rewarded! Now had come to her the bliss of which she had dreamed, that of belonging to a man to whom she felt that she was bound by all the chords of her heart. Then she repeated his name to herself, — Abraham Hall, and tried in a lowest whisper the sound of that other name, — Lucy Hall. And she opened her arms wide as she sat upon the chair as though in that way she could at once take his child to her bosom.

She had been sitting so nearly an hour when she started up suddenly and again put on her old hat and hurried off towards her office. She felt now that as regarded her clothes she did not care about herself. There was a paradise prepared for her so dear and so near that the present was made quite bright by merely being the short path to such a future. But for his sake she cared. As belonging to him she would fain, had it been possible, not have shown herself in a garb unfitting for his wife. Everything about him had always been decent, fitting, and serviceable! Well! It was his own doing. He had chosen her as she was. She would not run in debt to make herself fit for his notice, because such debts would have been debts to be paid by him. But if she could squeeze from her food what should supply her with garments fit at any rate to stand with at the altar it should be done.

Then as she hurried on to the office, she remembered what he had said about money. No! She would not have his money till it was hers of right. Then with what perfect satisfaction would she take from him whatever he pleased to give her, and how hard would she work for him in order that he might never feel that he had given her his good things for nothing!

It was five o'clock before she was at the office and she had promised to be back in the lodgings at six, to get for him his tea. It was quite out of the question that she should work to-day. "The truth is, ma'am," she said to the female superintendent, "I have received and accepted an offer of marriage this afternoon. He is going out of town to-night, and I want to be with him before he goes." This is a plea against which official rigour cannot prevail. I remember once when a young man applied to a saturnine pundit who ruled matters in a certain office for leave of absence for a month to get married. "To get married!" said the saturnine pundit. "Poor fellow! But you must have the leave." The lady at the telegraph office was no doubt less caustic, and dismissed our Lucy for the day with congratulation rather than pity.

She was back at the lodging before her lover, and had borrowed the little back parlour, and had spread the tea-things, and herself made the toast in the kitchen before he came. "There's something I suppose more nor friendship betwixt you and Mr. Hall, and better," said the landlady smiling. "A great deal better, Mrs. Green," Lucy had replied, with her face intent upon the toast. "I thought it never could have been that other young lady," said Mrs. Green.

"And now, my dear, about money," said Abraham as he rose to prepare himself for the journey. Many things had been settled over that meal, — how he was to get a house ready, and was then to say when she should come to him, and how she should bring the boy with her, and how he would have the banns called in the church, and how they would be married as soon as possible after her arrival in the new country. "And now, my dear about money?"

She had to take it at last. "Yes," she said, "it is right that I should have things fit to come to you in. It is right that you shouldn't be disgraced."

"I'd marry you in a sack from the poor-house, if it were necessary," he said with vehemence.

"As it is not necessary, it shall not be so. I will get things, — but they shall belong to you always; and I will not wear them till the day that I also shall belong to you."

She went with him that night to the station, and kissed him openly as she parted from him on the platform. There was nothing in her love now of which she was ashamed. How, after some necessary interval, she followed him down into Gloucestershire, and how she became his wife standing opposite to him in the bright raiment which his liberality had supplied, and how she became as good a wife as ever blessed a man's household, need hardly here be told.

That Miss Wilson recovered her health and married the hairdresser may be accepted by all anxious readers as an undoubted fact.

"The Telegraph Girl" appeared first in *Good Cheer*, the Christmas issue of *Good Words* for 1877.

Alice Dugdale

I

T USED TO BE SAID in the village of Beetham that nothing ever went wrong with Alice Dugdale, — the meaning of which, perhaps, lay in the fact that she was determined that things should be made to go right. Things as they came were received by her with a gracious welcome, and "things," whatever they were, seemed to be so well pleased with the treatment afforded to them, that they too for most part made themselves gracious in return.

Nevertheless she had had sorrows — as who has not? But she had kept her tears for herself, and had shown her smiles for the comfort of those around her. In this little story it shall be told how in a certain period of her life she suffered much; — how she still smiled, and how at last she got the better of her sorrow.

Her father was the country doctor in the populous and strag- gling parish of Beetham. Beetham is one of those places so often found in the south of England, half village, half town, for the existence of which there seems to be no special reason. It had no mayor, no municipality, no market, no pavements, and no gas. It was therefore no more than a village; — but it had a doctor, and Alice's father, Dr. Dugdale, was the man. He had been estab- lished at Beetham for more than thirty years, and knew every pulse and every tongue for ten miles around. I do not know that he was very great as a doctor; — but he was a kind-hearted, liberal man, and he enjoyed the confidence of the Beethamites, which is everything. For thirty years he had worked hard and had brought up a large family, at any rate without want. He was still working hard, though turned sixty, at the time of which we are speaking. He had, even in his old age, many children dependent on him, and, though he had fairly prospered, he had not become a rich man.

He had been married twice, and Alice was the only child left at home by his first wife. Two elder sisters were married, and an elder brother was away in the world. Alice had been much younger than they, and had been the only child living with him when he had brought to his house a second mother for her. She was then fifteen. Eight or nine years had since gone, and almost every year had brought an increase to the doctor's family. There were now seven little Dugdales in and about the nursery; and what the seven would do when Alice should go away the folk of Beetham always declared that they were quite at a loss even to guess. For Mrs. Dugdale was one of those women who succumb to difficulties, — who seem originally to have been made of soft material and to have become warped, out of joint, tattered, and almost useless under the wear of the world. But Alice had been constructed of thoroughly seasoned timber, so that, let her be knocked about as she might, she was never out of repair. Now the doctor, excellent as he was at doctoring, was not very good at household matters, — so that the folk at Beetham had reason to be at a loss when they bethought themselves as to what would happen when Alice should "go away."

Of course there is always that prospect of a girl's "going away." Girls not unfrequently intend to "go away." Sometimes they "go away" very suddenly, without any previous intention. At any rate, such a girl as Alice cannot be regarded as a fixture in a house. Binding as may be her duties at home, it is quite understood that should any adequate provocation to "go away" be brought within her reach, she will go, let the duties be what they may. Alice was a thoroughly good girl, — good to her father, good to her little brothers and sisters, unutterably good to that poor foolish stepmother; — but, no doubt she would "go away" if duly asked.

When that vista of future discomfort in the doctor's house first made itself clearly apparent to the Beethamites, an idea that Alice might perhaps go very soon had begun to prevail in the village. The eldest son of the vicar, Parson Rossiter, had come back from India as Major Rossiter, with an appointment, as some said, of £2,000 a year; — let us put it down as £1,500; — and had renewed his acquaintance with his old playfellow. Others, more than one or two, had endeavoured before this to entice Alice to "go away," but it was said that the dark-visaged warrior, with his swarthy face and black beard, and bright eyes, — probably, too, something in him nobler than those outward bearings, — had whispered words which had prevailed. It was supposed that Alice now had a fitting lover, and that therefore she would "go away."

There was no doubt in the mind of any single inhabitant of Beetham as to the quality of the lover. It was considered on all sides that he was fitting, — so fitting that Alice would of course go when asked. John Rossiter was such a man that every Beethamite looked upon him as a hero, — so that Beetham was proud to have produced him. In small communities a man will come up now and then as to whom it is surmised that any young lady would of course accept him. This man, who was now about ten years older than Alice, had everything to recommend him. He was made up of all good gifts of beauty, conduct, dignity, good heart, — and fifteen hundred a year at the very least. His official duties required him to live in London, from which Beetham was seventy miles distant; but those duties allowed him ample time for visiting the parsonage. So very fitting he was to take any girl away upon whom he might fix an eye of approbation, that there were others, higher than Alice in the world's standing, who were said to grudge the young lady of the village so great a prize. For Alice Dugdale was a young lady of the village and no more; whereas there were county families around, with daughters, among whom the Rossiters had been in the habit of mixing. Now that such a Rossiter had come to the fore, the parsonage family was held to be almost equal to county people.

To whatever extent Alice's love affairs had gone, she herself had been very silent about them; nor had her lover as yet taken the final step of being closeted for ten minutes with her father. Nevertheless everybody had been convinced in Beetham that it would be so, — unless it might be Mrs. Rossiter. Mrs. Rossiter was ambitious for her son, and in this matter sympathized with the county people. The county people certainly were of opinion that John Rossiter might do better, and did not altogether see what there was in Alice Dugdale to make such a fuss about. Of course she had a sweet countenance, rather brown, with good eyes. She had not, they said, another feature in her face which could be called handsome. Her nose was broad. Her mouth was large. They did not like that perpetual dimpling of the cheek which, if natural, looked as if it were practised. She was stout, almost stumpy, they thought. No doubt she danced well, having a good ear and being active and healthy: but with such a waist no girl could really be graceful. They acknowledged her to be the best nursemaid that ever a mother had in her family; but they thought it a pity that she should be taken away from duties for which her pressence was so much desired, at any rate by such a one as John Rossiter. I, who knew Beetham well, and who though turned the hill of middle life had still an eye for female charms, used to declare to myself that Alice, though she was decidedly village and not county, was far, far away the prettiest girl in that part of the world.

The old parson loved her, and so did Miss Rossiter, — Miss Janet Rossiter, — who was four or five years old than her brother and therefore quite an old maid. But John was so great a man that neither of them dared to say much to encourage him, — as neither did Mrs. Rossiter to use her eloquence on the other side. It was felt by all of them that any persuasion might have on John anything but the intended effect. Whan a man of the age of 33 is Deputy Assistant Inspector General of Cavalry, it is not easy to talk him this way or that in a matter of love. And John Rossiter, though the best fellow in the world, was apt to be taciturn on such a subject. Men frequently marry almost without thinking about it at all. "Well, perhaps I might as well. At any rate, I cannot very well help it." That too often is the frame of mind. Rossiter's discussion to himself was of a higher nature than that, but perhaps not quite what it should have been. "This is a thing of such moment that it requires to be pondered again and again. A man has to think of himself, and of her, and of the children which have to come after him; — of the total good or total bad which may come of such a decision." As in the one manner there is too much of negligence, so in the other there may be too much of care. The "perhaps I might as wells," — so good is Providence,

— are sometimes more successful than those careful, long-pondering heroes. The old parson was very sweet to Alice, believing that she would be his daughter-in-law, and so was Miss Rossiter, thoroughly approving of such a sister. But Mrs. Rossiter was a little cold; — all of which Alice could read plainly and digest, without saying a word. If it was to be, she would welcome her happy lot with heartfelt acknowledgment of the happiness provided for her; but if it was not to be, no human being should know that she had sorrowed. There should be nothing lack-a-daisical in her life or conduct. She had her work to do, and she knew that as long as she did that, grief would not overpower her.

In her own house it was taken for granted that she was to "go," in a manner that distressed her. "You'll never be here to lengthen 'em," said her stepmother to her, almost whinning, when there was a question as to flounces in certain juvenile petticoats which might require to be longer than they were first made before they should be finally abandoned.

"That I certainly shall if Tiny grows as she does now."

"I suppose he'll pop regularly when he next comes down," said Mrs. Dugdale.

There was ever so much in this which annoyed Alice. In the first place the word "pop" was to her abominable. Then she was almost called upon to deny that he would "pop," when in her heart she thought it very probable that he might. And the word, she knew, had become intelligible to the eldest of her little sisters who was present. Moreover, she was most unwilling to discuss the subject at all, and could hardly leave it undiscussed when such direct questions were asked. "Mamma," she said, "don't let us think about anything of the kind." This did not at all satisfy herself. She ought to have repudiated the lover altogether; and yet she could not bring herself to tell the necessary lie.

"I suppose he will come — some day," said Minnie, the child old enough to understand the meaning of such coming.

> "For men may come and men may go,
> But I go on for ever, — for ever,"

said or sang Alice, with a pretence of drollery as she turned herself to her little sister. But even in her little song there was a purpose. Let any man come or let any man go, she would go on, at any rate apparently untroubled, in her walk of life.

"Of course he'll take you away, and then what am I to do?" said Mrs. Dugdale, moaning. It is sad enough for a girl thus to have her lover thrown in her face when she is by no means sure of her lover.

A day or two afterwards another word, much more painful, was said to her up at the parsonage. Into the parsonage she went frequently to show that there was nothing in her heart to prevent her visiting her old friends as had been her wont.

"John will be down here next week," said the parson, whom she met on the gravel drive just at the hall door.

"How often he comes! What do they do at the Horse Guards, or wherever it is that he goes to?"

"He'll be more steady when he has taken a wife," said the old man.

"In the meantime what becomes of the cavalry?"

"I dare say you'll know all about that before long," said the parson, laughing.

"Now, my dear, how can you be so foolish as to fill the girl's head with nonsense of that kind?" said Mrs. Rossiter, who at that moment came out from the front door. "And you're doing John an injustice. You are making people believe that he has said that which he has not said."

Alice at the moment was very angry, — as angry as she well could be. It was certain that Mrs. Rossiter did not know what her son had said or had not said. But it was at any rate cruel that she who had put forward no claim, who had never been forward in seeking her lover, should be thus almost publicly rebuked. Quiet as she wished to be, it was at any rate necessary that she should say one word in her own defence. "I don't think Mr. Rossiter's little joke will do John any injustice or me any harm," she said. "But, as it may be taken seriously, I hope he will not repeat it."

"He could not do better for himself. That's my opinion," said the old man, turning back into the house. There had been words before on the subject between him and his wife, and he was not well pleased with her at this moment.

"My dear Alice, I am sure you know that I mean everything the best for you," said Mrs. Rossiter.

"If nobody would mean anything, but just let me alone, that would be best. And as for nonsense, Mrs. Rossiter, don't you know of me that I'm not likely to be carried away by foolish ideas of that kind?"

"I do know that you are very good."

"Then why should you talk at me as though I were very bad?" Mrs. Rossiter felt that she had been reprimanded, and was less inclined than ever to accept Alice as a daughter-in-law.

Alice, as she walked home, was low in spirits, and angry with herself because it was so. People would be fools: of course that was to be expected. She had known all along that Mrs. Rossiter wanted a grander wife for her son, whereas the parson was anxious to have her for his daughter-in-law. Of course she loved the parson better than his wife. But why was it that she felt at this moment that Mrs. Rossiter would prevail?

"Of course it will be so," she said to herself. "I see it now. And I suppose he is right. But then certainly he ought not to have come here. But perhaps he comes because he wishes to—see Miss Wanless." She went a little out of her road home, not only to dry a tear, but to rid herself of the effect of it, and then spent the remainder of the afternoon swinging her brothers and sisters in the garden.

Chapter II
Major Rossiter

"Perhaps he is coming here to see Miss Wanless," Alice said to herself. And in the course of that week she found that her surmise was correct. John Rossiter stayed only one night at the parsonage, and then went over to Brook Park, where lived Sir Walter Wanless and all the Wanlesses. The parson had not so declared when he told Alice that his son was coming, but John himself said on his arrival that this was a special visit made to Brook Park, and not to Beetham. It had been promised for the last three months, though only fixed lately. He took the trouble to come across to the doctor's house with the express purpose of explaining the fact. "I suppose you have always been intimate with them," said Mrs. Dugdale, who was sitting with Alice and a little crowd of children round them. There was a tone of sarcasm in the words not at all hidden. "We all know that you are a great deal finer than we mere village folk. We don't know the Wanlesses, but of course you do. You'll find yourself much more at home at Brook Park than you can in such a place as this." All that, though not spoken, was contained in the tone of the lady's speech.

"We have always been neighbours," said John Rossiter.

"Neighbours ten miles off!" said Mrs. Dugdale.

"I dare say the Good Samaritan lived thirty miles off," said Alice.

"I don't think distance has much to do with it," said the Major.

"I like my neighbours to be neighbourly. I like Beetham neighbours," said Mrs. Dugdale. There was a reproach in every word of it. Mrs. Dugdale had heard of Miss Georgiana Wanless, and Major Rossiter knew that she had done so. After her fashion, the lady was accusing him for deserting Alice.

Alice understood it also, and yet it behoved her to hold herself well up and be cheerful. "I like Beetham people best myself," she said; "but then it is because I don't know any other. I remember going to Brook Park once, when there was a party of children, a hundred years ago, and I thought it quite a paradise. There was a profusion of strawberries, by which my imagination has been troubled ever since. You'll just be in time for the strawberries, Major Rossiter." He had always been John till quite lately, —John with the memories of childhood; but now he had become Major Rossiter.

She went out into the garden with him for a moment as he took his leave, — not quite alone, as a little boy of two years old was clinging to her hand. "If I had my way," she said, "I'd have my neighbours everywhere, — at any distance. I envy a man chiefly for that."

"Those one loves best should be very near, I think."

"Those one loves best of all? Oh yes, so that one may do something. It wouldn't do not to have you every day, would it Bobby?" Then she allowed the willing little urchin to struggle up into her arms and to kiss her, all smeared as was his face with bread-and-butter.

"Your mother meant to say that I was running away from my old friends."

"Of course she did. You see, you loom so very large to us here. You are—such a swell, as Dick says, that we are a little sore when you pass us by. Everybody likes to be bowed to by royalty: don't you know that. Brook Park is, of course, the proper place for you; but you don't expect but what we are going to express our little disgusts and little prides when we find ourselves left behind!" No words could have less declared her own feelings on the matter than those she was uttering; but she found herself compelled to laugh at him, lest, in the other direction, something of tenderness might escape her, whereby he might be injured worse than by her raillery. In nothing that she might say could there be less of real reproach to him than in this.

"I hate that word 'swell,'" he said.

"So do I."

"Then why do you use it?"

"To show you how much better Brook Park is than Beetham. I am sure they don't talk about swells at Brook Park."

"Why do you throw Brook Park in my teeth?"

"I feel an inclination to make myself disagreeable to-day. Are you never like that?"

"I hope not."

"And then I am bound to follow up what poor dear mamma began. But I won't throw Brook Park in your teeth. The ladies, I know, are very nice. Sir Walter Wanless is a little grand; — isn't he?"

"You know," said he, "that I should be much happier here than there."

"Because Sir Walter is so grand?"

"Because my friends here are dearer friends. But still it is right that I should go. One cannot always be where one would be happiest."

"I am happiest with Bobby," said she; "and I can always have Bobby." Then she gave him her hand at the gate, and he went down to the parsonage.

That night Mrs. Rossiter was closeted for a while with her son before they both went to bed. She was supposed, in Beetham, to be of a higher order of intellect, — of a higher stamp generally, — than her husband or daughter, and to be in that respect nearly on a par with her son. She had not travelled as he had done, but she was of an ambitious mind and had thoughts beyond Beetham. The poor dear parson cared for little outside the bounds of his parish. "I am so glad you are going to stay for a while over at Brook Park," she said.

"Only for three days."

"In the intimacy of a house three days is a lifetime. Of course I do not like to interfere." When this was said the Major frowned, knowing well that his mother was going to interfere. "But I cannot help thinking how much a connection with the Wanlesses would do for you."

"I don't want anything from any connection."

"That is all very well, John, for a man to say; but in truth we all depend on connections one with another. You are beginning the world."

"I don't know about that, mother."

"To my eyes, you are. Of course, you look upwards."

"I take all that as it comes."

"No doubt; but still you must have it in your mind to rise. A man is assisted very much by the kind of wife he marries. Much would be done for a son-in-law of Sir Walter Wanless."

"Nothing I hope ever for me on that score. To succeed by favour is odious."

"But even to rise by merit so much outside assistance is often necessary! Though you will assuredly deserve all that you will ever get, yet you may be more likely to get it as son-in-law to Sir Walter Wanless than if you were married to some obscure girl. Men who make the most of themselves in the world do think of these things. I am the last woman in the world to recommend my boy to look after money in marriage."

"The Miss Wanlesses will have none."

"And therefore I can speak the more freely. They will have very little, — as coming from such a family. But he has great influence. He has contested the county five times. And then — where is there a handsomer girl than Georgiana Wanless?" The Major thought that he knew one, but did not answer the question. "And she is all that such a girl ought to be. Her manners are perfect, — and her conduct. A constant performance of domestic duties is of course admirable. If it comes to one to have to wash linen, she who washes her linen well is a good woman. But among mean things high spirits are not to be found."

"I am not so sure of that."

"It must be so. How can the employment of every hour in the day on menial work leave time for the mind to fill itself? Making children's frocks may be a duty, but it must also be an impediment."

"You are speaking of Alice."

"Of course I am speaking of Alice."

"I would wager my head that she has read twice more in the last two years than Georgiana Wanless. But, mother, I am not disposed to discuss either the one young lady or the other. I am not going to Brook Park to look for a wife; and if ever I take one, it will be simply because I like her best, and not because I wish to use her as a rung of a ladder by which to climb upwards into the world." That all this and just this would be said to her Mrs. Rossiter had been aware; but still she had thought that a word in season might have its effect.

And it did have its effect. John Rossiter, as he was driven over to Brook Park on the following morning, was unconsciously mindful of that allusion to the washerwoman. He had seen that Alice's cheek had been smirched by the greasy crumbs from her little brother's mouth; he had seen that the tips of her fingers showed the mark of the needle; he had seen fragments of thread about her dress, and the mud even from the children's boots on her skirts. He had seen this, and had been aware that Georgiana Wanless was free from all such soil on her outward raiment. He liked the perfect grace of unspotted feminine apparel, and he had, too, thought of the hours in which Alice might probably be employed amidst the multifarious needs of a nursery, and had argued to himself much as his mother had argued. It was good and homely, — worthy of a thousand praises; but was it exactly that which he wanted in a wife? He had repudiated with scorn his mother's cold, worldy doctrine; but yet he had felt that it would be a pleasant thing to have it known in London that his wife was the daughter of Sir Walter Wanless. It was true that she was wonderfully handsome, — a complexion perfectly clear, a nose cut as out of marble, a mouth delicate as of goddess, with a waist quite to match it. Her shoulders were white as alabaster. Her dress was at all times perfect. Her fingers were without mark or stain. There might perhaps be a want of expression; but faces so symmetrical are seldom expressive. And then, to crown all this, he

117

was justified in believing that she was attached to himself. Almost as much had been said to him by Lady Wanless herself, —a word which would amount to as much, coupled as it was with an immediate invitation to Brook Park. Of this he had given no hint to any human being; but he had been at Brook Park once before, and some rumour of something between him and Miss Georgiana Wanless had reached the people at Beetham, — had reached, as we have seen, not only Mrs. Rossiter, but also Alice Dugdale.

There had been moments up in London when his mind had veered round towards Miss Wanless. But there was one little trifle which opposed the action of his mind, and that was his heart. He had begun to think that it might be his duty to marry Georgiana; — but the more he thought so the more clearly would the figure of Alice stand before him, so that no veil could be thrown over it. When he tried to summon to his imagination the statuesque beauty of the one girl, the bright eyes of the other would look at him, and the words from her speaking mouth would be in his ears. He had once kissed Alice, immediately on his return, in the presence of her father, and the memory of the halcyon moment was always present to him. When he thought most of Miss Wanless he did not think much of her kisses. How grand she would be at his dining-table, how glorious in his drawing-room! But with Alice how sweet would it be to sit by some brook-side and listen to the waters!

And now since he had been at Beetham, from the nature of things which sometimes makes events to come from exactly contrary causes, a new charm had been added to Alice, simply by the little effort she had made to annoy him. She had talked to him of "swells," and had pretended to be jealous of the Wanlesses, just because she had known that he would hate to hear such a word from her lips, and that he would be vexed by exhibition of such a feeling on her part. He was quite sure that she had not committed these sins because they belonged to her as a matter of course. Nothing could be more simple than her natural language of her natural feelings. But she had chosen to show him that she was ready to run into little faults which might offend him. The reverse of her ideas came upon him. She had said, as it were, — "See how little anxious I must be to dress myself in your mirror, when I put myself in the category with my poor stepmother." Then he said to himself that he could see her as he was fain to see her, in her own mirror, and he loved her the better because she had dared to run the risk of offending him.

As he was driven up to the house at Brook Park he knew that it was his destiny to marry either the one girl or the other; and he was afraid of himself, — that before he left the house he might be engaged to the one he did not love. And he was thoroughly ashamed of himself as he felt that it might be so. He knew that it behoved him to be so strong, that no inducements from without should be powerful enough to turn him from any purpose on which he had fixed his mind. A word had been said to him, — the merest word, — but which he had still not failed to understand. That word, spoken by Lady Wanless, had told him that if he should choose to offer himself as a son-in-law to that family he would not be refused. Having fancied that so much was said to him, — even were it no more than a fancy, — ought he not to have remained altogether away from Brook Park? Should he have allowed himself to enter the precincts of the place after such an offer had in truth been made to him, unless he were disposed to accept the offer and do as Lady Wanless would have him? He knew that he was not prepared to accept the offer. He knew that he would not act in accordance with Lady Wanless's advice. And yet he did not like to have to own to himself that there was any house or any park in England in which he did not dare to show himself, regardless of consequences. Therefore he had himself driven up to the house.

Chapter III
Lady Wanless

Sir Walter Wanless was one of those great men who never do anything great, but achieve their greatness partly by their tailors, partly by a breadth of eyebrow and carriage of the body, — what we may call deportment, — and partly by the outside gifts of fortune. Taking his career altogether, we must say that he had been unfortunate. He was a baronet with a fine house and park, — and with an income hardly sufficient for the place. He had contested the county four times on old Whig principles, and had once been in Parliament for two years. There he had never opened his mouth; but in his struggle to get there had greatly embarrassed his finances. His tailor had been well chosen, and had always turned him out as the best-dressed old baronet in England. His eyebrow was all his own, and certainly commanded respect from those with whom eyebrows are efficacious. He never read; he eschewed farming, by which he had lost money in early life; and had, so to say, no visible occupation at all. But he was Sir Walter Wanless, and, what with his tailor and what with his eyebrow, he did command a great deal of respect in the country round Beetham. He had, too, certain good gifts for which people were thankful as coming from so great a man. He paid his bills, he went to church, he was well behaved, and still maintained certain old-fashioned family charities, though money was not plentiful with him.

He had two sons and five daughters. The sons were in the army, and were beyond his control. The daughters were all at home, and were altogether under the control of their mother. Indeed, everything at Brook Park was under the control of Lady Wanless, — though no man alive gave himself airs more autocratic than Sir Walter. It was on her shoulders that fell the burden of the five daughters, and of maintaining with straitened means the hospitality of Brook Park on their behoof. A hard-worked woman was Lady Wanless, in doing her duty, — with imperfect lights no doubt, but to the best of her abilities with such lights as she possessed. She was somewhat fine in her dress, not for any comfort that might accrue to herself, but from a feeling that an alliance with the Wanlesses would not be valued by the proper sort of young men unless she were grand herself. The girls were beautifully dressed; but oh, with such care and economy and daily labour among them, herself, and the two lady's-maids up-stairs! The father, what with his election and his farming, and a period of costly living early in his life, had not done well for the family. That she knew, and never rebuked him. But it was for her to set matters right, which she could only do by getting husbands for the daughters. That this might be achieved, the Wanless prestige must be maintained; and with crippled means it is so hard to maintain a family prestige! A poor duke may do it, or perhaps an earl; but a baronet is not high enough to give bad wines to his guests without serious detriment to his unmarried daughters.

A beginning to what might be hoped to be a long line of successes had already been made. The eldest girl, Sophia, was engaged. Lady Wanless did not look very high, knowing that failure in such operations will bring with it such unutterable misfortune. Sophia was engaged to the eldest son of a neighbouring squire, —whose property indeed was not large, nor was the squire likely to die very soon; but there were the means of present living and a future rental of £4,000 a year. Young Mr. Cobble was now staying at the house, and had been duly accepted by Sir Walter himself. The youngest girl, who was only nineteen, had fallen in love with a young clergyman in the neighbourhood. That would not do at all, and the young clergyman was not allowed within the Park. Georgiana was the beauty; and for her, if for any, some great destiny might have been hoped. But it was her turn, a matter of which Lady Wanless thought a great deal, and the Major was too good to be allowed to escape. Georgiana, in her cold, impassive way, seemed to like the Major, and therefore Lady Wanless paired them off instantly, with that decision which was necessary amidst the labours of her life. She had no scruples in what she did, feeling sure that her daughters would make honest, good wives, and that the blood of the Wanlesses was a dowry in itself.

The Major had been told to come early, because a party was made to visit certain ruins about eight miles off, —Castle Owless, as it was called, —to which Lady Wanless was accustomed to take her guests, because the family history declared that the Wanlesses had lived there at some remote period. It still belonged to Sir Walter, though unfortunately the intervening lands had for the most part fallen into other hands. Owless and Wanless were supposed to be the same, and thus there was room for a good deal of family tattle.

"I am delighted to see you at Brook Park," said Sir Walter as they met at the luncheon table. "When I was at Christchurch your father was at Wadham, and I remember him well." Exactly the same words had been spoken when the Major, on a former occasion, had been made welcome at the house, and clearly implied a feeling that Christchurch, though much superior, may condescend to know Wadham—under certain circumstances. Of the Baronet nothing further was heard or seen till dinner.

Lady Wanless went in the open carriage with three daughters, Sophie being one of them. As her affair was settled, it was not necessary that one of the two side-saddles should be alloted to her use. Young Cobble, who had been asked to send two horses over from Cobble Hall so that Rossiter might ride one, felt this to be hard. But there was no appeal from Lady Wanless. "You'll have plenty enough of her all the evening," said the mother, patting him affectionately, "and it is so necessary just at present that Georgiana and Edith should have horse exercise." In this way it was arranged that Georgiana should ride with the Major, and Edith, the third daughter, with young Burmeston, the son of Cox and Burmeston, brewers at the neighbouring town of Slowbridge. A country brewer is not quite what Lady Wanless would have liked; but with difficulties such as hers a rich young brewer might be worth having. All this was hard upon Mr. Cobble, who would not have sent his horses had he known it.

Our Major saw at a glance that Georgiana rode well. He liked ladies to ride, and doubted whether Alice had ever been on horseback in her life. After all, how many advantages does a girl lose by having to pass her days in a nursery! For a moment some such idea crossed his mind. Then he asked Georgiana some question as to the scenery through which they were passing. "Very fine, indeed," said Georgiana. She looked straight before her, and sat with her back square to the horse's tail. There was no hanging in the saddle, no shifting about in uneasiness. She could rise and fall easily, even gracefully, when the horse trotted. "You are fond of riding I can see," said the Major. "I do like riding," answered Georgiana. The tone in which she spoke of her present occupation was much more lively than that in which she had expressed her approbation of scenery.

At the ruin they all got down, and Lady Wanless told them the entire story of the Owlesses and the Wanlesses, and filled the brewer's mind with wonder as to the antiquity and dignity of the family. But the Major was the fish just as this moment in hand. "The Rossiters are very old too," she said smiling; "but perhaps that is a kind of thing you don't care for."

"Very much indeed," said he. Which was true, — for he was proud of knowing that he had come from the Rossiters who had been over four hundred years in Herefordshire. "A remembrance of old merit will always be an incitement to new."

"It is just that, Major Rossiter. It is strange how very nearly in the same words Georgiana said the same thing to me yesterday." Georgiana happened to overhear this, but did not contradict her mother, though she made a little grimace to her sister which was seen by no one else. Then Lady Wanless slipped aside to assist the brewer and Edith, leaving the Major and her second daughter together. The two younger girls, of whom the youngest was the wicked one with the penchant for the curate, were wandering among the ruins by themselves.

"I wonder whether there ever were any people called Owless," said Rossiter, not quite knowing what subject of conversation to choose.

"Of course there were. Mamma always says so."

"That settles the question; — does it not?"

"I don't see why there shouldn't be Owlesses. No, I won't sit on the wall thank you, because I should stain my habit."

"But you'll be tired."

"Not particularly tired. It is not so very far. I'd go back in the carriage, only of course we can't, because of the habits. Oh, yes; I'm very fond of dancing, — very fond indeed. We always have two balls every year at Slowbridge. And there are some others about the county. I don't think you ever have balls at Beetham."

"There is no one to give them."

"Does Miss Dugdale ever dance?"

The major had to think for a moment before he could answer the question. Why should Miss Wanless ask as to Alice's dancing? "I am sure she does. Now I think of it I have heard her talk of dancing. You don't know Alice Dugdale?" Miss Wanless shook her head. "She is worth knowing."

"I am quite sure she is. I have always heard that you thought so. She is very good to all those children; isn't she?"

"Very good indeed."

"She could be almost pretty if she wasn't so, — so dumpy, I should say." Then they got on their horses again and rode back to Brook Park. Let Georgiana be ever so tired she did not show it, but rode in under the portico with perfect equestrian grace.

"I'm afraid you took too much out of her," said Lady Wanless to the Major that evening. Georgiana had gone to bed a little earlier than the others.

This was in some degree hard upon him, as he had not proposed the ride, — and he excused himself. "It was you arranged it all, Lady Wanless."

"Yes, indeed," said she, smiling; "I did arrange the little excursion, but it was not I who kept her talking the whole day." Now this again was felt to be unfair, as nearly every word of conversation between the young people had been given in this little chronicle.

On the following day the young people were again thrust together, and before they parted for the night another little word was spoken by Lady Wanless which indicated very clearly that there was some special bond of friendship between the Major and her second daughter. "You are quite right," she had said in answer to some extracted compliment; "she does ride very well. When I was up in town in May I thought I saw no one with such a seat in the Row. Miss Green, who taught the Duchess of Ditchwater's daughters, declared that she knew nothing like it."

On the third morning he returned to Beetham early, as he intended to go up to town the same afternoon. Then there was prepared for him a little valedictory opportunity in which he could not but press the young lady's fingers for a moment. As he did so no one was looking at him, but then he knew that it was so much the more dangerous because no one was looking. Nothing could be more knowing than the conduct of the young lady, who was not in any way too forward. If she admitted that slight pressure, it was done with a retiring rather than obtrusive favour. It was not by her own doing that she was alone with him for a moment. There was no casting down or casting up of her eyes. And yet it seemed to him, as he left her and went out into the hall, that there had been so much between them that he was almost bound to propose to her. In the hall there was the Baronet to bid him farewell, — an honour which he did to his guests only when he was minded to treat them with great distinction. "Lady Wanless and I are delighted to have had you here," he said.

"Remember me to your father, and tell him that I remember him very well when I was at Christchurch and he was at Wadham." It was something to have had one's hand taken in so paternal a manner by a baronet with such an eyebrow and such a coat.

And yet when he returned to Beetham he was not in a good humour with himself. It seemed to him that he had been almost absorbed among the Wanlesses without any action or will of his own. He tried to comfort himself by declaring that Georgiana was, without doubt, a remarkably handsome young woman, and that she was a perfect horsewoman, — as though all that were a matter to him of any moment! Then he went across to the doctor's house to say a word of farewell to Alice.

"Have you had a pleasant visit?" she asked.

"Oh yes; all very well."

"That second Miss Wanless is quite beautiful, is she not?"

"She is handsome, certainly."

"I call her lovely," said Alice. "You rode with her yesterday over to that old castle."

Who could have told this of him already? "Yes; there was a party of us went over."

"When are you going there again?" Now something had been said of a further visit, and Rossiter had almost promised that he would return. It is impossible not to promise when undefined invitations are given. A man cannot declare that he is engaged for ever and ever. But how was it that Alice knew all that had been said and done? "I cannot say that I have fixed any exact day," he replied almost angrily.

"I've heard all about you, you know. That young Mr. Burmeston was at Mrs. Tweed's and told them what a favourite you are. If it be true I will congratulate you, because I do really think that the young lady is the most beautiful that I ever saw in my life." This she said with a smile and a good-humoured little shake of the head. If it was to be that her heart must be broken, he at least should not know it. And she still hoped, she still thought, that by being very constant at her work she might get over it.

Chapter IV
The Beethamites

It was told all through Beetham, before a week was over, that Major Rossiter was to marry the second Miss Wanless, and Beetham liked the news. Beetham was proud that one of her sons should be introduced into the great neighbouring family, and especially that he should be honoured by the hand of the acknowledged beauty. Beetham, a month ago, had declared that Alice Dugdale, a Beethamite herself from her babyhood, — who had been born and bred at Beetham and had ever lived there, — was to be honoured by the hand of the young hero. But it may be doubted whether Beetham had been altogether satisfied with the arrangement. We are apt to envy the good luck of those who have always been familiar with us. Why should it have been Alice Dugdale any more than one of the Tweed girls, or Miss Simkins, the daughter of the attorney, who would certainly have a snug little fortune of her own, — which unfortunately would not be the case with Alice Dugdale? It had been felt that Alice was hardly good enough for their hero, — Alice who had been seen about with all the Dugdale children, pushing them in per-ambulators almost every day since the eldest was born! We prefer the authority of a stranger to that of one chosen from among our-selves. As the two Miss Tweeds, and Miss Simkins, with Alice and three or four others, could not divide the hero among them, it was better than that the hero should go from among them, and choose a fitting mate in a higher realm. They all felt the greatness of the Wanlesses, and argued with Mrs. Rossiter that the rising star of the village should obtain such assistance in rising as would come to him from an almost noble marriage.

There had been certainly a decided opinion that Alice was to be the happy woman. Mrs. Dugdale, the stepmother, had boasted of the promotion; and old Mr. Rossiter had whispered his secret conviction into the ear of every favoured parishioner. The doctor himself had allowed his patients to ask questions about it. This had become so common that Alice herself had been inwardly indignant, — would have been outwardly indignant but that she could not allow herself to discuss the matter. That having been so, Beetham ought to have been scandalized by the fickleness of her hero. Beetham ought to have felt that her hero was most unheroic. But, at any rate among the ladies, there was no shadow of such a feeling. Of course such a man as the Major was bound to do the best for himself. The giving away of his hand in marriage was a very serious thing, and was not to be obligatory on a young hero because he had been carried away by the fervour of old friendship to kiss a young lady immediately on his return home. The history of the kiss was known all over Beetham, and was declared by competent authorities to have amounted to nothing. It was a last lingering touch of childhood's happy embracings, and if Alice was such a fool as to take it for more, she must pay the penalty of her folly. "It was in her father's presence," said Mrs. Rossiter, defending her son to Mrs. Tweed, and Mrs. Tweed had expressed her opinion that the kiss ought to go for nothing. The Major was to be acquitted, — and the fact of the acquittal made its way even to the doctor's nursery; so that Alice knew that the man might marry that girl at Brook Park with clean hands. That, as she declared to herself, did not increase her sorrow. If the man were minded to marry the girl, he was welcome for her. And she apologized for him to her own heart. What a man generally wants, she said, is a beautiful wife; and of the beauty of Miss Georgiana Wanless there could be no doubt. Only, — only — only, there had been a dozen words which he should have left unspoken!

That which riveted the news on the minds of the Beethamites was the stopping of the Brook Park carriage at the door of the parsonage one day about a week after the Major's visit. It was not altogether an unprecedented occurrence. Had there been no precedent it could hardly have been justified on the present occasion. Perhaps, once in two years Lady Wanless would call at the parsonage, and then there would be a return visit, during which a reference would always be made to Wadham and Christchurch. The visit was now out of its order, only nine months having elapsed, — of which irregularity Beetham took due notice. On this occasion Miss Wanless and the third young lady accompanied their mother, leaving Georgiana at home. What was whispered between the two old ladies Beetham did not quite know, — but made its surmises. It was in this wise.

"We were so glad to have the Major over with us," said her ladyship.

"It was so good of you," said Mrs. Rossiter.

"He is a great favourite with Sir Walter."

127

"That is so good of Sir Walter."

"And we are quite pleased to have him among our young people." That was all, but it was quite sufficient to tell Mrs. Rossiter that John might have Georgiana Wanless for the asking, and that Lady Wanless expected him to ask. Then the parting was much more affectionate than it had ever been before, and there was a squeezing of the hand and a nodding of the head which meant a great deal.

Alice held her tongue, and did her work, and attempted to be cheery through it all. Again and again she asked herself, — what did it matter? Even though she were unhappy, even though she felt a keen, palpable, perpetual aching at her heart, what would it matter so long as she could go about and do her business? Some people in this world had to be unhappy; — perhaps most people. And this was a sorrow which, though it might not wear off, would by wearing become dull enough to be bearable. She distressed herself in that there was any sorrow. Providence had given to her a certain condition of life to which many charms were attached. She thoroughly loved the people about her, — her father, her little brothers and sisters, even her overworn and somewhat idle stepmother. She was a queen in the house, a queen among her busy toils; and she liked being a queen, and liked being busy. No one ever scolded her or crossed her or contradicted her. She had the essential satisfaction of the consciousness of usefulness. Why should not that suffice to her? She despised herself because there was a hole in her heart, — because she felt herself to shrink all over when the name of Georgiana Wanless was mentioned in her hearing. Yet she would mention the name herself, and speak with something akin to admiration of the Wanless family. And she would say how well it was that men should strive to rise in the world, and how that the world progressed through such individual efforts. But she would not mention the name of John Rossiter, nor would she endure that it should be mentioned in her hearing, with any special reference to herself.

Mrs. Dugdale, though she was overworn and idle, — a warped and almost useless piece of furniture, made, as was said before, of bad timber, — yet saw more of this than any one else, and was indignant. To lose Alice, to have no one to let down those tucks and take up those stitches, would be to her the loss of all her comforts. But, though she was feckless, she was true-hearted, and she knew that Alice was being wronged. It was Alice that had a right to the hero and not that stuck-up young woman at Brook Park. It was thus she spoke of the affair to the doctor, and after a while found herself unable to be silent on the subject to Alice herself. "If what they say does take place, I shall think worse of John Rossiter than I ever did of any man I ever knew." This she said in the presence both of her husband and her stepdaughter.

"John Rossiter will not be very much the worse for that," said Alice without relaxing a moment from her work. There was a sound of drolling in her voice, as though she were quizzing her stepmother for her folly.

"It seems to me that men may do anything now," continued Mrs. Dugdale.

"I suppose they are the same now as they always were," said the doctor. "If a man chose to be false he could always be false."

"I call it unmanly," said Mrs. Dugdale. "If I were a man I would beat him."

"What would you beat him for?" said Alice, getting up, and as she did so throwing down on the table before her the little frock which she was making. "If you had the power of beating him, why would you beat him?"

"Because he is ill using you."

"How do you know that? Did I ever tell you so? Have you ever heard a word that he has said to me, either direct from himself, or secondhand, that justifies you in saying that he has ill used me? You ill use when you speak like that."

"Alice, do not be so violent," said the doctor.

"Father, I will speak of this once and once for all; — and then pray, pray, let there be no further mention of it. I have no right to complain of anything in Major Rossiter. He has done me no wrong. Those who love me should not mention his name in reference to me."

"He is a villain," said Mrs. Dugdale.

"He is no villain. He is a gentleman, as far as I know, from the crown of his head to the sole of his foot. Does it ever occur to you how little you make of me when you talk of him in this way? Dismiss it all from your mind, father, and let things be as they were. Do you think that I am pining for any man's love? I say that

Major Rossiter is a true man and a gentleman; — but I would not give my Bobby's little finger for all his whole body." Then there was silence, and afterwards the doctor told his wife that the Major's name had better not be mentioned again among them. Alice on this occasion was, or appeared to be, very angry with Mrs. Dugdale; but on that evening and on the next morning there was an accession of tenderness in her usually sweet manner to her mother-in-law. The expression of her mother's anger against the Major had been wrong; — but the feeling of anger was not the less endearing.

Some time after that, one evening, the parson came upon Alice as she was picking flowers in one of the Beetham lanes. She had all the children with her, and was filling Minnie's apron with roses from the hedge. Old Mr. Rossiter stopped and talked to them, and after a while succeeded in getting Alice to walk on with him. "You haven't heard from John?" he said.

"Oh, no," replied Alice, almost with a start. And then she added quickly, "There is no one at our house likely to hear from him. He does not write to any one there."

"I did not know whether any message might have reached you."

"I think not."

"He is to be here again before long," said the parson.

"Oh, indeed." She had but a moment to think of it all; but, after thinking, she continued, "I suppose he will be going over to Brook Park."

"I fear he will."

"Fear; — why should you fear, Mr. Rossiter? If that is true, it is the place where he ought to be."

"But I doubt its truth, my dear."

"Ah! I know nothing about that. If so, he had better stay up in London, I suppose."

"I don't think John can care much for Miss Wanless."

"Why not? She is the most thoroughly beautiful young woman I ever saw."

"I don't think he does, because I believe his heart is elsewhere. Alice, you have his heart."

"No."

"I think so, Alice."

"No, Mr. Rossiter; I have not. It is not so. I know nothing of Miss Wanless, but I can speak of myself."

"It seems to me that you are speaking of him now."

"Then why does he go there?"

"That is just what I cannot answer. Why does he go there? Why do we do the worse thing so often, when we see the better?"

"But we don't leave undone the thing which we wish to do, Mr. Rossiter."

"That is just what we do do, —under constraint. Alice, I hope, I hope that you may become his wife." She endeavoured to deny that it could ever be so — she strove to declare that she herself was much too heartfree for that; but the words would not come to her lips, and she could only sob while she struggled to retain her tears. "If he does come to you give him a chance again, even though he may have been untrue to you for a moment."

Then she was left alone among the children. She could dry her tears and suppress her sobs, because Minnie was old enough to know the meaning of them if she saw them; but she could not for a while go back into the house. She left them in the passage and then went out again, and walked up and down a little pathway that ran through the shrubs at the bottom of the garden. "I believe that his heart is elsewhere." Could it be that it was so? And if so, of what nature can be a man's love, if when it be given in one direction, he can go in another with his hand! She could understand that there had not been much heart in it; —that he, being a man and not a woman, could have made this turning point of his life an affair of calculation, and had taken himself here or there without much love at all; —that as he would seek a commodious house, so would he also a convenient wife. Resting on that suggestion to herself, she had dared to declare to her father and mother that Major Rossiter was, not a villain, but a perfect gentleman. But all that was not compatible with his father's story. "Alice, you have his heart," the old man had said. How had it come to pass that the old man had known it? And yet the assurance was so sweet, so heavenly, so laden to her eyes with divine music, that at this moment she would not even ask herself to disbelieve it. "If he does come to you, give him a chance again." Why, — yes! Though she never spoke a word of Miss Wanless without praise, though she had tutored herself to swear that Miss Wanless was the very wife for him, yet she knew herself too well not to know that she was better than Miss Wanless. For his sake, she could, with a clear conscience — give him a chance again. The dear old parson! He had seen it all. He had known. He had appreciated. If it should ever come to pass that she was to be his daughter-in-law, he should have his reward. She would not tell herself that she expected him to come again; but, if he did come, she would give the parson's son his chance. Such was her idea at that moment. But she was forced to change it before long.

Chapter V

The Invitation

When Major Rossiter discussed his own conduct with himself, as men are so often compelled to do by their own conscience, in opposition to their own wishes, he was not well pleased with himself. On his return home from India he had found himself possessed of a liberal income, and had begun to enjoy himself without thinking much about marrying. It is not often that a man looks for a wife because he has made up his mind that he wants the article. He roams about unshackled, till something, which at the time seems to be altogether desirable, presents itself to him; and then he meditates marriage. So it had been with our Major. Alice had presented herself to him as something altogether desirable, — a something which, when it was touched and looked at, seemed to be so full of sweetnesses, that to him it was for the moment of all things the most charming. He was not a forward man, — one of those who can see a girl for the first time on a Monday, and propose to her on the Tuesday. When the idea first suggested itself to him of making Alice his wife, he became reticent and undemonstrative. The kiss had in truth meant no more than Mrs. Tweed had said. When he began to feel that he loved her, then he hardly dared to dream of kissing her.

But though he felt that he loved her, — liked perhaps it would be fairer to say in that early stage of his feelings, — better than any other woman, yet when he came to think of marriage, the importance of it all made him hesitate; and he was reminded, by little hints from others, and by words plain enough from one person, that Alice Dugdale was after all a common thing. There is a fitness in such matters, — so said Mrs. Rossiter, — and a propriety in like being married to like. Had it been his lot to be a village doctor, Alice would have suited him well. Destiny, however, had carried him, — the Major, — higher up, and would require him to live in London, among ornate people, with polished habits, and peculiar manners of their own. Would not Alice be out of her element in London? See the things among which she passed her life! Not a morsal of soap or a pound of sugar was used in the house, but what she gave it out. Her hours were passed in washing, teaching, and sewing for the children. In her very walks she was always pushing a perambulator. She was, no doubt, the doctor's daughter; but, in fact, she was the second Mrs. Dugdale's nursemaid. Nothing could be more praiseworthy. But there is a fitness in things: and he, the hero of Beetham, the Assistant Deputy Inspector-General of the British Cavalry, might surely do better than marry a praiseworthy nursery girl. It was thus that Mrs. Rossiter argued with her son, and her arguments were not without avail.

Then Georgiana Wanless had been, as it were, thrown at his head. When one is pelted with sugar-plums one can hardly resent the attack. He was clever enough to feel that he was pelted, but at first he liked the sweetmeats. A girl riding on horseback with her back square to the horse's tail, with her reins well held, and a chimney-pot hat on her head, is an object, unfortunately, more attractive to the eyes of ordinary men, than a young woman pushing a perambulator with two babies. Unfortunately, I say, because in either case the young woman should be judged by her personal merits and not by externals. But the Major declared to himself that the personal merits would be affected by the externals. A girl who had pushed a perambulator for many years, would hardly have a soul above perambulators. There would be wanting the flavour of the aroma of romance, that something of poetic vagueness without which a girl can hardly be altogether charming to the senses of an appreciative lover. Then, a little later on, he asked himself whether Georgiana Wanless was romantic and poetic, — whether there was much of true aroma there.

But yet he thought that fate would require him to marry Georgiana Wanless, whom he certainly did not love, and to leave

Alice to her perambulator, — Alice, whom he certainly did love. And as he thought of this, he was ill at ease with himself. It might be well that he should give up his Assistant Deputy Inspector-Generalship, go back to India, and so get rid of his two troubles together. Fate, as he personified fate to himself in this matter, — took the form of Lady Wanless. It made him sad to think that he was but a weak creature in the hands of an old woman, who wanted to use him for a certain purpose; — but he did not see his way of escaping. When he began to console himself by reflecting that he would have one of the handsomest women in London at his dinner table, he knew that he would be unable to escape.

About the middle of July he received the following letter from Lady Wanless: —

"DEAR MAJOR ROSSITER, — The girls have been at their father for the last ten days to have an archery meeting on the lawn, and have at last prevailed, though Sir Walter has all a father's abhorrence to have the lawn knocked about. Now it is settled. 'I'll see about it,' Sir Walter said at last, and when so much as that had been obtained they all knew that the archery meeting was to be. Sir Walter likes his own way, and is not always to be persuaded. But when he has made the slightest show of concession, he never goes back from it. Then comes the question as to the day, which is now in course of discussion in full committee. In that matter Sir Walter is supposed to be excluded from any voice. 'It cannot matter to him what day of the week or what day of the month,' said Georgiana very irreverently. It will not, however, much matter to him so long as it is all over before St. Partridge comes around.

"The girls one and all declared that you must be here, — as one of the guests in the house. Our rooms will be mostly full of young ladies, but there will be one at any rate for you. Now, what day will suit you, — or rather, what day will suit the Cavalry generally? Everything must of course depend on the Cavalry. The girls say that the Cavalry is sure to go out of town after the tenth of August. But they would put it off for a week longer rather than not have the Inspector-General. Would Wednesday 14th suit the Cavalry? They are all reading every word of my letter as it is written, and bid me say that if Thursday or Friday in that week or

Wednesday or Thursday in the next, will do better, the accom-modation of the Cavalry shall be consulted. It cannot be a Mon-day or Saturday because there would be some Sunday encroach-ment. On Tuesday we cannot get the band from Slowbridge.

"Now you know our great purpose and our little difficulties. One thing you cannot know, — how determined we are to accommodate ourselves to the Cavalry. *The meeting is not to take place without the Inspector-General.* So let us have an early answer from that august functionary. The girls think that the Inspector had better come down before the day, so as to make himself useful in preparing.

"Pray believe me, with Sir Walter's kind regards, yours most sincerely,

"MARGARET WANLESS."

The Major felt that the letter was very flattering, but that it was false and written for a certain purpose. He could read between the lines at every sentence of it. The festival was to be got up, not at the instance of the girls, but of Lady Wanless her-self, as a final trap for the catching of himself, — and perhaps for Mr. Burmeston. Those irreverent words had never come from Georgiana, who was too placid to have said them. He did not believe a word of the girls looking over the writing of the letter. In all such matters Lady Wanless had more life, more energy than her daughters. All that little fun about the Cavalry came from Lady Wanless herself. The girls were too like their father for such ebullitions. The little sparks of joke with which the names of the girls were connected, — with which in his hearing the name of Georgiana had been specially connected, — had, he was aware, their origin always with Lady Wanless. Georgiana had said this funny thing and that, — but Georgiana never spoke after that fashion in his hearing. The traps were plain to his eyes, and yet he knew that he would sooner or later be caught in the traps.

He took a day to think of it before he answered the letter, and meditated a military tour to Berlin just about the time. If so, he must be absent during the whole of August, so as to make his presence at the toxophilite meeting an impossibility. And yet at last he wrote and said that he would be there. There would be something mean in flight. After all, he need not ask the girl to be his wife unless he chose to do so. He wrote a very pretty note to Lady Wanless saying that he would be at Brook Park on the 14th, as she had suggested.

Then he made a great resolution and swore an oath to himself, —— that he would not be caught on that occasion, and that after this meeting he would go no more either to Brook Park or to Beetham for a while. He would not marry the girl to whom he was quite indifferent, nor her who from her position was hardly qualified to be his wife. Then he went about his duties with a quieted conscience, and wedded himself for once and for always to the Cavalry.

Some tidings of the doings proposed by the Wanlesses had reached the parson's ears when he told Alice in the lane that his son was soon coming down to Beetham again, and that he was again going to Brook Park. Before July was over the tidings of the coming festivity had been spread over all that side of the county. Such a thing had not been done for many years, — not since Lady Wanless had been herself a young wife, with two sisters for whom husbands had to be, and were, provided. There were those who could still remember how well Lady Wanless had behaved on that occasion. Since those days hospitality on a large scale had not been rife at Brook Park — and the reason why it was so was well known. Sir Walter was determined not to embarrass himself further and would do nothing that was expensive. It could not be but that there was great cause for such a deviation as this. Then the ladies of the neighbourhood put their heads together — and some of the gentlemen — and declared that a double stroke of business was to be done in regard to Major Rossiter and Mr. Burmeston. How great a relief that would be to the mother's anxiety, if the three eldest girls could be married and got rid of all on the same day!

Beetham, which was ten miles from Brook Park, had a station of its own, whereas Slowbridge, with its own station, was only six miles from the house. The Major would fain have reached his destination by Slowbridge, so as to have avoided the chance of seeing Alice, were it not that his father and mother would have felt themselves aggrieved by such desertion. On this occasion his mother begged him to give them one night. She had much that she wished to say to him, and then, of course, he could have the parsonage horse and the parsonage phaeton to take him over to

Brook Park free of expense. He did go down to Beetham, did spend an evening there, and did go on to the park without having spoken to Alice Dugdale.

"Everybody says you are to marry Georgiana Wanless," said Mrs. Rossiter.

"If there were no other reason why I should not, the saying of everybody would be sufficient against it."

"That is unreasonable, John. The thing should be looked at itself, whether it is good or bad. It may be the case that Lady Wanless talks more than she ought to do. It may be the case that, as people say, she is looking for husbands for her daughters. I don't know but that I should do the same if I had five of them on my hands, and very little means for them. And if I did, how could I get a better husband for one of them than—such a one as Major John Rossiter?" Then she kissed his forehead.

"I hate the kind of thing altogether," said he. He pretended to be stern, but yet he showed that he was flattered by his mother's softness.

"It may well be, John, that such a match shall be desirable to them and to you too. If so, why should there not be a fair bargain between the two of you? You know that you admire the girl." He would not deny this, lest it should come to pass hereafter that she should become his wife. "And everybody knows that, as far as birth goes, there is not a family in the county stands higher. I am so proud of my boy that I wish to see him mated with the best."

He reached the parsonage that evening only just before dinner, and on the next morning he did not go out of the house till the phaeton came round to take him to Brook Park. "Are you not going up to see the old doctor?" said the parson after breakfast.

"No; — I think not. He is never at home, and the ladies are always surrounded by the children."

"She will take it amiss," said the father almost in a whisper.

"I will go as I come back," said he, blushing as he spoke at his own falsehood. For, if he held to his present purpose, he would return by Slowbridge. If fate intended that there should be nothing further between him and Alice, it would certainly be much better that they should not be brought together any more. He knew too what his father meant, and was more unwilling to take counsel from his father even than his mother. Yet he blushed because he knew that he was false.

"Do not seem to slight her," said the old man: "she is too good for that."

Then he drove himself over to Brook Park, and, as he made his way by one of the innumerable turnings out of Beetham, he saw at one of the corners Alice, still with the children and still with the perambulator. He merely lifted his hat as he passed, but did not stop to speak to her.

Chapter VI
The Archery Meeting

The Assistant Deputy Inspector-General, when he reached Brook Park, found that things were to be done on a great scale. The two drawing-rooms were filled with flowers, and the big dining-room was laid out for to-morrow's lunch, in preparation for those who would prefer the dining-room to the tent. Rossiter was first taken into the Baronet's own room, where Sir Walter kept his guns and administered justice. "This is a terrible bore, Rossiter," he said.

"It must disturb you a great deal, Sir Walter."

"Oh, dear — dreadfully! What would my old friend, your father, think of having to do this kind of thing? Though, when I was at Christchurch and he at Wadham, he used to be gay enough. I'm not quite sure that I don't owe it to you."

"To me, Sir Walter!"

"I rather think you put the girls up to it." Then he laughed as though it were a very good joke and told the Major where he would find the ladies. He had been expressly desired by his wife to be genial to the Major, and had been as genial as he knew how.

Rossiter, as he went out on to the lawn, saw Mr. Burmeston, the brewer, walking with Edith, the third daughter. He could not but admire the strategy of Lady Wanless when he acknowledged to himself how well she managed all these things. The brewer would not have been allowed to walk with Gertrude, the fourth daughter, nor even with Maria, the naughty girl who liked the curate, — because it was Edith's turn. Edith was certainly the plainest of the family, and yet she had her turn. Lady Wanless was by far too good a mother to have favourites among her own children.

He then found the mother, the eldest daughter, and Gertrude overseeing the decoration of a tent, which had been put up as an addition to the dining-room. He expected to find Mr. Cobble, to whom he had taken a liking, a nice, pleasant, frank young country gentleman; but Mr. Cobble was not wanted for any express purpose, and might have been in the way. Mr. Cobble was landed and safe. Before long he found himself walking round the garden with Lady Wanless herself. The other girls, though they were to be his sisters, were never thrown into any special intimacy with him. "She will be down before long now that she knows you are here," said Lady Wanless. "She was fatigued a little, and I thought it better that she should lie down. She is so impressionable, you know." "She" was Georgiana. He knew that very well. But why should Georgiana be called "She" to him, by her mother? Had "She" been in truth engaged to him it would have been intelligible enough. But there had been nothing of the kind. As "She" was thus dinned into his ears, he thought of the very small amount of conversation which had ever taken place between himself and the young lady.

Then there occurred to him an idea that he would tell Lady Wanless in so many words that there was a mistake. The doing so would require some courage, but he thought he could summon up manliness for the purpose, — if only he could find the words and occasion. But though "She" were so frequently spoken of, still nothing was said which seemed to give him the opportunity required. It is hard for a man to have to reject a girl when she has been offered, — but harder to do so before the offer has in truth been made. "I am afraid there is a little mistake in your ideas as to me and your daughter." It was thus that he would have had to speak, and then to have endured the outpouring of her wrath, when she would have declared that the ideas were only in his own arrogant brain. He let it pass by and said nothing, and before long he was playing lawn-tennis with Georgiana, who did not seem to have been in the least fatigued.

"My dear, I will not have it," said Lady Wanless about an hour afterwards, coming up and disturbing the game. "Major Rossiter, you ought to know better." Whereupon she playfully took the racket out of the Major's hand. "Mamma is such an old bother," said Georgiana as she walked back to the house with the Major. The Major had on a previous occasion perceived that the second Miss Wanless rode very well, and now he saw that she was very stout at lawn-tennis; but he observed none of that peculiarity of mental or physical development which her mother had described as "impressionable." Nevertheless she was a handsome girl, and if to play lawn-tennis would help to make a husband happy, so much at any rate she could do.

This took place on the day before the meeting, — before the great day. When the morning came the girls did not come down early to breakfast, and our hero found himself left alone with Mr. Burmeston. "You have known the family a long time," said the Major as they were sauntering about the gravel paths together, smoking their cigars.

"No, indeed," said Mr. Burmeston. "They only took me up about three months ago, — just before we went over to Owless. Very nice people; — don't you think so?"

"Very nice," said the Major.

"They stand so high in the county, and all that sort of thing. Birth does go a long way, you know."

"So it ought," said the Major.

"And though the Baronet does not do much in the world, he has been in the House, you know. All those things help." Then the Major understood that Mr. Burmeston had looked the thing in the face, and had determined that for certain considerations it was worth his while to lead one of the Miss Wanlesses to the hymeneal altar. In this Mr. Burmeston was behaving with more manliness than he, — who had almost made up his mind half-a-dozen times, and had never been satisfied with the way in which he had done it.

About twelve the visitors had begun to come, and Sophia with Mr. Cobble were very soon trying their arrows together. Sophia had not been allowed to have her lover on the previous day, but was now making up for it. That was all very well, but Lady Wanless was a little angry with her eldest daughter. Her success was insured for her; her business was done. Seeing how many sacrifices had been made to her during the last twelve-months, surely now she might have been active in aiding her sisters, instead of merely amusing herself.

The Major was not good at archery. He was no doubt an excellent Deputy Inspector-General of Cavalry; but if bows and arrows had still been the weapons used in any part of the British army, he would not, without further instruction, have been qualified to inspect that branch. Georgiana Wanless, on the other hand, was a proficient. Such shooting as she made was marvellous to look at. And she was a very image of Diana, as with her beautiful figure and regular features, dressed up to the work, she stood with her bow raised in her hand and let twang the arrows. The circle immediately outside the bull's-eye was the farthest from the mark she ever touched. But good as she was and bad as was the Major, nevertheless they were appointed always to shoot together. After a world of failures the Major would shoot no more, — but not the less did he go backwards and forwards with Georgiana when she changed from one end to the other, and found himself absolutely appointed to that task. It grew upon him during the whole day that this second Miss Wanless was supposed to be his own, — almost as much as was the elder the property of Mr. Cobble. Other young men would do no more than speak to her. And when once, after the great lunch in the tent, Lady Wanless came and put her hand affectionately upon his arm, and whispered some word into his ear, in the presence of all the assembled guests, he knew that the entire county had recognised him as caught.

There was old Lady Deepbell there. How it was that towards the end of the day's delights Lady Deepbell got hold of him he never knew. Lady Deepbell had not been introduced to him, and yet she got hold of him. "Major Rossiter, you are the luckiest man of the day," she said to him.

"Pretty well," said he, affecting to laugh; "but why so?"

"She is the handsomest young woman out. There hasn't been one in London this season with such a figure."

"You are altogether wrong in your surmise, Lady Deepbell."

"No, no; I am right enough. I see it all. Of course the poor girl won't have any money; but then how nice it is when a gentleman like you is able to dispense with that. Perhaps they do take after their father a little, and he certainly is not bright; but upon my word, I think a girl is all the better for that. What's the good of having such a lot of talkee-talkee."

"Lady Deepbell, you are alluding to a young lady without the slightest warrant," said the Major.

"Warrant enough — warrant enough," said the old woman, toddling off.

Then young Cobble came to him, and talked to him as though he were a brother of the house. Young Cobble was an honest fellow, and quite in earnest in his matrimonial intentions. "We shall be delighted if you'll come to us on the first," said Cobble. The first of course meant the first of September. "We ain't badly off just for a week's shooting. Sophia is to be there, and we'll get Georgiana too."

The Major was fond of shooting and would have been glad to accept the offer; but it was out of the question that he should allow himself to be taken in at Cobble Hall under a false pretext. And was it not incumbent on him to make this young man understand that he had no pretensions whatever to the hand of the second Miss Wanless? "You are very good," said he.

"We should be delighted," said young Cobble.

"But I fear there is a mistake. I can't say anything more about it now because it doesn't do to name people; — but there is a mistake. Only for that I should have been delighted. Good-bye." Then he took his departure, leaving young Cobble in a state of mystified suspense

The day lingered on to a great length. The archery and the lawn-tennis were continued till late after the so-called lunch, and towards the evening a few couples stood up to dance. It was evident to the Major that Burmeston and Edith were thoroughly comfortable together. Gertrude amused herself well, and even Maria was contented, though the curate as a matter of course was not there. Sophia with her legitimate lover was as happy as the day and evening were long. But there came a frown upon Georgiana's brow, and when at last the Major, as though forced by destiny, asked her to dance, she refused. It had seemed to her a matter of course that he should ask her, and at last he did; — but she refused. The evening with him was very long, and just as he thought that he would escape to bed, and was meditating how early he would be off on the morrow, Lady Wanless took possession of him and carried him off alone into one of the desolate chambers. "Is she very tired?" asked the anxious mother.

"Is who tired?" The Major at that moment would have given twenty guineas to have been in bed in his lodgings near St. James's Street.

"My poor girl," said Lady Wanless, assuming a look of great solicitude.

It was vain for him to pretend not to know who was the "She" intended. "Oh, ah, yes; Miss Wanless."

"Georgiana."

"I think she is tired. She was shooting a great deal. Then there was a quadrille; — but she didn't dance. There has been a great deal to tire young ladies."

"You shouldn't have let her do so much."

How was he to get out of it? What was he to say? If a man is clearly asked his intentions he can say that he has not got any. That used to be the old fashion when a gentleman was supposed to be dilatory in declaring his purpose. But it gave the oscillating lover so easy an escape! It was like the sudden jerk of the hand of the unpractised fisherman; if the fish does not succumb at once it goes away down the stream and is no more heard of. But from this new process there is no mode of immediate escape. "I couldn't prevent her because she is nothing to me." That would have been the straightforward answer; — but one most difficult to make. "I hope she will be none the worse to-morrow morning," said the Major.

"I hope not, indeed. Oh, Major Rossiter!" The mother's position was also difficult, as it is of no use to play with a fish too long without making an attempt to stick the hook into his gills.

"Lady Wanless!"

"What am I to say to you? I am sure you know my feelings. You know how sincere is Sir Walter's regard."

"I am very much flattered, Lady Wanless."

"That means nothing." This was true, but the Major did not intend to mean anything. "Of all my flock she is the fairest." That was true also. The Major would have been delighted to accede to the assertion of the young lady's beauty, if this might have been the end of it. "I had thought —"

"Had thought what, Lady Wanless?"

"If I am deceived in you, Major Rossiter, I never will believe in a man again. I have looked upon you as the very soul of honour."

"I trust that I have done nothing to lessen your good opinion."

"I do not know. I cannot say. Why do you answer me in this way about my child?" Then she held her hands together and looked up into his face imploringly. He owned to himself that she was a good actress. He was almost inclined to submit and to declare his passion for Georgiana. For the present that way out of the difficulty would have been so easy!

"You shall hear from me to-morrow morning," he said, almost solemnly.

"Shall I?" she asked, grasping his hand. "Oh, my friend, let it be as I desire. My whole life shall be devoted to making you happy, — you and her." Then he was allowed to escape.

Lady Wanless, before she went to bed, was closeted for a while with the eldest daughter. As Sophia was now almost as good as a married woman, she was received into closer counsel than the others. "Burmeston will do," she said; "but, as for that Cavalry man, he means it no more than the chair." The pity was that Burmeston might have been secured without the archery meeting, and that all the money, spent on behalf of the Major, should have been thrown away.

Chapter VII
After the Party

When the Major left Brook Park, on the morning after the archery amusements, he was quite sure of this, — that under no circumstances whatever would he be induced to ask Miss Georgiana Wanless to be his wife. He had promised to write a letter, — and he would write one instantly. He did not conceive it possible but that Lady Wanless should understand what would be the purport of that letter, although as she left him on the previous night she had pretended to hope otherwise. That her hopes had not been very high we know from the words which she spoke to Sophia in the privacy of her own room.

He had intended to return by Slowbridge, but when the morning came he changed his mind and went to Beetham. His reason for doing so was hardly plain, even to himself. He tried to make

himself believe that the letter had better be written from Beetham, — hot, as it were, from the immediate neighbourhood,
— than from London; but, as he thought of this, his mind was
crowded with ideas of Alice Dugdale. He would not propose to
Alice. At this moment, indeed, he was averse to matrimony,
having been altogether disgusted with female society at Brook
Park; but he had to acknowledge a sterling worth about Alice,
and the existence of a genuine friendship between her and himself, which made it painful to him to leave the country without
other recognition than that raising of his hat when he saw her at
the corner of the lane. He had behaved badly in this Brook Park
affair, — in having been tempted thither in opposition to those
better instincts which had made Alice so pleasant a companion
to him, — and was ashamed of himself. He did not think that he
could go back to his former ideas. He was aware that Alice must
think ill of him, — would not believe him to be now such as she
had once thought him. England and London were distasteful to
him. He would go abroad on that foreign service which he had
proposed to himself. There was an opening for him to do so if he
liked, and he could return to his present duties after a year or two.
But he would see Alice again before he went. Thinking of all
this, he drove himself back to Beetham.

On that morning tidings of the successful festivities at Brook
Park reached the doctor's house. Tidings of the coming festivities, then of the preparations, and at last of the festal day itself,
had reached Alice, so that it seemed to her that all Beetham
talked of nothing else. Old Lady Deepbell had caught a cold,
walking about on the lawn with hardly anything on her old
shoulders, — stupid old woman, — and had sent for the doctor
the first thing in the morning. "Positively settled," she had said
to the doctor, "absolutely arranged, Dr. Dugdale. Lady Wanless
told me so herself, and I congratulated the gentleman." She did
not go on to say that the gentleman had denied the accusation,
— but then she had not believed the denial. The doctor, coming
home, had thought it his duty to tell Alice, and Alice had
received the news with a smile. "I knew it would be so, father."

"And you?" This he said, holding her hand and looking tenderly into her eyes.

145

"Me! It will not hurt me. Not that I mean to tell a lie to you, father," she added after a moment. "A man isn't hurt because he doesn't get a prize in the lottery. Had it ever come about, I dare say I should have liked him well enough."

"No more than that?"

"And why should it have come about?" she went on saying, avoiding her father's last question, determined not to lie if she could help it, but determined, also, to show no wound. "I think my position in life very happy, but it isn't one from which he would choose a wife."

"Why not, my dear?"

"A thousand reasons; I am always busy, and he would naturally like a young lady who had nothing to do." She understood the effect of the perambulator and the constant needle and thread. "Besides, though he might be all very well, he could never, I think, be as dear to me as the bairns. I should feel that I lost more than I got by going." This she knew to be a lie, but it was so important that her father should believe her to be contented with her home duties! And she was contented, though very unhappy. When her father kissed her, she smiled into his face, — oh, so sweetly, so pleasantly! And the old man thought that she could not have loved very deeply. Then she took herself to her own room, and sat awhile alone with a countenance much changed. The lines of sorrow about her brow were terrible. There was not a tear; but her mouth was close pressed, and her hand was working constantly by her side. She gazed at nothing, but sat with her eyes wide open, staring straight before her. Then she jumped up quickly, and striking her hand upon her heart, she spoke aloud to herself. "I will cure it," she said. "He is not worthy, and it should therefore be easier. Though he were worthy, I would cure it. Yes, Bobby, I am coming." Then she went about her work.

That might have been about noon. It was after their early dinner with the children that the Major came up to the doctor's house. He had reached the parsonage in time for a late breakfast, and had then written his letter. After that he had sat idling about on the lawn, — not on the best terms with his mother, to whom he had sworn that under no circumstances would he make Georgiana Wanless his wife. "I would sooner marry a girl from a troop of tight-rope dancers," he had said in his anger. Mrs. Rossiter knew that he intended to go up to the doctor's house, and therefore the immediate feeling between the mother and son was not pleasant. My readers, if they please, shall see the letter to Lady Wanless.

"MY DEAR LADY WANLESS, — It is a great grief to me to say that there has been, I fear, a misconception between you and me on a certain matter. This is the more a trouble to me because you and Sir Walter have been so very kind to me. From a word or two which fell from you last night I was led to fear that you suspected feelings on my part which I have never entertained, and aspirations to which I have never pretended. No man can be more alive than I am to the honour which has been suggested, but I feel bound to say that I am not in a condition to accept it.

"Pray believe me to be,
"Dear Lady Wanless,
"Yours always very faithfully,
"JOHN
ROSSITER."

The letter, when it was written, was, to himself, very unsatisfactory. It was full of ambiguous words and namby-pamby phraseology which disgusted him. But he did not know how to alter it for the better. It is hard to say an uncivil thing civilly without ambiguous namby-pamby language. He could not bring it out in straightforward stout English: "You want me to marry your daughter, but I won't do anything of the kind." So the letter was sent. The conduct of which he was really ashamed did not regard Miss Wanless, but Alice Dugdale.

At last, very slowly, he took himself up to the doctor's house. He hardly knew what it was that he meant to say when he found himself there, but he was sure that he did not mean to make an offer. Even had other things suited, there would have been something distasteful to him in doing this so quickly after the affair of Miss Wanless. He was in no frame now for making love; but yet it would be ungracious in him, he thought, to leave Beetham without seeing his old friend. He found the two ladies together, with the children still around them, sitting near a window which opened down to the ground. Mrs. Dugdale had a novel in hand, and, as usual, was leaning back in a rocking-chair. Alice had also a book open on the table before him, but she was bending over a sewing-machine. They had latterly divided the cares of the family between them. Mrs. Dugdale had brought the children into the world, and Alice had washed, clothed, and fed them when they were there. When the Major entered the room, Alice's mind was, of course, full of tidings she had heard from her father, — which tidings, however, had not been communicated to Mrs. Dugdale.

Alice at first was very silent while Mrs. Dugdale asked as to the festivities. "It has been the grandest thing anywhere about here for a long time."

"And, like other grand things, a great bore," said the Major.

"I don't suppose you found it so, Major Rossiter," said the lady.

Then the conversation ran away into a description of what had been done during the day. He wished to make it understood that there was no permanent link binding him to Brook Park, but he hardly knew how to say it without going beyond the lines of ordinary conversation. At last there seemed to be an opening, — not exactly what he wished, but still an opening. "Brook Park is not exactly the place," said he, "at which I should ever feel myself quite at home." This was in answer to some chance word which had fallen from Mrs. Dugdale.

"I am sorry for that," said Alice. She would have given a guinea to bring the word back after it had been spoken; but spoken words cannot be brought back.

"Why sorry?" he asked, smiling.

"Because — Oh, because it is so likely that you may be there often."

"I don't know that at all."

"You have become so intimate with them!" said Alice. "We are told in Beetham that the party was got up all for your honour."

So Sir Walter had told him, and so Maria, the naughty girl, had said also — "Only for your *beaux yeux*, Major Rossiter, we shouldn't have had any party at all." This had been said by Maria when she was laughing at him about her sister Georgiana. "I don't know how that may be," said the Major; "but all the same I shall never be at home at Brook Park."

"Don't you like the young ladies?" asked Mrs. Dugdale.

148

"Oh yes, very much; and Lady Wanless; and Sir Walter. I like them all, in a way. But yet I shall never find myself at home at Brook Park."

Alice was very angry with him. He ought not to have gone there at all. He must have known that he could not be there without paining her. She thoroughly believed that he was engaged to marry the girl of whose family he spoke in this way. He had thought, — so it seemed to her, — that he might lessen the blow to her by making little of the great folk among whom his future lot was to be cast. But what could be more mean? He was not the John Rossiter to whom she had given her hand. There had been no such man. She had been mistaken. "I am afraid you are one of those," she said, "who, wherever they find themselves, at once begin to wish for something better."

"That is meant to be severe."

"My severity won't go for much."

"I am sure you have deserved it," said Mrs. Dugdale, most indiscreetly.

"Is this intended for an attack?" he asked, looking from one to the other.

"Not at all," said Alice, affecting to laugh. "I should have said nothing if I thought mamma would take it up so seriously. I was only sorry to hear you speak of your new friends so slightingly."

After that the conversation between them was very difficult, and he soon got up to go away. As he did so, he asked Alice to say a word to him out in the garden, having already explained to them both that it might be some time before he would be again down at Beetham. Alice rose slowly from her sewing-machine, and, putting on her hat, led the way with a composed and almost dignified step out through the window. Her heart was beating within her, but she looked as though she were mistress of every pulse. "Why did you say that to me?" he asked.

"Say what?"

"That I always wished for better things and better people than I found."

"Because I think you ambitious, — and discontented. There is nothing disgraceful in that; — though it is not the character which I myself like the best."

"You meant to allude specially to the Wanlesses?"

149

"Because you have just come from there, and were speaking of them."

"And to one of that family specially?"

"No, Major Rossiter. There you are wrong. I alluded to no one in particular. They are nothing to me. I do not know them; but I hear that they are kind and friendly people, with good manners and very handsome. Of course I know, as we all know everything of each other in this little place, that you have of late become very intimate with them. Then when I hear you aver that you are already discontented with them, I cannot help thinking that you are hard to please. I am sorry that mamma spoke of deserving. I did not intend to say anything so seriously."

"Alice!"

"Well, Major Rossiter."

"I wish I could make you understand me."

"I do not know that that would do any good. We have been old friends, and of course I hope that you may be happy. I must say good-bye now. I cannot go beyond the gate, because I am wanted to take the children out."

"Good-bye then. I hope you will not think ill of me."

"Why should I think ill of you? I think very well, — only that you are ambitious." As she said this, she laughed again, and then she left him.

He had been most anxious to tell her that he was not going to marry that girl, but he had not known how to do it. He could not bring himself to declare that he would not marry a girl, when by such declaration he would have been forced to assume that he might marry her if he pleased. So he left Alice at the gate, and she went back to the house still convinced that he was betrothed to Georgiana Wanless.

Chapter VIII
Sir Walter Up in London

The Major, when he left the doctor's house, was more thoroughly in love with Alice than ever. There had been something in her gait as she led the way out through the window, and again as with determined purpose she bade him speedily farewell at the gate, which forced him to acknowledge that the dragging of perambulators and the making of petticoats had not detracted from her feminine charm or from her feminine dignity. She had been dressed in her ordinary morning frock, — the very frock on which he had more than once seen the marks of Bobby's dirty heels; but she had pleased his eye better than Georgiana, clad in all the glory of her toxophilite array. The toxophilite feather had been very knowing, the tight leathern belt round her waist had been bright in colour and pretty in design. The looped-up dress, fit for the work in hand, had been gratifying. But with it all there had been the show of a thing got up for ornament and not for use. She was like a box of painted sugar-plums, very pretty to the eye, but of which no one wants to extract any for the purpose of eating them. Alice was like a housewife's store, kept beautifully in order, but intended chiefly for comfortable use. As he went up to London he began to doubt whether he would go abroad. Were he to let a few months pass by would not Alice be still there, and willing perhaps to receive him with more kindness when she should have heard that his follies at Brook Park were at an end?

Three days after his return, when he was sitting in his offices thinking perhaps more of Alice Dugdale than of the whole British cavalry, a soldier who was in waiting brought a card to him. Sir Walter Wanless had come to call upon him. If he were disengaged Sir Walter would be glad to see him. He was not at all anxious to see Sir Walter; but there was no alternative, and Sir Walter was shown into the room.

In explaining the purport of Sir Walter's visit, we must go back for a few minutes to Brook Park. When Sir Walter came down to breakfast on the morning after the festivities he was surprised to hear that Major Rossiter had taken his departure. There sat young Burmeston. He at any rate was safe. And there sat young Cobble, who by Sophia's aid had managed to get himself accommodated for the night, and all the other young people, including the five Wanless girls. The father, though not observant, could see that Georgiana was very glum. Lady Wanless herself affected a good-humour which hardly deceived him, and certainly did not deceive any one else. "He was obliged to be off this morning, because of his duties," said Lady Wanless. "He told me that it was to be so, but I did not like to say anything about it yesterday." Georgiana turned up her nose, as much as to say that the going and coming of Major Rossiter was not a matter of much importance to any one there, and, least of all, to her. Except the father, there was not a person in the room who was not aware that Lady Wanless had missed her fish.

But she herself was not quite sure even yet that she had failed altogether. She was a woman who hated failure, and who seldom failed. She was brave of heart too, and able to fight a losing battle to the last. She was very angry with the Major, who she well knew was endeavoring to escape from her toils. But he would not on that account be the less useful as a son-in-law; — nor on that account was she the more willing to allow him to escape. With five daughters without fortunes it behoved her as a mother to be persistent. She would not give it up, but must turn the matter well in her mind before she took further steps. She feared that a simple invitation could hardly bring the Major back to Brook Park. Then there came the letter from the Major, — which did not make the matter easier.

"My dear," she said to her husband, sitting down opposite to him in his room, "that Major Rossiter isn't behaving quite as he ought to do."

"I'm not a bit surprised," said the Baronet angrily. "I never knew anybody from Wadham behave well."

"He's quite a gentleman, if you mean that," said Lady Wanless; "and he's sure to do very well in the world; and poor Georgiana is really fond of him, — which doesn't surprise me in the least."

"Has he said anything to make her fond of him? I suppose she has gone and made a fool of herself, — like Maria."

"Not at all. He has said a great deal to her; — much more than he ought to have done, if he meant nothing. But the truth is, young men nowadays never know their own minds unless there is somebody to keep them up to the mark. You must go and see him."

"I!" said the afflicted father.

"Of course, my dear. A few judicious words in such a case may do so much. I would not ask Walter to go," — Walter was the eldest son, who was with his regiment, — "because it might lead to quarrelling. I would not have anything of that kind, if only for the dear girl's sake. But what you would say would be known to nobody; and it might have the desired effect. Of course, you will be very quiet, — and very serious also. Nobody could do it better

152

than you will. There can be no doubt that he has trifled with the dear girl's affections. Why else has he been with her whenever he has been here? It was so visible on Wednesday that every body was congratulating me. Old Lady Deepbell asked whether the day was fixed. I treated him quite as though it were settled. Young men do so often get these sudden starts of doubt. Then, sometimes, just a word afterwards will put it all right." In this way the Baronet was made to understand that he must go and see the Major.

He postponed the unwelcome task till his wife at last drove him out of the house. "My dear," she said, "will you let your child die broken-hearted for want of a word?" When it was put to him in that way he found himself obliged to go, though, to tell the truth, he could not find any sign of heart-breaking sorrow about his child. He was not allowed to speak to Georgiana herself, his wife telling him that the poor child would be unable to bear it.

Sir Walter, when he was shown into the Major's room, felt himself to be very ill able to conduct the business in hand, and to the Major himself the moment was one of considerable trouble. He had thought it possible that he might receive an answer to his letter, a reply that might be indignant, or piteous, or minatory, or simply abusive, as the case might be, —one which might too probably require a further correspondence; but it had never occurred to him that Sir Walter would come in person. But here he was, —in the room—by no means with that pretended air of geniality with which he had last received the Major down at Brook Park. The greeting, however, between the gentlemen was courteous if not cordial, and then Sir Walter began his task. "We were quite surprised you should have left us so early that morning."

"I had told Lady Wanless."

"Yes; I know. Nevertheless we were surprised. Now, Major Rossiter, what do you mean to do about, — about, — about this young lady?" The Major was silent. He could not pretend to be ignorant what young lady was intended after the letter which he had himself written to Lady Wanless. "This, you know, is a very painful kind of thing, Major Rossiter."

"Very painful indeed, Sir Walter."

"When I remembered that I had been at Christchurch and your excellent father at Wadham both at the same time, I thought that I might trust you in my house without the slightest fear."

"I make bold to say, Sir Walter, that you were quite justified in that expectation, whether it was founded on your having been at Christchurch or on my position and character in the world." He knew that the scene would be easier to him if he could work himself up to a little indignation on his part.

"And yet I am told, — I am told—"

"What are you told, Sir Walter?"

"There can, I think, be no doubt that you have — in point of fact, paid attention to my daughter." Sir Walter was a gentleman, and felt that the task imposed upon him grated against his better feelings.

"If you mean that I have taken steps to win her affections, you have been wrongly informed."

"That's what I do mean. Were you not received just now at Brook Park as, — as paying attention to her?"

"I hope not."

"You hope not, Major Rossiter?"

"I hope no such mistake was made. It certainly was not made by me. I felt myself much flattered by being received at your house. I wrote the other day a line or two to Lady Wanless and thought I had explained all this."

Sir Walter opened his eyes when he heard, for the first time, of the letter, but was sharp enough not to exhibit his ignorance at the moment. "I don't know about explaining," he said. "There are some things which can't be so very well explained. My wife assures me that that poor girl has been deceived, — cruelly deceived. Now I put it to you, Major Rossiter, what ought you as a gentleman to do?"

"Really, Sir Walter, you are not entitled to ask me any such question."

"Not on behalf of my own child?"

"I cannot go into the matter from that view of the case. I can only declare that I have said nothing and done nothing for which I can blame myself. I cannot understand how there should have been such a mistake; but it did not, at any rate, arise with me."

Then the Baronet sat dumb. He had been specially instructed not to give up the interview till he had obtained some sign of weakness from the enemy. If he could only induce the enemy to promise another visit to Brook Park that would be much. If he could obtain some expression of liking or admiration for the young lady that would be something. If he could induce the Major to allude to delay as being necessary, further operations would be founded on that base. But nothing had been obtained. "It's the most, — the most — the most astonishing thing I ever heard," he said at last.

"I do not know that I can say anything further."

"I'll tell you what," said the Baronet: "come down and see Lady Wanless. The women understand these things much better than we do. Come down and talk it over with Lady Wanless. She won't propose anything that isn't proper." In answer to this the Major shook his head. "You won't?"

"It would do no good, Sir Walter. It would be painful to me, and must, I should say, be distressing to the young lady."

"Then you won't do anything!"

"There is nothing to be done."

"Upon my word, I never heard such a thing in all my life, Major Rossiter. You come down to my house; and then, — then, — then you won't, — you won't come again! To be sure he was at Wadham, but I did think your father's son would have behaved better." Then he picked up his hat from the floor and shuffled out of the room without another word.

Tidings that Sir Walter had been up to London and had called upon Major Rossiter made their way into Beetham and reached the ears of the Dugdales, — but not correct tidings as to the nature of the conversation. "I wonder when it will be," said Mrs. Dugdale to Alice. "As he has been up to town I suppose it'll be settled soon."

"The sooner the better for all parties," said Alice cheerily. "When a man and a woman have agreed together, I can't see why they shouldn't at once walk off to the church arm in arm."

"The lawyers have so much to do."

"Bother the lawyers! The parson ought to do all that is necessary, and the sooner the better. Then there would not be such peraphernalia of presents and gowns and eatings and drinkings, all of which is got up for the good of the tradesmen. If I were to be married, I should like to slip out round the corner, just as though I were going to get an extra loaf of bread from Mrs. Bakewell."

"That wouldn't do for my lady at Brook Park."

"I suppose not."

"Nor yet for the Major."

Then Alice shook her head and sighed, and took herself out to walk alone for a few minutes among the lanes. How could it be that he should be so different from that which she had taken him to be! It was now September, and she could remember an early evening in May, when the leaves were beginning to be full, and they were walking together with the spring air fresh around them, just where she was now creeping alone with the more per- fect and less fresher beauty of the autumn around her. How dif- ferent a person he seemed to her to be now from that which he had seemed to be then; — not different because he did not love her, but different because he was not fit to be loved! "Alice," he had said, "you and I are alike in this, that simple, serviceable things are dear to both of us." The words had meant so much to her that she had never forgotten them. Was she simple and ser- viceable, so that she might be dear to him? She had been sure then that he was simple, and that he was serviceable, so that she could love him. It was thus that she had spoken of him to herself, thinking herself to be sure of his character. And now, before the summer was over, he was engaged to marry such a one as Geor- giana Wanless and to become the hero of a fashionable wedding!

But she took pride to herself, as she walked alone, that she had already overcome the bitterness of the malady which, for a day or two, had been so heavy that she had feared for herself that it would oppress her. For a day or two after that farewell at the gate she had with a rigid purpose tied herself to every duty, — even to the duty of looking pleasant in her father's eyes, of joining in the children's games, of sharing the gossip of her stepmother. But this she had done with an agony that nearly crushed her. Now she had won her way through it, and could see her path before her. She had not cured altogether that wound in her heart; but she had assured herself that she could live on without further inter- ference from the wound.

Chapter IX
Lady Deepbell

Then by degrees it began to be rumoured about the country, and at last through the lanes of Beetham itself, that the alliance between Major Rossiter and Miss Georgiana Wanless was not quite a settled thing. Mr. Burmeston had whispered in Slow-bridge that there was a screw loose, perhaps thinking that if another could escape, why not he also? Cobble, who had no idea of escaping, declared his conviction that Major Rossiter ought to be horsewhipped; but Lady Deepbell was the real town-crier, who carried the news far and wide. But all of them heard it before Alice, and when others believed it Alice did not believe it, — or, indeed, care to believe or not to believe.

Lady Deepbell filled a middle situation, half way between the established superiority of Brook Park and the recognised humility of Beetham. Her title went for something; but her husband had been only a Civil Service Knight, who had deserved well of his country by a meritorious longevity. She lived in a pretty little cottage half way between Brook Park and Beetham, which was just large enough to enable her to talk of her grounds. She loved Brook Park dearly, and all the county people; but in her love for social intercourse generally she was unable to eschew the more frequent gatherings of the village. She was intimate not only with Mrs. Rossiter, but with the Tweeds and Dugdales and Simkinses, and, while she could enjoy greatly the grandeur of the Wanless aristocracy, so could she accommodate herself comfortably to the cosy gossip of the Beethamites. It was she who first spread the report in Beetham that Major Rossiter was, — as she called it, — "off."

She first mentioned the matter to Mrs. Rossiter herself; but this she did in a manner more subdued than usual. The "alliance" had been high, and she was inclined to think that Mrs. Rossiter would be disappointed. "We did think, Mrs. Rossiter, that these young people at Brook Park had meant something the other day."

Mrs. Rossiter did not stand in awe of Lady Deepbell, and was not pleased at the allusion. "It would be much better if young people could be allowed to arrange their own affairs without so much tattling about it," she said angrily.

"That's all very well, but tongues will talk, you know, Mrs. Rossiter. I am sorry for both their sakes, because I thought that it would do very well."

"Very well indeed, if the young people, as you call them, liked each other."

"But I suppose it's over now, Mrs. Rossiter?"

"I really know nothing about it, Lady Deepbell." Then the old woman, quite satisfied after this that the "alliance" had fallen to the ground, went on to the Tweeds.

"I never thought it would come to much," said Mrs. Tweed.

"I don't see why it shouldn't," said Matilda Tweed. "Georgiana Wanless is good-looking in a certain way; but they none of them have a penny, and Major Rossiter is quite a fashionable man." The Tweeds were quite outside the Wanless pale; and it was the feeling of this that made Matilda love to talk about the second Miss Wanless by her Christian name.

"I suppose he will go back to Alice now," said Clara, the younger Tweed girl.

"I don't see that at all," said Mrs. Tweed.

"I never believed much in that story," said Lady Deepbell.

"Nor I either," said Matilda. "He used to walk about with her, but what does that come to? The children were always with them. I never would believe that he was going to make so little of himself."

"But is it quite sure that all the affair at Brook Park will come to nothing, after the party and everything?" asked Mrs. Tweed.

"Quite positive," said Lady Deepbell authoritatively. "I am able to say certainly that that is all over." Then she toddled off and went to the Simkinses.

The rumour did not reach the doctor's house on that day. The conviction that Major Rossiter had behaved badly to Alice, — that Alice had been utterly thrown over by the Wanless "alliance," had been so strong, that even Lady Deepbell had not dared to go and probe wilfully that wound. The feeling in this respect had been so general that no one in Beetham had been hard-hearted enough to speak to Alice either of the triumph of Miss Wanless, or of the misconduct of the Major; and now Lady Deepbell was afraid to carry her story thither.

It was the doctor himself who first brought the tidings to the house, and did not do this till some days after Lady Deepbell had been in the village. "You had better not say anything to Alice about it." Such at first had been the doctor's injunction to his wife. "One way or the other, it will only be a trouble to her." Mrs. Dugdale, full of her secret, anxious to be obedient, thinking that the gentleman relieved from his second love, would be ready at once to be on again with his first, was so fluttered and fussy that Alice knew that there was something to be told. "You have got some great secret, mamma," she said.

"What secret, Alice?"

"I know you have. Don't wait for me to ask you to tell it. If it is to come, let it come."

"I am not going to say anything."

"Very well, mamma. Then nothing shall be said."

"Alice, you are the most provoking young woman I ever had to deal with in my life. If I had twenty secrets I would not tell you one of them."

On the next morning Alice heard it all from her father. "I knew there was something by mamma's manner," she said.

"I told her not to say anything.."

"So I suppose. But what does it matter to me, papa, whether Major Rossiter does or does not marry Miss Wanless? If he has given her his word, I am sure I hope that he will keep it."

"I don't suppose he ever did."

"Even then it doesn't matter. Papa, do not trouble yourself about him."

"But you?"

"I have gone through the fire, and have come out without being much scorched. Dear papa, I do so wish that you should understand it all. It is so nice to have some dear one to whom everything can be told. I did like him."

"And he?"

"I have nothing to say about that; — not a word. Girls, I suppose, are often foolish, and take things for more than they are intended to mean. I have no accusation to make against him. But I did, — I did allow myself to be weak. Then came this about Miss Wanless, and I was unhappy. I woke from a dream, and the waking was painful. But I have got over it. I do not think that you will ever know from your girl's manner that anything has been the matter with her."

"My brave girl!"

"But don't let mamma talk to me as though he could come back because the other girl has not suited him. He is welcome to the other girl, — welcome to do without her, — welcome to do with himself as it may best please him; but he shall not trouble me again." There was a stern strength in her voice as she said this, which forced her father to look at her almost with amazement. "Do not think that I am fierce, papa."

"Fierce, my darling!"

"But that I am in earnest. Of course, if he comes to Beetham we shall see him. But let him be just like anybody else. Don't let it be supposed that because he flitted here once, and was made welcome, like a bird that comes in at the window, and then flitted away again, that he can be received in at the window just as before, should he fly this way any more. That's all, papa." Then, as before, she went off by herself, — to give herself renewed strength by her solitary thinkings. She had so healed the flesh round that wound that there was no longer danger of mortification. She must now take care that there should be no further wound. The people around her would be sure to tell her of this breach between her late lover and the Wanless young lady. The Tweeds and the Simkinses, and old Lady Deepbell would be full of it. She must take care so to answer them at the first word that they should not dare to talk to her of Major Rossiter. She had cured herself so that she no longer staggered under the effects of the blow. Having done that, she would not allow herself to be subject to the little stings of the little creatures around her. She had had enough of love, — of a man's love, and would make herself happy now with Bobby and the other bairns.

"He'll be sure to come back," said Mrs. Dugdale to her husband.

"We shall do no good by talking about it," said the doctor. "If you will take my advice, you will not mention his name to her. I fear that he is worthless and unworthy of mention." That might be very well, thought Mrs. Dugdale; but no one in the village doubted that he had at the very least £1,500 a year, and that he was a handsome man, and such a one as is not to be picked up under every hedge. The very men who go about the world most like butterflies before marriage "steady down the best" afterwards. These were her words as she discussed the matter with Mrs. Tweed, and they both agreed that if the hero showed himself again at the doctor's house "bygones ought to be bygones."

Lady Wanless, even after her husband's return from London, declared to herself that even yet the game had not been altogether played out. Sir Walter, who had been her only possible direct messenger to the man himself, had been, she was aware, as bad a messenger as could have been selected. He could be neither authoritative nor persuasive. Therefore when he told her, on coming home, that it was easy to perceive that Major Rossiter's father could not have been educated at Christchurch, she did not feel very much disappointed. As her next step she determined to call on Mrs. Rossiter. If that should fail she must beard the lion in his den, and go herself to Major Rossiter at the Horse Guards. She did not doubt but that she would at least be able to say more than Sir Walter. Mrs. Rossiter, she was aware, was herself favourable to the match.

"My dear Mrs. Rossiter," she said in her most confidential manner, "there is a little something wrong among these young people, which I think you and I can put right if we put our heads together."

"If I know one of the young people," said Mrs. Rossiter, "it will be very hard to make him change his mind."

"He has been very attentive to the young lady."

"Of course I know nothing about it, Lady Wanless. I never saw them together."

"Dear Georgiana is so very quiet that she said nothing even to me, but I really thought that he had proposed to her. She won't say a word against him, but I believe he did. Now, Mrs. Rossiter, what has been the meaning of it?"

"How is a mother to answer for her son, Lady Wanless?"

"No; — of course not: I know that. Girls, of course are different. But I thought that perhaps you might know something about it, for I did imagine you would like the connection."

"So I should. Why not? Nobody thinks more of birth than I do, and nothing in my opinion could have been nicer for John.

161

But he does not see with my eyes. If I were to talk to him for a week it would have no effect."

"Is it that girl of the doctor's, Mrs. Rossiter?"

"I think not. My idea is that when he has turned it all over in his mind he has come to the conclusion that he will be better without a wife than with one."

"We might cure him of that, Mrs. Rossiter. If I could only have him down there at Brook Park for another week, I am sure he would come to." Mrs. Rossiter, however, could not say that she thought it probable that her son would be induced soon to pay another visit to Brook Park.

A week after this Lady Wanless absolutely did find her way into the Major's presence at the Horse Guards, — but without much success. The last words at that interview only shall be given to the reader, — the last words as they were spoken both by the lady and by the gentleman. "Then I am to see my girl die of a broken heart?" said Lady Wanless, with her handkerchief up to her eyes.

"I hope not, Lady Wanless; but in whatever way she might die, the fault would not be mine." There was a frown on the gentleman's brow as he said this which cowed even the lady.

As she went back to Slowbridge that afternoon, and then home to Brook Park, she determined at last that the game must be looked upon as played out. There was no longer any ground on which to stand and fight. Before she went to bed that night she sent for Georgiana. "My darling child," she said, "that man is unworthy of you."

"I always thought he was," said Georgiana. And so there was an end of that little episode in the family of the Wanlesses.

Chapter X
The Bird That Pecked at the Window

The bird that had flown in at the window and been made welcome, had flown away ungratefully. Let him come again pecking as he might at the window, no more crumbs of love should be thrown to him. Alice, with a steady purpose, had resolved on that. With all her humble ways, her continual darning of stockings, her cutting of bread and butter for the children, her pushing of the perambulator in the lanes, there was a pride about her, a knowledge of her own dignity as a woman, which could have been stronger in the bosom of no woman of title, of wealth, or of fashion. She claimed nothing. She had expected no admiration. She had been contented to take the world as it came to her, without thinking much of love or romance. When John Rossiter had first shown himself at Beetham, after his return from India, and when he had welcomed her so warmly, — too warmly, — as his old playfellow, no idea had occurred to her that he would ever be more to her than her old playfellow. Her own heart was too precious to herself to be given away idly to the first comer. Then the bird has flown in at the window, and it had been that the coming of the stranger had been very sweet to her. But even for the stranger, she would not change her ways, — unless, perchance, some day she might appertain to the stranger. Then it would be her duty to fit herself entirely to him. In the meantime, when he gave her little hints that something of her domestic slavery might be discontinued, she would not abate a jot from her duties. If he liked to come with her when she pushed the children, let him come. If he cared to see her when she was darning a stocking or cutting bread and butter, let him pay his visits. If he thought those things derogatory, certainly let him stay away. So the thing had grown till she had found herself surprised, and taken, as it were, into a net, — caught in a pitfall of love. But she held her peace, stuck manfully to the perambulator, and was a little colder in her demeanour than heretofore. Whereupon Major Rossiter, as the reader is aware, made two visits to Brook Park. The bird might peck at the window, but he should never again be taken into the room.

But the bird, from the moment in which he had packed up his portmanteau at Brook Park, had determined that he would be taken in at the window again, — that he would at any rate return to the window, and peck at the glass with constancy, soliciting that it might be opened. As he now thought of the two girls, the womanliness of the one, as compared with the worldliness of the other, conquered him completely. There had never been a moment in which his heart had in truth inclined itself towards the young athlete of Brook Park, — never a moment, hardly a moment, in which his heart had been untrue to Alice. But glitter had for a while prevailed with him, and he had, just for a moment, allowed himself to be discontented with the homely colour of unalloyed gold. He was thoroughly ashamed of himself, knowing well that he had given pain. He had learned, clearly enough, from what her father, mother, and others had said to him, that there were those who expected him to marry Alice Dugdale, and others who hoped that he would marry Georgiana Wanless. Now, at last, he could declare that no other love than that which was warm within his heart at present could ever have been possible to him. But he was aware that he had much to do to recover his footing. Alice's face and her manner as she bade him good-bye at the gate were very clear before his eyes.

Two months passed by before he was again seen at Beetham. It had happened that he was, in truth, required elsewhere, on duty, during that period, and he took care to let it be known at Beetham that such was the case. Information to this effect was in some shape sent to Alice. Openly, she took no notice of it; but, inwardly, she said to herself that they who troubled themselves by sending her such tidings, troubled themselves in vain. "Men may come and men may go," she sang to herself, in a low voice. How little they knew her, to come to her with news as to Major Rossiter's coming and going!

Then one day he came. One morning early in December the absolute fact was told at the dinner table. "The Major is at the parsonage," said the maid-servant. Mrs. Dugdale looked at Alice, who continued, however, to distribute hashed mutton with an equanimity which betrayed no flaw.

After that not a word was said about him. The doctor had warned his wife to be silent; and though she would fain have spoken, she restrained herself. After dinner the usual work went on, and then the usual playing in the garden. The weather was dry and mild for the time of year, so that Alice was swinging two of the children when Major Rossiter came up through the gate. Minnie, who had been a favourite, ran to him, and he came slowly across the lawn to the tree on which the swing was hung. For a moment Alice stopped her work that she might shake hands with him, and then at once went back to her place. "If I were to stop a moment before Bobby has had his turn," she said, "he would feel the injustice."

"No, I isn't," said Bobby. "Oo may go 'is time."

"But I don't want to go, Bobby, and Major Rossiter will find mamma in the drawing-room." The Major went into the drawing-room, and Alice for a moment thought of getting her hat and going off from the place. Then she reflected that to run away would be cowardly. She went on swinging the children, — very deliberately, in order that she might be sure of herself, that the man's coming had not even flurried her.

In ten minutes the Major was there again. It had been natural to suppose that he should not be detained long in conversation by Mrs. Dugdale. "May I swing one of them for a time?" he asked.

"Well, no; I think not. It is my allotted exercise, and I never give it up." But Minnie, who knew what a strong arm could do, was imperious, and the Major got possession of the swing.

Then of a sudden he stopped. "Alice," he said, "I want you to take a turn with me up the road."

"I am not going out at all today," she said. Her voice was steady and well preserved; but there was a slight rising of colour on her cheeks.

"But I wish it expressly. You must come to-day."

She could consider only for a moment, — but for a moment she did think the matter over. If the man chose to speak to her seriously, she must listen to him, — once, and once only. So much he had a right to demand. When a bird of that kind pecks in that manner some attention must be paid to him. So she got her hat, and, leading the way down the road, opened the gate and turned up the lane away from the street of the village. For some yards he did not speak. She, indeed, was the first to do so. "I cannot stay out very long, Major Rossiter; so, if there is anything —?"

"There is a something, Alice." Of course she knew, but she was quite resolved. Resolved! Had not every moment of her life since last she had parted with him been given up to the strengthening of this resolution? Not a stitch had gone through the calico which had not been pulled the tighter by the tightening of her purpose! And now he was there. Oh, how more than earthly sweet it had been to have him there, when her resolutions had been of another kind! But she had been punished for that, and was strong against such future ills. "Alice, it had better come out simply. I love you, and have ever loved you with all my heart." Then there was a frown and a little trampling of the ground

165

beneath her foot, but she said not a word. Oh, if it only could have come sooner, — a few weeks sooner! "I know what you would say to me, but I would have you listen to me, if possible, before you say it. I have given you cause to be angry with me."

"Oh no!" she cried, interrupting him.

"But I have never been untrue to you for a moment. You seemed to slight me."

"And if I did!"

"That may pass. If you should slight me now, I must bear it. Even though you should deliberately tell me that you cannot love me, I must bear that. But with such a load of love as I have at my heart, it must be told to you. Day and night it covers me from head to foot. I can think of nothing else. I dream that I have your hand in mine, but when I wake I think that it can never be so."

There was an instinct with her at the moment to let her fingers glide into his; but it was shown only by the gathering together of her two hands, so that no rebellious fingers straying from her in that direction might betray her. "If you have never loved me, never can love me, say so, and I will go away." She should have spoken now, upon the instant; but she simply moved her foot upon the gravel and was silent. "That I should be punished might be right. If it could be possible that the punishment should extend to two, that could not be right."

She did not want to punish him, — only to be brave herself. If to be obdurate would in truth make him unhappy, then would it be right that she should still be firm? It would be bad enough, after so many self-assurances, to succumb at the first word; but for his sake, — for his sake, — would it not be possible to bear even that? "If you never have loved me, and never can love me, say so, and I will go." Even to herself, she had not pledged herself to lie. If he asked her to be his wife in the plain way, she could say that she would not. Then the way would be plain before her. But what reply was she to make in answer to such a question as this? Could she say that she had not loved him, — or did not love him? "Alice," he said, putting his hand up to her arm.

"No!"

"Alice, can you not forgive me?"

"I have forgiven."

"And will you not love me?"

She turned her face upon him with a purpose to frown, but the fulness of his eyes upon her was too much, and the frown gave way, and a tear came into her eye, and her lips trembled; and then she acknowledged to herself that her resolution had not been worth a straw to her.

It should be added that considerably before Alice's wedding, both Sophia and Georgiana Wanless were married, — Sophia, in due order, as of course, to young Cobble, and Georgiana to Mr. Burmeston, the brewer. This, as the reader will remember, was altogether unexpected; but it was a great and guiding principle with Lady Wanless that the girls should not be taken out of their turns.

"Alice Dugdale" appeared first in *Good Cheer*, the Christmas issue of *Good Words* for 1878.

The Courtship of Susan Bell

J OHN MUNROE BELL had been a lawyer in Albany, and as such had thriven well. He had thriven well as long as thrift and thriving on this earth had been allowed to him. But the Almighty had seen fit to shorten his span.

Early in life he had married a timid, anxious, pretty, good little wife, whose whole heart and mind had been given up to do his bidding and deserve his love. She had not only deserved it but had possessed it, and as long as John Munroe Bell had lived Henrietta Bell—Hetta as he called her—had been a woman rich in blessings. After twelve years of such blessings he had left her, and had left her with two daughters, a second Hetta, and the heroine of our little story, Susan Bell.

A lawyer in Albany may thrive passing well for eight or ten years, and yet not leave behind him any very large sum of money if he dies at the end of that time. Some small modicum, some few thousand dollars John Bell had amassed, so that his widow and daughters were not absolutely driven to look for work or bread.

In those happy days when cash had begun to flow in plenteously to the young father of the family, he had taken it into his head to build for himself, or rather for his young female brood, a small neat house on the outskirts of Saratoga Springs. In doing so he was instigated as much by the excellence of the investment for his pocket as by the salubrity of the place for his girls. He furnished the house well; and then, during some summer weeks, his wife lived there, and sometimes he let it.

How the widow grieved when the lord of her heart and master of her mind was laid low in the grave I need not tell. At the commencement of my story she had already counted ten years of widowhood, and her children had grown to be young women beside her. Since that sad day on which they had left Albany they had lived together at the cottage at the Springs. In winter their life had been lonely enough; but as soon as the hot weather began to drive the fainting citizens from New York, they had always received two or three boarders — old ladies generally, and occasionally an old gentleman — persons of very steady habits, with whose pockets the widow's moderate demands agreed better than the hotel charges. And so the Bells lived for ten years.

That Saratoga is a gay place in July, August, and September the world knows well enough. To girls who go there with trunks full of muslin and crinoline, for whom a carriage and pair of horses is always waiting immediately after dinner, whose fathers' pockets are bursting with dollars, it is a very gay place. Dancing and flirtations come as a matter of course, and matrimony follows after with only too great rapidity. But the place was not very gay for Hetta or Susan Bell.

In the first place, the widow was a timid woman, and, among other fears, feared greatly that she should be thought guilty of setting traps for husbands. Poor mothers! how often are they charged with this sin when their honest desires go no farther than that their bairns may be "respectit like the lave." Then she feared flirtations — flirtations that should be nothing more; flirtations that are so destructive of the heart's peace. She feared love also, though she longed for that as well as feared it — for her girls I mean: all such feelings for herself had been long laid under ground. And then, like a timid creature as she was, she had other indefinite fears, and among them a great fear that those girls of hers would be left husbandless — a phase of life which, after her twelve years of bliss, she regarded as any thing but desirable. But the upshot was, the upshot of so many fears and such small means, that Hetta and Susan Bell had but a dull life of it.

Were not my respected friend, Mr. Fletcher Harper, disposed to be so mean in the number of his allotted pages, I would describe at full length the merits and beauties of Hetta and Susan Bell. As it is, I can but say a few words. At our period of their

THE COURTSHIP OF SUSAN BELL

lives Hetta was nearly one-and-twenty, and Susan just nineteen. Hetta was a short, plump, demure young woman, with the softest, smoothest hair, and the brownest, brightest eyes. She was very useful in the house, good at corn cakes, and thought much, particularly in these latter months, of her religious duties. Her sister, in the privacy of their own little room, would sometimes twit her with the admiring patience with which she would listen to the lengthened eloquence of Mr. Phineas Beckard, the Baptist minister. Now Mr. Phineas Beckard was a bachelor.

Susan was not so good a girl in the kitchen or about the house as was her sister; but she was brighter in the parlor; and if that motherly heart could have been made to give out its inmost secret — which, however, it could not have been made to give out in any way painful to dear Hetta — perhaps it might have been found that Susan was loved with the most eager love. She was taller than her sister and lighter; her eyes were blue as were her mother's; her hair was brighter than Hetta's, but not always so scrupulously neat. She had a dimple on her chin, whereas Hetta had none; dimples on her cheek, too, when she smiled; and, oh, such a mouth! There, my allowance of pages permits no more.

One piercing cold winter day there came knocking at the widow's door — a young man. Winter days, when the ice of January is refrozen by the winds of February, are very cold at Saratoga Springs. In those days there was not often much to disturb the serenity of Mrs. Bell's house; but on the day in question there came knocking at the door — a young man.

Mrs. Bell kept an old domestic who had lived with them in those happy Albany days. Her name was Kate O'Brien; but though picturesque in name she was hardly so in person. She was a thick-set, noisy, good-natured old Irishwoman, who had joined her lot to that of Mrs. Bell when the latter first began housekeeping, and knowing when she was well off, had remained in the same place from that day forth. She had known Hetta as a baby; and, so to say, had seen Susan's birth.

"And what might you be wanting, Sir?" said Kate O'Brien, apparently not quite pleased as she opened the door and let in all the cold air.

"I wish to see Mrs. Bell. Is not this Mrs. Bell's house?" said the young man, shaking the snow from out of the breast of his coat.

171

He did see Mrs. Bell; and we will now tell who he was, and why he had come, and how it came to pass that his carpet-bag was brought down to the widow's home, and one of the front bedrooms was prepared for him, and that he drank tea that night in the widow's parlor.

His name was Aaron Dunn, and by profession he was an engineer. What peculiar misfortune in those days of frost and snow had befallen the line of rails which runs from Schenectady to Lake Champlain I never quite understood. Banks and bridges had in some way come to grief, and on Aaron Dunn's shoulders was thrown the burden of seeing that they were duly repaired. Saratoga Springs was the centre of these mishaps, and therefore at Saratoga Springs it was necessary that he should take up his temporary abode.

Now there was at that time in New York City a Mr. Bell great in railway matters, an uncle of the once thriving but now departed Albany lawyer. He was a rich man; but he liked his riches himself, or, at any rate, had not found himself called upon to share them with the widow and daughters of his nephew. But when it chanced to come to pass that he had a hand in dispatching Aaron Dunn to Saratoga, he took the young man aside, and recommended him to lodge with the widow. "There," said he, "show her my card." So much the rich uncle thought he might vouchsafe to do for the nephew's widow.

Mrs. Bell and both her daughters were in the parlor when Aaron Dunn was shown in, snow and all. He told his story in a rough, shaky voice, for his teeth chattered; and he gave the card, almost wishing that he had gone to the empty big hotel, for the widow's welcome was not at first quite warm.

The widow listened to him as he gave his message, and then she took the card and looked at it. Hetta, who was sitting on the side of the fire-place facing the door, went on demurely with her work. Susan gave one glance round — her back was to the stranger — and then another; and then she moved her chair a little nearer to the wall, so as to give the young man room to come to the fire if he would. He did not come; but his eye glanced upon Susan Bell, and he thought that the old man in New York was right, and that the big hotel would be cold and dull. It was a pretty face to look on that cold evening as she turned it up from the stocking she was mending.

"Perhaps you don't wish to take winter boarders, ma'am?" said Aaron Dunn.

"We never have done so yet, Sir," said Mrs. Bell, timidly. Could she let the young wolf in among her lamb-fold? He might be a wolf — who could tell?

"Mr. Bell seemed to think it would suit," said Aaron.

Had he acquiesced in her timidity, and not pressed the point, it would have been all up with him. But the widow did not like to go against the big uncle, and so she said, "Perhaps it may, Sir."

"I guess it will, finely," said Aaron; and then the widow, seeing that the matter was so far settled, put down her work and came round into the passage. Hetta followed her, for there would be housework to do. Aaron gave himself another shake, settled the weekly number of dollars — with very little difficulty on his part, for he had caught another glance at Susan's face — and then went after his bag. 'Twas thus that Aaron Dunn obtained an entrance into Mrs. Bell's house. "But what if he be a wolf?" she said to herself over and over again that night, though not exactly in those words. Ay, but there is another side to that. What if he be a stalwart man, honest-minded, with clever eye, cunning hand, ready brain, broad back, and warm heart, in want of a wife may-hap? A man that can earn his own and another's — half a dozen others when the half dozen come? Would not that be a good sort of lodger? Such a question as that did just flit across the widow's sleepless mind. But then she thought so much more of the wolf! Wolves, she had taught herself to think, were more common than stalwart, honest-minded wife-desirous men.

"I wonder mother consented to take him," said Hetta, when they were in the little room together.

"And why shouldn't she?" said Susan. "It will be a help."

"Yes, it will be a little help," said Hetta. "But we have done very well hitherto without winter lodgers."

"But Uncle Bell said she was to."

"What is Uncle Bell to us?" said Hetta, who had a spirit of her own; and she began to surmise within herself whether Aaron Dunn would join the Baptist congregation, and whether Phineas Beckard would approve of this new move.

"He is a very well-behaved young man, at any rate," said Susan, "and draws beautifully. Did you see those things he was doing?"

"He draws very well, I dare say," said Hetta, who regarded this as but a poor warranty for good behavior. Hetta also had some fear of wolves — not for herself, perhaps, but for her sister.

Aaron Dunn's work — the commencement of his work — lay at some distance from the Springs, and he left every morning with a lot of workmen by an early train, almost before daylight; and every morning, cold and wintry as the mornings were, the widow got him his breakfast with her own hands. She took his dollars, and would not leave him altogether to the awkward mercies of Kate O'Brien; nor would she trust her girls to attend upon the young man. Hetta she might have trusted; but then Susan would have asked why she was spared her share of such hardship.

In the evening, leaving his work when it was dark, Aaron always returned, and then the remaining hours of the day were passed together. But they were passed with the most demure propriety. The three women would make the tea, cut the bread and butter, and then sew; while Aaron Dunn, when the cups were removed, would always go to his plans and his drawings.

On Sundays they were more together; but even on that day there was cause of separation, for Aaron went to the Episcopalian Church, rather to the disgust of Hetta. In the afternoon, however, they were together, and then Phineas Beckard came in to tea on Sundays and he and Aaron got talking on religion; and though they disagreed pretty much, and would not give an inch, either one or the other, nevertheless the minister told the widow, and Hetta, too, probably, that the lad had good stuff in him, though he was so stiff-necked.

"But he sould be more modest in talking on such matters with a minister," said Hetta.

The Rev. Phineas acknowledged that perhaps he should; but he was honest enough to repeat that the lad had good stuff in him. "Perhaps after all he is not a wolf," said the widow to herself.

Things went on this way for above a month. Aaron had declared to himself over and over again that that face was sweet to look upon, and had unconsciously promised to himself certain delights in talking, and, perhaps, in walking, with the owner of it. But the walkings had not been achieved—nor even the talk-ings as yet. The truth was that Dunn was bashful with young women, though he could be so stiff-necked with the minister.

And then he felt angry with himself, inasmuch as he had advanced no further; and as he lay in his bed—which, perhaps, those pretty hands had helped to make — he resolved that he would be a thought bolder in his bearing. He had no idea of mak-ing love to Susan Bell—of course not. But why should he not amuse himself by talking to a pretty girl when she sat so near him, evening after evening?

"What a very quiet young man he is!" said Susan to her sister.

"He has his bread to earn, and sticks to his work," said Hetta. "No doubt he has amusement when he is in the city," added the elder sister, not wishing to leave too strong an impression of the young man's virtues.

They had all now their settled places in the parlor. Hetta sat on one side of the fire, close to the table, having that side to her-self. There she sat always busy. She must have made every dress and bit of linen worn in the house, and hemmed every sheet and towel, so busy was she always. Sometimes, once in a week or so, Phineas Beckard would come in, and then place was made for him between Hetta's usual seat and the table. For when there he would read out loud. On the other side, close also to the table, sat the widow—busy, but not savagely busy, as her elder daugh-ter. Between Mrs. Bell and the wall, with her feet ever on the fender, Susan used to sit—not absolutely idle, but doing work of some slender, pretty sort — and talking ever and anon to her mother. Opposite to them all, at the other side of the table, far away from the fire, would Aaron Dunn place himself with his plans and drawings before him.

"Are you a judge of bridges, ma'am?" said Aaron, the evening after he made his resolution. 'Twas thus he began his courtship.

"Of bridges!" said Mrs. Bell, "Oh, dear no, Sir;" but she put out her hand to take the little drawing which Aaron handed to her.

"Because that's one I've planned for our bit of a new branch from Moreau up to Lake George. I guess Miss Susan knows some-thing about bridges."

"I guess I don't," said Susan; "only that they oughtn't to tumble down when the frost comes."

"Ha, ha, ha! no more they ought; I'll tell M'Evoy that." Mr. M'Evoy had been a former engineer on the line. "Well, that won't burst with any frost, I guess."

"Oh, my! how pretty!" said the widow; and then Susan, of course, jumped up to look over her mother's shoulder.

The artful dodger! He had drawn and colored a beautiful little sketch of a bridge — not an engineer's plan with sections and measurements, vexatious to a woman's eye — but a graceful little bridge with a string of cars running under it. You could almost hear the bell going.

"Well, that is a pretty bridge," said Susan; "isn't it, Hetta?"

"I don't know any thing about bridges," said Hetta, to whose clever eyes the dodge was quite apparent. But in spite of her cleverness Mrs. Bell and Susan had soon moved their chairs round to the table, and were looking at the contents of Aaron's port-folio. "But yet he may be a wolf," thought the poor widow, just as she was kneeling down to say her prayers.

That evening certainly made a commencement. Though Hetta went on pertinaciously with the body of a new dress, the other two ladies did not put in another stitch that night. From his drawings Aaron got to his instruments, and, before bedtime, was teaching Susan how to draw parallel lines. Susan found that she had quite an aptitude for parallel lines, and altogether had a good time of it that evening. It is dull to go on, week after week, and month after month, talking only to one's mother and sister. It is dull, though one does not one's self recognize it to be so. A little change in such matters is so very pleasant. Susan had not the slightest idea of regarding Aaron as even a possible lover. But young ladies do like the conversation of young gentlemen. Oh, my exceedingly proper prim old lady — you, who are so shocked at this as a general doctrine, has it never occurred to you that the Creator has so intended it?

Susan, understanding little of the how and why, knew that she had had a good time, and was rather in spirits as she went to bed. But Hetta had been frightened by the dodge.

"Oh, Hetta, you should have looked at those drawings. He is so clever!" said Susan.

"I don't know that they would have done me much good," replied Hetta.

"Good? Well; they did me more good than a long sermon, I know," said Susan; "except on a Sunday, of course," she added, apologetically. This was an ill-natured attack both on Hetta and Hetta's admirer; but then why had Hetta been so snappish?

"I'm sure he's a wolf," thought Hetta, as she went to bed.

"What a clever young man he is!" thought Susan, as she pulled the warm clothes round about her shoulders and ears.

"Well, that certainly was an improvement," thought Aaron, as he went through the same operation, with a stronger feeling of self-approbation than he had enjoyed for some time past.

In the course of the next fortnight the family arrangements all altered themselves. Unless when Beckard was there, Aaron would sit in the widow's place, the widow would take Susan's chair, and the two girls would be opposite. And then Dunn would read to them; not sermons, but passages from Shakespeare, and Byron, and Longfellow. "He reads much better than Mr. Beckard," Susan had said one night. "Of course you are a competent judge," had been Hetta's retort. "I mean that I like it better," said Susan. "It's well that all people don't think alike," replied Hetta.

And then there was a deal of talking. The widow herself, as unconscious in this respect as her youngest daughter, certainly did find that a little variety was agreeable on those long winter nights, and talked herself with unaccustomed freedom. And Beckard came there oftener, and talked very much. When he was there the two men did all the talking; and they pounded each other immensely. But still there grew up a sort of friendship between them.

"Mr. Beckard seems quite to take to him," said Mrs. Bell to her eldest daughter.

"It is his great good-nature, mother," replied Hetta.

It was at the end of the second month when Aaron took another step in advance — a perilous step. Sometimes on evenings he still went on with his drawing for an hour or so; but during three or four evenings he never asked any one to look at what he was about. On one Friday he sat over his work late without any reading or talking at all — so late that at last Mrs. Bell said,

"If you're going to sit much longer, Mr. Dunn, I'll get you to put out the candles;" thereby showing, had he known it or had she, that the mother's confidence in the young man was growing fast. Hetta knew all about it, and dreaded that the growth was too quick.

"I've finished now," said Aaron; and he looked carefully at the card-board on which he had washed in his water-colors. "I've finished now." He then hesitated a moment; but ultimately he put the card into his port-folio and carried it up to his bedroom. Who does not perceive that it was intended as a present to Susan Bell?

The question which Aaron asked himself that night, and which he hardly knew how to answer, was this: Should he offer the drawing to Susan in the presence of her mother and sister, or on some occasion when they two might be alone together? No such occasion had ever yet occurred, but Aaron thought that it might probably be brought about. But then he wanted to make no fuss about it. His first intention had been to chuck the drawing lightly across the table when it was completed, and so make nothing of it. But he had finished it with more care than he had at first intended; and then he had hesitated when he had finished it. It was too late now for that plan of chucking it over the table.

On the Saturday evening when he came down from his room Mr. Beckard was there, so that he found no opportunity that night. On the Sunday, in conformity with a previous engagement, he went to hear Mr. Beckard preach, and walked to and from meeting with the family. This pleased Mrs. Bell, and they were all very gracious that afternoon. But Sunday was no day for the picture.

On Monday the thing had become of importance to him. Things always do when they are kept over. Before tea that night, when he came down, Mrs. Bell and Susan only were in the room. He knew Hetta for his foe, and therefore determined to use this occasion.

"Miss Susan," he said, stammering somewhat, and blushing too, poor fool! — "I have done a little drawing which I want you to accept." And he put his port-folio down on the table.

"Oh! I don't know," said Susan, who had seen the blush.

Mrs. Bell had seen the blush also, and pursed her mouth up, and looked grave. Had there been no stammering and no blush she might have thought nothing of it.

Aaron saw at once that his little gift was not to go down smoothly. He was, however, in for it now; so he picked it out from among the other papers in the case and brought it to Susan. He endeavored to hand it to her with an air of indifference, but I can not say that he succeeded.

It was a very pretty, well-finished water-colored drawing, representing still the same bridge, but with more adjuncts. In Susan's eyes it was a work of high art. Of pictures probably she had seen but little, and her liking for the artist no doubt added to her admiration. But the more she admired it and wished for it the stronger was her feeling that she ought not take it.

Poor Susan! she stood for a minute looking at the drawing, but she said nothing — not even a word of praise. She felt that she was red in the face, and uncourteous to their lodger; but her mother was looking at her, and she did not know how to behave herself.

Mrs. Bell put out her hand for the sketch, trying to bethink herself as she did so in what least uncivil way she could refuse the present. She took a moment to look at it, collecting her thoughts, and as she did so her woman's wit came to her aid.

"Oh dear, Mr. Dunn, it is very pretty; quite a beautiful picture. I can not let Susan rob you of that. You must keep that for some of your own particular friends."

"But I did it for her," said Aaron, innocently.

Susan looked down at the ground half-pleased at the declaration. The drawing would look very pretty in a small gilt frame just over her dressing-table. But the matter now was altogether in her mother's hands.

"I am afraid it is too valuable, Sir, for Susan to accept it."

"It is not valuable at all," said Aaron, declining to take it back from the widow's hands.

"Oh, I am quite sure it is. It is worth ten dollars at least, or twenty," said poor Mrs. Bell, not in the very best taste. But she was perplexed, and did not know how to get out of the scrape. The article in question now lay upon the table-cloth, appropriated by no one, and at this moment Hetta came into the room.

"It is not worth ten cents," said Aaron, with something like a frown on his brow; "but as we had been talking about the bridge, I thought Miss Susan would accept it."

"Accept what?" said Hetta, and then her eye fell upon the drawing, and she took it up.

"It is beautifully done," said Mrs. Bell, wishing much to soften the matter; perhaps the more so that Hetta the demure was now present. "I'm telling Mr. Dunn that we can't take a present of any thing so valuable."

"Oh dear no," said Hetta. "It wouldn't be right."

It was a cold frosty evening in March, and the fire was burning brightly on the hearth. Aaron Dunn took up the drawing quietly, very quietly, and rolling it up, as such drawings are rolled, put it between the blazing logs. It was the work of four evenings, and his *chef-d'oeuvre* in the way of art.

Susan, when she saw what he had done, burst into tears. The widow could very readily have done so also; but she was able to restrain herself, and merely exclaimed,

"Oh, Mr. Dunn!"

"If Mr. Dunn chooses to burn his own picture he has certainly a right to do so," said Hetta.

Aaron immediately felt ashamed of what he had done; and he also could have cried, but for his manliness. He walked away to one of the parlor windows and looked out upon the frosty night. It was dark, but the stars were bright, and he thought that he should like to be walking fast by himself along the line of rails toward Balston. There he stood, perhaps for three minutes. He thought it would be proper to give Susan time to recover from her tears.

"Will you please to come to your tea, Sir?" said the soft voice of Mrs. Bell.

He turned round to do so, and found that Susan was gone. It was not quite in her power to recover from her tears in three minutes. And then the drawing had been so beautiful! It had been done expressly for her too! And there had been something, she knew not what, in his eye as he had so declared. She had watched him intently over those four evenings' work, wondering why he did not show it, till her feminine curiosity had become rather strong. It was something very particular, she was sure. And now she knew that all that precious work had been for her; and all that precious work was destroyed. How was it possible that she should not cry for more than three minutes?

The others took ther meal in perfect silence, and when it was over the two women sat down to their work. Aaron had a book which he pretended to read; but instead of reading, he was bethinking himself that he had behaved badly. What right had he to throw them all into such confusion by indulging in his passion? He was ashamed of what he had done, and fancied that Susan would hate him. Fancying that, he began to find at the same time that he by no means hated her.

At last Hetta got up and left the room. She knew that her sister was sitting alone in the cold. And Hetta was as affectionate as she was severe. Susan had not been in fault, and therefore Hetta went up to console her.

"Mrs. Bell," said Aaron, as soon as the door was closed, "I beg your pardon for what I did just now."

"Oh, Sir, I'm so sorry that the picture is burned," said poor Mrs. Bell.

"The picture does not matter a straw," said Aaron. "But I see that I have disturbed you all. And I'm afraid I have made Miss Susan unhappy."

"She was grieved because your picture was burned," said Mrs. Bell, putting some emphasis on the "your," intending to show that her daughter had not regarded the drawing as her own. But the emphasis bore another meaning; and so the widow perceived as soon as she had spoken.

"Oh, I can do twenty more of the same, if any body wanted them," said Aaron. "If I do another like it, will you let her take it, Mrs. Bell; just to show that you have forgiven me, and that we are friends as we were before?"

Was he or was he not a wolf? That was the question which Mrs. Bell scarcely knew how to answer. Hetta had given her voice, saying that he probably was lupine. Mr. Beckard's opinion she had not liked to ask directly. Mr. Beckard she thought would probably propose to Hetta; but as yet he had not done so. And as he was still a stranger in the family, she did not like in any way to compromise Susan's name. Indirectly she had asked the question; and, indirectly also, Mr. Beckard's answer had been favorable.

"But it mustn't mean any thing, Sir," was the widow's weak answer, when she had paused on the question for a moment.

"Oh no, of course not," said Aaron, joyously; and his face became radiant and happy. "And I do beg your pardon for burning it; and the young ladies' pardon too;" and then he rapidly got out his card-board, and set himself to work about another bridge. The widow, meditating many things in heart, commenced the hemming of a handkerchief.

In about an hour the two girls came back to the room and silently took their accustomed places. Aaron hardly looked up but went on diligently with his drawing. This bridge should be a better bridge than that other. Its acceptance was now assured. Of course it was to mean nothing. That was a matter of course. So he worked away diligently and said not a word — nothing to any body.

When they went off to bed the girls turned into the mother's room. "Oh, mother, I hope he is not very angry," said Susan.

"Angry!" said Hetta. "If any body should be angry it is mother. He might have known that Susan could not accept it. He should never have offered it."

"But he's doing another," said Mrs. Bell.

"Not for her?" said Hetta.

"Yes he is," said Mrs. Bell. "And I have promised that she shall take it." Susan as she heard this sank gently into the chair behind her, and her eyes became full of tears. The intimation was almost too much for her.

"Oh, mother!" said Hetta.

"But I particularly said that it was to mean nothing."

"Oh, mother, that makes it worse."

Why should Hetta interfere in this way, thought Susan to herself. Had she interfered when Mr. Beckard gave Hetta a Testament bound in morocco? Had she not smiled, and looked gratified, and kissed her sister, and declared that Phineas Beckard was a nice, dear man, and by far the most elegant preacher at the Springs? Why should Hetta be so cruel?

"I don't see that, my dear," said the mother.

182

Hetta could not explain before her sister, so they all went to bed.

On Thursday evening the drawing was finished. Not a word had been said about it, at any rate in his presence, and he had gone on working in silence. "There," said he, late on Thursday evening, "I don't know that it will be any better if I go on daub-ing for another hour. There, Miss Susan, there's another bridge. I hope that will neither burst with the frost nor yet be destroyed by fire;" and he gave it a light flip with his finger and sent it skim-ming over the table."

Susan blushed, and smiled, and took it up. "Oh, it is beauti-ful!" she said. "Isn't it beautifully done, mother?" And then all the three got up to look at it, and all confessed that it was excel-lently done.

"And I am sure we are very much obliged to you," said Susan, after a pause, remembering that she had not yet thanked him.

"Oh, it's nothing," said he, not quite liking the word "we."

On the following day he returned from his work to Saratoga about noon. This he had never done before, and therefore no one expected that he would be seen in the house before the evening. On this occasion, however, he went straight thither, and, as chance would have it, both the widow and her elder daughter were out. Susan was alone in charge of the house.

He walked in and opened the parlor door. There she sat, with her feet on the fender, with her work unheeded on the table behind her, and the picture — Aaron's drawing — lying on her knees. She was gazing at it intently as he entered, thinking in her young heart that it possessed all the beauties which any picture could possibly possess.

"Oh, Mr. Dunn!" she said, getting up and holding the tell-tale sketch behind the skirt of her dress.

"Oh, Miss Susan! I have come to tell your mother that I must start for New York this afternoon, and be there for six weeks or perhaps longer."

"Mother is out," said she. "I'm so sorry!"

"Is she?" said Aaron.

"And Hetta too. Dear me! And you'll be wanting dinner. I'll go and see about it."

Aaron began to swear that he could not possibly eat any dinner — he had dined once, and was going to dine again — any thing to keep her from going.

"But you must have something, Mr. Dunn;" and she walked toward the door.

But he put his back to it. "Miss Susan," said he, "I guess I've been here nearly two months."

"Yes, Sir, I believe you have," she replied, shaking in her shoes, and not knowing which way to look.

"And I hope we have been good friends."

"Yes, Sir," said Susan, almost beside herself as to what she was saying.

"I'm going away now, and it seems to be such a time before I'll be back!"

"Will it, Sir?"

"Six weeks, Miss Susan!" and he paused, looking into her eyes to see what he could read there. She leaned against the table, pulling to pieces a morsel of half-raveled muslin which she held in her hands; but her eyes were turned to the ground, and he could hardly see them.

"Miss Susan," he continued, "I may as well speak out now as at another time." He, too, was looking toward the ground, and clearly did not know what to do with his hands. "The truth is just this: I — I love you dearly, with all my heart. I never saw any one I ever thought so beautiful, so nice, and so good; and what's more, I never shall. I'm not very good at this sort of thing, I know; but I couldn't go away from Saratoga for six weeks and not tell you." And then he ceased. He did not ask for any love in return. His presumption had not got so far as that yet. He merely declared his passion, leaning there against the door, and then stood twiddling his thumbs.

Susan had not the slightest conception of the way in which she ought to receive such a declaration. She had never had a lover before. Nor had she ever thought of Aaron absolutely as a lover, though something very like love for him had been creeping over her spirit. Now at this moment she felt that he was the beau-ideal of manhood, though his boots were covered with the railway mud, and though his pantaloons were tucked up in rolls around his ankles. He was a fine, well-grown, open-faced fellow, whose eye was bold and yet tender, whose brow was full and broad, and all his bearing manly. Love him! Of course she loved him. Why else had her heart melted with pleasure when her mother said that that second picture was to be accepted?

But what was she to say? Any thing but the open truth. She well knew that. The open truth would not do at all. What would her mother say, and Hetta, if she were rashly to say that? Hetta, she knew, would be dead against such a lover, and of her mother's approbation she had hardly more hope. Why they should disapprove of Aaron as a lover she had never asked herself. There are many nice things which seem to be wrong only because they are so nice. May be that Susan regarded a lover as one of them.

"Oh, Mr. Dunn! you shouldn't." That, at first, was all that she could say.

"Should not I?" said he. "Well, perhaps not. But there's the truth, and no harm ever comes of that. Perhaps I'd better not ask you for an answer now. But I thought it right you should know it all. And remember this: I care for one thing now in the world, and that is your love." And then he paused, thinking it probable that, in spite of what he had said, he might perhaps get some sort of answer, some inkling in the state of her heart's disposition toward him.

But Susan had at once resolved to take him at his word, when he suggested that an immediate reply was not necessary. To say that she loved him was of course impossible; and to say that she did not was equally so. She determined, therefore, to close at once with the offer of silence.

When he ceased speaking there was a moment's pause, during which he strove hard to read what might be written on her down-turned face. But he was not good at such reading. "Well, I guess I'll go and get my things ready now," he said, and then turned round to open the door.

"Mother will be in before you are gone, I suppose," said Susan.

"I have only got twenty minutes," said he, looking at his watch. "But, Susan, tell her what I have said to you. Good-by," and he put out his hand. He knew he should see her again, but this had been his dodge to get her hand in his.

"Good-by, Mr. Dunn," and she gave him her hand.

He held it tight for a moment, so that she could not draw it away — could not if she would. "Will you tell your mother?" he asked.

"Yes," she answered, quite in a whisper, "I guess I'd better tell her." And then she gave a long sigh. He pressed her hand again, and got it up to his lips.

"Mr. Dunn, don't," she said. But he did kiss it.

"God bless you, my own dearest, dearest girl. I'll just open the door as I come down. Perhaps Mrs. Bell will be here," and then he rushed up stairs.

But Mrs. Bell did not come in. She and Hetta were at a weekly service at Mr. Beckard's meeting-house, and Mr. Beckard, it seemed, had much to say. Susan, when left alone, sat down and tried to think. But she could not think; she could only love. She could use her mind only in recounting to herself the perfection of that demigod whose heavy steps were so audible overhead, as he walked to and fro collecting his things and putting them into his bag.

And then, just when he had finished, she bethought herself that he must be hungry. She flew to the kitchen, but she was too late. Before she could even reach at the loaf of bread he descended the stairs with a clattering noise, and heard her voice as she spoke quickly to Kate O'Brien.

"Miss Susan," he said, "don't get any thing for me, for I'm off."

"Oh! Mr. Dunn, I'm so sorry. You'll be so hungry on your journey," and she came out to him in the passage.

"I shall want nothing on the journey, dearest, if you'll say one kind word to me."

Again her eyes went to the ground. "What do you want me to say, Mr. Dunn?"

"Say God bless you, Aaron."

"God bless you, Aaron," said she; and yet she was sure that she had not declared her love! He, however, thought otherwise, and went up to New York with a happy heart.

Things happened in the next fortnight rather quickly. Susan at once resolved to tell her mother, but she resolved also not to tell Hetta. That afternoon she got her mother to herself in Mrs. Bell's own room, and there she made a clean breast of it.

"And what did you say to him, Susan?"

"I said nothing, mother."

"Nothing, dear!"

"No, mother, not a word. He told me he didn't want it." She forgot how she had used his Christian name in bidding God bless him.

"Oh, dear!" said the widow.

"Was it very wrong?" asked Susan.

"But what do you think yourself, my child?" asked Mrs. Bell, after a while. "What are your own feelings?"

Mrs. Bell was sitting on a chair, and Susan was standing opposite to her against the foot of the bed. She made no answer, but moving from her place, she threw herself into her mother's arms and hid her face on her mother's shoulder. It was easy enough to guess what were her feelings.

"But, my darling," said the mother, "you must not think that it is an engagement."

"No," said Susan, sorrowfully.

"Young men say these things to amuse themselves." Wolves she would have said had she spoken out her mind freely.

"Oh, mother, he is not like that!"

The daughter contrived to extract a promise from the mother that Hetta should not be told just at present. Mrs. Bell calculated that she had six weeks before her. As yet Mr. Beckard had not spoken out. But there was reason to suppose that he would do so before those six weeks would be over, and then she would be able to seek counsel from him.

Mr. Beckard spoke out at the end of six days, and Hetta frankly accepted him. "I hope you'll love your brother-in-law," said she to Susan.

"Oh! I will, indeed," said Susan, and in the softness of her heart at the moment she almost made up her mind to tell. But Hetta was full of her own affairs, and thus it passed off.

It was then arranged that Hetta should go and spend a week with Mr. Beckard's parents. Old Mr. Beckard was a farmer living near Utica; and now that the match was declared and approved of, it was thought well that Hetta should know her future husband's family. So she went for a week, and Mr. Beckard went with her. "He will be back in plenty of time for me to speak to him before Aaron Dunn's six weeks are over," said Mrs. Bell to herself.

But things did not go exactly as she expected. On the very morning after the departure of the engaged couple there came a letter from Aaron saying that he would be at Saratoga that very evening. The railway people had ordered him down again for some days' special work. Then he was to go elsewhere, and not to return to Saratoga till June. "But he hoped," so said the letter, "that Mrs. Bell would not turn him out into the street even then, though the summer might have come, and her regular lodgers might be expected."

"Oh dear, oh dear!" said Mrs. Bell to herself, reflecting that she had no one of whom she could ask advice, and that she must decide that very day. Why had she let Mr. Beckard go without telling him? Then she told Susan, and Susan spent the day trembling. Perhaps, thought Mrs. Bell, he will say nothing about it. In such case, however, would it not be her duty to say something? Poor mother! She trembled nearly as much as Susan.

It was dark when the fatal knock came at the door. The tea things were already laid, and the tea-cake was already baked; for it would, at any rate, be necessary to give Mr. Dunn his tea. Susan, when she heard the knock, rushed from her chair and took refuge up stairs. The widow gave a long sigh, and settled her dress. Kate O'Brien, with willing step, opened the door, and bade her old friend welcome.

"How are the ladies?" asked Aaron, trying to gather something from the face and voice of the domestic.

"Miss Hetta and Mr. Beckard be gone off to Utica, just man-and-wife like. And so they are; more power to them."

"Oh, indeed; I'm very glad," said Aaron. And so he was; very glad to have Hetta the demure out of the way. And then he made his way into the parlor, doubting much and hoping much.

Mrs. Bell rose from her chair, and tried to look grave. Aaron glanced round the room and saw that Susan was not there. He walked straight up to the widow, and offered his hand, which she took. It might be that Susan had not thought fit to tell, and in such case it would not be right for him to compromise her; so he said never a word.

But the subject was too important to the mother to allow of her being silent when the young man stood before her. "Oh, Mr. Dunn," said she, "what is this you have been saying to Susan?"

"I have asked her to be my wife," said he, drawing himself up and looking her full in the face. Mrs. Bell's heart was almost as soft as her daughter's, and it was nearly gone; but at the moment she had nothing to say but, "Oh dear, oh dear!"

"May I not call you mother?" said he, taking both her hands in his.

"Oh dear, oh dear! But will you be good to her? Oh, Aaron Dunn, if you deceive my child —"

In another quarter of an hour Susan was kneeling at her mother's knees with her face in her mother's lap; the mother was wiping tears out of her eyes; and Aaron was standing by, holding one of the widow's hands.

"You are *my* mother too now," said he. What would Hetta and Mr. Beckard say when they came back? But then he surely was not a wolf!

There were four or five days left for the courtship before Hetta and Mr. Beckard would return — four or five days during which Susan might be happy, Aaron triumphant, and Mrs. Bell nervous. Days I have said, but after all it was only the evenings that were so left. Every morning Susan got up to give Aaron his breakfast, but Mrs. Bell got up also. Susan boldly declared her right to do so, and Mrs. Bell found no objection which she could urge. But after that Aaron was always absent till seven or eight o'clock in the evening, when he would return to his tea. Then came the hour or two of lover's intercourse.

But they were very tame those hours. The widow still felt an undefined fear that she was wrong, and though her heart yearned to know that her daughter was happy in the sweet happiness of accepted love, yet she dreaded to be too confident. Not a word had been said about money matters; not a word of Aaron Dunn's relatives. So she did not leave them by themselves, but waited with what patience she could for the return of her wise counselors.

And then Susan hardly knew how to behave herself with her accepted suitor. She felt that she was very happy; but perhaps she was most happy when she was thinking about him through the long day, assisting in fixing little things for his comfort, and waiting for his evening return. And as he sat there in the parlor, she could be happy there too, if she were but allowed to sit still and look at him; not stare at him, but raise her eyes every now and again to his face for the shortest possible glance, as she had been used to do ever since he came there.

But he, unconscionable lover, wanted to hear her speak, was desirous of being talked to, and perhaps thought that he should by right be allowed to sit by her, and hold her hand. No such privileges were accorded to him. If they had been alone together, walking side by side on the green turf as lovers should walk, she would soon have found the use of her tongue — have talked fast enough no doubt. Under such circumstances, when a girl's shyness has given way to real intimacy, there is, in general, no end to her power of chatting. But though there was much love between Aaron and Susan, there was as yet but little intimacy; and then, let a mother be ever so motherly — and no mother could have more of a mother's tenderness than Mrs. Bell — still her presence must be a restraint. Aaron was very fond of Mrs. Bell; but nevertheless he did sometimes wish that some domestic duty would take her out of the parlor for a few happy minutes. Susan went out very often, but Mrs. Bell seemed to be a fixture.

Once for a moment he did find her alone, immediately as he came into the house.

"My own Susan, do you love me? Do say so to me once;" and he contrived to get his arm round her waist.

"Yes," she whispered; but she slipped like an eel from his hands, and left him only preparing himself for a kiss; and then, when she got to her room, half frightened, she clasped her hands together, and bethought herself that she did really love him with a strength and depth of love which filled her whole existence. Why should she not have told him something of all this?

And so the few days of his second sojourn at Saratoga passed away, not altogether satisfactorily. It was settled that he should return to New York on Saturday night, leaving Saratoga on that evening; and as the Beckards — Hetta was already regarded quite as a Beckard — were to be back to dinner on that day, Mrs. Bell would have an opportunity of telling her wondrous tale. It might be well that Mr. Beckard should see Aaron before his return.

On that Saturday the Beckards did arrive just in time for dinner. It may be imagined that Susan's appetite was not very keen, nor her manners very collected. But all this passed by unobserved in the importance attached to the various Beckard arrangements which came under discussion. Ladies and gentlemen circumstanced as were Hetta and Mr. Beckard are, perhaps, a little too apt to think that their own affairs are paramount. But after dinner Susan vanished at once, and when Hetta prepared to follow her, desirous of further talk about matrimonial arrangements, her mother stopped her, and the disclosure was made.

"Proposed to her!" said Hetta, who perhaps thought that one marriage in a family was enough at a time.

"Yes, my love. And he did it, I must say, in a very honorable way; telling her not to make any answer till she had spoken to me. Now that was very nice; was it not, Phineas?" Mrs. Bell had become very anxious that Aaron should not be voted a wolf.

"And what has been said to him since?" asked the discreet Phineas.

"Why, nothing absolutely decisive." Oh, Mrs. Bell! "You see I know nothing as to his means."

"Nothing at all," said Hetta.

"He is a man that will always earn his bread," said Mr. Beckard; and Mrs. Bell blessed him in her heart for saying it.

"But has he been encouraged?" asked Hetta.

"Well, yes he has," said the widow.

"Then Susan, I suppose, likes him?" asked Phineas.

"Well, yes she does," said the widow. And the conference ended in a resolution that Phineas Beckard should have a conversation with Aaron Dunn as to his worldly means and position; and that he, Phineas, should decide whether Aaron might, or might not, be at once accepted as a lover, according to the tenor of that conversation. Poor Susan, she was not told any thing of all this.

"Better not," said Hetta the demure. "It will only flurry her the more."

How would she have liked it if, without consulting her, they had left it to Aaron to decide whether or no she might marry Phineas?

They knew where on the works Aaron was to be found, and thither Mr. Beckard rode after dinner. We need not narrate at length the conference between the young men. Aaron at once declared that he had nothing but what he made as an engineer, and explained that he held no permanent situation on the line. He was well paid at that present moment, but at the end of the summer he would have to look for employment.

"Then you can hardly marry at present?" said the discreet minister.

"Perhaps not quite immediately."

"And long engagements are never wise," said the other.

"Three or four months," suggested Aaron. But Mr. Beckard shook his head.

The afternoon at Mrs. Bell's house was melancholy. The final decision of the three judges was as follows: There was to be no engagement; of course no correspondence. Aaron was to be told that it would be better that he should get lodgings elsewhere when he returned; but that he would be allowed to visit at Mrs. Bell's house, and at Mrs. Beckard's, which was very considerate. If he should succeed in getting a permanent appointment, and if he and Susan still held the same mind, why then — etc., etc., etc. Such was Susan's fate, as communicatetd to her by Mrs. Bell and Hetta. She sat still and wept when she heard it; but she did not complain. She had always felt that Hetta would be against her.

"Mayn't I see him, then?" she said, through her tears.

Hetta thought she had better not. Mrs. Bell thought she might. Phineas decided that they might shake hands, but only in full conclave. There was to be no lovers' farewell. Aaron was to leave the house at half past five, but before he went Susan should be called down. Poor Susan! she sat down and bemoaned herself; uncomplaining, but very sad.

Susan was soft, feminine, and manageable. But Aaron Dunn was not very soft, was especially masculine, and in some matters not easily manageable. When Mr. Beckard, in the widow's presence — Hetta had retired in obedience to her lover — informed him of the court's decision there came over his face the look he had worn when he burned the picture. "Mrs. Bell," he said, "had encouraged his engagement; and he did not understand why other people should now come and disturb it."

"Not an engagement, Aaron," said Mrs. Bell, piteously.

"He was able and willing to work," he said, "and knew his profession. What young man of his age had done better than he had?" and he glanced round at them with perhaps more pride than was quite becoming.

Then Mr. Beckard spoke out, very wisely no doubt, but perhaps a little too much at length. Sons and daughters, as well as fathers and mothers, will know very well what he said; so I need not repeat his words. I can not say that Aaron listened with much attention, but he understood perfectly what the upshot of it was. Many a man understands the purport of many a sermon without listening to one word in ten. Mr. Beckard meant to be kind in his manner; and indeed was so, only that Aaron could not accept as kindness any interference on his part.

"I'll tell you what, Mrs. Bell," said he, "I look upon myself as engaged to her, and I look on her as engaged to me. I tell you so fairly; and I believe that's her mind as well as mine."

"But, Aaron, you won't try to see her, or to write to her; not in secret, will you?"

"When I try to see her, I'll come and knock at this door; and if I write to her, I'll write to her full address by the post. I never did and never will do any thing in secret."

"I know you're good and honest," said the widow, with her handkerchief to her eyes.

"Then why do you separate us?" asked he, almost roughly. "I suppose I may see her, at any rate, before I go. My time's nearly up now, I guess."

And then Susan was called for, and she and Hetta came down together. Susan crept in behind her sister. Her eyes were red with weeping, and her appearance was altogether disconsolate. She had had a lover for a week, and now she was to be robbed of him.

"Good-by, Susan," said Aaron, and he walked up to her without bashfulness or embarrassment. Had they all been compliant and gracious to him he would have been as bashful as his love; but now his temper was hot. "Good-by, Susan," and she took his hand, and he held hers till he had finished; "and remember this, I look upon you as my promised wife, and I don't fear that you'll deceive me. At any rate, I sha'n't deceive you. Good-by."

"Good-by, Aaron," she sobbed.

"Good-by, and God bless you, my own darling!" and then, without saying a word to any one else, he turned his back upon them and went his way.

There had been something very consolatory and very sweet to the poor girl in her lover's last words; and yet they had almost made her tremble. He had been so bold, and stern, and confident. He had seemed so utterly to defy the impregnable discretion of Mr. Beckard, so to despise the demure propriety of Hetta. But of this she felt sure, when she came to question her heart, that she could never, never, never cease to love him better than all the world besides. She would wait—patiently if she could find patience; and then, if he deserted her, she would die.

In another month Hetta became Mrs. Beckard. Susan brushed up a little for the occasion, and looked very pretty as bridemaid. She was serviceable, too, in arranging household matters, hemming linen and sewing tablecloths, though, of course, in those matters she did not do a tenth of what Hetta did.

Then the summer came, the Saratoga summer of July, August, and September, during which the widow's house was full; and Susan's hands saved the pain of her head, for she was forced into occupation. Now that Hetta was gone to her own duties, it was necessary that Susan's part in the household should be more prominent.

Aaron did not come back to his work at Saratoga. Why he did not they could not then learn. During the whole long summer they heard no word of him nor from him; and then, when the cold winter months came and their boarders had left them, Mrs. Beckard congratulated her sister in that she had given no further encouragement to a lover who had cared so little for her. This was very hard to bear, but Susan did bear it.

That winter was very sad. They learned nothing of Aaron Dunn till about January, and then they heard that he was doing very well. He was engaged on the Erie trunk line, was paid highly, and was much esteemed. And yet he neither came nor sent.

"He has an excellent situation," their informant told them.

"And a permanent one?" asked the widow.

"Oh yes, no doubt," said the gentleman; "for I happen to know that they count greatly on him."

And yet he sent no word of love.

After that the winter became very sad indeed. Mrs. Bell thought it to be her duty now to teach her daughter that, in all probability, she would see Aaron Dunn no more. It was open to him to leave her without being absolutely a wolf. He had been driven from the house when he was poor, and they had no right to expect that he would return now that he had made some rise in the world. "Men do amuse themselves in that way," the widow tried to teach her.

"He is not like that, mother," she said again.

"But they do not think so much of those things as we do," urged the mother.

"Don't they?" said Susan, oh so sorrowfully. And so through the whole long winter months she became paler and paler, and thinner and thinner.

And then Hetta tried to console her with religion; and that, perhaps, did not make things any better. Religious consolation is the best cure for all grief; but it must not be looked for specially with regard to any individual sorrow. A religious man, should he become bankrupt through the misfortunes of the world, will find true consolation in his religion even for that sorrow; but a bankrupt who has not thought much of such things will hardly find solace by taking up religion for that special occasion.

And Hetta, perhaps, was hardly prudent in her attempts. She thought that it was wicked on Susan's part to grow thin and pale for love of Aaron Dunn, and she hardly hid her thoughts. Susan was not sure but that it might be wicked; but this doubt in no way tended to make her plump and rosy. So that in those days she found no comfort in her sister.

But her mother's pity and soft love did ease her sufferings, though it could not make them cease. Her mother did not tell her that she was wicked, or bid her read long sermons, or force her to go oftener to the meeting-house.

"He will never come again, I think," she said one day as, with a shawl wrapped round her shoulders, she leaned with her head on her mother's bosom.

"My own darling!" said the mother, pressing her child closely to her side.

"You think he never will — eh, mother?"

What could Mrs. Bell say? In her heart of hearts she did not think he ever would come again.

"No, my child, I do not think he will."

And then the hot tears ran down, and the sobs came thick and frequent.

"My darling! my darling'" exclaimed the mother; and they wept together.

"Was I wicked to love him at the first?" she asked that night.

"No, my child; you were not wicked at all — at least I think not."

"Then why — why was he sent away?" It was on her tongue to ask that question, but she paused and spared her mother. This was as they were going to bed. The next morning Susan did not get up. She was not ill, she said, but weak and weary. Would her mother let her lie that day? And then Mrs. Bell went down alone to her room, and sorrowed with all her heart for the sorrow of her child. Why, oh why had she driven away from her door-sill the love of an honest man?

On the next morning Susan again did not get up. Nor did she hear, or, if she heard, did she recognize, the steps of the postman who brought a letter to the door. Early, before the widow's breakfast, the postman came, and the letter which he brought was as follows:

"MY DEAR MRS. BELL, — I have now got a permanent situation on the Erie line, and the salary is enough for myself and a wife — at least I think so — and I hope you will too. I shall be down at Saratoga to-morrow evening, and I hope neither Susan nor you will refuse to receive me.

Yours, affectionately,
"AARON DUNN."

That was all. It was very short, and did not contain one word of love; but it made the widow's heart leap for joy. She was rather afraid that Aaron was angry, he wrote so curtly, and with such a brusque, business-like attention to mere facts; but surely he could have but one object in coming there. And then he alluded specially to a wife. So the widow's heart leaped with joy.

But how was she to tell Susan? She ran up stairs, almost breathless with haste, to the bedroom door. But then she stopped. Too much joy, she had heard, was as dangerous as too much sorrow. She must think it over for a while; so she crept back again.

But after breakfast — that is, when she had sat for a while over her tea-cup — she returned to the room, and this time she entered it. The letter was in her hand, but held so as to be hidden — in her left hand — as she sat down with her right arm toward the invalid.

"Susan dear," she said, and smiled at her child, "you'll be able to get up this morning — eh, dear?"

"Yes, mother," said Susan, thinking that her mother objected to this idleness of her lying in bed. And so she began to bestir herself.

"I don't mean this very moment, love. Indeed, I want to sit with you for a little while." And she put her right arm affectionately round her daughter's waist.

"Dearest mother!" said Susan.

"Ah! there's one dearer than me, I guess." And Mrs. Bell smiled sweetly as she made the maternal charge against her daughter.

Susan raised herself quickly in the bed, and looked straight into her mother's face.

"Mother, mother!" she said, "what is it? You've something to tell. Oh, mother!" And stretching herself over, she struck her hand against the corner of Aaron's letter. "Mother, you've a letter! Is he coming, mother?" And with eager eyes and open lips she sat up, holding tight to her mother's arm.

"Yes, love, I have got a letter."

"Is he — is he coming?"

How the mother answered I can hardly tell; but she did answer, and they were soon lying in each other's arms, warm with each other's tears. It would be hard to say which was the happier.

Aaron was to be there that evening — that very evening.

"Oh, mother, let me get up," said Susan.

But Mrs. Bell said no, not yet. Her darling was pale and thin; and she almost wished that Aaron was not coming for another week. What if he should come and look at her, and finding her beauty gone, vanish again, and seek a wife elsewhere!

So Susan lay in bed thinking of her happiness, dozing now and again, and fearing, as she waked, that it was a dream — looking constantly at that drawing of his, which she kept outside upon the bed — nursing her love, and thinking of it, and endeavoring — vainly endeavoring — to arrange what she would say to him.

"Mother," she said, when Mrs. Bell went up to her, "you won't tell Hetta and Phineas, will you? Not to-day, I mean."

Mrs. Bell agreed that it would be better not to tell them. Perhaps she thought that she had already depended too much on Hetta and Phineas in this matter.

Susan's finery in the way of dress had never been extensive; and now, lately, in those last sad winter days, she had thought but little of her clothes. But when she began to dress herself for this evening she did ask her mother, with some anxiety, what she had better wear.

"If he loves you, he'll hardly see what you have on," said the mother. But not the less was she careful to smooth her daughter's hair, and make the most that might be made of those faded roses.

How Susan's heart beat — how both their heats beat — as the hands of the clock came round to seven! And then, sharp at seven, came the knock — that same bold, ringing knock which Susan had so soon learned to know as belonging to Aaron Dunn.

"Oh! mother, I had better go up stairs," she cried, starting from her chair.

"No, dear; you would only be more nervous."

"Yes, mother, I will go."

'No, no, dear; you have not time."

And then Aaron Dunn was in the room.

She had thought much what she would say to him; but had not yet quite made up her mind. It mattered, however, but very little. On whatever she might have resolved, her resolution would have vanished to the wind. Aaron Dunn came into the room; and in one second she found herself in the centre of a whirlwind, and his arms were the storms that enveloped her on every side.

"My own, own darling girl!" he said, over and over again, as he pressed her to his heart, quite regardless of Mrs. Bell, who stood by, sobbing with joy. "My own Susan!"

"Aaron, dear Aaron!" she whispered.

But she had already recognized the fact that, for the present meeting, a passive part would become her well, and save her a deal of trouble. She had her lover there quite safe — safe beyond any thing that Mr. or Mrs. Beckard might have to say to the contrary. She was quite happy, only that there were symptoms, now and again, that the whirlwind was about to engulf her once more.

"Dear Aaron, I am so glad you are come," said the innocent-minded widow, as she went up stairs with him to show him his room; and then he embraced her also.

"Dear, dear mother!" he said.

On the next day there was, as a matter of course, a family conclave. Hetta and Phineas came down, and discussed the whole subject of the coming marriage with Mrs. Bell. Hetta, at first, was not quite certain. Ought they not to inquire whether the situation was permanent?

"I won't inquire at all," said Mrs. Bell, with an energy that startled both the daughter and son-in-law. "I would not part them now—no, not if—" And the widow shuddered as she thought of her daughter's sunken eye and pale checks.

"He is a good lad," said Phineas; "and I trust she will make him a sober and steady wife."

And so the matter was settled.

During this time Susan and Aaron were walking along the Balston Road; and they also had settled the matter — quite as satisfactorily.

Such was the courtship of Susan Bell.

"The Courtship of Susan Bell" appeared first in the August issue of *Harper's New Monthly Magazine* for 1860.

Miss Ophelia Gledd

WHO CAN SAY WHAT IS A LADY? My intelligent and well bred reader of either sex will at once declare that he and she know very well who is a lady. So, I hope, do I. But the present question goes further than that. What is it, and whence does it come? Education does not give it, nor intelligence, nor birth, — not even the highest. The thing, which in its presence or absence is so well known and understood, may be wanting to the most polished manners, to the sweetest disposition, to the truest heart. There are thousands among us who know it at a glance, and can recognise its presence from the sound of a dozen words; — but there is not one among us who can tell us what it is.

Miss Ophelia Gledd was a young lady of Boston, Massachusetts, and I should be glad to know whether in the estimation of my countrymen and countrywomen she is to be esteemed a lady. An Englishman, even of the best class, is often at a loss to judge of the "ladyship" of a foreigner, unless he has really lived in foreign cities and foreign society; but I do not know that he is ever so much puzzled in this matter by any nationality as he is by the American. American women speak his own language, read his own literature, and in many respects think his own thoughts; but there has crept into American society so many little social ways at variance with our social ways, — there have been wafted thither so many social atoms which there fit into their places, but which with us would clog the wheels, that the words and habits and social carriage of an American woman of the best class too often offend the taste of an Englishman; as do, quite as strongly, those of the Englishwoman offend the American. There are those who declare that there are no American ladies; — but these are people who would probably declare the same of the French and the Italians if the languages of France and Italy were as familiar to their ears, as is the language of the States. They mean that American women do not grow up to be English ladies — not bethinking themselves that such a growth was hardly to be expected. Now, I will tell my story and ask my readers to answer this question: Was Miss Ophelia Gledd a lady?

When I knew her she was at any rate great in the society of Boston, Massachusetts, in which city she had been as well known for the last four or five years as the yellow dome of the State House. She was as pure and perfect a specimen of a Yankee girl as ever it was my fortune to know. Standing about five feet eight, she seemed to be very tall because she always carried herself at her full height. She was thin, too, and rather narrower at the shoulders than the strictest rules of symmetry would have made her. Her waist was very slight, — so much so that to the eye it would seem that some bond of obligation had enforced its slender compass; but I have fair ground for stating my belief that no such bond of obligation had existed. But yet, though she was slight and thin, and even narrow, there was a vivacity and quickness about all her movements, and an aptitude in her mode of moving, which made it impossible to deny to her the merit of a pleasing figure. No man would, I think, at first sight declare her to be pretty, — and certainly no woman would do so; and yet I have seldom known a face in the close presence of which it was more gratifying to sit and talk and listen. Her brown hair was always brushed close off from her forehead. Her brow was high, and her face narrow and thin; but that face was ever bright with motion, and her clear, deep, grey eyes, full of life and light, were always ready for some combat or some enterprise. Her nose and mouth were the best features in her face, and her teeth were perfect, — miracles of perfection; but her lips were too thin for feminine beauty; and indeed such personal charms as she had were not the charms which men love most, — sweet changing colour, soft, full, flowing lines of grace, and womanly gentleness in every movement. Ophelia Gledd had none of these. She was hard and sharp in shape, of a good brown steady colour, hard and sharp also in her gait; with no full flowing lines, with no softness; — but she was bright as burnished steel.

And yet she was the belle of Boston. I do now know that any man of Boston, or stranger knowing Boston, would have ever declared that she was the prettiest girl in the city; but this was certain almost to all, — that she received more of that admiration which is generally given to beauty than did any other lady there; and that the upper social world of Boston had become so used to her appearance, such as it was, that no one ever seemed to question the fact of her being a beauty. She had been passed as a beauty by examiners whose certificate in that matter was held to be good, and had received high rank as a beauty in the drawing-rooms at Boston. The fact was never questioned now, unless by some passing stranger who would be told in flat terms that he was wrong. "Yes, Sir; you'll find you're wrong. You'll find you are, if you'll bide here awhile." I did bide there awhile, and did find I was wrong. Before I left I was prepared to allow that Miss Ophelia Gledd was a beauty. And moreover, which was more singular, all the women allowed it. Ophelia Gledd, though the belle of Boston, was not hated by the other belles. The female feeling with regard to her was, I think, this; — that the time had arrived in which she should choose her husband, and settle down, so as to leave room for others less attractive than herself.

When I knew her she was very fond of men's society; but I doubt if anyone could fairly say that Miss Gledd ever flirted. In the proper sense of the word she certainly never flirted. Interesting conversations with interesting young men, at which none but themselves were present, she had by the dozen. It was as common for her to walk up and down Beacon Street, — the parade of Boston, — with young Jones or Smith, or more probably with young Mr. Optimus M. Opie, or young Mr. Hannibal H. Hoskins, as it is for our young Joneses and young Smiths and young Hoskinses to saunter out together. That is the way of the country, and no one took wider advantage of the ways of her own country than did Miss Ophelia Gledd. She told young men also when to call upon her, — if she liked them; and in seeking or in avoiding their society, did very much as she pleased. But these practices are right or wrong, not in accordance with a fixed rule of morality prevailing over all the earth, — such a rule, for instance, as that which orders men not to steal; but they are right or wrong according to the usages of the country in which they are practised. In Boston it is right that Miss Ophelia Gledd should walk up Beacon Street with Hannibal Hoskins the morning after she has met him at a ball, and that she should invite him to call upon her at twelve o'clock on the following day.

She had certainly a nasal twang in speaking. Before my intercourse with her was over her voice had become pleasant in my ears, and it may be that that nasal twang which had at first been so detestable to me, had recommended itself to my sense of hearing. At different periods of my life I have learned to love an Irish brogue, and a Northern burr. Be that as it may, I must acknowledge that Miss Ophelia Gledd spoke with a certain nasal twang. But then such is the manner of speech at Boston; and she only did that which the Joneses and Smiths, the Opies and Hoskinses were doing around her.

Ophelia Gledd's mother was, for a living being, the nearest thing to a nonentity that I ever met. Whether within her own house in Chestnut Street she exercised herself in her domestic duties and held authority over her maidens, I cannot say, but neither in her dining parlour nor in her drawing room did she hold any authority. Indeed, throughout the house Ophelia was paramount, and it seemed as though her mother could not venture on a hint in opposition to her daughter's behests. Mrs. Gledd never went out, but her daughter frequented all balls, dinners, and assemblies which she chose to honour. To all these she went alone, and had done ever since she was eighteen years of age. She went also to lectures, to meetings of wise men for which the western Athens is much noted, to political debates, and wherever her enterprising heart and inquiring head chose to carry her. But her mother never went anywhere, and it always seemed to me that Mrs. Gledd's intercourse with her domestics must have been nearer, closer, and almost dearer to her, than any that she could have with her daughter.

Mr. Gledd had been a merchant all his life. When Ophelia Gledd first came before the Boston world he had been a rich merchant, and as she was an only child she had opened her campaign with all the advantages which attach to an heiress. But now, in these days, Mr. Gledd was known to be a merchant without riches. He still kept the same house, and lived apparently as he had always lived; but the world knew that he had been a broken merchant and was now again struggling. That Miss Gledd felt the disadvantage of this no one can, I suppose, doubt. But she never showed that she felt it. She spoke openly of her father's poverty as of a thing that was known, — and of her own. Where she had been *exigéante* before, she was *exigéante* now. Those she disliked when rich, she disliked now that she was poor. Where she had been patronising before, she patronised now. Where she had loved, she still loved. In former days she had a carriage, and now she had none. Where she had worn silk, she now wore cotton. In her gloves, her laces, her little belongings there was all the difference which money makes or the want of money; — but in her manner there was none. Nor was there any difference in the manner of others to her. The loss of wealth seemed to entail on Miss Gledd no other discomfort than the actual want of those things which hard money buys. To go in a coach might have been a luxury to her, and that she had lost; — but she had lost none of her ascendancy, none of her position, none of her sovereignty.

I remember well where, when and how I first met Miss Gledd. At that time her father's fortune was probably already gone; but, if so, she did not then know that it was gone. It was in winter, — towards the end of winter, when the passion for sleighing becomes ecstatic. I expect all my readers to know that sleighing is the grand winter amusement of Boston. And indeed it is not bad fun. There is the fashionable course for sleighing, — the Brighton road, and along that you drive, seated among furs, with a young lady beside you if you can get one to trust you; your horse or horses carry little bells which add to the charm; the motion is rapid and pleasant; and — which is the great thing — you see and are seen by everybody. Of course it is expedient that the frost should be sound and perfect, so that the sleigh should run over a dry smooth surface. But as the season draws to an end, and when sleighing intimacies have become close and warm, the horses are made to travel through slush and wet, and the scene becomes one of peril and discomfort, — though one also of excitement and not unfrequently of love.

Sleighing was fairly over at the time of which I now speak, so that the Brighton road was deserted in its slush and sloppiness. Nevertheless there was a possibility of sleighing, and as I was a stranger newly arrived a young friend of mine took me—or rather allowed me to take him—out, so that the glory of the charioteer might be mine. "I guess we're not alone," said he, after we'd passed the bridge out of the town. "There's young Hoskins with Pheely Gledd just ahead of us." That was the first I had ever heard of Ophelia, and then as I jingled along after her, instigated by a foolish Briton's ambition to pass the Yankee whip, I did hear a good deal about her; and in addition to what has been already told I then heard that this Mr. Hannibal Hoskins, to pass whom on the road was now my only earthly desire, was Miss Gledd's professed admirer; — in point of fact, that it was known to all Boston that he had offered his hand to her more than once already. "She has accepted him now, at any rate," said I, looking at their close contiguity on the sleigh before me. But my friend explained to me that such was by no means probable;—that Miss Gledd had twenty hangers-on of the same description, with any one of whom she might be seen sleighing, walking, or dancing, but that no argument as to any further purport on her part was to be deduced from any such practice. "Our girls," said my friend, "don't go about tied to their mothers' aprons, as yours do in the old country. Our free institutions—&c. &c. &c." I confessed my blunder, and acknowledged that a wide and perhaps salutary latitude was allowed to the feminine creation on his side of the Atlantic.

But, do what I would, I could not pass Hannibal Hoskins. Whether he guessed that I was an ambitious Englishman, or whether he had a general dislike to be passed on the road, I don't know; but he raised his whip to his horses and went away from me suddenly and very quickly through the slush. The snow was half gone, and hard ridges of it remained across the road, so that his sleigh was bumped about most uncomfortably. I soon saw that his horses were running away, and that Hannibal Hoskins was in a fix. He was standing up, pulling at them with all his strength and weight, and the carriage was yawing about and across the road in a manner that made me fear it would go to pieces. Miss

Ophelia Gledd, however, kept her seat, and there was no shrieking.

In about five minutes they were well planted into a ditch, and we were alongside of them. "You've fixed that pretty straight, Hoskins," said my friend. "Darn them for horses!" said Hoskins, as he wiped the perspiration from his brow and looked down upon the fiercest of his quadrupeds sprawling up to his withers in the snow. Then he turned to Miss Gledd, who was endeavouring to unroll herself from her furs. "Oh, Miss Gledd, I *am* so sorry. What *am* I to say?" "You'd better say that the horses ran away, I think," said Miss Gledd. Then she stepped carefully out on to a buffalo robe, and moved across from that, quite dry-footed, on to our sleigh.

As my friend and Hoskins were very intimate, and could as I thought get on very well by themselves with the débris in the ditch, I offered to drive Miss Gledd back to town. She looked at me with eyes which gave me, as I thought, no peculiar thanks, and then remarked that she had come out with Mr. Hoskins, and that she would go back with him. "Oh, don't mind me," said Hoskins, who was at that time up to his middle in snow. "Ah, but I do mind you," said Ophelia. "Don't you think we could go back and send some people to help these gentlemen?" It was the coolest proposition that I had ever heard, but in two minutes Miss Gledd was putting it into execution. Hannibal Hoskins was driving her back in the sleigh which I had hired, and I was left with my friend to extricate those other two brutes from the ditch. "That's so like Pheely Gledd," said my friend. "She always has her own way." Then it was that I questioned Miss Gledd's beauty, and was told that before long I should find myself to be wrong. I had almost acknowledged myself to be wrong before that night was over.

I was at a tea-party that same evening at which Miss Gledd was present; it was called a tea-party, though I saw no tea. I did, however, see a large hot supper, and a very large assortment of long-necked bottles. I was standing rather listlessly near the door, being short of acquaintance, when a young Yankee dandy with a very stiff neck informed me that Miss Gledd wanted to speak to me. Having given me the intimation, he took himself off, with an air of disgust, among the long-necked bottles. "Mr. Green," she said, — I had just been introduced to her as she was being whisked away by Hoskins in my sleigh, — "Mr. Green, I believe I owe you an apology. When I took your sleigh from you, I didn't know you were a Britisher; I didn't indeed." I was a little nettled, and endeavoured to explain to her that an Englishman would be just as ready to give up his carriage to a lady as any American. "Oh dear, yes; of course," she said. "I didn't mean that; and now I've put my foot into it worse than ever. I thought you were at home here, and knew our ways, and if so you wouldn't mind being left with a broken sleigh." I told her that I didn't mind it. That what I had minded was the being robbed of the privilege of driving her home, which I had thought to be justly mine. "Yes," she said. "And I was to leave my friend in the ditch! That's what I never do. You didn't suffer any disgrace by remaining there till the men came."

"I didn't remain there till any men came. I got it out and drove it home."

"What a wonderful man! But then you're English. However, you can understand that if I had left my driver he would have been disgraced. If ever I go out anywhere with you, Mr. Green, I'll come home with you. At any rate, it shan't be my fault if I don't." After that I couldn't be angry with her, and so we became great friends.

Shortly afterwards the crash came, but Miss Gledd seemed to disregard the crash altogether, and held her own in Boston. As far as I could see there were just as many men desirous of marrying her as ever, and among the number Hannibal H. Hoskins was certainly no defaulter. My acquaintance with Boston had become intimate; but, after a while, I went away for twelve months, and when I returned Miss Gledd was still Miss Gledd. "And what of Hoskins?" I said to my friend, — the same friend who had been with me on the sleighing expedition. "He's just on the old tack. I believe he proposes once a year regularly. But they say now that she's going to marry an Englishman."

It was not long before I had an opportunity of renewing my friendship with Miss Gledd, for our acquaintance had latterly amounted to a friendship, and of seeing the Englishman with her. As it happened, he also was a friend of my own, an old friend, and the last man in the world whom I should have picked out as a husband for Ophelia. He was a literary man of some mark, fifteen years her senior, very sedate in his habits, nor much given to love-making, and possessed of a small fortune sufficient for his own wants, but not sufficient to enable him to marry with what he would consider comfort. Such was Mr. Pryor, and I was given to understand that Mr. Pryor was a suppliant at the feet of Ophelia. He was a suppliant, too, with so much hope that Hannibal Hoskins and the other suitors were up in arms against him.

I saw them together at some evening assembly, and on the next morning I chanced to be in Miss Gledd's drawing-room. On my entrance there were others there, but the first moment that we were alone, she turned round sharp upon me with a question. "You know your countryman, Mr. Pryor; — what sort of a man is he?"

"But you know him also," I answered. "If the rumours in Boston are true, he is already a favourite in Chestnut Street."

"Well, then; for once in a way the rumours in Boston are true, for he is a favourite. But that is no reason you shouldn't tell me what sort of a man he is. You've known him these ten years."

"Pretty nearly twenty," I said. I had known him ten or twelve.

"Ah,' said she, "you want to make him out to be older than he is. I know his age to a day."

"And does he know yours?"

"He may if he wishes it. Everybody in Boston knows it, — including yourself. Now tell me what sort of man is Mr. Pryor?"

"He is a man highly esteemed in his own country."

"So much I knew before; and he is highly esteemed here also. But I hardly understand what high estimation means in your country."

"It is much the same thing in all countries, as I take it," said I.

"There you are absolutely wrong. Here, in the States, if a man be highly esteemed it amounts almost to everything. Such estimation will cary him everywhere, and will carry his wife everywhere too, so as to give her a chance of making standing ground for herself."

"But Mr. Pryor has not got a wife."

"Don't be stupid; of course he hasn't got a wife, and of course you know what I mean."

But I did not know what she meant. I knew that she was meditating whether or not it would be good for her to become Mrs.
Pryor, and that she was endeavouring to get from me some information which might assist her in coming to a decision on that
matter; but I did not understand the exact gist and point of her
inquiry.

"You have so many prejudices of which we know nothing!" she
continued. "Now don't put your back up and fight for that
blessed old country of yours, as though I were attacking it."

"It is a blessed old country," said I, patriotically.

"Quite so; — very blessed and very old, — and very nice too,
I'm sure. But you must admit that you have prejudices. You are
very much the better, perhaps, for having them. I often wish that
we had a few." Then she stopped her tongue, and asked no further
questions about Mr. Pryor; but it seemed to me that she wanted
me to go on with the conversation.

"I hate discussing the relative merits of the two countries," said
I, "and I especially hate to discuss them with you. You always
begin as though you meant to be fair, and end by an amount of
unfairness — that — that —"

"Which would be insolent if I were not a woman, and which
is pert as I am one. That is what you mean."

"Something like it."

"And yet I love your country so dearly, that I would sooner live
there than in any other land in the world, — if I only thought
that I could be accepted. You English people," she continued,
"are certainly wanting in intelligence, or you would read, in the
anxiety of all we say about England, how much we all think of
you. What will England say of us? — what will England think of
us? — what will England do in this or that matter as it concerns
us? — that is our first thought as to every matter that is of importance to us. We abuse you, and admire you. You abuse us, and
despise us. That is the difference. So you won't tell me anything
about Mr. Pryor? Well, I shan't ask you again! — I never again
ask a favour that has been refused." Then she turned away to some
old gentleman that was talking to her mother, and the conversation was at an end.

I must confess that as I walked away from Chestnut Street into
Beacon Street, and across the Common, my anxiety was more

keen with regard to Mr. Pryor than as concerned Miss Gledd. He was an Englishman and an old friend, and being also a man not much younger than myself, he was one regarding whom I might, perhaps, form some correct judgment as to what would or would not suit him. Would he do well in taking Ophelia Gledd home to England with him as his wife? Would she be accepted there, as she herself phrased it, — accepted in such fashion as to make him contented? She was intelligent, — so intelligent that few women whom she would meet in her proposed new country could beat her there; — she was pleasant, good humoured, and true, as I believed; — but would she be accepted in London? There was a freedom and easiness about her, — a readiness to say anything that came into her mind — an absence of all reticence, which would go very hard with her in London. But I had never heard her say anything that she should not have said. Perhaps, after all, we have got our prejudices in England.

When next I met Pryor I spoke to him about Miss Gledd. "The long and the short of it is," I said, "that people say that you are going to marry her."

"What sort of people?"

"They were backing you against Hannibal Hoskins the other night at the club, and it seemed clear that you were the favourite."

"The vulgarity of these people surpasses anything that I ever dreamed of," said Pryor. "That is, of some of them. It's all very well for you to talk, but would such a bet as that be proposed in the open room of any club in London?"

"The clubs in London are too big; but I daresay it might, down in the country. It would be just the thing for Little Pedlington."

"But Boston is not Little Pedlington. Boston assumes to be the Athens of the States. I shall go home by the first boat next month." He had said nothing to me about Miss Gledd; but it was clear that if he went home by the first boat next month he would go home without a wife; and as I certainly thought that the suggested marriage was undesirable, I said nothing then to persuade him to remain at Boston.

It was again sleighing time, and some few days after my meeting with Pryor I was out upon the Brighton road in the thick of the crowd. Presently I saw the hat and back of Hannibal Hoskins,

211

and by his side was Ophelia Gledd. Now, it must be understood that Hannibal Hoskins, though he was in many respects most unlike an English gentleman, was neither a fool nor a bad fellow. A fool he certainly was not. He had read much. He could speak glibly, — as is the case with all Americans. He was scientific, classical, and poetical, — probably not to any great depth. And he knew how to earn a large income with the full approbation of his fellow-citizens. I had always hated him since the day on which he had driven Miss Gledd home, but I had generally attributed my hatred to the manner in which he wore his hat on one side. I confess I had often felt amazed that Miss Gledd should have so far encouraged him. I think I may at any rate declare that he would not have been accepted in London, — not accepted for much! And yet Hannibal Hoskins was not a bad fellow. His true devotion to Ophelia Gledd proved that.

"Miss Gledd," said I, speaking to her from my sleigh, "do you remember your calamity? There is the very ditch, not a hundred yards ahead of you."

"And here is the very knight that took me home in your sleigh," said she, laughing. Hoskins sat bolt upright and took off his hat. Why he took off his hat I don't know, unless that thereby he got an opportunity to putting it on again a little more on one side.

"Mr. Hoskins would not have the goodness to upset you again, I suppose?" said I.

"No, Sir," said Hoskins; and he raised the reins and squared up his elbows, meaning to look like a knowing charioteer. "I guess we'll go back; — eh, Miss Gledd?"

"I guess we will," said she. "But, Mr. Green, don't you remember that I once told you, if you'd take me out, I'd be sure to come home with you? You've never tried me, and I take it bad of you." So encouraged I made an engagement with her, and in two or three days' time from that I had her beside me in my sleigh on the same road.

By this time I had quite become a convert to the general opinion, and was ready to confess in any presence that Miss Gledd was a beauty. As I started with her out of the city warmly enveloped in buffalo furs, I could not but think how nice it would be to drive on, and on, so that nobody should ever catch us. There was a sense of companionship about her in which no woman that I have ever known excelled her. She had a way of adapting herself to the friend of the moment which was beyond anything winning. Her voice was decidedly very pleasant; — and as to that nasal twang I am not sure that I was ever right about it. I wasn't in love with her myself, and didn't want to fall in love with her. But I felt that I should have liked to cross the Rocky Mountains with her, over to the Pacific, and to have come home round by California, Peru, and the Pampas. And for such a journey I should not at all have desired to hamper the party with the society either of Hannibal Hoskins or of Mr. Pryor!

"I hope you feel that you're having your revenge," said she.

"But I don't mean to upset you."

"I almost wish you would, — so as to make it even. And my poor friend Mr. Hoskins would feel himself so satisfied. He says you Englishmen are conceited about your driving."

"No doubt he thinks we are conceited about everything."

"So you are, and so you should be. Poor Hannibal! He is wild with despair, because, —"

"Because what?"

"Oh never mind. He is an excellent fellow,, but I know you hate him."

"Indeed I don't."

"Yes, you do and so does Mr. Pryor. But he is so good! You can't either understand or appreciate the kind of goodness which our young men have. Because he pulls his hat about, and can't wear his gloves without looking stiff, you won't remember that out of his hard earnings he gives his mother and sisters everything that they want."

"I didn't know anything of his mother and sisters."

"No, of course you didn't. But you knew a great deal about his hat and gloves. You are too hard and polished and well mannered in England to know anything about anybody's mother or sisters, — or indeed to know anything about anybody's anything. It is nothing to you whether a man be moral or affectionate, or industrious, or good tempered. As long as he can wear his hat properly, and speak as though nothing on the earth, or over the earth, or under the earth, could ever move him, — that is sufficient."

"And yet I thought you were so fond of England?"

"So I am. I too like, — nay love that ease of manner which you all possess and which I cannot reach."

There was a silence between us, for perhaps half a mile; and yet I was driving slow, as I did not wish to bring our journey to an end. I had fully made up my mind that it would be in every way better for my friend Pryor that he should give up all thoughts of this Western Aspasia, and yet I was anxious to talk to her about him as though such a marriage were still on the cards. It had seemed lately that she had thrown herself much into an intimacy with myself, and that she was anxious to speak openly to me if I would only allow it. But she had already declared, on a former occasion, that she would ask no further questions about Mr. Pryor. At last I plucked up courage, and put to her a direct proposition about the future tenor of her life.

"After all that you have said about Mr. Hoskins, I suppose I may expect to hear that you have at last accepted him?"

I could not have asked such a question of any English girl that I ever knew — not even of my own sister in those plain terms. And yet she took it not only without anger, but even without surprise. And she answered it as though I had asked her the most ordinary question in the world. "I wish I had," she said. "That is, I think I wish I had. It is certainly what I ought to do."

"Then why do you not do it?"

"Ah; why do I not? Why do we not all do just what we ought to do. But why am I to be cross-questioned by you? You would not answer me a question when I asked you the other day."

"You tell me that you wish you had accepted Mr. Hoskins. Why do you not do so?" said I, continuing my cross-examination.

"Because I have a vain ambition; a foolish ambition, a silly mothlike ambition, by which, if I indulge it, I shall only burn my wings. Because I am such an utter ass that I would fain make myself an Englishwoman."

"I don't see that you need burn your wings."

"Yes! Should I go there I shall find myself to be nobody, whereas here I am in good repute. Here I could make my husband a man of mark by dint of my own power. There I doubt whether even his esteem would so shield and cover me, as to make me endurable. Do you think that I do not know the difference; that I am not aware of what makes social excellence there? And yet, though I know it all, and covet it, I despise it. Social distinction with us is given on sounder terms than it is with you, and is more frequently the deserved reward of merit. Tell me; if I go to London will they ask who was my grandfather?"

"Indeed no; they will not ask even of your father, unless you speak of him."

"No; their manners are too good. But they will speak of their fathers, and how shall I talk with them? Not but what my grandfather was a good man; and you are not to suppose that I am ashamed of him because he stood in a store and sold leather with his own hand. Or rather I am ashamed of it. I should tell his old friends and my new acquaintances that it was so, because I am not a coward; and yet as I told them I should be ashamed. His brother is what you call a baronet."

"Just so."

"And what would the baronet's wife say to me with all my sharp Boston notions? Can't you see her looking at me over the length of her drawing room? And can't you fancy how pert I should be, and what snappish words I should say to the she baronet? Upon the whole, don't you think I should do better with Mr. Hoskins?"

Again I sat silent for some time. She had now asked me a question to which I was bound to give her a true answer—an answer that should be true as to herself without reference to Pryor. She was sitting back in the sleigh, tamed as it were by her own thoughts, and she had looked at me as though she really wanted council. "If I am to answer you in truth," I said.

"You are to answer me in truth."

"Then," said I, "I can only bid you take him of the two whom you love;—that is, if it be the case that you love either."

"Love!" she said.

"And if it be the case," I continued, "that you love neither, —then leave them both as they are."

"I am not then to think of the man's happiness."

"Certainly not by marrying him without affection."

"Ah;—but I may reject him,—with affection."

"And for which of them do you feel affection?" I asked;—and as I asked, we were already within the streets of Boston. She again remained silent, almost till I placed her at her own door;

—then she looked at me with eyes full, not only of meaning, but of love also; — with that in her eyes for which I had not hitherto given her credit. "You know the two men," she said, "and do you ask me that?" When these words were spoken she jumped from the sleigh and hurried up the steps to her father's door. In very truth the hat and gloves of Hannibal Hoskins had influenced her as they had influenced me, — and they had done so, although she knew how devoted he was as a son and a brother.

For a full month after that I had no further conversation either with Miss Gledd or with Mr. Pryor on the subject. At this time I was living in habits of daily intimacy with Pryor, but as he did not speak to me about Ophelia, I did not often mention her name to him. I was aware that he was often with her, — or at any rate often in her company. But I did not believe that he had any daily habit of going to the house, as he would have done had he been her accepted suitor. And indeed I believed him to be a man who would be very persevering in offering his love, but who, if persistently refused, would not probably tender it again. He still talked of returning to England, though he had fixed no day. I myself proposed doing so early in May, and used such influence as I had in endeavouring to keep him at Boston till that time. Miss Gledd also I constantly saw. Indeed, one could not live in the society of Boston without seeing her almost daily, and I was aware that Mr. Hoskins was frequently with her. But as regarded her, this betokened nothing, as I have before endeavoured to explain. She never deserted a friend, and had no idea of being reserved in her manners with a man because it was reported that such man was her lover. She would be very gracious to Hannibal in Mr. Pryor's presence; and yet it was evident, at any rate to me, that in doing so she had no thought of piquing her English admirer.

I was one day seated in my room at the hotel when a servant brought me up a card. "Misther Hoskins; — he's a waiting below and wants to see yer honour very partickler," said the raw Irishman. Mr. Hoskins had never done me the honour of calling on me before, nor had I ever become intimate with him, even at the club; but, nevertheless, as he had come to me, of course I was willing to see him, and so he was shown up into my room. When he entered, his hat was, I suppose, in his hand; but it looked as though it had been on one side of his head the moment before, and as though it would be one one side again the moment he left me.

"I beg your pardon, Mr. Green," said he. "Perhaps I ought not to intrude upon you here."

"No intrusion at all. Won't you take a chair and put your hat down?" He did take a chair, but he wouldn't put his hat down. I confess that I had been actuated by a foolish desire to see it placed for a few minutes in a properly perpendicular position.

"I've just come, — I'll tell you why I've come. There are some things, Mr. Green, in which a man doesn't like to be interfered with." I could not but agree with this, but, in doing so, I expressed a hope that Mr. Hoskins had not been interfered with to any very disagreeable extent.

"Well!" — I scorn to say that the Boston dandy said "wa'all," but if this story were written by any Englishman less conscientious than myself, the latter form of letters is the one which he would adopt in his endeavour to convey the sound as uttered by Mr. Hoskins. "Well; I don't quite know about that. Now, Mr. Green, I'm not a quarrelsome man. I don't go about with six-shooters in my pockets, and I don't want to fight, no how, if I can help it." In answer to this I was obliged to tell him that I sincerely hoped that he would not have a fight; but that if fighting became necessary to him, I trusted that his fighting propensities would not be directed against any friend of mine. "We don't do much in that way on our side of the water," said I.

"I am well aware of that," said he. "I don't want any one to teach me what are usages of genteel life in England. I was there the whole fall, two years ago."

"As regards myself," said I, "I don't think much good was ever done by duelling."?

"That depends, Sir, on how things eventuate. But, Mr. Green, satisfaction of that description is not what I desiderate on the present occasion. I wish to know whether Mr. Pryor is or is not engaged to marry Miss Ophelia Gledd."

"If he is, Mr. Hoskins, I don't know it."

"But, Sir, you are his friend."

This I admitted; but again assured Mr. Hoskins that I knew nothing of any such engagement. He pleaded also that I was her friend as well as his. This too I admitted, but again declared that from neither side had I been made aware of the fact of any such engagement.

"Then, Mr. Green," said he, "may I ask you for your own private opinion?" Upon the whole I was inclined to think that he might not, and so I told him in what most courteous words I could find for the occasion. His back at first grew very long and stiff, and his hat became more and still more sloped as he held it. I began to fear that, though he might not have a six-shooter in his pocket, he had nevertheless some kind of pistol in his thoughts. At last he started up on his feet and confronted me, as I thought, with a look of great anger. But his words, when they came, were no longer angry. "Mr. Green," said he, "if you knew all that I've done to get that girl!" My heart was instantly softened to him. "For aught that I know," said I, "you may have her this moment for asking." "No," said he; "no." His voice was very melancholy, and as he spoke he looked into his sloping hat. "No. I've just come from Chestnut Street, and I think she's rather more turned against me than ever."

He was a tall man, good looking after a fashion, with thick black shining hair, and a huge bold moustache. I myself do not like his style of appearance, but he certainly had a manly bearing. And in the society of Boston generally he was regarded as a stout fellow, well able to hold his own, — as a man by no means soft, or green, or feminine. And yet now, in the presence of me, a stranger to him, he was almost crying about his lady love. In England no man tells another that he has been rejected; but then, in England, so few men tell to others anything of their real feeling. As Ophelia had said to me, we are hard and polished, and nobody knows anything about anybody's anything. What could I say to him? I did say something. I went so far as to assure him that I had heard Miss Gledd speak of him in the highest language; and at last, perhaps, I hinted, — though I don't think I did quite hint it, — that if Pryor were out of the way, Hoskins might find the lady more kind.

He soon became quite confidential, as though I were his bosom friend. He perceived, I think, that I was not anxious that Pryor should carry off the prize, and he wished me to teach Pryor that the prize was not such a prize as would suit him. "She's the very girl for Boston," he said in his energy; "but I put it to you, Mr. Green; she hasn't the gait of going that would suit London." Whether her gait of going would or would not suit our metropolis I did not undertake to say in the presence of Mr. Hoskins, but I did at last say that I would speak to Pryor, so that the field might be left open for others, if he had no intention of running for the cup himself.

I could not but be taken, and indeed charmed, by the honest strength of affection which Hannibal Hoskins felt for the object of his adoration. He had come into my room determined to display himself as a man of will, of courage, and of fashion. But he had broken down in all that under his extreme desire to obtain assistance in getting the one thing which he wanted. When he parted with me he shook hands with me almost boisterously, while he offered me most exuberant thanks. And yet I had not suggested that I could do anything for him. I did think that Ophelia Gledd would accept his offer as soon as Pryor was gone; but I had not told him that I thought so.

About two days afterwards I had a very long and a very serious conservation with Pryor, and at that time I do not think that he had made up his mind as to what he intended to do. He was the very opposite of Hoskins in all his ways and all his moods. There was not only no swagger with him, but a propriety and quiescence of demeanour the very opposite to swagger. In conversation his most violent opposition was conveyed by a smile. He displayed no other energy than what might be shown in the slight curl of his upper lip. If he reproved you he did it by silence. There could be no greater contrast than that between him and Hoskins, and there could be no doubt which man would recommend himself most to our English world by his gait and demeanour. But I think there may be a doubt as to which was the best man, and a doubt also as to which would make the best husband. That my friend was not then engaged to Miss Gledd I did learn; but I learned nothing further, — except this, that he would take his departure with me the first week in May, unless anything special should occur to keep him in Boston.

It was some time early in April that I got a note from Miss Gledd, asking me to call on her. "Come at once," she said, "as I want your advice above all things," and she signed herself, "In all truth, yours, O. G." I had had many notes from her, but none written in this strain; and therefore, feeling that there was some circumstance to justify such instant motion, I got up and went to her then, at ten o'clock in the morning.

She jumped up to meet me, giving me both her hands. "Oh! Mr. Green," she said, "I am so glad you have come to me. It is all over."

"What is over?" said I.

"My chance of escape from the she baronet. I gave in last night. Pray tell me that I was right. And yet I want you to tell me the truth. And yet, above all things, you must not tell me that I have been wrong."

"Then you have accepted Mr. Pryor."

"I could not help it," she said. "The temptation was too much for me. I love the very cut of his coat, the turn of his lip, the tone of his voice. The very sound which he makes as he closes the door behind him is too much for me. I believe that I ought to have let him go, but I could not do it."

"And what will Mr. Hoskins do?"

"I wrote to him immediately, and told him everything; of course I had John's leave for doing so." This calling of my sedate friend by the name of John was, to my feeling, a most wonderful breaking down of all proprieties! "I told him the exact truth. This morning I got an answer from him, saying that he should visit Russia. I am so sorry, because of his mothers and sisters."

"And when is it to be?"

"Oh! at once; immediately. So John says. When we resolve on doing these things here, on taking the plunge we never stand shilly-shallying on the brink, as your girls do in England. And that is one reason why I have sent for you. You must promise to go over with us. Do you know, I am half afraid of him, — much more afraid of him that I am of you."

They were to be married very early in May, and of course I promised to put off my return for a week or two to suit them. "And then for the she baronet," she said, "and for all the terrible grandeur of London!" When I endeavoured to explain to her that she would encounter no great grandeur, she very quickly corrected me. "It is not grandeur of that sort, but the grandeur of coldness that I mean; — I fear that I shall not do for them. But,

Mr. Green, I must tell you one thing, I have not cut off from myself all means of retreat."

"Why; what do you mean? You have resolved to marry him."

"Yes, I have promised to do so; but I did not promise till he had said that if I could not be made to suit his people in Old England, he would return here with me, and teach himself to suit my people in New England. The task will be very much easier."

They were married in Boston, not without some considerable splendour of ceremony, — as far as the splendour of Boston went. She was so universal a favourite that every one wished to be at her wedding, and she had no idea of giving herself airs and denying her friends a favour. She was married with much *éclât*, and, as far as I could judge, seemed to enjoy the marriage herself.

Now comes the question: Will she, or will she not, be received in London as a lady, — as such a lady as my friend Pryor might have been expected to take for his wife?

"Miss Ophelia Gledd" appeared first in A *Welcome* (London: Emily Faithfull and Company, 1863).

The Lady of Launay

H

Chapter I

OW GREAT IS THE DIFFERENCE between
doing our duty and desiring to do it; between doing our duty and
a conscientious struggle to do it; between duty really done and
that satisfactory state of mind which comes from a conviction
that it has been performed. Mrs. Miles was a lady who through
her whole life had thought of little else than duty. Though she
was possessed of wealth and social position, though she had been
a beautiful woman, though all phases of self-indulgent life had
been open to her, she had always adhered to her own idea of duty.
Many delights had tempted her. She would fain have travelled,
so as to see the loveliness of the world; but she had always
remained at home. She could have enjoyed the society of the
intelligent sojourners in capitals; but she had confined herself to
that of her country neighbours. In early youth she had felt herself
to be influenced by a taste for dress; she consequently compelled
herself to use raiment of extreme simplicity. She would buy no
pictures, no gems, no china, because when young she found that
she liked such things too well. She would not leave the parish
church to hear a good sermon elsewhere, because even a sermon
might be a snare. In the early days of her widowed life it became,
she thought, her duty to adopt one of two little motherless, fatherless girls, who had been left altogether unprovided for in the
world; and having the choice between the two, she took the
plain one, who had weak eyes and a downcast, unhappy look,
because it was her duty to deny herself. It was not her fault that

the child, who was so unattractive at six, had become beautiful at sixteen, with sweet soft eyes, still downcast occasionally, as though ashamed of their own loveliness; nor was it her fault that Bessy Pryor had so ministered to her in her advancing years as almost to force upon her the delights of self-indulgence. Mrs. Miles had struggled manfully against these wiles, and, in the performance of her duty, had fought with them, even to an attempt to make herself generally disagreeable to the young child. The child, however, had conquered, having wound herself into the old woman's heart of hearts. When Bessy at fifteen was like to die Mrs. Miles for a while broke down altogether. She lingered by the bedside, caressed the thin hands, stroked the soft locks, and prayed to the Lord to stay his hand, and to alter his purpose. But when Bessie was strong again she strove to return to her wonted duties. But Bessy, through it all, was quite aware that she was loved.

Looking back at her own past life, and looking also at her days as they were passing, Mrs. Miles thought that she did her duty as well as it is given to frail man or frail women to perform it. There had been lapses, but still she was conscious of great strength. She did believe of herself that should a great temptation come in her way she would stand strong against it. A great temptation did come in her way, and it is the purport of this little story to tell how far she stood and how far she fell.

Something must be communicated to the reader of her condition in life, and of Bessy's; something, but not much. Mrs. Miles had been a Miss Launay, and, by the death of four brothers almost in their infancy, had become heiress to a large property in Somersetshire. At twenty-five she was married to Mr. Miles, who had a property of his own in the next county, and who at the time of their marraige represented that county in Parliament. When she had been married a dozen years she was left a widow, with two sons, the younger of whom was then about three years old. Her own property, which was much the larger of the two, was absolutely her own; but was intended for Philip, who was her younger boy. Frank Miles, who was ten years older, inherited the other. Circumstances took him much away from his mother's wings. There were troubles among trustees and executors; and the father's heir, after he came of age, saw but little of his mother.

She did her duty, but what she suffered in doing it may be imagined.

Philip was brought up by his mother, who, perhaps, had some consolation in remembering that the younger boy, who was always good to her, would become a man of a higher standing in the world than his brother. He was called Philip Launay, the family name having passed on through the mother to the intended heir of the Launay property. He was fifteen when Bessy Pryor was brought home to Launay Park, and, as a school-boy, had been good to the poor little creature, who for the first year or two had hardly dared to think her life her own amidst the strange, huge spaces of the great house. He had despised her, of course; but had not been boyishly cruel to her, and had given her his old play-things. Everybody at Launay had at first despised Bessy Pryor; though the mistress of the house had been thoroughly good to her. There was no real link between her and Launay. Mrs. Pryor had, as a humble friend, been under great obligations to Mrs. Launay, and these obligations, as is their wont, had produced deep love in the heart of the person conferring them. Then both Mr. and Mrs. Pryor had died, and Mrs. Miles had declared that she would take one of the children. She fully intended to bring the girl up sternly and well, with hard belongings, such as might suit her condition. But there had been lapses, occasioned by those unfortunate female prettinesses, and by that equally unfortunate sickness. Bessy never rebelled, and gave, therefore, no scope to an exhibition of extreme duty; and she had a way of kissing her adopted mamma which Mrs. Miles knew to be dangerous. She struggled not to be kissed, but ineffectually. She preached to herself, in the solitude of her own room, sharp sermons against the sweet softness of the girl's caresses; but she could not put a stop to them. "Yes; I will," the girl would say, so softly, but so persistently! Then there would be a great embrace, which Mrs. Miles felt to be as dangerous as a diamond, as bad as a box at the opera.

Bessy had been despised at first all around Launay. Unattractive children are despised, especially when, as in this case, they are nobodies. Bessy Pryor was quite nobody. And certainly there had never been a child more powerless to assert herself. She was for a year or two inferior to the parson's children, and was not thought much of by the farmers' wives. The servants called her Miss Bessy, of course; but it was not till after that illness that there existed among them any of that reverence which is generally felt in the servants' hall for the young ladies of the house. It was then, too, that the parson's daughters found that Bessy was nice to walk with, and that the tenants began to make much of her when she called. The old lady's secret manifestations in the sick bedroom had, perhaps, been seen. The respect paid to Mrs. Miles in that and the next parish was of the most reverential kind. Had she chosen that a dog should be treated as one of the Launays, the dog would have received all the family honours. It must be acknowledged of her that in the performance of her duty she had become a rural tyrant. She gave away many petticoats; but they all had to be stitched according to her idea of stitching a petticoat. She administered physic gratis to the entire estate; but the estate had to take the doses as she chose to have them mixed. It was because she had fallen something short of her acknowledged duty in regard to Bessy Pryor that the parson's daughters were soon even proud of an intimacy with the girl, and that the old butler, when she once went away for a week in the winter, was so careful to wrap her feet up warm in the carriage.

In this way, during the two years subsequent to Bessy's illness, there had gradually come up an altered condition of life at Launay. It could not have been said before that Bessy, though she had been Miss Bessy, was as a daughter in the house. But now a daughter's privileges were accorded to her. When the old squiress was driven out about the county, Bessy was expected, but was asked, rather than ordered, to accompany her. She always went; but went because she decided on going, not because she was told. And she had a horse to ride; and she was allowed to arrange flowers for the drawing-room; and the gardener did what she told him. What daughter could have more extensive privileges? But poor Mrs. Miles had her misgivings, often asking herself what would come of it all.

When Bessy had been recovering from her illness, Philip, who was seven years her senior, was making a grand tour about the world. He had determined to see, not Paris, Vienna, and Rome, which used to make a grand tour, but Japan, Patagonia, and the South Sea Islands. He had gone in such a way as to ensure the consent of his mother. Two other well-minded young men of fortune had accompanied him, and they had been intent on botany, the social condition of natives, and the progress of the world generally. There had been no harum-scarum rushing about without an object. Philip had been away for more than two years, and had seen all there was to be seen in Japan, Patagonia, and the South Sea Islands. Between them, the young men had written a book, and the critics had been unanimous in observing how improved in those days were the aspirations of young men. On his return he came to Launay for a week or two, and then went up to London. When, after four months, he returned to his mother's house, he was twenty-seven years of age; and Bessy was just twenty. Mrs. Miles knew that there was cause for fear; but she had already taken steps to prevent the danger, which she had foreseen.

Chapter II
How Bessy Pryor Wouldn't Marry the Parson

Of course there would be danger. Mrs. Miles had been aware of that from the commencement of things. There had been to her a sort of pleasure in feeling that she had undertaken a duty which might possibly lead to circumstances which would be altogether heartbreaking. The duty of mothering Bessy was so much more a duty because, even when the little girl was blear-eyed and thin, there was present to her mind all the horror of a love affair between her son and the little girl. The Mileses had always been much, and the Launays very much, in the west of England. Bessy had not a single belonging that was anything. Then she had become beautiful and attractive, and, worse than that, so much of a person about the house that Philip himself might be tempted to think that she was fit to be his wife!

Among the duties prescribed to herself by Mrs. Miles was none stronger than that of maintaining the family position of the Launays. She was one of those who not only think that blue blood should remain blue, but that blood not blue should be allowed no azure mixture. The proper severance of classes was a religion to her. Bessy was a gentlewoman, so much had been admitted, and therefore she had been brought into the drawing-room instead of being relegated among the servants, and had thus grown up to

227

be, oh, so dangerous! She was a gentlewoman, and fit to be a gentleman's wife, but not fit to be the wife of the heir of the Launays. The reader will understand, perhaps, that I, the writer of this little history, think her to have been fit to become the wife of any man who might have been happy enough to win her young heart, however blue his blood. But Mrs. Miles had felt that precautions and remedies and arrangements were necessary.

Mrs. Miles had altogether approved of the journey to Japan. That had been a preventive, and might probably afford time for an arrangement. She had even used her influence to prolong the travelling till the arrangements should be complete; but in this she had failed. She had written to her son, saying that, as his sojourn in strange lands would so certainly tend to the amelioration of the human races generally — for she had heard of the philanthropic enquires, of the book, and the botany—she would by no means press upon him her own natural longings. If another year was required, the necessary remittances should be made with a liberal hand. But Philip, who had chosen to go because he liked it, came back when he liked it, and there he was at Launay before a certain portion of the arrangements had been completed, as to which Mrs. Miles had been urgent during the last six months of his absence.

A good-looking young clergyman in the neighbourhood, with a living of £400 a year, and a fortune of £6,000 of his own, had during the time been proposed to Bessy by Mrs. Miles. Mr. Morrison, the Rev. Alexander Morrison, was an excellent young man; but it may be doubted whether the patronage by which he was put into the living of Budcombe at an early age, over the head of many senior curates, had been exercised with sound clerical motives. Mrs. Miles was herself the patroness, and, having for the last six years felt the necessity of providing a husband for Bessy, had looked about for a young man who should have good gifts and might probably make her happy. A couple of thousand pounds added had at first suggested itself to Mrs. Miles. Then love had ensnared her, and Bessy had become dear to everyone, and money was plenty. The thing should be made so beautiful to all concerned that there should be no doubt of its acceptance. The young parson didn't doubt. Why should he? The living had been a wonderful stroke of luck for him! The portion proposed would put him at once among the easy-living gentlemen of the county; and then the girl herself! Bessy had loomed upon him as feminine perfection from the first moment he had seen her. It was to him as though the heavens were raining their choicest blessings on his head.

Nor had Mrs. Miles any reason to find fault with Bessy. Had Bessy jumped into the man's arm directly he had been offered to her as a lover, Mrs. Miles would herself have been shocked. She knew enough of Bessy to be sure that there would be no such jumping. Bessy had at first been startled, and, throwing herself into her old friend's arms, had pleaded her youth. Mrs. Miles had accepted the embrace, had acknowledged the plea, and had expressed herself quite satisfied, simply saying that Mr. Morrison would be allowed to come about the house, and use his own efforts to make himself agreeable. The young parson had come about the house, and had shown himself to be good-humoured and pleasant. Bessy never said a word against him; did in truth try to persuade herself that it would be nice to have him as a lover; but she failed. "I think he is very good," she said one day, when she was pressed by Mrs. Miles.

"And he is a gentleman."

"Oh, yes," said Bessy.

"And good-looking."

"I don't know that that matters."

"No, my dear, no; only he is handsome. And then he is so very fond of you." But Bessy would not commit herself, and certainly had never given any encouragement to the gentleman himself.

This had taken place just before Philip's return. At that time his stay at Launay was to be short; and during his sojourn his hands were to be very full. There would not be much danger during that fortnight, as Bessy was not prone to put herself forward in any man's way. She met him as his little pet of former days, and treated him quite as though he were a superior being. She ran about for him as he arranged his botanical treasures, and took in all that he said about the races. Mrs. Miles, as she watched them, still trusted that there might be no danger. But she went on with her safeguards. "I hope you like Mr. Morrison," she said to her son.

"Very much indeed, mother; but why do you ask?"

229

"It is a secret; but I'll tell you. I think he will become the husband of our dear Bessy."

"Marry Bessy!"

"Why not?" Then there was a pause. "You know how dearly I love Bessy. I hope you will not think me wrong when I tell you that I propose to give what will be for her a large fortune, considering all things."

"You should treat her just as though she were a daughter and a sister," said Philip.

"Not quite that! But you will not begrudge her six thousand pounds?"

"It is not half enough."

"Well, well. Six thousand pounds is a large sum of money to give away. However, I am sure we shall not differ about Bessy. Don't you think Mr. Morrison would make her a good husband?" Philip looked very serious, knitted his brows, and left the room, saying that he would think about it.

To make him think that the marriage was all but arranged would be a great protection. There was a protection to his mother also in hearing him speak of Bessy as being almost a sister. But there was still a further protection. Down away in Cornwall there was another Launay heiress coming up, some third or fourth cousin, and it had long since been settled among certain elders that the Launay properties should be combined. To this Philip had given no absolute assent; had even run away to Japan just when it had been intended that he should go to Cornwall. The Launay heiress had then only been seventeen, and it had been felt to be almost as well that there should be delay, so that the time was not passed by the young man in dangerous neighbourhoods. The South Sea Islands and Patagonia had been safe. And now when the idea of combining the properties was again mooted, he at first said nothing against it. Surely such precautions as these would suffice, especially as Bessy's retiring nature would not allow her to fall in love with any man within the short compass of a fortnight.

Not a word more was said between Mrs. Miles and her son as to the prospects of Mr. Morrison; not a word more then. She was intelligent enough to perceive that the match was not agreeable to him; but she attributed this feeling on his part to an idea that

Bessy ought to be treated in all respects as though she were a daughter of the house of Launay. The idea was absurd, but safe. The match, if it could be managed, would of course go on, but should not be mentioned to him again till it could be named as a thing absolutely arranged. But there was no present danger. Mrs. Miles felt sure that there was no present danger. Mrs. Miles had seen Bessy grow out of meagre thinness and early want of ruddy health, into gradual proportions of perfect feminine loveliness; but, having seen the gradual growth, she did not know how lovely the girl was. A woman hardly ever does know how omnipotent may be the attraction which some feminine natures, and some feminine forms, diffuse unconsciously on the young men around them.

But Philip knew, or rather felt. As he walked about the park he declared to himself that Alexander Morrison was an insufferably impudent clerical prig; for which assertion there was, in truth, no ground whatsoever. Then he accused his mother of a sordid love of money and property, and swore to himself that he would never stir a step towards Cornwall. If they chose to have that red-haired Launay girl up from the far west, he would go away to London, or perhaps back to Japan. But what shocked him most was that such a girl as Bessy, a girl whom he treated always just like his own sister, should give herself to such a man as that young parson at the very first asking! He struck the trees among which he was walking with his stick as he thought of the meanness of feminine nature. And then such a greasy, ugly brute! But Mr. Morrison was not at all greasy, and would have been acknowledged by the world at large to be much better looking than Philip Launay.

Then came the day of his departure. He was going up to London in March to see his book through the press, make himself intimate at his club, and introduce himself generally to the ways of that life which was to be his hereafter. It had been understood that he was to pass the season in London, and that then the combined-property question should come on in earnest. Such was his mother's understanding; but by this time, by the day of his departure, he was quite determined that the combined-property question should never receive any consideration at his hands.

Early on that day he met Bessy somewhere about the house. She was very sweet to him on this occasion, partly because she loved him dearly, — as her adopted brother; partly because he was going; partly because it was her nature to be sweet! "There is one question I want to ask you," he said suddenly, turning round upon her with a frown. He had not meant to frown, but it was his nature to do so when his heart frowned within him.

"What is it, Philip?" She turned pale as she spoke, but looked him full in the face.

"Are you engaged to that parson?" She went on looking at him, but did not answer a word. "Are you going to marry him? I have a right to ask." Then she shook her head. "You certainly are not?" Now as he spoke his voice was changed, and the frown had vanished. Again she shook her head. Then he got hold of her hand, and she left her hand with him, not thinking of him as other than a brother. "I am so glad. I detest that man."

"Oh, Philip; he is very good!"

"I do not care two-pence for his goodness. You are quite sure?" Now she nodded her head. "It would have been most awful, and would have made me miserable; miserable. Of course, my mother is the best woman in the world; but why can't she let people alone to find husbands and wives for themselves?" There was a slight frown, and then with a visible effort he completed his speech. "Bessy, you have grown to be the loveliest woman that ever I looked upon."

She withdrew her hand very suddenly. "Philip, you should not say such a thing as that."

"Why not, if I think it?"

"People should never say anything to anybody about themselves."

"Shouldn't they?"

"You know what I mean. It is not nice. It's the sort of stuff which people who ain't ladies and gentlemen put into books."

"I should have thought I might say anything."

"So you may; and of course you are different. But there are things that are so disagreeable!"

"And I am one of them?"

"No, Philip, you are the truest and best of brothers."

"At any rate you won't —" Then he paused.

"No, I won't."

"That's a promise to your best and dearest brother?" She nodded her head again, and he was satisfied.

He went away, and when he returned to Launay at the end of four months he found that things were not going on pleasantly at the Park. Mr. Morrison had been refused, with a positive assurance from the young lady that she would never change her mind, and Mrs. Miles had become more stern than ever in the performance of her duty to her family.

Chapter III
How Bessy Pryor Came to Love the Heir of Launay

Matters became very unpleasant at the Park soon after Philip went away. There had been something in his manner as he left, and a silence in regard to him on Bessy's part, which created, not at first surprise, but uneasiness in the mind of Mrs. Miles. Bessy hardly mentioned his name, and Mrs. Miles knew enough of the world to feel that such restraint must have a cause. It would have been natural for a girl so circumstanced to have been full of Philip and his botany. Feeling this she instigated the parson to renewed attempts; but the parson had to tell her that there was no chance for him. "What has she said?" asked Mrs. Miles.

"That it can never be."

"But it shall be," said Mrs. Miles, stirred on this occasion to an assertion of the obstinacy which was in her nature. Then there was a more unpleasant scene between the old lady and her dependent. "What is it that you expect?" she asked.

"Expect, aunt!" Bessy had been instructed to call Mrs. Miles her aunt.

"What do you think is to be done for you?"

"Done for me! You have done everything. May I not stay with you?" Then Mrs. Miles gave utterance to a very long lecture, in which many things were explained to Bessy. Bessy's position was said to be one very peculiar in its nature. Were Mrs. Miles to die there would be no home for her. She could not hope to find a home in Philip's house as a real sister might have done. Everybody loved her because she had been good and gracious, but it was her duty to marry—especially her duty—so that there might be no future difficulty. Mr. Morrison was exactly the man that such a girl as Bessy ought to want as a husband. Bessy through her tears declared that she didn't want any husband, and that she certainly did not want Mr. Morrison.

"Has Philip said anything?" asked the imprudent old woman. Then Bessy was silent. "What has Philip said to you?"

"I told him, when he asked, that I should never marry Mr. Morrison." Then it was — in that very moment — that Mrs. Miles in truth suspected the blow that was to fall upon her; and in that same moment she resolved that, let the pain be what it might to any or all of them, she would do her duty by her family.

"Yes," she said to herself, as she sat alone in the unadorned, unattractive sanctity of her own bed-room, "I will do my duty at any rate now." With deep remorse she acknowledged to herself that she had been remiss. For a moment her anger was very bitter. She had warmed a reptile in her bosom. The very words came to her thoughts, though they were not pronounced. But the words were at once rejected. The girl had been no reptile. The girl had been true. The girl had been as sweet a girl as had ever brightened the hearth of an old woman. She acknowledged so much to herself even in this moment of her agony. But not the less would she do her duty by the family of the Launays. Let the girl do what she might, she must be sent away — got rid of — sacrificed in any way rather than that Philip should be allowed to make himself a fool.

When for a couple of days she had turned it all in her mind she did not believe that there was as yet any understanding between the girl and Philip. But still she was sure that the danger existed. Not only had the girl refused her destined husband — just such a man as such a girl as Bessy ought to have loved — but she had communicated her purpose in that respect to Philip. There had been more of confidence between them than between her and the girl. How could they two have talked on such a subject, unless there had been between them something of stricter, closer friendship even than that of brother and sister? There had been something of a conspiracy between them against her — her who at Launay was held to be omnipotent, against her who had in her hands all the income, all the power, all the ownership — the mother of one of them and the protectress and only friend of the other! She would do her duty, let Bessy be ever so sweet. The girl must be made to marry Mr. Morrison — or must be made to go.

But whither should she go, and if that "whither" should be found, how should Philip be prevented from following her? Mrs. Miles, in her agony conceived an idea that it would be easier to deal with the girl herself than with Philip. A woman, if she thinks it to be a duty, will more readily sacrifice herself in the performance of it than will a man. So at least thought Mrs. Miles, judging from her own feelings; and Bessy was very good, very affectionate, very grateful, had always been obedient. If possible she should be driven into the arms of Mr. Morrison. Should she stand firm against such efforts as could be made in that direction, then an appeal should be made to herself. After all that had been done for her, would she ruin the family of the Launays for the mere whim of her own heart?

During the process of driving her into Mr. Morrison's arms — a process which from first to last was altogether hopeless — not a word had been said about Philip. But Bessy understood the reticence. She had been asked as to her promise to Philip, and never forgot that she had been asked. Nor did she ever forget those words which at the moment so displeased her — "You have grown to be the loveliest woman that I have ever looked upon." She remembered now that he had held her hand tightly while he had spoken them, and that an effort had been necessary as she withdrew it. She had been perfectly serious in decrying the personal compliment; but still, still there had been a flavour of love in the words which now remained among her heartstrings. Of course he was not her brother — not even her cousin. There was not a touch of blood between them to warrant such a compliment as a joke. He, as a young man, had told her that he thought her, as a young woman, to be lovely above all others. She was quite sure of this — that no possible amount of driving should drive her into the arms of Mr. Morrison.

The old woman became more and more stern. "Dear aunt," Bessy said to her one day, with an air of firmness which had evidently been assumed purposely for the occasion, "indeed, indeed, I cannot love Mr. Morrison." Then Mrs. Miles had resolved that she must resort to the other alternative. Bessy must go. She did believe that when everything should be explained Bessy herself would raise no difficulty as to her own going. Bessy had no more right to live at Launay than had any other fatherless, motherless, penniless living creature. But how to explain it? What reason should be given? And whither should the girl be sent?

Then there came delay, caused by another great trouble. On a sudden Mrs. Miles was very ill. This began about the end of May, when Philip was still up in London inhaling the incense which came up from the success of his book. At first she was very eager that her son should not be recalled to Launay. "Why should a young man be brought into the house with a sick old woman?" Of course she was eager. What evils might not happen if they two were brought together during her illness? At the end of three weeks, however, she was worse — so much worse that the people around her were afraid; and it became manifest to all of them that the truth must be told to Philip in spite of her injunctions. Bessy's position became one of great difficulty, because words fell from Mrs. Miles which explained to her almost with accuracy the con- dition of her aunt's mind. "You should not be here," she said over and over again. Now, it had been the case, as a matter of course, that Bessy, during the old lady's illness, had never left her bedside day or night. Of course she had been the nurse, of course she had tended the invalid in everything. It had been so much a matter of course that the poor lady had been impotent to prevent it, in her ineffectual efforts to put an end to Bessy's influence. The ser- vants, even the doctors, obeyed Bessy in regard to the household matters. Mrs. Miles found herself quite unable to repel Bessy from her bedside. And then, with her mind always intent on the necessity of keeping the young people apart, and when it was all but settled that Philip should be summoned, she said again and again, "You should not be here, Bessy. You must not be here, Bessy."

But whither should she go? No place was even suggested to her. And were she herself to consult some other friend as to a place — the clergyman of their own parish for instance, who out of that house was her most intimate friend — she would have to tell the whole story, a story which could not be told by her lips. Philip had never said a word to her, except that one word: "You have grown to be the loveliest woman that ever I looked upon." The word was very frequent in her thoughts, but she could tell no one of that!

If he did think her lovely, if he did love her, why should not things run smoothly? She had found it to be quite out of the question that she should be driven into the arms of Mr. Morrison, but she soon came to own to herself that she might easily be enticed into those other arms. But then perhaps he had meant nothing — so probably had meant nothing! But if not, why should she be driven away from Launay? As her aunt became worse and worse, and when Philip came down from London, and with Philip a London physician, nothing was settled about poor Bessy, and nothing was done. When Philip and Bessy stood together at the sick woman's bedside she was nearly insensible, wandering in her mind, but still with that care heavy at her heart. "No, Philip; no, no, no," she said. "What is it, mother?" asked Philip. Then Bessy escaped from the room and resolved that she would always be absent when Philip was by his mother's bedside.

There was a week in which the case was almost hopeless; and then a week during which the mistress of Launay crept slowly back to life. It could not but be that they two should see much of each other during such weeks. At every meal they sat together. Bessy was still constant at the bedside of her aunt, but now and again she was alone with Philip. At first she struggled to avoid him, but she struggled altogether in vain. He would not be avoided. And then of course he spoke. "Bessy, I am sure you know that I love you."

"I am sure I hope you do.," she replied, purposely misinterpreting him.

Then he frowned at her. "I am sure, Bessy, you are above all subterfuges."

"What subterfuges? Why do you say that?"

"You are no sister of mine; no cousin even. You know what I mean when I say that I love you. Will you be my wife?"

Oh! if she might only have knelt at his feet and hidden her face among her hands, and have gladly answered him with a little "Yes," extracted from amidst her happy blushes! But, in every way, there was no time for such joys. "Philip, think how ill your mother is," she said.

"That cannot change it. I have to ask you whether you can love me. I am bound to ask you whether you will love me." She would not answer him then; but during that second week in which Mrs. Miles was creeping back to life she swore that she did love him, and would love him, and would be true to him for ever and ever.

Chapter IV
How Bessy Pryor Owned that She Was Engaged

When these pretty oaths had been sworn, and while Mrs. Miles was too ill to keep her eyes upon them or to separate them, of course the two lovers were much together. For whispering words of love, for swearing oaths, for sweet kisses and looking into each other's eyes, a few minutes now and again will give ample opportunities. The long hours of the day and night were passed by Bessy with her aunt; but there were short moments, heavenly moments, which sufficed to lift her off the earth into an Elysium of joy. His love for her was so perfect, so assured! "In a matter such as this," he said in his fondly serious air, "my mother can have no right to interfere with me."

"But with me she may," said Bessy, foreseeing in the midst of her Paradise the storm which would surely come.

"Why should she wish to do so? Why should she not allow me to make myself happy in the only way in which it is possible?" There was such an ecstacy of bliss coming from such words as these, such a perfection of the feeling of mutual love, that she could not but be exalted to the heavens, although she knew that the storm would surely come. If her love would make him happy, then, then surely he should be happy. "Of course she has given up her idea about that parson," he said.

"I fear she has not, Philip."

"It seems to me too monstrous that any human being should go to work and settle whom two other human beings are to marry."

"There was never a possibility of that."

"She told me it was to be so."

"It never could have been," said Bessy with great emphasis. "Not even for her, much as I love her—not even for her to whom I owe everything—could I consent to marry a man I did not love. But —"

"But what?"

"I do not know how I shall answer her when she bids me give you up. Oh, my love, how shall I answer her?"

Then he told her at considerable length what was the answer which he thought should in such circumstances be made to his mother. Bessy was to declare that nothing could alter her intentions, that her own happiness and that of her lover depended on her firmness, and that they two did, in fact, intend to have their own way in this matter sooner or later. Bessy, as she heard the lesson, made no direct reply, but she knew too well that it could be of no service to her. All that it would be possible for her to say, when the resolute old woman should declare her purpose, would be that come what might she must always love Philip Launay; that she never, never, never could become the wife of any other man. So much she thought she would say. But as to asserting her right to her lover, that she was sure would be beyond her.

Everyone in the house except Mrs. Miles was aware that Philip and Bessy were lovers, and from the dependents of the house the tidings spread through the parish. There had been no special secrecy. A lover does not usually pronounce his vows in public. Little half-lighted corners and twilight hours are chosen, or banks beneath the trees supposed to be safe from vulgar eyes, or lonely wanderings. Philip had followed the usual way of the world in his love-making, but had sought his secret moments with no special secrecy. Before the servants he would whisper to Bessy with that look of thorough confidence in his eyes which servants completely understand; and thus while the poor old woman was still in her bed, while she was unaware both of the danger and of her own immediate impotence, the secret — as far as it was a secret — became known to all Launay. Mr. Morrison heard it over at Budcombe, and, with his heart down in his boots, told himself that now certainly there could be no chance for him. At Launay Mr. Gregory was the rector, and it was with his daughters that Bessy had become intimate. Knowing much of the mind of the first lady of the parish, he took upon himself to say a word or two to Philip. "I am so glad to hear that your mother is much better this morning."

"Very much better."

"It has been a most serious illness."

"Terribly serious, Mr. Gregory."

Then there was a pause, and sundry other faltering allusions were made to the condition of things up at the house, from which Philip was aware that words of counsel or perhaps reproach were coming. "I hope you will excuse me, Philip, if I tell you something."

"I think I shall excuse anything from you."

"People are saying about the place that during your mother's illness you have engaged yourself to Bessy Pryor."

"That's very odd," said Philip.

"Odd!" repeated the parson.

"Very odd indeed, because what the people about the place say is always supposed to be untrue. But this report is true."

"It is true?"

"Quite true, and I am proud to be in a position to assure you that I have been accepted. I am really sorry for Mr. Morrison, you know."

"But what will your mother say?"

"I do not think that she or anyone can say that Bessy is not fit to be the wife of the finest gentleman in the land." This he said with an air of pride which showed plainly enough that he did not intend to be talked out of his purpose.

"I should not have spoken, but that your dear mother is so ill," rejoined the parson.

"I understand that. I must fight my own battle and Bessy's as best I may. But you may be quite sure, Mr. Gregory, that I mean to fight it."

Nor did Bessy deny the fact when her friend Mary Gregory interrogated her. The question of Bessy's marriage with Mr. Morrison had, somewhat cruelly in regard to her and more cruelly still in regard to the gentleman, become public property in the neighbourhood. Everybody had known that Mrs. Miles intended to marry Bessy to the parson of Budcombe, and everybody had thought that Bessy would, as a matter of course, accept her destiny. Everybody now knew that Bessy had rebelled; and, as Mrs. Miles's autocratic disposition was well understood, everybody was waiting to see what would come of it. The neighbourhood generally thought that Bessy was unreasonable and ungrateful. Mr. Morrison was a very nice man, and nothing could have been more appropriate. Now, when the truth came out, everybody was very much interested indeed. That Mrs. Miles should assent to a marriage between the heir and Bessy Pryor was quite out of the question. She was too well known to leave a doubt on the mind of anyone either in Launay or Budcombe on that matter. Men and women drew their breath and looked at each other. It was just when the parishes thought that she was going to die that the parishioners first heard that Bessy would not marry Mr. Morrison because of the young squire. And now, when it was known that Mrs. Miles was not going to die, it was known that the young squire was absolutely engaged to Bessy Pryor. "There'll be a deal o' vat in the voir," said the old head ploughman of Launay, talking over the matter with the wife of Mr. Gregory's gardener. There was going to be "a deal of fat in the fire."

Mrs. Miles was not like other mothers. Everything in respect to present income was in her hands. And Bessy was not like other girls. She had absolutely no "locus standi" in the world, except what came to her from the bounty of the old lady. By favour of the Lady of Launay she held her head among the girls of that part of the country as high as any girl there. She was only Bessy Pryor; but, from love and kindness, she was the recognised daughter of the house of Launay. Everybody knew it all. Everybody was aware that she had done much towards reaching her present position by her own special sweetness. But should Mrs. Miles once frown, Bessy would be nobody. "Oh, Bessy, how is this all to be?" asked Mary Gregory.

"As God pleases," said Bessy, very solemnly.

"What does Mrs. Miles say?"

"I don't want anybody to ask me about it," said Bessy. "Of course I love him. What is the good of denying it? But I cannot talk about it." Then Mary Gregory looked as though some terrible secret had been revealed to her — some secret of which the burden might probably be too much for her to bear.

The first storm arose from an interview which took place between the mother and son as soon as the mother found herself able to speak on a subject which was near her heart. She sent for him and once again besought him to take steps towards that combining of the properties which was so essential to the Launay interests generally. Then he declared his purpose very plainly. He did not intend to combine the properties. He did not care for the red-haired Launay cousin. It was his intention to marry — Bessy Pryor; yes — he had proposed to her and she had accepted him. The poor sick mother was at first almost overwhelmed with despair. "What can I do but tell you the truth when you ask me?" he said.

"Do!" she screamed. "What could you do? You could have remembered your honour! You could have remembered your blood! You could have remembered your duty!" Then she bade him leave her, and after an hour passed in thought she sent for Bessy. "I have had my son with me," she said, sitting bolt upright in her bed, looking awful in her wanness, speaking with low, studied, harsh voice, with her two hands before her on the counterpane. "I have had my son with me and he has told me." Bessy felt that she was trembling. She was hardly able to support herself. She had not a word to say. The sick old woman was terrible in her severity. "Is it true?"

"Yes, it is true," whispered Bessy.

"And this is to be my return?"

"Oh, my dearest, my darling, oh, my aunt, dear, dearest, dearest aunt. Do not speak like that! Do not look at me like that! You know I love you. Don't you know I love you?" Then Bessy prostrated herself on the bed, and getting hold of the old woman's hand covered it with kisses. Yes, her aunt did know that the girl loved her, and she knew that she loved the girl perhaps better than any other human being in the world. The eldest son had become estranged from her. Even Philip had not been half so much to her as this girl. Bessy had wound herself round her very heartstrings. It made her happy even to sit and look at Bessy. She had denied herself all pretty things; but this prettiest of all things had grown up beneath her eyes. She did not draw away her hand; but, while her hand was being kissed, she made up her mind that she would do her duty.

"Of what service will be your love," she said, "if this is to be my return?" Bessy could only lie and sob and hide her face. "Say that you will give it up." Not to say that, not to give him up, was the only resolution at which Bessy had arrived. "If you will not say so, you must leave me, and I shall send you word what you are to do. If you are my enemy you shall not remain here."

"Pray — pray do not call me an enemy."

"You had better go." The woman's voice as she said this was dreadful in its harshness. Then Bessy, slowly creeping down from the bed, slowly slunk out of the room.

Chapter V
How Bessy Pryor Ceased to be a
Young Lady of Importance

When the old woman was alone she at once went to work in her own mind resolving what should be her course of proceeding. To yield in the matter, and to confirm the happiness of the young people, never occurred to her. Again and again she repeated to herself that she would do her duty; and again and again she repeated to herself that in allowing Philip and Bessy to come together she had neglected her duty. That her duty required her to separate them, in spite of their love, in spite of their engagement, though all the happiness of their lives might depend upon it, she did not in the least doubt. Duty is duty. And it was her duty to aggrandize the house of Launay, so that the old autocracy of the land might, so far as in her lay, be preserved. That it would be a good and pious thing to do, — to keep them apart, to force Philip to marry the girl in Cornwall, to drive Bessy into Mr. Morrison's arms, was to her so certain that it required no further thought. She had never indulged herself. Her life had been so led as to maintain the power of her own order, and relieve the wants of those below her. She had done nothing for her own pleasure. How should it occur to her that it would be well for her to change the whole course of her life in order that she might administer to the joys of a young man and a young woman?

It did not occur to her to do so. Lying thus all alone, white, sick, and feeble, but very strong of heart, she made her resolutions. As Bessy could not well be sent out of the house till a home should be provided for her elsewhere, Philip should be made to go. As that was to be the first step, she again sent for Philip that day. "No mother; not while you are so ill." This he said in answer to her first command that he should leave Launay at once. It had not occurred to him that the house in which he had been born and bred, the house of his ancestors, the house which he had always supposed was at some future day to be his own, was not free to him. But, feeble as she was, she soon made him understand her purpose. He must go, — because she ordered him, because the house was hers and not his, because he was no longer welcome there as a guest unless he would promise to abandon Bessy. "This is tyranny, mother," he said.

"I do not mean to argue the question," said Mrs. Miles, leaning back among the pillows, gaunt, with hollow cheeks, yellow with her long sickness, seeming to be all eyes as she looked at him. "I tell you that you must go."

"Mother!"

Then, at considerable length, she explained her intended arrangements. He must go, and live upon the very modest income which she proposed. At any rate he must go, and go at once. The house was hers and she would not have him there. She would have no one in the house who disputed her will. She had been an over-indulgent mother to him, and this had been the return made to her! She had condescended to explain to him her intention in regard to Bessy, and he had immediately resolved to thwart her. When she was dead and gone it might perhaps be in his power to ruin the family if he chose. As to that she would take further thought. But she, as long as she lived, would do her duty. "I suppose I may understand," she said, "that you will leave Launay early after breakfast to-morrow."

"Do you mean to turn me out of the house?"

"I do," she said, looking full at him, all eyes, with her grey hair coming dishevelled from under the large frill of her nightcap, with cheeks gaunt and yellow. Her extended hands were very thin. She had been very near death, and seemed, as he gazed at her, to be very near it now. If he went it might be her fate never to see him again.

"I cannot leave you like this," he said.

"Then obey me."

"Why should we not be married, mother?"

"I will not argue. You know as well as I do. Will you obey me?"

"Not in this, mother. I could not do so without perjuring myself."

"Then go you out of this house at once." She was sitting now bolt upright on her bed, supporting herself on her hands behind her. The whole thing was so dreadful that he could not endure to prolong the interview, and he left the room.

Then there came a message from the old housekeeper to Bessy, forbidding her to leave her own room. It was thus that Bessy first understood that her great sin was to be made public to all the household. Mrs. Knowl, who was the head of the domestics, had been told, and now felt that a sort of authority over Bessy had been confided to her. "No, Miss Bessy; you are not to go into her room at all. She says that she will not see you till you promise to be said by her."

"But why, Mrs. Knowl?"

"Well, miss; I suppose it's along of Mr. Philip. But you know that better than me. Mr. Philip is to go to-morrow morning and never come back any more."

"Never come back to Launay?"

"Not while things is as they is, miss. But you are to stay here and not go out at all. That's what Madam says." The servants about the place all called Mrs. Miles Madam.

There was a potency about Mrs. Miles which enabled her to have her will carried out, although she was lying ill in bed, — to have her will carried out as far as the immediate severance of the lovers was concerned. When the command had been brought by the mouth of a servant, Bessy determined that she would not see Philip again before he went. She understood that she was bound by her position, bound by gratitude, bound by a sense of propriety, to so much obedience as that. No earthly authority could be sufficient to make her abandon her troth. In that she could not allow even her aunt to sway her, — her aunt though she were sick and suffering, even though she were dying! Both her love and her vow were sacred to her. But obedience at the moment she did owe, and she kept her room. Philip came to the door but she sat mute and would not speak to him. Mrs. Knowl, when she brought her some food, asked her whether she intended to obey the order. "Your aunt wants a promise from you, Miss Bessy?"

"I am sure my aunt knows that I shall obey her," said Bessy.

On the following morning Philip left the house. He sent a message to his mother, asking whether she would see him; but she refused. "I think you had better not disturb her, Mr. Philip," said Mrs. Knowl. Then he went, and as the waggonette took him away from the door, Bessy sat and listened to the sound of the wheels on the gravel.

All that day and all the next passed on and she was not allowed to see her aunt. Mrs. Knowl repeated that she could not take upon herself to say that Madam was better. No doubt the worry of the last day or two had been a great trouble to her. Mrs. Knowl grew much in self-importance at the time, and felt that she was overtopping Miss Bessy in the affairs of Launay.

It was no less true than singular that all the sympathies of the place should be on the side of the old woman. Her illness probably had something to do with it. And then she had been so autocratic, all Launay and Budcombe had been so accustomed to bow down to her, that rebellion on the part of anyone seemed to be shocking. And who was Bessy Pryor that she should dare to think of marrying the heir? Who, even, was the supposed heir that he should dare to think of marrying anyone in opposition to the actual owner of the acres? Heir though he was called, he was not necessarily the heir. She might do as she pleased with all Launay and all Budcombe, and there were those who thought that if Philip was still obstinate she would leave everything to her elder son. She did not love her elder son. In these days she never saw him. He was a gay man of the world who had never been dutiful to her. But he might take the name of Launay, and the family would be perpetuated as well that way as the other. Philip was very foolish. And as for Bessy; Bessy was worse than foolish. That was the verdict of the place generally.

I think Launay liked it. The troubles of our neighbours are generally endurable, and any subject for conversation is a blessing. Launay liked the excitement; but, nevertheless, felt itself to be compressed into whispers and a solemn demeanour. The Gregory girls were solemn, conscious of the iniquity of their friend, and deeply sensitive of the danger to which poor Philip was exposed. When a rumour came to the vicarage that a fly had been up at the great house, it was immediately conceived that Mr. Jones, the lawyer from Taunton, had been sent for, with a view to an alteration of the will. This suddenness, this anger, this disruption of all things was dreadful! But when it was discovered that the fly contained no one but the doctor there was disappointment.

On the third day there came a message from Mrs. Miles to the rector. Would Mr. Gregory step up and see Mrs. Miles. Then it was thought at the rectory that the dear old lady was again worse, and that she had sent for her clergyman that she might receive the last comforts of religion. But this again was wrong. "Mr. Gregory," she said very suddenly, "I want to consult you as to a future home for Bessy Pryor."

"Must she go from this?"

"Yes; she must go from this. You have heard, perhaps, about her and my son." Mr. Gregory acknowledged that he had heard. "Of course she must go. I cannot have Philip banished from the house which is to be his own. In this matter he probably has been the most to blame."

"They have both, perhaps, been foolish."

"It is wickedness rather than folly. But he has been the wickeder. It should have been a duty to him, a great duty, and he should have been the stronger. But he is my son, and I cannot banish him."

"Oh, no!"

"But they must not be brought together. I love Bessy Pryor dearly, Mr. Gregory; — oh, so dearly! Since she came to me, now so many years ago, she has been like a gleam of sunlight in the house. She has always been gentle with me. The very touch of her hand is sweet to me. But I must not on that account sacrifice the honour of the family. I have a duty to do; and I must do it, though I tear my heart in pieces. Where can I send her?"

"Permanently?"

"Well, yes; permanently. If Philip were married, of course she might come back. But I will still trust that she herself may be married first. I do not mean to cast her off; — only she must go. Anything that may be wanting in money shall be paid for her. She shall be provided for comfortably. You know what I had hoped about Mr. Morrison. Perhaps he may even yet be able to persuade her; but it must be away from here. Where can I send her?"

This was a question not very easy to answer, and Mr. Gregory said that he must take time to think of it. Mrs. Miles, when she asked the question, was aware that Mr. Gregory had a maiden sister, living at Avranches in Normandy, who was not in opulent circumstances.

Chapter VI
How Bessy Pryor Was to Be Banished

When a man is asked by his friend if he knows of a horse to be sold he does not like immediately to suggest a transfer of the animal which he has in his own stable, though he may at the moment be in want of money and anxious to sell his steed. So it was with Mr. Gregory. His sister would be delighted to take as a boarder a young lady for whom liberal payment would be made; but at the first moment he had hesitated to make an offer by which his own sister would be benefited. On the next morning, however, he wrote as follows: —

"Dear Mrs. Miles, — My sister Amelia is living at Avranches, where she has a pleasant little house on the outskirts of the town, with a garden. An old friend was living with her, but she died last year, and my sister is now alone. If you think that Bessy would like to sojourn for a while in Normandy, I will write to Amelia and make the proposition. Bessy will find my sister good-tempered and kind-hearted. — Faithfully yours, Joshua Gregory."

Mrs. Miles did not care much for the good temper and the kind heart. Had she asked herself whether she wished Bessy to be happy she would no doubt have answered herself in the affirmative. She would probably have done so in regard to any human being or animal in the world. Of course, she wanted them all to be happy. But happiness was to her thinking of much less importance than duty; and at the present moment her duty and Bessy's duty and Philip's duty were so momentous that no idea of happiness ought, to her thinking, to be considered in the matter at all. Had Mr. Gregory written to say that his sister was a woman of severe morals, of stern aspect, prone to repress all youthful ebullitions, and supposed to be disagreeable because of her temper, all that would have been no obstacle. In the present condition of things suffering would be better than happiness; more in accord with the feelings and position of the person concerned. It was quite intelligible to Mrs. Miles that Bessy should really love Philip almost to the breaking of her heart, quite intelligible that Philip should have set his mind upon the untoward marriage with all the obstinacy of a proud man. When young men and young women neglect their duty, hearts have to be broken. But it is not a soft and silken operation, which can be made pleasant by good temper and social kindness. It was necesesary, for certain quite adequate reasons, that Bessy should be put on the wheel, and be racked and tormented. To talk to her of the good temper of the old woman who would have to turn the wheel would be to lie to her. Mrs. Miles did not want her to think that things could be made pleasant for her.

Soon after the receipt of Mr. Gregory's letter she sent for Bessy, who was then brought into the room under the guard, as it were, of Mrs. Knowl. Mrs. Knowl accompanied her along the corridor, which was surely unnecessary, as Bessy's door had not been locked upon her. Her imprisonment had only come from obedience. But Mrs. Knowl felt that a great trust had been confided to her, and was anxious to omit none of her duties. She opened the door so that the invalid on the bed could see that this duty had been done, and then Bessy crept into the room. She crept in, but very quickly, and in a moment had her arms around the old woman's back and her lips pressed to the old woman's forehead. "Why may not I come and be with you?" she said.

"Because you are disobedient."

"No, no; I do all that you tell me. I have not stirred from my room, though it was hard to think you were ill so near me, and that I could do nothing. I did not try to say a word to him, or even to look at him; and now that he has gone, why should I not be with you?"

"It cannot be."

"But why not, aunt? Even though you would not speak to me I could be with you. Who is there to read to you?"

"There is no one. Of course it is dreary. But there are worse things than dreariness."

"Why should not I come back, now that he has gone?" She still had her arm round the old woman's back, and had now succeeded in dragging herself on to the bed and in crouching down by her aunt's side. It was her perseverance in this fashion that had so often forced Mrs. Miles out of her own ordained method of life, and compelled her to leave for a moment the strictness which was congenial to her. It was this that had made her declare to Mr. Gregory, in the midst of her severity, that Bessy had been like a gleam of sunshine in the house. Even now she knew not how to escape from the softness of an embrace which was in truth so grateful to her. It was a consciousness of this, — of the potency of Bessy's charm even over herself, — which had made her hasten to send her away from her. Bessy would read to her all the day, would hold her hand when she was half dozing, would assist in every movement with all the patience and much more than the tenderness of a waiting-maid. There was no voice so sweet, no hand so cool, no memory so mindful, no step so soft as Bessy's. And now Bessy was there, lying on her bed, caressing her, more closely bound to her than had ever been any other being in the world, and yet Bessy was an enemy from whom it was imperatively necessary that she should be divided.

"Get down, Bessy," she said; "go off from me."

"No, no, no," said Bessy, still clinging to her and kissing her.

"I have that to say to you which must be said calmly."

"I am calm, — quite calm. I will do whatever you tell me; only pray, pray, do not send me away from you."

"You say that you will obey me."

"I will; I have. I always have obeyed you."

"Will you give up your love for Philip?"

"Could I give up my love for you, if anybody told me? How can I do it? Love comes of itself. I did not try to love him. Oh, if you could know how I tried not to love him! If somebody came and said I was not to love you, would it be possible?"

"I am speaking of another love."

"Yes; I know. One is a kind of love that is always welcome. The other comes first as a shock, and one struggles to avoid it. But when it has come, how can it be helped? I do love him, better than all the world." As she said this she raised herself upon the bed, so as to look round upon her aunt's face; but still she kept her arm upon the old woman's shoulder. "Is it not natural? How could I have helped it?"

"You must have known that it was wrong."

"No.!"

"You did not know that it would displease me?"

"I knew that it was unfortunate, — not wrong. What did I do that was wrong? When he asked me, could I tell him anything but the truth?"

"You should have told him nothing." At this reply Bessy shook her head. "It cannot be that you should think that in such a matter there should be no restraint. Did you expect that I should give my consent to such a marriage? I want to hear from yourself what you thought of my feelings."

"I knew you would be angry."

"Well?"

"I knew you must think me unfit to be Philip's wife."

"Well?"

"I knew that you wanted something else for him, and something else also for me."

"And did such knowledge go for nothing?"

"It made me feel that my love was unfortunate, — but not that it was wrong. I could not help it. He had come to me, and I loved him. The other man came, and I could not love him. Why should I be shut up for this in my own room? Why should I be sent away from you, to be miserable because I know that you want things done? He is not here. If he were here and you bade me not to go near him, I would not go. Though he were in the next room I would not see him. I will obey you altogether, but I must love him. And as I love him I cannot love another. You would not wish me to marry a man when my heart has been given to another."

The old woman had not at all intended that there should be such arguments as these. It had been her purpose simply to communicate her plan, to tell Bessy that she would have to live probably for a few years at Avranches, and then to send her back to her prison. But Bessy had again got the best of her, and then had come caressing, talking, and excuses. Bessy had been nearly an hour in her room before Mrs. Miles had disclosed her purpose, and had hovered round her aunt, doing as had been her wont when she was recognised as having all the powers of head nurse in her hands. Then at last, in a manner very different from that which had been planned, Mrs. Miles proposed the Normandy scheme. She had been, involuntarily, so much softened that she condescended even to repeat what Mr. Gregory had said as to the good temper and general kindness of his maiden sister. "But why should I go?" asked Bessy, almost sobbing.

"I wonder that you should ask."

"He is not here."

"But he may come."

"If he came ever so I would not see him if you bade me not. I think you hardly understand me, aunt. I will obey you in every-thing. I am sure you will not now ask me to marry Mr. Morrison."

She could not say that Philip would be more likely to become amenable and marry the Cornish heiress if Bessy were away at Avranches than if she still remained shut up at Launay. But that was her feeling. Philip, she knew, would be less obedient than Bessy. But then, too, Philip might be less obstinate of purpose. "You cannot live here, Bessy, unless you will say that you will never become the wife of my son."

"Never?"

"Never!"

"I cannot say that." There was a long pause before she found the courage to pronounce these words, but she did pronounce them at last.

"Then you must go."

"I may stay and nurse you till you are well. Let me do that. I will go whenever you may bid me."

"No. There shall be no terms between us. We must be friends, Bessy, or we must be enemies. We cannot be friends as long as you hold yourself to be engaged to Philip Launay. While that is so I will not take a cup of water from your hands. No, no," for the girl was again trying to embrace her. "I will not have your love, nor shall you have mine."

"My heart would break were I to say it."

"Then let it break! Is my heart not broken? What is it though our hearts do break — what is it though we die, — if we do our duty? You owe me this for what I have done for you."

"I owe you everything."

"Then say that you will give him up."

"I owe you everything, except this. I will not speak to him, I will not write to him, I will not even look at him, but I will not give him up. When one loves, one cannot give it up." Then she was ordered to go back to her room, and back to her room she went.

Chapter VII
How Bessy Pryor was Banished to Normandy

There was nothing for it but to go, after the interview described in the last chapter. Mrs. Miles sent a message to the obstinate girl, informing her that she need not any longer consider herself as a prisoner, but that she had better prepare her clothes so as to be ready to start within a week. The necessary correspondence had taken place between Launay and Avranches, and within ten days from the time at which Mr. Gregory had made the proposition, — in less than a fortnight from the departure of her lover, — Bessy came down from her room all equipped, and took her place in the same waggonette which so short a time before had taken her lover away from her. During the week she had had liberty to go where she pleased, except into her aunt's room. But she had, in truth, been almost as much a prisoner as before. She did for a few minutes each day go out into the garden, but she would not go beyond the garden into the park, nor did she accept an invitation from the Gregory girls to spend an evening at the rectory. It would be so necessary, one of them wrote, that everything should be told to her as to the disposition and ways of life of Aunt Amelia! But Bessy would not see the Gregory girls. She was being sent away from home because of the wickedness of her love, and all Launay knew it. In such a condition of things she could not go out to eat sally-lunn and pound-cake, and to be told of the delights of a small Norman town. She would not even see the Gregory girls when they came up to the house, but wrote an affectionate note to the elder of them explaining that her misery was too great to allow her to see any friend.

She was in truth very miserable. It was not only because of her love, from which she had from the first been aware that misery must come, — undoubted misery, if not misery that would last through her whole life. But now there was added to this the sorrow of absolute banishment from her aunt. Mrs. Miles would not see her again before she started. Bessy was well aware of all that she owed to the mistress of Launay; and, being intelligent in the reading of character, was aware also that through many years she had succeeded in obtaining from the old woman more than the intended performance of an undertaken duty. She had forced the old woman to love her, and was aware that by means of that love the old women's life had been brightened. She had not only received but had conferred kindness, — and it is by conferring kindness that love is created. It was an agony to her that she should be compelled to leave this dearest friend, who was still sick and infirm, without seeing her. But Mrs. Miles was inexorable. These four words written on a scrap of paper were brought to her on that morning; — "Pray, pray, see me?" She was still inexorable. There had been long pencil-written notes between them on the previous day. If Bessy would pledge herself to give up her lover all might yet be changed. The old women at Avranches should be compensated for her disappointment. Bessy should be restored to all her privileges at Launay. "You shall be my own, own child," said Mrs. Miles. She condescended even to promise that not a word more should be said about Mr. Morrison. But Bessy also could be inexorable. "I cannot say that I will give him up," she wrote. Thus it came to pass that she had to get into the waggonette without seeing her old friend. Mrs. Knowl went with her, having received instructions to wait upon Miss Bessy all the way to Avranches. Mrs. Knowl felt that she was sent as a guard against the lover. Mrs. Miles had known Bessy too well to have fear of that kind, and had sent Mrs. Knowl as general guardian against the wild beasts which are supposed to be roaming about the world in quest of unprotected young females.

In the distribution of her anger Mrs. Miles had for the moment been very severe towards Philip as to pecuniary matters. He had chosen to be rebellious, and therefore he was not only turned out of the house, but told that he must live on an uncomfortably small income. But to Bessy Mrs. Miles was liberal. She had astounded Miss Gregory by the nobility of the terms she had proposed, and on the evening before the journey had sent ten five-pound notes in a blank envelope to Bessy. Then in a subsequent note she had said that a similar sum would be paid to her every half-year. In none of these notes was there any expression of endearment. To none of them was there even a signature. But they all conveyed evidence of the amount of thought which Mrs. Miles was giving to Bessy and her affairs.

Bessy's journey was very comfortless. She had learned to hate Mrs. Knowl, who assumed all the airs of a duenna. She would not leave Bessy out of sight for a moment, as though Philip might have been hidden behind every curtain or under every table. Once or twice the duenna made a little attempt at persuasion herself; "It ain't no good, miss, and it had better be give up." Then Bessy looked at her, and desired that she might be left alone. This had been at the hotel at Dover. Then again Mrs. Knowl spoke as the carriage was approaching Avranches; "If you wish to come back, Miss Bessy, the way is open." "Never mind my wishes, Mrs. Knowl," said Bessy. When, on her return to Launay, Mrs. Knowl once attempted to intimate to her mistress that Miss Bessy was very obstinate, she was silenced so sternly, so shortly, that the housekeeper began to doubt whether she might not have made a mistake and whether Bessy would not at last prevail. It was evident that Mrs. Miles would not hear a word against Bessy.

On her arrival at Avranches Miss Gregory was very kind to her. She found that she was received not at all as a naughty girl who had been sent away from home in order that she might be subjected to severe treatment. Miss Gregory fulfilled all the promises which her brother had made on her behalf, and was thoroughly kind and good-tempered. For nearly a month not a word was said about Philip or the love affairs. It seemed to be understood that Bessy had come to Avranches quite at her own desire. She was introduced to the genteel society with which that placed abounds and was conscious that a much freer life was vouchsafed to her than she had ever known before. At Launay she had of course been subject to Mrs. Miles. Now she was subject to no one. Miss Gregory exercised no authority over her, — was indeed rather subject to Bessy, as being the recipient of the money paid for Bessy's board and lodging.

But by the end of the month there had grown up so much of friendship between the elder and the younger lady that something came to be said about Philip. It was impossible that Bessy should be silent as to her past life. By degrees she told all that Mrs. Miles had done for her; how she herself had been a penniless orphan; how Mrs. Miles had taken her in from simple charity; how love had grown up between them two, — the warmest, truest love; and then how that other love had grown! The telling of secrets begets the telling of secrets. Miss Gregory, though she was now old, with the marks of little feeble crow's-feet round her gentle eyes, though she wore a false front and was much withered, had also had her love affair. She took delight in pouring forth her little tale; how she had loved an officer and had been beloved; how there had been no money; how the officer's parents had besought her to set the officer free, so that he might marry money; how she had set the officer free, and how, in consequence, the officer had married money and was now a major-general, with a large family, a comfortable house, and the gout. "And I have always thought it was right," said the excellent spinster. "What could I have done for him?"

"It couldn't be right if he loved you best," said Bessy.

"Why not, my dear? He has made an excellent husband. Perhaps he didn't love me best when he stood at the altar."

"I think love should be more holy."

"Mine has been very holy, — to me, myself. For a time I wept; but now I think I am happier than if I had never seen him. It adds something to one's life to have been loved once."

Bessy, who was of a stronger temperament, told herself that happiness such as that would not suffice for her. She wanted not only to be happy herself, but also to make him so. In the simplicity of her heart she wondered whether Philip would be different from that easy-changing major-general; but in the strength of her heart she was sure he would be very different. She would certainly not release him at the request of any parent; — but he should be free as air at the slightest hint of a request from himself. She did not believe, for a moment, that such a request would come; but, if it did, — if it did, — then there should be no difficulty. Then would she submit to banishment, — at Avranches or elsewhere as it might be decided for her, — till it might please the Lord to release her from her troubles.

At the end of six weeks Miss Gregory knew the whole secret of Philip and Bessy's love, and knew also that Bessy was quite resolved to persevere. There were many discussions about love, in which Bessy always clung to the opinion that when it were once offered and taken, given and received, it ought to be held as more sacred than any other bond. She owed much to Mrs. Miles; — she acknowledged that; — but she thought that she owed more to Philip. Miss Gregory would never quite agree with her; — was strong in her own opinion that women are born to yield and suffer and live mutilated lives, like herself; but not the less did they become fast friends. At the end of six weeks it was determined between them that Bessy should write to Mrs. Miles. Mrs. Miles had signified her wish not to be written to, and had not herself written. Messages as to the improving state of her health had come from the Gregory girls, but no letter had as yet passed. Then Bessy wrote as follows, in direct disobedience to her aunt's orders; —

"Dearest Aunt, — I cannot help writing a line because I am so anxious about you. Mary Gregory says you have been up and out on the lawn in the sunshine, but it would make me so happy if I could see the words in your own dear handwriting. Do send me one little word. And though I know what you told me, still I think you will be glad to hear that your poor affectionate loving Bessy is well. I will not say that I am quite happy. I cannot be quite happy away from Launay and you. But Miss Gregory has been very, very kind to me, and there are nice people here. We live almost as quietly as at Launay, but sometimes we see the people. I am reading German and making lace, and I try not to be idle.

"Good-bye, dear, dearest aunt. Try to think kindly of me. I pray for you every morning and night. If you will send me a little note from yourself it will fill me with joy. — Your most affectionate and devoted niece,

"Bessy Pryor."

This was brought up to Mrs. Miles when she was still in bed, for as yet she had not returned to the early hours of her healthy life. When she had read it she at first held it apart from her. Then she put it close to her bosom and wept bitterly as she thought how void of sunshine the house had been since that gleam had been turned away from it.

Chapter VIII
How Bessy Pryor Received Two Letters from Launay

The same post brought Bessy two letters from England about the middle of August, both of which the reader shall see; — but first shall be given that which Bessy read the last. It was from Mrs. Miles, and had been sent when she was beginning to think that her aunt was still resolved not to write to her. The letter was as follows, and was written on square paper, which in these days is only used even by the old-fashioned when the letter to be sent is supposed to be one of great importance.

"My dear Bessy, — Though I had told you not to write to me still I am glad to hear that you are well and that your new home has been made as comfortable for you as circumstances will permit. Launay has not been comfortable since you went. I miss you very much. You have become so dear to me that my life is sad without you. My days have never been bright, but now they are less so than ever. I should scruple to admit so much as this to you, were it not that I intend it as a prelude to that which will follow.

"We have been sent into this world, my child, that we may do our duties, independent of that fleeting feeling which we call happiness. In the smaller affairs of life I am sure you would never seek a pleasure at the cost of your conscience. If not in the smaller things, then certainly should you not do so in the greater. To deny yourself, to remember the welfare of others, when temptation is urging you to do wrong, then do that which you know to be right, — that is your duty as a Christian, and especially your duty as a woman. To sacrifice herself is the special heroism which a woman can achieve. Men who are called upon to work may gratify their passions and still be heroes. A woman can soar only by suffering.

"You will understand why I tell you this. I and my son have been born into a special degree of life which I think it to be my duty and his to maintain. It is not that I or that he may enjoy any special delights that I hold fast to this opinion, but that I may do my part towards maintaining that order of things which has made my country more blessed than others. It would take me long to explain all this, but I know you will believe me when I say that an imperative sense of duty is my guide. You have not been born into that degree. That this does not affect my own personal feeling to you, you must know. You have had many signs how dear you are to me. At this moment my days are heavy to bear because I have not my Bessy with me, — my Bessy who has been so good to me, so loving, such an infinite blessing that to see the hem of her garments, to hear the sound of her foot, has made things bright around me. Now, there is nothing to see, nothing to hear,

258

that is not unsightly and harsh of sound. Oh, Bessy, if you could come back to me!

"But I have to do that duty of which I have spoken, and I shall do it. Though I were never to see you again I shall do it. I am used to suffering, and sometimes think it wrong even to wish that you were back with me. But I write to you thus that you may understand everything. If you will say that you will give him up, you shall return to me and be my own, own beloved child. I tell you that you are not of the same degree. I am bound to tell you so. But you shall be so near my heart that nothing shall separate us.

"You two cannot marry while I am living. I do not think it possible that you should be longing to be made happy by my death. And you should remember that he cannot be the first to break away from this foolish engagement without dishonour. As he is the wealthy one, and the higher born, and as he is the man, he ought not to be the first to say the word. You may say it without falsehood and without disgrace. You may say it, and all the world will know that you have been actuated only by a sense of duty. It will be acknowledged that you have sacrificed yourself, — as it becomes a woman to do.

"One word from you will be enough to assure me. Since you came to me you have never been false. One word, and you shall come back to me and to Launay, my friend and my treasure! If it be that there must be suffering we will suffer together. If tears are necessary there shall be joint tears. Though I am old still I can understand. I will acknowledge the sacrifice. But, Bessy, my Bessy, dearest Bessy, the sacrifice must be made.

"Of course he must live away from Launay for a while. The fault will have been his, and what of inconvenience there may be he must undergo. He shall not come here till you yourself shall say that you can bear his presence without an added sorrow.

"I know you will not let this letter be in vain. I know you will think it over deeply, and that you will not keep me too long waiting for an answer. I need hardly tell you that I am

"Your most loving friend,
"M. Miles."

When Bessy was reading this, when the strong words with which her aunt had pleaded her cause were harrowing her heart, she had clasped in her hand this other letter from her lover. This too was written from Launay.

"My own dearest Bessy, — It is absolutely only now that I have found out where you are, and have done so simply because the people at the rectory could not keep the secret. Can anything be more absurd than supposing that my mother can have her way by whisking you away and shutting you up in Normandy? It is too foolish! She has sent for me, and I have come like a dutiful son. I have, indeed, been rejoiced to see her looking again so much like herself. But I have not extended my duty to obeying her in a matter in which my own future happiness is altogether bound up; and in which, perhaps, the happiness of another person may be slightly concerned. I have told her that I would venture to say nothing of the happiness of the other person. The other person might be indifferent, though I did not believe it was so; but I was quite sure of my own. I have assured her that I know what I want myself, and that I do not mean to abandon my hope of achieving it. I know that she is writing to you. She can of course say what she pleases.

"The idea of separating two people who are as old as you and I, and who completely know our own minds, — you see that I do not really doubt as to yours, — is about as foolish as anything well can be. It is as though we were going back half a dozen centuries into the tyrannies of the middle ages. My object shall be to induce her to let you come home and be married properly from Launay. If she will not consent by the end of this month I shall go over to you, and we must contrive to be married at Avranches. When the thing has been once done all this rubbish will be swept away. I do not believe for a moment that my mother will punish us by any injustice as to money.

"Write and tell me that you agree with me, and be sure that I shall remain, as I am, always altogether your own,
"Truly and affectionately,
"Philip Miles."

When Bessy Pryor began to consider these two letters together, she felt that the task was almost too much for her. Her lover's letter had been the first read. She had known his handwriting, and of course had read his the first. And as she had read it everything seemed to be of rose colour. Of course she had been filled with joy. Something had been done by the warnings of Miss Gregory, something, but not much, to weaken her strong faith in her lover. The major-general had been worldly and untrue, and it had been possible that her Philip should be as had been the major-general. There had been moments of doubt in which her heart had fainted a little; but as she read her lover's words she acknowledged to herself how wrong she had been to faint at all. He declared it to be "a matter in which his own future happiness was altogether bound up." And then there had been his playful allusion to her happiness, which was not the less pleasant to her because he had pretended to think that the "other person might be indifferent." She pouted her lips at him, as though he were present while she was reading, with a joyous affectation of disdain. No, no; she could not consent to an immediate marriage at Avranches. There must be some delay. But she would write to him and explain all that. Then she read her aunt's letter.

It moved her very much. She had read it all twice before there came upon her a feeling of doubt, an acknowledgment to herself that she must reconsider the matter. But even when she was only reading it, before she had begun to consider, her former joy was repressed and almost quenched. So much of it was too true, terribly true. Of course her duty should be paramount. If she could persuade herself that duty required her to abandon Philip, she must abandon him, let the suffering to herself or to others be what it might. But then, what was it that duty required of her? "To sacrifice herself is the special heroism which a woman can achieve." Yes, she believed that. But then, how about sacrificing Philip, who, no doubt, was telling the truth when he said that his own happiness was altogether bound up in his love?

She was moved too by all that which Mrs. Miles said as to the grandeur of the Launay family. She had learned enough of the manners of Launay to be quite alive to the aristocratic idiosyncrasies of the old woman. She, Bessy Pryor, was nobody. It would have been well that Philip Launay should have founded his happiness on some girl of higher birth. But he had not done so. King Cophetua's marriage had been recognised by the world at large. Philip was no more than King Cophetua, nor was she less than the beggar-girl. Like to like in marriages was no doubt expedient, —but not indispensable. And, though she was not Philip's equal;

yet she was a lady. She would not disgrace him at his table, or among his friends. She was sure that she could be a comfort to him in his work.

But the parts of the old woman's letter which moved her most were those in which she gave full play to her own heart, and spoke, without reserve, of her own love for her dearest Bessy. "My days are heavy to bear because I have not my Bessy with me." It was impossible to read this and not to have some desire to yield. How good this lady had been to her! Was it not through her that she had known Philip? But for Mrs. Miles, what would her own life have been? She thought that had she been sure of Philip's happiness, could she have satisfied herself that he would bear the blow, she would have done as she was asked. She would have achieved her heroism, and shown the strength of her gratitude, and would have taken her delight in administering to the comforts of her old friend, — only that Philip had her promise. All that she could possibly owe to all the world beside must be less, so infinitely less, than what she owed to him.

She would have consulted Miss Gregory, but she knew so well what Miss Gregory would have advised. Miss Gregory would only have mentioned the major-general and her own experiences. Bessy determined, therefore, to lie awake and think of it, and to take no other counsellor beyond her own heart.

Chapter IX
How Bessy Pryor Answered the Two Letters, and What Came of It

The letters were read very often, and that from Mrs. Miles I think the oftener. Philip's love was plainly expressed, and what more is expected from a lover's letter than a strong, manly expression of love? It was quite satisfactory, declaring the one important fact that his happiness was bound up in hers. But Mrs. Miles' was the stronger letter, and by far the more suggestive. She had so mingled hardness and softness, had enveloped her stern lesson of feminine duty in so sweet a frame of personal love, that it was hardly possible that such a girl as Bessy Pryor should not be shaken by her arguments. Then were moments during the night in which she had almost resolved to yield. "A woman can soar only by suffering." She was not sure that she wanted to soar, but she certainly did want to do her duty, even though suffering should come of it. But there was one word in her aunt's letter which militated against the writer's purpose rather than assisted it. "Since you first came to me, you have never been false." False! no; she hoped she had not been false. Whatever might be the duty of a man or a woman that duty should be founded on truth. Was it not her special duty at this moment to be true to Philip? I do not know that she was altogether logical. I do not know but that in so supporting herself in her love there may have been a bias of personal inclination. Bessy perhaps was a little prone to think that her delight and her duty went together. But that flattering assurance, that she had never yet been false, strengthened her resolution to be true, now, to Philip.

She took the whole of the next day to think, abstaining during the whole day from a word of confidential conversation with Miss Gregory. Then on the following morning she wrote her letters. That to Philip would be easily written. Words come readily when one has to give a hearty assent to an eager and welcome proposition. But to deny, to make denial to one loved and respected, to make denial of that which the loved one has a right to ask, must be difficult. Bessy, like a brave girl, went to the hard task first, and she rushed instantly at her subject, as a brave horseman rides at his fence without craning.

"Dearest Aunt, — I cannot do as you bid me. My word to him is so sacred to me that I do not dare to break it. I cannot say that I won't be his when I feel that I have already given myself to him.

"Dear, dearest aunt, my heart is very sad as I write this, because I feel that I am separating myself from you almost for ever. You know that I love you. You know that I am miserable because you have banished me from your side. All the sweet kind words of your love to me are like daggers to me, because I cannot show my gratitude by doing as you would have me. It seems so hard! I know it is probable that I may never see him again, and yet I am to be separated from you, and you will be my enemy. In all the world there are but two that I really love. Though I cannot and will not give him up, I desire to be back at Launay now only that I might be with you. My love for him would be contented with a simple permission that it should exist. My love for you cannot be satisfied unless I am allowed to be close to you once again. You say that a woman's duty consists of suffering. I am striving to do my duty, but I know how great is my suffering in doing it. However angry you may be with your Bessy, you will not think that she can appear even to be ungrateful without a pang.

"Though I will not give him up, you need not fear that I shall do anything. Should he come here I could not, I suppose, avoid seeing him, but I should ask him to go at once; and I should beg Miss Gregory to tell him that she could not make him welcome to her house. In all things I will do as though I were your daughter — though I know so well how far I am from any right to make use of so dear a name!

"But dear, dear aunt, no daughter could love you better, nor strive more faithfully to be obedient.

"I shall always be, even when you are most angry with me, your own, poor, loving, most affectionate
"Bessy."

The other letter need perhaps be not given in its entirety. Even in such a chronicle as this there seems to be something of treachery, something of a want of that forbearance to which young ladies are entitled, in making public the words of love which such a one may write to her lover. Bessy's letter was no doubt full of love, but it was full of prudence also. She begged him not to come to Avranches. As to such a marriage as that of which he had spoken, it was, she assured him, quite impossible. She would never give him up, and so she had told Mrs. Miles. In that respect her duty to him was above her duty to her aunt. But she was so subject to her aunt that she would not in any other matter disobey her. For his sake — for Philip's sake — only for Philip's sake, she grieved that there should be more delay. Of course she was aware that it might possibly be a trouble in life too many for him to bear. In that case he might make himself free from it without a word of reproach from her. Of that he alone must be the judge. But, for the present, she could be no partner to any plans for the future. Her aunt had desired her to stay at Avranches, and at Avranches she must remain. There were words of love, no doubt; but the letter, taken altogether, was much sterner and less demonstrative of affection than that written to her aunt.

There very soon came a rejoinder from Mrs. Miles, but it was so curt and harsh as almost to crush Bessy by its laconic severity.

"You are separated from me, and I am your enemy." That was all. Beneath that one line the old woman had signed her name, M. Miles, in large plain angry letters. Bessy, who knew every turn of the woman's mind, understood exactly how it had been with her when she wrote those few words, and when, with care, she had traced the indignant signature. "Then everything shall be broken, and though there was but one gleam of sunshine left to me, that gleam shall be extinguished. No one shall say that I, as Lady of Launay, did not do my duty." It was thus the Lady of Launay had communed with herself when she penned that dreadful line. Bessy understood it all, and could almost see the woman as she wrote it.

Then in her desolation she told everything to Miss Gregory — showed the two former letters, showed that dreadful denunciation of lasting wrath, and described exactly what had been her own letter, both to Mrs. Miles and to her lover. Miss Gregory had but one recipe to offer in such a malady; that namely, which she had taken herself in a somewhat similar sickness. The gentleman should be allowed to go forth into the world and seek a fitter wife, whereas Bessy should content herself, for the remainder of her life, with the pleasures of memory. Miss Gregory thought that it was much even to have been once loved by the major-general. When Bessy almost angrily declared that this would not be enough for her, Miss Gregory very meekly suggested that possibly affection might change in the lapse of years, and that some other suitor — perhaps Mr. Morrison — might in course of time suffice. But at the idea Bessy became indignant, and Miss Gregory was glad to confine herself to the remedy pure and simple which she acknowledged to have been good for herself.

Then there passed a month — a month without a line from Launay or from Philip. That Mrs. Miles should not write again was to be expected. She had declared her enmity, and there was an end of everything. During the month there had come a cheque to Miss Gregory from some man of business, and with the cheque there had been no intimation that the present arrangement was to be brought to a close. It appeared therefore that Mrs. Miles, in spite of her enmity, intended to provide for the mutinous girl a continuation of the comforts which she now enjoyed. Certainly nothing more than this could have been expected from her. But, in regard to Philip, though Bessy had assured herself, and had assured Miss Gregory also, that she did not at all desire a correspondence in the present condition of affairs, still she felt so total a cessation of all tidings to be hard to bear. Mary Gregory, when writing to her aunt, said nothing of Philip — merely remarked that Bessy Pryor would be glad to know that her aunt had nearly recovered her health, and was again able to go out among the poor. Then Bessy began to think — not that Philip was like the major-general, for to that idea she would not give way at all — but that higher and nobler motives had induced him to yield to his mother. If so she would never reproach him. If so she would accept her destiny and entreat her old friend to allow her to return once more to Launay, and thenceforth to endure the evil thing which fate would have done to her in patient submission. If once the word should have come to her from Philip, then would she freely declare that everything should be over, then and for always, between her and her lover. After such suffering as that, while she was undergoing agony so severe, surely her friend would forgive her. That terrible word, "I am your enemy," would surely then be withdrawn.

But if it were to be so, if this was to be the end of her love, Philip, at least, would write. He would not leave her in doubt, after such a decision on his part. That thought ought to have sustained her; but it was explained to her by Miss Gregory that the major-general had taken three months before he had been inspirited to send the fatal letter, and to declare his purpose of marrying money. There could be but little doubt, according to Miss Gregory, that Philip was undergoing the same process. It was, she thought, the natural end to such an affair. This was the kind of thing which young ladies without dowry, but with hearts to love, are doomed to suffer. There could be no doubt that Miss Gregory regarded the termination of the affair with a certain amount of sympathetic satisfaction. Could she have given Bessy all Launay, and her lover, she would have done so. But sadness and disappointment were congenial to her, and a heart broken, but still constant, was, to her thinking, a pretty feminine acquisition. She was to herself the heroine of her own romance, and she thought it good to be a heroine. But Bessy was indignant; not that Philip should be false, but that he should not dare to write and say so. "I think he ought to write," was on her lips, when the door was opened, and, lo, all of a sudden, Philip Miles was in the room.

Chapter X
How Bessy Pryor's Lover Argued His Case

We must now to back to Launay. It will be remembered that Bessy received both her letters on the same day — those namely from Mrs. Miles and from Philip — and that they both came from Launay. Philip had been sent away from the place when the fact of his declared love was first made known to the old lady, as though into a banishment which was to be perpetual till he should have repented of his sin. Such certainly had been his mother's intention. He was to be sent one way, and the girl another, and everyone concerned was to be made to feel the terrible weight of her displeasure, till repentance and retraction should come. He was to be starved into obedience by a minimised allowance, and she by the weariness of her life at Avranches. But the person most grievously punished by these arrangements was herself. She had declared to herself that she would endure anything, everything, in the performance of her duty. But the desolation of her life was so extreme that it was very hard to bear. She did not shrink and tell herself that it was unendurable, but after a while she persuaded herself that now that Bessy was gone there could be no reason why Philip also should be exiled. Would not her influence be more potent over Philip if he were at Launay? She therefore sent for him, and he came. Thus it was that the two letters were written from the same house.

Philip obeyed his mother's behest in coming as he had obeyed it in going; but he did not hesitate to show her that he felt himself to be aggrieved. Launay of course belonged to her. She could leave it and all the property to some hospital if she chose. He was well aware of that. But he had been brought up as the heir, and he could not believe that there should come such a ruin of heaven and earth as would be produced by any change in his mother's intentions as to the Launay property. Touching his marriage, he felt that he had a right to marry whom he pleased, as long as she was a lady, and that any dictation from his mother in such a matter was a tyranny not to be endured. He had talked it all over with the rector before he went. Of course it was possible that his mother should commit such an injustice as that at which the rector hinted. "There are," said Philip, "no bounds to possibilities." It was, however, he thought, all but impossible; and whether probable or improbable, no fear of such tyranny should drive him from his purpose. He was a little magniloquent, perhaps, in what he said, but he was very resolved.

It was, therefore, with some feeling of an injury inflicted upon him that he first greeted his mother on his return to the house. For a day or two not a word passed about Bessy. "Of course, I am delighted to be with you, and glad enough to have the shooting," he said, in answer to some word of hers. "I shouldn't have gone, as you know, unless you had driven me away." This was hard on the old woman; but she bore it, and, for some days, was simply affectionate and gentle to her son — more gentle than was her wont. Then she wrote to Bessy and told her son that she was writing. "It is so impossible," she said, "that I cannot conceive that Bessy should not obey me when she comes to regard it at a distance!"

"I see no impossibility; but Bessy can, of course, do as she pleases," replied Philip, almost jauntily. Then he determined that he also would write.

There were no further disputes on the matter till Bessy's answer came, and then Mrs. Miles was very angry indeed. She had done her best so to write her letter that Bessy should be conquered both by the weight of her arguments and by the warmth of her love. If reason would not prevail, surely gratitude would compel her to do as she was bidden. But the very first words of Bessy's letter contained a flat refusal. "I cannot do as you bid me." Who was this girl, that had been picked out of a gutter, that she should persist in the right of becoming the mistress of Launay? In a moment the old woman's love was turned into a feeling of condemnation, nearly akin to hatred. Then she sent off her short rejoinder, declaring herself to be Bessy's enemy.

On the following morning regret had come, and perhaps remorse. She was a woman of strong passion, subject to impulses which were, at the time, uncontrollable; but she was one who was always compelled by her conscience to quick repentance, and sometimes to an agonising feeling of wrong done by herself. To declare that Bessy was her enemy — Bessy, who, for so many years, had prevented all her wishes, who had never been weary of well-doing to her, who had been patient in all things, who had been her gleam of sunshine, of whom she had sometimes said to herself in her closet that the child was certainly nearer to perfection than any other human being that she had known! True, it was not fit that the girl should become mistress of Launay! A misfortune had happened which must be cured — if even by the severance of persons so dear to each other as she and her Bessy. But she knew that she had sinned in declaring one so good, and one so dear, to be her enemy.

But what should she do next? Days went on and she did nothing. She simply suffered. There was no pretext on which she could frame an affectionate letter to her child. She could not write and ask to be forgiven for the harshness of her letter. She could not simply revoke the sentence she had pronounced without any reference to Philip and his love. In great misery, with a strong feeling of self-degradation because she had allowed herself to be violent in her wrath, she went on, repentant but still obstinate, till Philip himself forced the subject upon her.

"Mother," he said, one day, "is it not time that things should be settled?"

"What things, Philip?"

"You know my intention."

"What intention?"

"As to making Bessy my wife."

"That can never be."

"But it will be. It has to be. If as regards my own feelings I could bring myself to yield to you, how could I do so with honour in regard to her? But, for myself, nothing on earth would induce me to change my mind. It is a matter on which a man has to judge for himself, and I have not heard a word from you or from anyone to make me think that I have judged wrongly."

"Do birth and rank go for nothing?"

He paused a moment, and then he answered her very seriously, standing up and looking down upon her as he did so. "For very much—with me. I do not think that I could have brought myself to choose a wife, whatever might have been a woman's charms, except among ladies. I found this one to be the chosen companion and dearest friend of the finest lady I know." At this the old woman, old as she was, first blushed, and then, finding herself to be sobbing, turned her face away from him. "I came across a girl of whose antecedents I could be quite sure, of whose bringing up I knew all the particulars, as to whom I could be certain that every hour of her life had been passed among the best possible associations. I heard testimony as to her worth and her temper which I could not but believe. As to her outward belongings, I had eyes of my own to judge. Could I be wrong in asking such a one to be my wife? Can I be regarded as unhappy in having succeeded with her? Could I be acquitted of dishonour if I were to desert her? Shall I be held to be contemptible if I am true to her?"

At every word he spoke he grew in her esteem. At this present crisis of her life she did not wish to think specially well of him, though he was her son, but she could not help herself. He became bigger before her than he had ever been before, and more of a man. It was, she felt, almost vain for a woman to lay her commands, either this way or that, upon a man who could speak to her as Philip had spoken.

But not the less was the power in her hands. She could bid him go and marry — and be a beggar. She could tell him that all Launay should go to his brother, and she could instantly make a will to that effect. So strong was the desire for masterdom upon her that she longed to do it. In the very teeth of her honest wish to do what was right, there was another wish — a longing to do what she knew to be wrong. There was a struggle within during which she strove to strengthen herself for evil. But it was vain. She knew of herself that were she to swear to-day to him that he was disinherited, were she to make a will before nightfall carrying out her threat, the pangs of conscience would be so heavy during the night that she would certainly change it all on the next morning. Of what use is a sword in your hand if you have not the heart to use it? Why seek to be turbulent with a pistol if your bosom be of such a nature that your finger cannot be forced to pull the trigger? Power was in her possession — but she could not use it. The power rather was in her hands. She could not punish her boy, even though he had deserved it. She had punished her girl, and from that moment she had been crushed by torments, because of the thing that she had done. Others besides Mrs. Miles have felt, with something of regret, that they have lacked the hardness necessary for cruelty and the courage necessary for its doing.

"How shall it be, mother?" asked Philip. As she knew not what to answer she rose slowly from her chair, and leaving the room went to the seclusion of her own chamber.

Days again passed before Philip renewed his question, and repeated it in the same words: "How shall it be, mother?" Wistfully she looked up at him, as though even yet something might be accorded by him to pity; as though the son might even yet be induced to accede to his mother's prayers. It was not that she thought so. No. She had thought much, and was aware that it could not be so. But as a dog will ask with its eyes when it knows that asking is in vain, so did she ask. "One word from you, mother, will make us all happy."

"No; not all of us."

"Will not my happiness make you happy?" Then he stooped over her and kissed her forehead. "Could you be happy if you knew that I were wretched?"

"I do not want to be happy. It should be enough that one does one's duty."

"And what is my duty? Can it be my duty to betray the girl I love in order that I may increase an estate which is already large enough?"

"It is for the family."

"What is a family but you, or I, or whoever for the moment may be its representative? Say that it shall be as I would have it, and then I will go to her and let her know that she may come back to your arms."

Not then, or on the next day, or on the next, did she yield; though she knew well during all these hours that it was her fate to yield. She had indeed yielded. She had confessed to herself that it must be so, and as she did so she felt once more the soft pressure of Bessy's arms as they would cling round her neck, and she could see once more the brightness of Bessy's eyes as the girl would hang over her bed early in the morning. "I do not want to be happy," she had said; but she did want, sorely want, to see her girl. "You may go and tell her," she said one night as she was preparing to go to her chamber. Then she turned quickly away, and was out of the room before he could answer her with a word.

Chapter XI
How Bessy Pryor Received Her Lover

Miss Gregory was certainly surprised when, on the entrance of the young man, Bessy jumped from her chair and rushed into his arms. She knew that Bessy had no brother, and her instinct rather than her experience told her that the greeting which she saw was more than fraternal, — more than cousinly. She did not doubt but that the young man was Philip Launay, and knowing what she knew she was not disposed to make spoken complaints. But when Bessy lifted her face to be kissed, Miss Gregory became red and very uneasy. It is probable that she herself had never progressed as far as this with the young man who afterwards became the major-general.

Bessy herself, had a minute been allowed to her for reflection, would have been less affectionate. She knew nothing of the cause which had brought Philip to Avranches. She only knew that her dear friend at Launay had declared her to be an enemy, and that she had determined that she could not, for years, become the wife of Philip Launay, without the consent of her who had used that cruel word. And at the moment of Philip's entering the room her heart had been sore with reproaches against him. "He ought at any rate to write." The words had been on her lips as the door had been opened, and the words had been spoken in the soreness of heart coming from a fear that she was to be abandoned.

Then he was there. In the moment that sufficed for the glance of his eye to meet hers she knew that she was not abandoned. With whatever tidings he had come that was not to be the burden of his news. No man desirous of being released from his vows ever looked like that. So up she jumped and flew to him, not quite knowing what she intended, but filled with delight when she found herself pressed to his bosom. Then she had to remember herself, and to escape from his arms. "Philip," she said, "this is Miss Gregory. Miss Gregory, I do not think you ever met Mr. Launay."

Then Miss Gregory had to endeavour to look as though nothing particular had taken place, — which was a trial. But Bessy bore her part, if not without a struggle, at least without showing it. "And now, Philip," she said, "how is my aunt?"

"A great deal stronger than when you left her."

"Quite well?"

"Yes; for her, I think I may say quite well."

"She goes out every day?"

"Every day, — after the old plan. The carriage toddles round to the door at three, and then toddles about the parish at the rate of four miles an hour, and toddles home exactly at five. The people at Launay, Miss Gregory, don't want clocks to tell them the hour in the afternoon."

"I do love punctuality," said Miss Gregory.

"I wish I were with her," said Bessy.

"I have come to take you," said Philip.

"Have you?" Then Bessy blushed, — for the first time. She blushed as a hundred various thoughts rushed across her mind. If he had been sent to take her back, sent by her aunt, instead of Mrs. Knowl, what a revulsion of circumstances must there not have been at Launay! How could it all have come to pass? Even to have been sent for at all, to be allowed to go back even in disgrace, would have been an inexpressible joy. Had Knowl come for her, with a grim look and an assurance that she was to be brought back because a prison at Launay was thought to be more secure than a prison at Avranches, the prospect of a return would have been hailed with joy. But now, — to be taken back by Philip to Launay! There was a whole heaven of delight in the thought of the very journey.

Miss Gregory endeavoured to look pleased, but in truth the prospect to her was not so pleasant as to Bessy. She was to be left alone again. She was to lose her pensioner. After so short a fruition of the double bliss of society and pay, she was to be deserted without a thought. But to be deserted without many thoughts had been her lot in life, and now she bore her misfortune like a heroine. "You will be glad to go back to your aunt, Bessy; will you not?"

"Glad!" The ecstacy was almost unkind, but poor Miss Gregory bore it, and maintained that pretty smile of gratified serenity as though everything were well with all of them.

But Bessy felt that she had as yet heard nothing of the real news, and that the real news could not be told in the presence of Miss Gregory. It had not even yet occurred to her that Mrs. Miles had actually given her sanction to the marriage. "This is a very pretty place," said Philip.

"What, Avranches?" said Miss Gregory, mindful of future possible pensioners. "Oh, delightful. It is the prettiest place in Normandy, and I think the most healthy town in all France."

"It seemed nice as I came up from the hotel. Suppose we go out for a walk, Bessy. We have to start back to-morrow."

"To-morrow!" ejaculated Bessy. She would have been ready to go in half an hour had he demanded it.

"If you can manage it. I promised my mother to be as quick as I could; and, when I arranged to come, I had ever so many engagements."

"If she must go to-morrow, she won't have much time for walking," said Miss Gregory, with almost a touch of anger in her voice. But Bessy was determined to have her walk. All her fate in life was to be disclosed to her within the next few minutes. She was already exultant, but she was beginning to think that there was a heaven, indeed, opening for her. So she ran away for her hat and gloves, leaving her lover and Miss Gregory together.

"It is very sudden," said the poor old lady with a gasp.

"My mother felt that, and bade me tell you that, of course, the full twelvemonth —"

"I was not thinking about that," said Miss Gregory. "I did not mean to allude to such a thing. Mrs. Miles has always been so kind to my brother, and anything I could have done I should have been so happy, without thinking of money. But" Philip sat with the air of an attentive listener, so that Miss Gregory could get no answer to her question without absolutely asking it. "But there seems to be a change."

"Yes, there is a change, Miss Gregory."

"We were afraid that Mrs. Miles had been offended."

"It is the old story, Miss Gregory. Young people and old people very often will not think alike; but it is the young people who generally have their way."

She had not had her way. She remembered that at the moment. But then, perhaps, the major-general had had his. When a period of life has come too late for success, when all has been failure, the expanding triumphs of the glorious young grate upon the feelings even of those who are generous and self-denying. Miss Gregory was generous by nature and self-denying by practice, but Philip's pæan and Bessy's wondrous prosperity were for a moment a little hard upon her. There had been a comfort to her in the conviction that Philip was no better than the major-general. "I suppose it is so," she said. "That is, if one of them has means."

"Exactly."

"But if they are both poor, I don't see how their being young can enable them to live upon nothing." She intended to imply that Philip probably would have been another major-general, but that he was heir to Launay.

Philip, who had never heard of the major-general, was a little puzzled; nevertheless, he acceded to the proposition, not caring, however, to say anything as to his own circumstances on so very short an acquaintance.

Then Bessy came down with her hat, and they started for their walk. "Now tell me all about it," she said, in a fever of expectation, as soon as the front door was closed behind them.

"There is nothing more to tell," said he.

"Nothing more?"

"Unless you want me to say that I love you."

"Of course I do."

"Well, then, —I love you. There!"

"Philip, you are not half nice to me."

"Not after coming all the way from Launay to say that?"

"There must be so much to tell me? Why has my aunt sent for me?"

"Because she wants you?"

"And why has she sent you?"

"Because I want you too."

"But does she want me?"

"Certainly she does."

"For you?" If he could say this, then everything would have been said. If he could say this truly, then everything would have been done necessary for the perfection of her happiness. "Oh, Philip, do tell me. It is so strange that she should send for me! Do you know what she said to me in her last letter? It was not a letter. It was only a word. She said that I was her enemy."

"All that is changed."

"She will be glad to have me again?"

"Very glad. I fancy that she has been miserable without you."

"I shall be as glad to be with her again, Philip. You do not know how I love her. Think of all she has done for me?"

"She has done something now that I hope will beat everything else."

"What has she done?"

"She has consented that you and I shall be man and wife. Isn't that more than all the rest?"

"But has she? Oh, Philip, has she really done that?"

Then at last he told his whole story. Yes; his mother had yielded. From the moment in which she had walked out of the room, having said that he might "go and tell her," she had never endeavoured to renew the fight. When he had spoken to her, endeavouring to draw from her some warmth of assent, she had generally been very silent. She had never brought herself absolutely to wish him joy. She had not as yet so crucified her own spirit in the matter as to be able to tell him that he had chosen his wife well; but she had shown him in a hundred ways that her anger was at an end, and that if any feeling was left opposed to his own happpiness, it was simply one of sorrow. And there were signs which made him think that even that was not deep-seated. She would pat him, stroking his hair, and leaning on his shoulder, administering to his comforts with a nervous accuracy as to little things which was peculiar to her. And then she gave him an infinity of directions as to the way in which it would be proper that Bessy should travel, being anxious at first to send over a maid for her behoof, — not Mrs. Knowl, but a younger woman, who would have been at Bessy's command. Philip, however, objected to the maid. And when Mrs. Miles remarked that if it was Bessy's fate to become mistress of Launay, Bessy ought to have a maid to attend her, Philip said that would be very well a month or two hence, when Bessy would have become, — not mistress of Launay, which was a place which he trusted might not be vacant for many a long day, — but first lieutenant to the mistress, by right of marriage. He refused altogether to take the maid with him, as he explained to Bessy with much laughter. And so they came to understand each other thoroughly, and Bessy knew that the great trouble of her life, which had been as a mountain in her way, had disappeared suddenly, as might some visionary mountain. And then, when they thoroughly understood each other, they started back to England and to Launay together.

Chapter XII
How Bessy Pryor Was Brought Back, and
What Then Became of Her

Bessy understood the condition of the old woman much better than did her son. "I am sad a little," she said on her way home, "because of her disappointment."

"Sad, because she is to have you, — you yourself, — for her daughter-in-law?"

"Yes, indeed, Philip; because I know that she has not wanted me. She will be kind because I shall belong to you, and perhaps partly because she loves me; but she will always regret that that young lady down in Cornwall has not been allowed to add to the honour and greatness of the family. The Launays are everything to her, and what can I do for the Launays?" Of course he said many pretty things to her in answer to this, but he could not eradicate from her mind the feeling that, in regard to the old friend who had been so kind to her, she was returning evil for good.

But even Bessy did not quite understand the old woman. When she found that she had yielded, there was disappointment in the old woman's heart. Who can have indulged in a certain longing for a lifetime, in a special ambition, and seen that ambition and that longing crushed and trampled on, without such a feeling? And she had brought this failure on herself, — by her own weakness, as she told herself. Why had she given way to Bessy and to Bessy's blandishments? It was because she had not been strong to do her duty that this ruin had fallen upon her hopes. The power in her own hands had been sufficient. But for her Philip need never have seen Bessy Pryor. Might not Bessy Pryor have been sent somewhere out of the way when it became evident that she had charms of her own with which to be dangerous? And even after the first evil had been done her power had been sufficient. She need not have sent for Philip back. She need have written no letter to Bessy. She might have been calm and steady in her purpose, so that there should have been no violent ebullition of anger, — so violent as to induce repentance, and with repentance renewed softness and all the pangs of renewed repentance.

When Philip had left her on his mission to Normandy her heart was heavy with regret, and heavy also with anger. But it was with herself that she was angry. She had known her duty and she had not done it. She had known her duty, and had neglected it, — because Bessy had been soft to her, and dear, and pleasant. It was here that Bessy did not quite understand her friend. Bessy reproached herself because she had made to her friend a bad return to all the kindness she had received. The old woman would not allow herself to entertain any such a thought. Once she had spoken to herself of having warmed a serpent in her bosom; but instantly, with infinite self-scorn, she had declared to herself that Bessy was no serpent. For all that she had done for Bessy, Bessy had made ample return, the only possible return that could be full enough. Bessy had loved her. She too had loved Bessy, but that should have had no weight. Though they two had been linked together by their very heartstrings, it had been her duty to make a severance because their joint affection had been dangerous. She had allowed her own heart to over-ride her own sense of duty, and therefore she was angry, — not with Bessy but with herself.

But the thing was done. To quarrel with Philip had been impossible to her. One feeling coming upon another, her own repentance, her own weakness, her acknowledgement of a certain man's strength on the part of her son, had brought her to such a condition that she had yielded. Then it was natural that she should endeavour to make the best of it. But even the doing of that was a trial to her. When she told herself that as far as the woman went, the mere woman, Philip could not have found a better wife had he searched the world all round, she found that she was being tempted from her proper path even in that. What right could she have to look for consolation there? For other reasons, which she still felt to be adequate, she had resolved that something else should be done. That something else had not been done, because she had failed in her duty. And now she was trying to salve the sore by the very poison which had created the wound. Bessy's sweet temper, and Bessy's soft voice, and Bessy's bright eye, and Bessy's devotion to the delight of others, were all so many temptations. Grovelling as she was in sackcloth and ashes because she had yielded to them how could she console herself by a prospect of these future enjoyments either for herself or her son?

But there were various duties to which she could attend, grievously afflicted as she was by her want of attention to that great duty. As Fate had determined that Bessy Pryor was to become mistress of Launay, it was proper that all Launay should know and recognise its future mistress. Bessy certainly should not be punished by any want of earnestness in this respect. No one should be punished but herself. The new mistress should be made as welcome as though she had been the red-haired girl from Cornwall. Knowl was a good deal put about because Mrs. Miles, remembering a few hard words which Knowl had allowed herself to use in the days of the imprisonment, became very stern. "It is settled that Miss Pryor is to become Mrs. Philip Launay, and you will obey her just as myself." Mrs. Knowl, who had saved a little money, began to consider whether it would not be as well to retire into private life.

When the day came on which the two travellers were to reach Launay Mrs. Miles was very much disturbed in her mind. In what way should she receive the girl? In her last communication, — her very last, — she had called Bessy her enemy; and now Bessy was being brought home to be made her daughter-in-law under her own roof. How sweet it would be to stand at the door and welcome her in the hall, among all the smiling servants, to make a tender fuss and hovering over her, as would be so natural with a mother-in-law who loved an adopted daughter as tenderly as Mrs. Miles loved Bessy! How pleasant to take her by the hand and lead her away into some inner sanctum where warm kisses as between mother and child would be given and taken; to hear her praises of Philip, and then to answer again with other praises; to tell her with words half serious and half drollery that she must now buckle on her armour and do her work, and take upon herself the task of managing the household! There was quite enough of softness in the old woman to make all this delightful. Her imagination revelled in thinking of it even at the moment in which she was telling herself that it was impossible. But it was impossible. Were she to force such a change upon herself Bessy would not believe in the sincerity of the change. She had told Bessy that she was her enemy!

At last the carriage which had gone to the station was here; not the waggonette on this occasion, but the real carriage itself, the carriage which was wont to toddle four miles an hour about the parish. "This is an honour meant for the prodigal daughter," said Philip, as he took his seat. "If you had never been naughty, we should only have had the waggonette, and we then should have been there in half the time." Mrs. Miles, when she heard the wheels on the gravel, was even yet uncertain where she would place herself. She was fluttered, moving about from the room into the hall and back, when the old butler spoke a careful word; "Go into the library, madam, and Mr. Philip will bring her to you there." Then she obeyed the butler, — as she had probably never done in her life before.

Bessy, as soon as her step was off the carriage, ran very quickly into the house. "Where is my aunt?" she said. The butler was there showing the way, and in a moment she had thrown her arms round the old woman. Bessy had a way of making her kisses obligatory, from which Mrs. Miles had never been able to escape. Then, when the old woman was seated, Bessy was at once upon her knees before her. "Say that you love me, aunt. Say that at once! Say that first of all!"

"You know I love you."

"I know I love you. Oh, I am so glad to have you again. It was so hard not to be with you when I thought that you were ill. I did not know how sick it would make me to be away from you." Neither then or at any time afterwards was there a word spoken on the one side or the other as to that declaration of enmity.

There was nothing then said in way of explanation. There was nothing perhaps necessary. It was clear to Bessy that she was received at Launay as Philip's future wife, — not only by Mrs. Miles herself, but by the whole household, — and that all the honours of the place were to be awarded to her without stint. For herself that would have sufficed. To her any explanation of the circumstances which had led to a change so violent was quite unnecessary. But it was not so with Mrs. Miles herself. She could not but say some word in justification of herself, — in excuse rather than justification. She had Bessy into her bedroom that night, and said the word, holding between her two thin hands the hand of the girl she addressed. "You have known, Bessy, that I did not wish this." Bessy muttered that she did know it. "And I think you knew why."

"How could I help it, aunt?"

Upon this the old woman patted the hand. "I suppose he could not help it. And, if I had been a young man, I could not have helped it. I could not help it as I was, though I am an old woman. I think I am as foolish as he is."

"Perhaps he is foolish, but you are not."

"Well; I do not know. I have my misgivings about that, my dear. I had objects which I thought were sacred and holy, to which I had been wedded through many years. They have had to be thrust aside."

"Then you will hate me!"

"No, my child; I will love you with all my heart. You will be my son's wife now, and, as such, you will be dear to me, almost as he is dear. And you will still be my own Bessy, my gleam of sunlight, without whom the house is so gloomy that it is like a prison to me. For myself, do you think I could want any other young woman about the house than my own dear Bessy; — that any other wife for Philip could come as near my heart as you do?"

"But if I have stood in the way?"

"We will not think of it any more. You, at any rate, need not think of it," added the old woman, as she remembered all the circumstances. "You shall be made welcome with all the honours and all the privileges due to Philip's wife; and if there be a regret, it shall never trouble your path. It may be a comfort to you to hear me say that you, at least, in all things have done your duty." Then, at last, there were more tears, more embracings, and before either of them went to their rest, a perfect ecstasy of love.

Little or nothing more is necessary for the telling of the story of the Lady of Launay. Before the autumn had quite gone, and the last tint had left the trees, Bessy Pryor became Bessy Launay, under the hand of Mr. Gregory, in the Launay parish church. Everyone in the neighbourhood around was there, except Mr. Morrison who had taken this opportunity of having a holiday and visiting Switzerland. But even he, when he returned, soon become reconciled to the arrangement, and again became a guest in the dining-room of the mansion. I hope I shall have no reader who will not think that Philip Launay did well in not following the example of the major-general.

"The Lady of Launay" appeared first in the April 6 to May 11 issues of *Light*: Belles Lettres Section for 1878.

THIS BOOK WAS DESIGNED BY
JUDITH OELFKE SMITH
TYPESET IN ELEVEN POINT GOUDY OLDSTYLE
BY FORT WORTH LINOTYPING COMPANY
PRINTED ON WARREN'S OLDE STYLE WOVE
BY MOTHERAL PRINTING COMPANY
AND BOUND BY UNIVERSAL BINDERY